BOYS

OF THE UNIVERSE EXPLORER

BOYS

OF THE UNIVERSE EXPLORER

Michael Lee-Allen Dawn

iUniverse, Inc.
Bloomington

BOYS OF THE UNIVERSE EXPLORER

iUniverse books may be ordered through booksellers or by contacting:

iUniverse
1663 Liberty Drive
Bloomington, IN 47403
www.iuniverse.com
1-800-Authors (1-800-288-4677)

ISBN: 978-1-4759-9200-7 (sc)
ISBN: 978-1-4759-9202-1 (hc)
ISBN: 978-1-4759-9201-4 (ebk)

Printed in the United States of America

iUniverse rev. date: 05/24/2013

PROLOGUE 1

THE BEGINNING

The war was finally over. After fifty long hard years, the war was over. About ten percent of Earth's population was confirmed lost, and sadly many more were still missing, or presumed dead. The Qaralon people tried hard to conquer Earth and its people, but they lost. Even though Earth was a young planet in the universe, in the grand scheme of things, they had ships that were good, very good, and they had people running them that were even better yet.

In the year 2158, Earth finally broke from their own solar system and entered the universe beyond. It took nearly a hundred years of nearly every country providing their most talented scientists to design and build a ship fast enough to make the trip, and durable enough to withstand the stresses of such trips. This was all made possible from the asteroid mining that was started around the middle of the 21st century.

Needing new sources of minerals to build Earth's ever expanding civilization, scientists decided to attempt to harness the nearly unlimited supply of asteroids and comets right in Earth's very own backyard. As it turned out, they struck proverbial gold. Some of the first asteroids the scientists were able to mine brought forth incredible metals, that when mixed properly, made super alloys that were of extreme strength, while being surprisingly light, especially in comparison to anything Earth was able to produce. The true payoff came however when they mined their fifth asteroid.

They were almost disappointed at first to find almost no metals on it, and nearly missed what the asteroid truly hid, and it was only dumb luck that they had found anything at all. One of the astronauts doing the survey accidentally blasted a section of what appeared to be rock, with one of his electrical charges that were used to test for metals, and the explosion that resulted would surely have killed him, had it not been for his space suit. When everyone found out what happened, some of the strange new rock was brought aboard, and stored in a very secure manner, to be brought back to the planet for testing. No one expected what they found though.

The material, they found, would end up being the new power source for nearly everything the planet used. When even just a small piece of the material was hit with a tiny amount of power, and when harnessed correctly, the new material, they decided to call Nutronium, provided enough electricity to power the average city. There were many mishaps at first, and a few people very nearly died due to these, but eventually it was worked out, and they came out of it with a power source of unbelievable potential. The Nutronium was given its name, simply because it was a hundred times more powerful than plutonium, and as best they could tell, was completely harmless, well unless someone went and blasted it incorrectly for some stupid reason. The rock was a dull greyish color, almost boring looking in fact, and no one would normally give it a second look for its appearance, yet it was far more than it appeared. Asteroids containing Nutronium in the solar system were found to be very plentiful, and regular mining of all the asteroids they could find was now a normal thing.

So armed with new metals, that were extremely strong, and a new power source, that could provide the massive amounts of raw energy needed, they started designing and building the first space ships destined to break Earth's inhabitants from their solar system. It took almost a hundred years, and many designs, but finally they had done it. They worked and worked, tested and tested, redesign after redesign was made to make sure that absolutely everything was perfect, and that it functioned even more so.

Their brand new ship was very sleek looking, powerful looking. It's propulsion pods were bottom mounted, so that they were able to land on a planetary surface. It was nearly three times longer, and quite a bit wider, than it was tall, nearly twice in fact, and given that it was ten decks high, that made it quite large by any standard that they had.

The upper deck housed the bridge, the captains office, some of the officers suites, and many other rooms. The observation deck was made with an almost entirely glass roof, although it was not actually glass, and it had a number of the very best computer systems in there, because it was to be their science hall as well.

Their engine and power rooms were in the very bottom of the ship, were two decks high, and very near to the middle, because they needed to be close to the propulsion systems for peak performance. They figured that they could put as much as three hundred people on the ship without problem, but the normal capacity would be far lower than that.

Their cargo bay in the rear of the ship was massive as well, three decks high, many storage rooms off of it, and more than a few people had joked that you could play football or hockey in there with ease. For the most part though, nothing was ever in the cargo bay, it was only where everything was stored until a proper home could be found for it. Some excess supplies would of course stay there, but for the most part, that was unnecessary.

Even with being as large as it was though, most of the space on the ship was used up by the massive systems that it took to run the ship, hence the reason its human capacity was not as high as it looked like it should be. In comparison to an ocean ship, it was almost the same size, or at least the same weight. They were just very different dimensions, and where an ocean cruise liner could hold a thousand or more people, the space ships could not.

By the time that 2158 was coming up, and the first ever flight outside the solar system was to take place, Earth was a thriving mecca of activity. It was still far from perfect, unfortunately there was still hate and prejudice, there was still poverty and starvation, there was still the rich and powerful running everything, there was still the poor and the starving barely scraping by, the way it had always been, and probably always would be.

Many of the rich and powerful had fought long and hard to keep the oil fields open, and protested that this new power source was too unstable, but after the almost hundred years since Nutronium was founded, and put into use, there had been no major accidents, not like the oil, which was polluting everything, but they still wanted to sell it, that however did stop, eventually.

Finally, on January first, of the year 2158, the very first universe break out of a manned vessel took place. With twenty of the planets finest astronauts, and twenty of the world's elite scientists, they boarded their brand new ship, and took off. The trip to the outer edges of the solar system would take only a few minutes, if they went top speed, with the new engines that had been designed and tested just for this ship, just for this trip.

Over the last hundred years, of course engines were the number one concern, and the number one time consumer. Finally the design that was built, that worked the best, and was tested in a number of smaller ships in a smaller size, was built to full size, and installed in the brand new ship. Within just an hour, the crew of the Universe Explorer, as it was aptly named, reached the outer barrier of what was thought to be the solar system, and ventured outside.

They had not even gone their maximum speed, which was roughly a hundred times the speed of light, because they would have been able to cross the entire solar system in just a few minutes, had they wanted to. None of them wanted to go quite that fast though, at least not yet. First and foremost, the engine was brand new, and almost totally untested, so they wanted to ease up to their top speed slowly, to get the engine more broken in. They also wanted to see all the sights on their way out as well, because most of them had never gone out nearly as far as they were heading, even in their solar system, although others had by then.

The engineers had had to design a system of controlling the speed, because they were working in the trillions of kilometers an hour, so it got sort of silly. They had sub light-year speeds, ranging from just a few hundred kilometers an hour, right up to, but not over one full light-year, and this was marked on a scale of zero to a hundred. They also had their one hundred light-year settings, but each one jumped one light-year at a time. Early on, the astronauts devised a system of telling others what speed they wanted, they called each notch a LY, for light-year, but pronounced lie, so sub light-year speeds were simply called sub LYS. It just made it faster and easier for them.

Of course nothing looked any different once they got out there, because nothing much changes in space, but they were further than any human had ever been before, and before this trip was through, they would go so much further. The Universe Explorer was scheduled to be out for approximately a year, and by their third day in space, they were seeing and recording many amazing things, and transmitting the information back home. By their sixth day, they found and landed on their very first planet. Using the absolute best scanners that could be designed, they found that it was very similar to Earth in climate and air composition, just a little more oxygen, as well as gravity being just slightly less. They were also able to determine that the planet was uninhabited, so they had no problems landing and checking it out.

What they found though was right out of fantasy novels; perfect beaches, shimmering waterfalls, dense foliage, and the most stunning sky anyone could ever imagine. The color of the sky was a deep blue, with a hint of green, it was just beautiful. It was wholeheartedly decided upon, that spending a day there would not harm any of them, so everyone went back in and changed, and then ran and jumped into the clearest water any of them had ever seen, and splashed and frolicked in the water like a bunch of school children. They camped out under the familiar, but unfamiliar stars, and told stories deep into the night.

The next morning they awoke, with a start, to a group of people standing around them. They were vaguely humanoid in appearance, but had green scaled skin, no hair, pointed features, and huge eyes. They were roughly as tall as the average human, stood on two legs, had two arms, and had they had tails, they probably would have looked almost lizard like.

"Welcome strange people, who are you, and why are you on our vacation planet?" The leader asked of the captain of the ship, moving his arm in an arc, pointing to the land all around them.

"Hello, I'm Captain Casey, and we're humans from the planet Earth. We apologize, we weren't aware that this planet was inhabited, because none of our scans showed any signs of intelligent life, and we didn't expect to find anyone here." He answered softly, hoping to have not offended the first people that they came across. He then went on to explain.

"There are also no dwellings here, so we felt that it was empty. If you wish though, we'll leave immediately, because we don't wish to intrude. This is our first trip outside of our solar system, and we were excited to find a planet that we could easily breath on, but we never thought that it was claimed."

"No need to apologize, there's no rush to leave, at least not yet. Normally this planet's crawling with people from our home world, and even a few others. However, we don't have dwellings here, because we didn't wish to harm the natural beauty of the planet, and if we decide to sleep on the planet, we often do just as you did." This time motioning toward the sleeping arrangements that the captain and his people had used.

"This is unfortunately the time of year that you wouldn't want to be here though, because random and violent storms are known to break out all over, and to be caught in one could spell certain death to nearly anyone. My name is Splenklar, I too am the captain of our ship, and we're Tenarians. We're familiar with your solar system, and have been patiently waiting for you to arrive, we knew it would be soon. We didn't wish to intrude on your learning, to do so wouldn't have been proper, so we waited for you to exit your home first in your own time."

"Well, I must say, if this is the off season, then we must truly visit in the peak season then." Captain Casey stated in obvious awe from the beauty that surrounded them all.

"Yes, you should, it is truly spectacular then." Captain Splenklar smiled widely, showing obvious pleasure at the mere mention of his favorite vacation place.

"Tell me, if you can, why is it you speak the same language as we do? We'd figured that language would be the largest barrier we'd face out here, so we have a massive computer system set up, just to try and decipher languages as we come across them."

"Well that's an easy one to answer. Your satellites broadcast their signals, even to us, and with our computers, we were able to program our internal translators with your language, so that we could talk freely. This is one of only a few pieces of technology that we'd be happy to share with you, should you desire it. We of course know all about your people, the fights that you've had to get to where you are now, your history, both the good and the bad, everything, you're much like we used to be." Captain Splenklar answered happily.

"Well that's an excellent idea, and a most generous offer, so on behalf of my crew and my planet, we would gladly accept, on one condition. I'd love for you and your people to join us on our ship for dinner this evening?" Captain Casey offered.

"I'm sure that that arrangement would be met with approval from all my people. I'll have a list of items, with design plans, for you at that time. You'll probably find a few things you'll recognize though, some of your peoples ideas were excellent, but didn't live up to their fullest potential, so they were redesigned. Now, I do have a friendly warning for your people though. Your satellites, like I said, broadcast all your information out, and there are people out there who aren't as friendly as we are, who'd love some of the information we have about you. A few of the systems around you do have this information, but it doesn't go beyond us, as far as we're aware. We'd recommend that using the encryption equipment, that we'll provide the plans of to you this evening, would help to greatly reduce the chances of the wrong people getting sensitive information about you." Captain Splenklar said.

"I'm guessing that our people weren't aware that our secret information was being broadcast out for all to see, and any help you can give us there would be much appreciated. Our governments will be happy to hear this report this evening I'm sure."

"Most of the information was secure, but the security that your people use isn't that good. We were able to crack it with ease, and that's the reason why we'll give you the designs to the equipment that we use to encrypt our data, it's the best. We should also be heading back to our ship now, so that we too may report our visit. We're in orbit above the planet, so just come on up, and we'll have dinner tonight. What time would be acceptable for us to arrive?" Captain Splenklar asked.

"Excellent! Why don't you come over at 1800 hours. I do however have one quick question for you though. What types of food do your people eat, and will we serve anything that goes against your religion, and or will insult anyone? We have issues like this on our planet with different races of people, and I wouldn't like for that to happen on our first dinner together." Captain Casey asked with a smile.

"Most of my people will have little trouble with anything that you might serve, because we too are omnivores such as you, and we'd all love to try some of the wine your people makes. We've tried making it ourselves, but it seems our fruit isn't as suited for the wine making you do. We'll also bring some of our dinner drink, I think you'll like it." Captain Splenklar answered, also with a smile.

In a short time, a life long friendship had formed, and while the captains had been talking, a few groups of the others had also broken off, and were all talking, and a few friends were made there as well. So with waves and farewells all around, the Tenarians teleported up to their ship.

"Now there's a useful technology I wouldn't mind having, I wonder how they do it? We still haven't managed to actually send anything in that fashion yet, even though we've tried time and time again." The lead scientist told Captain Casey.

"Yes, it'd be very useful. I'd say it'd be nice if they gave us that information as well, but I'm willing to bet they won't!"

"We can always dream right. Really, anything they're willing to give us is a bonus, so I won't look a gift horse in the mouth, that much is for certain."

"That's right, let's get back to the ship. I have a hell of a lot of information to report, and we need to prepare a feast fit for royalty for this evenings dinner."

A short while later found Captain Casey in his personal office, filling out a report to tell of everything that had so far been found. The three best cooks on board the ship were busy getting a huge feast prepared, while the rest of the crew were preparing the ship for takeoff. About the time that Captain Casey finished his report and sent it off, the ship was ready to take off, and with a quick approval from the captain on his personal communicator, which at all times was around every crew persons wrist, the ship was airborne.

They found the Tenarians Ship right away, and to say it was impressive, would be an understatement. It was nearly five times larger than the Universe Explorer was, it was large by any Earth standard. It was very smooth, no visible means of propulsion, and the lines were clean and straight. In comparison, the Earth ship looked like a toy. This of course bothered no one.

The groups of scientists, when they broke off, had found that the Tenarians had by then been capable of full space travel for nearly a thousand years, so naturally they had become very good ship builders. They had told the humans that their ships used to look much alike, but technology changed, and they would be pleasantly surprised at what the Tenarians ship looked like. They were.

PROLOGUE 2

DINNER WITH FRIENDS

Even though the Universe Explorer was not actively searching, its scanners were always active; this was a scientific excursion after all, and they were all surprised that they could almost not even see the ship with their scanners. They could tell it was there, but nothing else. Whatever shields they used must dull the senses of the scanners too much.

After much preparation and cleaning, Captain Casey and his crew welcomed the Tenarians aboard, and they brought gifts of many bottles of the drink Captain Splenklar had promised.

"We welcome you aboard our humble home of the sky, and thank you for the gifts that you've given. Would a tour of our ship be welcome?" Captain Casey graciously asked.

"Please, a tour of your ship would be much appreciated." Captain Splenklar answered.

"Would you follow me then please?"

For the next half an hour, the captains looked over the ship, followed by the rest of the crew members, and everyone explained what everything was as they came upon it.

"You have a very nice ship, very well built, nothing like what our first ships were. You however took a lot longer to get to where you are now. We weren't so patient, we are now, many mistakes happened before we learned the hard way. Space travel forced us to grow up. Your people are much further along in that aspect than we were." Captain Splenklar said.

"Thank you for the compliment, but it's nothing compared to your ship though, it's massive, and looks very nice. If you don't mind my asking, how fast can you go in that thing anyway?" Captain Casey asked curiously.

"Believe it or not, we go about the same speed as you do, in your measurements, our top speed is one hundred LYS. Our engines are amazingly similar in design, and currently it's the fastest that we can go. Not surprising really, since we use the same fuel source, because it's pretty much the standard fuel throughout the known universe."

"Well, I must say that that's somewhat of a surprise. Here we are the new kids on the block, and we seem to be as fast as the other kids are. Well I'm certain that you far surpass us in many ways, for instance, teleportation, it's something our top scientists have been working on for generations, but have yet to figure out why it won't work, yet we can clearly see that you've mastered that."

"Like I said though, your people were much more cautious and patient, and waited until everything was perfect before attempting this. Our scientists believe that it took the same amount of time for our peoples to design and build the engines we use, and ours haven't changed much at all in several hundred years or more. Yes, it's true, we do have many of the things that you've tried very hard to do, and with teleportation, your people almost had it, apparently many times. I'm sure you'll be happy to know that this is one of the items we're going to offer you. It uses the same basic design as what you already have, just with a few minor differences. It was your people that actually got ours working on it in fact, because we've only had the technology for a hundred and fifty years or so, about when your people came up with the first real good designs that made it seem plausible. Our people just took your design and worked on it to perfect it, and now it works perfectly."

"You mean all along they almost had it? When they see the plans, they'll probably kick themselves, saying 'why didn't we think of that.' Well, dinner's ready, why don't we make our way to the banquet hall, and sit down to a nice dinner?" Captain Casey asked.

"Please, lead the way!" Captain Splenklar answered with a bow.

The captains and the lead scientists took the head table, while the rest broke into smaller groups and enjoyed the dinner. The Tenarians loved the wine, and the humans nearly died at the first taste of the Tenarians drink. It was called Fire Drink in English.

"Now you know why we call it Fire Drink in your language, it's very good though. There's no direct translation to what we call it."

"Yes, I think I know why you call it Fire Drink, this stuff is some powerful. I've never had an alcohol burn so much going down, but it tastes very nice though. What's it made of?" Captain Casey asked.

The captain explained that it was made from a local berry on their planet called the zebla berry, and in looks was similar to Earth's strawberry. He did however warn them to never take an offer to eat a raw berry, though some do enjoy them, because they are incredibly hot. He explained it as being about five times hotter than the reported habanero peppers from Earth, and that they had been known to kill people. Captain Casey was not certain as to whether Captain Splenklar was pulling his leg or not.

As Captain Casey was enjoying the zebla berry wine, Captain Splenklar had been enjoying the wine that Captain Casey had provided. When asked, Captain Casey informed him that it was one of his personal favorites, apple wine.

As they sat there, eating and drinking, enjoying the excellent feast that the ships cooks had provided, they talked happily, everyone getting to know everyone, all of them enjoying the company a great deal. Captain Casey of course explained to them everything that they had been eating, a personal favorite of his as well, a full turkey dinner with all the trimmings, and ended with pumpkin pie, which Captain Splenklar actually admitted that they had almost the exact same dessert on their planet, and the flavor was surprisingly similar. Dinner and talk lasted very nearly two hours, all of them enjoying themselves a great deal, but finally it was decided that the Tenarians were ready to head out.

Captain Casey stood to say farewell.

"Thank you very much for joining us this evening for a wonderful meal, it was our great pleasure to have met you. We hope that you all enjoyed the meal and that we get the chance to once again do this."

"Yes, I agree, it was a very enjoyable evening and the food very nice, I too hope that we can do this again soon. I'd invite you to our ship for a similar feast, but sadly, soon after we leave here this evening, we must be off. We're having a bit of a border incident, someone wants to cross our space, and we're not inclined to let them. So I'll offer that the next time we see each other, that dinner will be on us." Captain Splenklar offered.

"Sorry to hear that, but is there any assistance that we can offer you?"

"No, you need not get mixed up in this mess. These people aren't at all friendly, and getting on their bad side so soon after entering the rest of the universe wouldn't be a nice thing."

"Nonsense, we can call our peoples friends, I hope, and friends help friends. Really, if they get through you guys, where can they go? One of the places is our home, so we'd only be helping to protect our home, and by the sounds of it, we'd soon be meeting these people anyway. At the very least, for our first contact with them, it'd be nice to be with friends to show support."

"Well then, you're welcome to join us! The trip there should take roughly two days at maximum speed, our far border is a considerable ways away. I'll offer dinner tomorrow evening then. Now, I have a pad with a few toys for your people to look over, to see if there's anything you can use." Captain Splenklar offered, handing over a pad much like the ones they used.

Captain Casey took the offered pad, and then handed it to the lead scientist, who took it with a silly grin and shaking hands, he was a true scientific geek. The others just smiled and laughed.

"We should be going then, I'll send the coordinates of where we're going to you. We'll be joined along the way by a few other ships, so you can meet more of our people. Thanks by the way." Captain Splenklar said with a bow.

"Nothing to be thankful for, I'd hope that should the situation ever be reversed, you too would offer assistance. I however thank you for your hospitality and friendship." Captain Casey said, offering his hand to shake.

"Well, then we're both thankful. We'll talk, I'm sure, so have a pleasant evening." Captain Splenklar said as his goodbyes, shaking the offered hand, and then he and his crew teleported back to their ship.

"Well folks, we've met the nice, now we go meet the not so nice. I want the entire ship to be tested to the maximum over the next couple days. I want every weapon and defense system triple checked, if we have to trade shots, I don't wish to get blown out of the sky on our very first mission. That wouldn't look so good on my record. Not that I'd care any mind you." Captain Casey said with a wry smile.

The crew, after giving their agreements, all took off to their assigned posts to look after what the captain wanted. Captain Casey headed to his office to call back home to tell home base what they were up to.

"Earth Command, this is Captain Casey calling." Captain Casey spoke into the communication system. Seconds later he was answered.

"Yes Captain, how may we help you, and so soon after the impressive report you sent us." Admiral Way, a graying blond man in his thirties, asked, coming up on the screen.

"Well, the Tenarians are having a bit of a border issue with a hostile people, and I've offered our help, so we're going. I have no idea if a battle will come or not, but we'll continue on after that's all settled, and we'll continue to give you reports as to what's happening. I also have to tell you, the Tenarian's have been kind enough to give us a few pieces of technology that we'll send out as soon as my people on board get finished looking it over, you'll be very happy with some of the things on the list I think." Captain Casey said flatly.

"Well, telling you to be careful would be pointless, you're the best we have, and that's the very reason you have that ship, we all trust you, so just come back alive. As for the technology, what all is there?"

"I haven't seen or heard the whole list, and even if I had, I wouldn't tell you Sir. You'll have to be patient and wait for the report to come down." He grinned evilly.

"You know I could order it out of you right?" The Admiral asked dryly.

"And you know I'd still refuse to answer, we've gone over this before Sir, you'll just have to wait, patience is good for you."

"Yeah, the last time you did this to me, I nearly had a coronary waiting, you're truly awful, and if you weren't the best captain in the entire space fleet, I'd gladly knock you down a peg or two."

"Ah, bring it on old man. You know, this is going to be the hardest part of this trip. I already miss having our late night bull sessions and rib fests. Well old friend, I need to go, so keep in touch." Captain Casey said.

"I too will miss that as well, but you keep in touch as well, and have a good night." Admiral Way said, signing off.

The following day the crew continued to test every system fully, and at the arranged time, went to the Tenarians ship for dinner. Captain Casey also brought a few bottles of various wines for dinner. They too were treated to a tour of the ship, after gracious welcomes were passed around.

"I must say you have an impressive ship, it feels so much larger inside, much more than it seems outside. How many people could this ship carry." Captain Casey asked curiously.

"Thank you, this ship is the pride of the fleet, it's brand new itself, and it was designed with the utmost comfort in mind. It can hold over a thousand people comfortably, but as you found last night, we're only running about 60 people right now. Why don't we head to the dining hall and have a nice dinner?"

"Please lead the way!"

They all sat down at the various tables, and this time it was only the two captains at the head table. As they sat they once again talked and found out more great information. Captain Splenklar told Captain Casey all about what they were eating, warning him to be careful of the dipping sauce, since it was zebla berry, but paired very nicely with the breaded baso bird that they were eating. He then had to explain that the bird was similar to Earths grouse, just larger. Captain Casey enjoyed it a great deal, it had a good strong, but not overpowering flavor, and did go well with the sauce, which was both hot and sweet. Captain Casey enjoyed everything a great deal, even though a few flavors were certainly new to him, but he would certainly try it all again any time.

"Well I thank you for the wonderful meal, it was very delicious." Captain Casey said once it was complete.

"And you are very welcome. So did your people look over the things we gave you, and if so, what do they think about it?"

"My people on board were all very excited, but I only saw a few of the items on the list, you're much too generous. They forwarded it to our people on Earth early this afternoon, but we haven't heard from them yet. I think they might be in shock. A few of my people on board almost had to be torn from their labs this evening just to come to dinner, they wanted to keep working on the things you gave them. I ended up having to order them to come. It was kinda funny really, they're all such nerds, they really love that type of thing, I personally don't understand it at all." He laughed.

"I know what you mean, some of my people are the exact same. If it weren't for the fact that they'd pass out without food or sleep, I sometimes believe they'd stay in their labs all day and night working." Captain Splenklar laughed as well.

"I can well imagine, but I believe that it's beyond time that we got back underway, so we should head back." Captain Casey said, offering his hand to shake.

"You're probably correct. Let us transport your people back, so that they can get a feel as to what it's like. It's not unpleasant, but for the first time it's a bit disconcerting. It just sorta feels real weird." He offered, shaking Captain Casey's hand.

"Sure, I'm always open to knew things, let's try it." Captain Casey said with a smile. "Gather around people, Captain Splenklar has offered to teleport us back to our ship. He says that it's not unpleasant, but feels weird."

The crew and Captain Casey gathered around, and Captain Splenklar gave the word, so within seconds, the whole Universe Explorer crew was on their own ship, on the bridge. A few people fell down from the dizzying experience, but most just wavered a bit, and more than a few groaned.

"Well that was an experience alright. It'd take a few times probably, but should be easy enough to get used to. When will you guys have ours built you figure?" Captain Casey asked.

"I think we have everything needed Sir, and if we do, it won't take long to construct, maybe three days, give or take a day. We'll start after we get back on our way. A couple of the other things also look promising, and are going to get priority. One of them was a shielding device that we can add to this ship easily, so I've already started on that, and hopefully by morning I'll have it installed and tested." The lead scientist told the captain.

"Excellent! What else was there? Anything we could use right now for this mission?"

"The rest of the stuff really won't help with the current mission, mostly they're just comfort things. We do have a few interesting things though. They included the designs for the translators they use, and it just gets inserted into almost any communicator, but ours aren't quite capable, they need to be modified slightly, it's nothing major though. We were also given designs for the communicators they use, much like our own, but smaller, yet with a larger screen, and a whole lot more powerful. They use a Nutronium core, and a much more advanced transmission system, which should triple our current range, should be interesting. I'll give you a full report once I have it ready."

"Excellent. Well, don't stay up all night, you do need to sleep as well. Have a good night."

"You too Sir, but I can't guarantee I'll obey that. We could really use those shields, so we'll build all night if we have to, because we need to have it done by a little after noon tomorrow, or nothing."

"Just remember, if you get too tired, you'll miss something important, and it won't work when we need it, and that'd be of no use to anyone, most especially us. If we don't have it, then we know our weakness, and will avoid getting into the more dangerous situations."

"True, I'll remember that, have a good night Sir." He said and turned and walked off before the captain could say anything further.

Captain Casey headed off himself as well, and took care of any business that he needed to attend to.

PROLOGUE 3

FIRST MEETING OF THE ENEMY

The following morning, Captain Casey was shown the fully functional, and thoroughly tested shielding device, and how it worked. He was informed excitedly that they tested a small version of it against one of their Nutronium missiles, and it hardly even flickered, but the asteroid they were targeting was unscathed. He was also informed how it had already been incorporated into their current weapons console, seeing as how that was the most logical placement for it.

"Well ladies and gentlemen, that's excellent news. We should ask Captain Splenklar to give it a good test then. Have him fire at us, and see how it really holds up. We'll abandon a section of the ship, and have him fire on that part only." Captain Casey said happily, but many of the faces around him dropped.

"Well, I can't say that I'd like to be shot at, but I guess it makes sense. It's better to know what we're working with, than to not." The lead scientist said, and the faces dropped further, because they all thought the two people leading them were clearly insane to ask to be fired upon, even if it did make perfect sense.

Half an hour later, and an equally bewildered Splenklar, their ship was fired upon, and other than being shaken up a bit, the ship was undamaged. Captain Casey thanked Captain Splenklar for his help to test their new systems, but he had just shook his head in amazement and disconnected, but was smiling. The other captains, that had by now joined them, all also thought Captain Casey was both brilliant and crazy, they all said they were not that brave to be willingly fired upon, but they agreed with Casey's logic behind it.

1300 hours came, and found a number of ships sitting and waiting at the border of the Tenarian systems, with a smaller number of ugly looking ships. The ships were still almost twice as large as the Universe Explorer, but they looked in very poor shape. There were obvious signs of damage to all the hulls that had either gone unrepaired, or had been shoddily repaired, and they were an ugly dull rusty color. It was also an ugly shape, very sharp pointed features, and kind of short and squat. The windows were also all sharp pointed shapes, none of them matching, none of them the same size, even on the same ship. It was like each ship was just built from spare parts from whatever they had kicking around at the time. Their propulsion systems were side mounted on short squat wing like things, and looked exceptionally weak. Everyone thought that they would be the very first target, because to remove their ability to move would be to remove their ability to fight as well.

Captain Splenklar was to be the ambassador to these dealings, so as soon as he arrived, and took the forward position, with the Universe Explorer and one of the other Tenarian ships flanking him, he signaled the the other ships.

What Captain Casey and his crew saw on their view screens made their skin crawl. They were faced with an ugly creature that looked like a cross between a human and a wild boar. They were short, squat little creatures, just like their ships, greyish brown in colour, with three fingered hands and sharp claws, course hair all over their bodies, and about six to eight inch long tusks sticking out their faces. Their faces looked much like a boars face, only with a shorter snout and all very sharp pointed teeth. The ears however were identical to a boars. Most of the beasts' tusks were noted to be stained a reddish tinge, more than likely from blood. They were all wearing simple, poorly made tunics of an odd skin, which were also a dull greyish brown colour, and more than a few of these garments appeared as if they should have been replaced years ago. They were quite possibly the ugliest and most unkempt creatures the humans had ever set eyes on, and hoped that they never would again have to.

"Qaralon fleet, your request for passage through our space has already been denied numerous times, we won't grant you passage now or ever. You were warned the last time that the next time you came to our borders, that you'd be escorted back to your system under heavy guard, and that if you ever came back, you'd be blown out of space. Apparently this warning was not strong enough for you, we're now going to escort you home, and any refusal to this, will be met with brutal force." Captain Splenklar barked out.

"Tenarian fleet, like say last time, if try stop us, we force way through. Last time we not 'nough ships, this time do. You little ships no stop us. And what that beastly looking thing, it look like piece of scrap metal." The beast asked of the Universe Explorer.

"Captain Casey, would you like to take this one?" Captain Splenklar asked with a wide grin.

"Certainly. I have no idea what to call you, but we're from Earth. We're new to the area, and the Tenarians are friends of ours, but while my ship may be smaller than yours, it's fast and strong, and certainly in far better shape than your rusting hunks of scrap metal." He answered calmly.

"Bah, you those people not even in space yet, three system over. We nothing fear from you, you not even fly that thing. Go home, you not b'long here, or we forced to show why no one messes with Qaralon people." It growled out.

"I don't take threats from people like you, but you're obviously mistaken, because the Tenarians obviously aren't afraid of you." Captain Casey said smoothly.

This seemed to anger the beasts further, because it and all the ones they could see very clearly bristled from it. In fact, their short bristly hair stood on end with that, and almost every last one of them growled.

"That's correct, the Qaralon people are of no threat to us, you've tried and failed, many times, to cross our borders, but each time you lose half the ships that you bring against us, while we may get damage to one, or maybe two ships on a bad day. Again you bring a pitiful gang of bullies with you, and against larger numbers than you've ever seen before, you have no hope, now come along peacefully, and we'll take you home." Captain Splenklar said calmly.

In answer, the Qaralon ships all closed off communication and started firing at will. Captain Splenklar was hit pretty hard by at least three of the Qaralon ships, but they did not seem to hurt him, even though it was clear that he was hit by the blackening of the areas that had been hit and by how the ship lurched.

None of the Qaralon ships used any sort of strategy though, they just fired randomly and sporadically, almost as if they were not aiming at all. They missed on almost as many shots as they hit, but they were bombarding the defenders with sheer numbers, because they just kept firing and firing, not caring at all that they were wasting more than they were using.

Captain Casey, in response to the hit he received, which had also caused them to lurch more than a bit, started calling out orders and maneuvers, and within seconds he was able to disable the lead ship. He left them sitting there stranded, and then went to the next victim. Because the Universe Explorer was so much smaller, but just as fast, it had incredible maneuverability in comparison to the larger ships, and they were able to destroy five of the twelve remaining ships. They dodged in and out of the larger ships, bobbing and weaving almost as if dancing, all of them doing their best to win this fight that they now found themselves in.

The remainder of the Tenarian's ships were able to either disable or destroy the rest of the Qaralon ships with relative ease. Within only twenty minutes, the entire Qaralon attack fleet had been disabled, and the few that were not destroyed outright, were sitting there now, waiting for what they had no idea.

The Tenarians used tractor beams to move the three Qaralon ships that were left, and the winners of the fight surrounded them. Captain Splenklar pinged the Qaralon ships and they answered.

"What, you plan slaughter us now? Get over with it." Snarled the beast.

"Oh no, much worse than that I'm afraid. We're going to let you go. I figure that on auxiliary power and engines, you should make it home in a week or two, unless you can repair your ships. Then when you get home, you get to tell them that you were handed your hearts on a platter, and the Earth people took out almost half your ships, with nothing more than a scratch to themselves. Not to mention that the most damage you could dish out, was to my ship, and it'll take all of maybe an hour to repair. Now get going, before I forget that I'm a nice person." Captain Splenklar snapped out, and shut down the communication.

The defenders all backed off and left the Qaralon some space. After maybe ten minutes, the Qaralon were able to reroute their auxiliary systems, and took off, limping home. As soon as they were out of firing range, which took well over an hour, Captain Splenklar called up Captain Casey.

"You guys were incredible, I never thought your ship would handle so well. I think we need to go a bit smaller in our designs if you can move like that, but what was that incredible weapon you guys used? You could've taken on their entire group and survived!" He asked in awe, and the others all nodded.

"Thanks. We've all trained very hard to get this good, and our ships, while being designed for exploring, will take a good beating, but dish out even more. As for the missiles, a little home grown brew I guess you can say. Sadly, Earth is really good at making extremely powerful and destructive weapons, as you may have found out already from our history, and these were specially designed for our protection out here. I'd be happy to give you the specifications, to pay you back some for all your generosity to us."

"I'm sure that that'd be very well received. Unfortunately now though, the Qaralon will want to try and save face and attack you, or your planet. They've tried a number of times on our planet, though thankfully they've never succeeded. They're a fierce creature, and they breed very rapidly, so there are trillions of them. We've barely kept them at bay, and we're not sure why they've never moved up to a full scale assault on us. We're very powerful yes, but I don't believe that that's all, they fear us for some reason. I have to wonder though, what they'll do to you if they get a chance!" He warned.

"We'll worry about that when, and if the time comes. After the defeat that we handed them today, I'd hope that they're not that stupid, but I feel that they are."

"Your feelings are correct, they are that stupid. They're also pure carnivores, and don't seem to care who, or what they kill for their food. They're very reckless, and not very smart, hence the reason they keep attacking us in these small numbers with those poor ships of theirs."

"Well, we should be going. I have to send a report back home, saying we're all okay, and then we should be on our way. We still have a lot to explore, this is our first trip after all, and we're all excited to go out exploring." Captain Casey smiled.

"I too must send a report. Be careful out there, the Qaralon are all over the place out there, they normally travel in packs, and there are also other hostile peoples out there, but I think you'll have no problems with them. Should you need any help at all, just call, and I'll come with friends to help however we can. Enjoy your trip, and keep us posted."

"You too, and if you need help as well, call, we'll also come, and you be sure to keep us posted as well. Be safe and talk to you soon." Captain Casey said and signed off.

Captain Casey ordered his crew on, while he went to his office and called Admiral Way to give his report. The admiral was very happy that they were still alive, with nothing more than a scratch, and ecstatic that they performed so well. Captain Casey warned the admiral about what his feelings of the Qaralon were, and that a ramp up of ship building might be wise. The admiral informed the captain that this was already in the works, and within a month, three more ships would launch with full crew, then at a rate of about five per month from each of the five factories, as soon as they were all up and running, which was still another month away.

After a good long chat and bull session, the two old friends signed off, and the captain went about his duties. He checked up on the scientists to see what they were all up to. They were broken up into groups of five and working on the projects that they had picked, and had some excellent progress already for only having started a few hours before.

The communicator, he was told, would be done by the end of the day, as well the teleporter was already started, and he was promised it would be done in three days or less. Captain Casey was pleased with the work that all the scientists were doing, so left them to their work.

The next five months for the crew of the Universe Explorer seemed to just fly by; they were all having a great time exploring the universe, and meeting all kinds of new people, some were friendly, some were not, some were cold and distant, while some were just plain mean. All in all, with the information the crew had gathered, the people they had met, and the things they had seen, the crew decided to turn around and head home. There was still much to explore, and they would all be happy to go further, once getting back home to make their one year scheduled return.

About half way back home, Captain Casey received a distress call from the Tenarians.

"Captain Casey, you need to get back as quick as you can. The Qaralon have sent a fleet of thousands of ships, and are about to attack our system, we only just picked them up. Almost half the fleet broke off and appear to be skirting our system, and we feel that they're heading to Earth, but they could be trying to sneak around to catch us from behind as well. You need to call home and warn them of the dangers, and you need to get there as soon as you can." Captain Splenklar intoned.

"Thank you Captain, we're on our way. We've been headed back for some time already, but taking a different route back, and taking the long way. We'll change course immediately and get there as soon as we can." Captain Casey said and then signed off. There was little need for politeness at this point.

On that vain, the captain called home.

"Admiral Way, we have a situation." Captain Casey said as soon as his friend came up on the screen. Admiral Way knew by the look on his friends face that he was not going to like this any.

"What is it Casey, you look like you've just seen a ghost." He asked worriedly.

"The Qaralon have sent in an entire armada of ships, thousands of them, in against the Tenarians. I've been informed, however, that half the ships have broken off, and are attempting to quietly skirt the Tenarian systems, and they feel they may be headed straight for you. By now you should have lots of ships, but you need to get the shields and weapons into anything that flies, and right away. As it stands, our entire fleet together couldn't withstand the sheer size of such a fight, and the Tenarians will be fighting on their own front. We're on our way back, and we'll get there as soon as we can, but we're still a long ways away. We have no idea, at this time, how far away the attack is, or if it's coming though, so we must prepare. If it's not, however, we need to go help the Tenarians, so we must still prepare everything we can." He said rapidly.

"Well old friend, that's grave news no doubt. All told we have a bit over a hundred of your ship design ready and flying. You're correct though, we're not yet prepared to face an enemy that large. We'll ramp up production as fast as we possibly can, we'll get any factory capable of ship building to start building what they can. We'll even equip rust bucket old cars with the large engines, shields, and weapons if we have to. I hope you get home before they arrive. I of course will be scanning for their arrival in every way possible." He said, looking more than a little sick at hearing such horrific news.

"Good. I say do it, just get as much in the sky as you can. These things are unpredictable apparently, and this attack took a lot more forethought than the Tenarians thought they had. I have a feeling someone else is helping them, and that same feeling also tells me we're in a lot of trouble."

"We will. I have to go now, I have a lot to prepare. Hope to see you soon." He said and signed off.

The admiral was sick though, because he had known Captain Casey for far too long, and trusted the captains gut instincts too much, so knew without a shadow of a doubt that they were in for a fight. He called everyone and told them the news, got everyone going as fast as they possibly could to prepare, but for what he had no clue at all, only he hoped it would not be a horrible loss. What it was though was sadly far from that, far surpassing a horrible loss, it was staggering, sickening, all things horrible.

Sadly, Captain Casey was not in time, although he may not have been able to help even if he had have made it in time. The Qaralon fleet did try and sneak in, and they made it far closer than anyone expected them to. Though by the time the Earth ships went to greet them, they were already turning around. At first the humans were baffled, thinking they decided the fight was not worth the effort, how wrong they were.

What the Qaralon had done was launch hundreds of large missiles, most aimed at Earth's extensive network of communication satellites, to knock out their systems. The largest of the missiles however were aimed at ten major cities throughout the world. The missiles were very well shielded, and being relatively small, they almost went completely undetected, but by the time they were noticed, it was too late, more than oner hundred million people were lost on that one day alone.

The Earth ships stood down in utter shock as to what had happened. The people on the planet, no matter where they were, knew instantly what had happened. Everyone had been warned that an attack was almost imminent, and when the world shook, they knew. Given that the satellite systems were down, there was nearly no way for everyone to be told immediately, everyone had radios of some sort still though, and when the signals on their computers and TV's went down, most switched those on. The news was slow in coming, but finally, they were all informed as to the gravity of the situation. The entire planet was in shock.

PROLOGUE 4

WAR IS UPON US

Back in Admiral Way's office at the World Space Exploration Center, or WSEC, in Vancouver Canada, he and every other commander of the fleet, and most Prime Ministers and Presidents of the world, were busy communicating as best they could. They all teleported in as soon as they were able to get clearance, and they all met at headquarters. Five of the people that should have been there, however, were not, due to the fact that they were either dead, or missing in the cities that were almost all lost. It was a sad meeting to say the least, for everywhere you looked you could see the great sadness in each and every person's eye there. Some you could see had shed a few tears as well, for they had many friends that were feared lost.

"Silence, everyone, please. We need to figure out where to go from here. Captain Casey and his crew should be here any time now, and I'd like to wait until he gets here." Admiral Way stated, his mood understandably very subdued.

"Admiral, do we yet know who all got hit, and how many lost?" Prime Minister Williams of Canada asked.

"Sir, at this time we know almost nothing. We believe that all of our satellites, and at least eight major cities around the globe were destroyed. We know they got New York and Los Angeles, as well as Beijing and Tokyo. Paris and London, however, we have yet to contact, and they too are feared to be lost. Toronto was also targeted, but the cities defenses managed to get it before it hit, although there's still major damage, because it was caught very close, and at this time we know of no deaths there, however I'm sure there are many. The death toll in the other cities though, may never truly be known. From pictures we were able to get of Los Angeles though, I'd have to say that the loss is total. When the missile detonated, it caused the San Andreas fault to simply open up, and swallow the cities around it whole. I'm honestly surprised though that they didn't hit us here, and the only reason that I can see that they didn't, was simply because they had no idea this was where our headquarters were. If I had to guess, I'd say that they just pointed their weapons at the largest concentrations of humans, and fired." Admiral Way stated sadly.

"This is truly a sad day, one that none of us ever hoped to see. Let's all take a minute in silence to honor the fallen." The Prime Minister said, equally as sad.

For one full minute not a sound was to be heard, and not one eye was dry. Once they all looked up, still no one said a word, no one felt that words were appropriate at this time. The room was still silent with everyone in thought an hour later when Captain Casey teleported in.

"Admirals, Prime Ministers and Presidents. Today is a grave day, and I fear this was all my fault. Had I not helped the Tenarians, we wouldn't have had this happen. My resignation will be written shortly. I apologize, and I hope that whomever you get to replace me is better than I at judging situations." Captain Casey bowed his head shamefully to those present.

"Your resignation is refused. We'll hear nothing of your quitting. This was in no way your fault, and you know it, just as well as every person in this room. The Qaralon are bullies, you and I both know it, and they want this planet and the people on it, simply for food. We all knew that it was a matter of time, and that they'd attack sooner or later. I for one believe that we have the best person in charge up there already, and now that you're here, we can talk strategy." Prime Minister Williams stated emphatically, and almost everyone else nodded their approval.

"Fine Sir, I won't resign then! What I'd like to know though, is how did the scum get in so close without being seen, and what kind of weapon did they use?"

"Their ships were equipped with a fairly good shield that prevented our long distance scanners from seeing them. We knew they were there, but couldn't see them. The missiles, however, we have no idea what they were made of. They launched them, and they were even more invisible than the ships were, we never even saw it coming 'til it was too late." Admiral Way said.

"From what I've seen and heard of the Qaralon, they don't have the skills necessary to carry out such a large scale attack, or build that kind of equipment. I'm now of firm belief that they were being helped, but by whom I don't know. On our mission we met many species, and I can name two, maybe three, that'd be capable of such a thing. Have the Tenarians been informed yet, and if not, they should be? I feel that when we call full war, which I'm sure we will be, they too will follow. I don't feel that we'll be alone. There are a number of races as well, I'm sure, that would be willing to join the fight." Captain Casey told the group.

"Captain I don't believe that it's appropriate that you say that we'll go to war, that's the decision of this council, and this council alone. And furthermore, if you were in my charge, I'd have you demoted, and jailed for the danger that you've put the planet in." The president of the United States finally spoke.

"Then it's a good thing that he isn't, and given I have the majority vote of this council, I'd have called war on his advice. Not to mention, what makes you believe we'd sit back and let the Qaralon use planet Earth· as a farm to feed their people. We're nothing more than farm animals to them, they'll try and beat us down, but we won't allow it." Admiral Way nearly whispered to the president, and he looked and sounded so deadly at that point, that the president actually took a step back, but he held his head up.

"I have no intentions of sitting back, and we'll be voting for war as well, it's however not the place of a captain to tell the leaders of the planet what to do." The president said as if he was not just verbally bashed.

"And I'd never presume to do so either Sir, that was simply what my opinion was, and I knew that there was no way the council would decide to do anything but. You have to remember that we're the ones out there fighting this, and my vote has to count for a lot, because until you get in a ship and go out and fight, I don't feel that anyone in this room has any right to not listen to me." Captain Casey stated calmly.

"Good point Captain, and believe me, the captains of the ships have a lot of say in here, especially in these cases. If needed though, every last one of us in this room will take command of a ship and help out!" Admiral Way stated.

"Glad to hear it. Now, what are the plans anyway?" Captain Casey asked, trying to break the obvious tension in the room.

"We were waiting for you to arrive, so that we could plan out our next move. We now know your point of view, anything else to add." The admiral asked.

"Yes, I'd like to add a few things. Our first priority must be to build as much as we can as fast as we can. Outfit every last freighter, survey ship, and hunk of rust we have with the best shields and weapons we can stuff into them, and get the people in them and training. I recommend that we do this until we're sure we have what we need to go after the beasts that did this. We'll also need to contact the Tenarians and get their input on this." Captain Casey added.

"I for one could not have put it any better myself." Prime Minister Williams said.

"I also have to agree! We've been overly patient so far, making sure our ships were perfect before leaving our system, even though many in this room would have left years ago. We can't make a rash decision in the heat of the moment. I understand that we need to show the enemy that we're not afraid of them, but to do so at this time would prove nothing, because we'd be outnumbered five hundred to one. We couldn't hope to overcome those odds. I'm going to go call the Tenarians, would the rest of you please start planning the building! Captain and Prime minister Williams, would you please come with me?" Admiral Way asked, and they nodded and followed.

"Well old friend, we're really in it up to our eyeballs, aren't we!" Admiral Way stated somberly to the captain.

"Yes, yes we are, and I don't know how we're gonna get out of it. Let me contact Captain Splenklar to see what he and his government have in mind." He said, and in answer the admiral just nodded.

"Hello Captain Splenklar, how's the fight on your front." Captain Casey asked once he brought the Captain up.

"There isn't one. Many hours ago now, they just backed off and left as quick as they could, and they appeared to be heading home.

We lost a few ships, and a few hundred good men and women though in the battle that did happen. I'd have to say though, that by the looks on your faces however, you didn't get off so lightly."

"I am afraid it's far worse than you can imagine. They somehow managed to sneak in, and they were too close, we never even saw it coming. Whomever is helping them has given them excellent shielding technology, they sent out hundreds of missiles, they destroyed probably every satellite the planet had, and then they targeted ten of our most populous cities, we simply have no idea how many people were lost, many many millions at the very least." Admiral Way said sadly.

"I am deeply saddened by this news, and our planets condolences go out to yours. Any help we can offer will be freely given. As for who was helping them, we now know that as well, we also know a bit about why, we think, but are pretty certain as well." Captain Splenklar told the two.

The meeting of all the world leaders in the other room however was getting very heated at times. Many of the countries could not decide who should do what, and some complained that they were getting too much to do. It was going nowhere fast, and before too long, a full out brawl would take place. The volume in there was already reaching yelling, and soon full out bellowing would ensue.

"We thank you for your kind words, and any help you could offer would be most appreciated, I assure you. We have decided to hold off on the retaliation, until we either have to go out and fight, or until we have the ships, and the crews ready to go. If we were to take on such an opponent at this time, we'd surely lose, and there'd be no point in that. Please give us any information that you're able to?" The prime minister asked.

"First I'd say that that's a very smart move on your part, you're right, such a fight you could not yet win. Even with us helping, I don't believe we could do it. We'll send what people we can spare to help in your ship building efforts, and we'll find other friendly races to help as much as they're able to as well. As for who the mysterious backers are, they're a long time ally of the Qaralon, they're called the Framgar."

"They're almost as mean, not quite so ugly, and unfortunately, a lot smarter. As for the reason they want your planet, well, it's two fold. The Qaralon need another planet to call home, theirs is full, and they also believe that your people look very tasty. They don't like us any from what it sounds, they say we taste bitter, and leave an even worse aftertaste, this is probably one of the reasons why they leave us alone, for the most part. They won't eat us, so there's no point in fighting us." Captain Splenklar said, kind of grinning.

"Well I can assure you, that even dead, I'll fight with every fiber of my being before I let one of those monsters eat me. So what's in it for the Framgar then? They can't be helping out just to be nice. Creatures like this, I'd think, only do things if there's something good in it for them." Captain Casey asked.

"You're most probably correct. What, however, it may be, we have as many ideas as you yourselves probably have. The Framgar are a small dying people, who really have nothing to lose by such an action. Maybe they're looking for a new home planet, and your Mars is just like their home world. If I had to give an educated guess, I'd say that that'd be the concession."

The arguments were starting to fly fast and furious throughout the meeting hall next door, and threats and insults were starting to truly become offensive. It was becoming painfully obvious that if this was not stopped soon, it would be an all out fist fight, and that was almost what it became, just as the three people that had left the room found, when they came back in.

"I'd say then that that's a very good guess. I hope we can meet sometime soon Sir, and we thank you for all your help. We however must be going, we have a lot of planning to do." The prime minister said.

"As do I. Myself, and many representatives of our government will be there in a few days, at the latest. See you then." Captain Splenklar stated and signed off.

"I can hear the others, and it doesn't sound very friendly out there, we better go!" The admiral stated as soon as the captain was gone.

"What the hell is going on here. Every last one of you sit down now, and don't say one word until you're spoken to, is that understood!" Admiral Way shouted out as they entered the room.

Everyone found a chair and sat down, and other than a few nasty glares, nothing was said.

"Okay, I understand that this has been a very stressful day on all of us, but the planet is depending on us to get us all through this, in some semblance of one piece. Acting like spoiled rotten two-year-old's will get you nowhere, and is certainly not appreciated right now. So did anyone actually come up with anything useful then, or were you fighting the entire time?" Admiral Way asked, his voice dripping with anger.

"No Sir, we were trying to figure out what countries could do what, when everyone started to complain and say they were getting too much." The president of the United States said.

"I see. So everyone thought they were getting more work than everyone else! Well then, let's make this simple then shall we. Every job that is NOT essential to the operation of your country, WLL be transferred to ship building. Any, and all people that can be taught, will either be building, and or flying the ships. No one under the age of eighteen may be allowed, and all children will go to school as normal as possible. The Tenarian people have offered a great deal of help, and a few leaders will be here in a few days. What I just witnessed in this room is definitely not to be repeated, because if you embarrass me, I'll move to have a vote of non-competence put against each and every one of the people involved. Now go." Admiral Way snapped.

Without a word spoken from them, everyone got up and left. Many of the country leaders more than a bit upset that a mere admiral, of the space department, was able to push them around like he could, but especially in a war footing, as they now certainly were, they were simply his advisers.

"You realize every last one of them probably hates you now, right!" Prime Minister Williams stated seriously.

"And I bet it hurts his feelings so bad, can't you see the look of hurt on his face Prime Minister." Captain Casey said with a grin.

"No, I'm certain he cares very little."

"You're both correct, they do hate me, and will continue to hate me for some time, but we all have a greater issue to deal with, and that's first and foremost. I don't care if they can't stand to look at me, my only care is to get us out of this mess, hopefully in one piece."

"And you will old friend, there's no better person for the job!" Captain Casey said reassuringly.

"I concur. You're the best one to get this mess straightened out. Have no fear about the others though, they'll come around when they cool down, and come to see that you're right."

As it turned out all the world leaders did finally come to understand Admiral Way was correct, and they did what he basically ordered them to do. The help that the Tenarians sent was also much appreciated. Within six months Earth had an army of ships in virtually every size and shape, ranging in man power from fifty to two hundred and they felt they could finally go get the revenge they felt they rightly deserved.

No one, however, could understand why the Qaralon and the Framgar did not attack when they clearly had an advantage. It was assumed that the Qaralon were fearful of the full might of the Humans and the Tenarians together, and figured, that after so much time, that they were safe. If that was the case, boy were they wrong. What it was, they found out later, was that they were now lightly fighting amongst themselves about spoils when they went back to finish the human planet off.

CHAPTER 1

THE WAR IS OVER

The war with the Qaralon was long and brutal. The Humans and the Tenarians were joined by quite a few other races, over the years, who were also fed up with the Qaralon raids, fed up with the Qaralon taking their children for food. The Qaralon and Framgar outnumbered the other races, in both man power and their sheer amount of ships, but that mattered very little in the long run. The other races had ships that were by far more superior in both build and handling. Because of this, the Qaralon and Framgar ended up losing nearly twenty ships to every one that they were able to damage or destroy.

They could afford to lose these though, for much too long a time. However, eventually at these losses, they could not sustain their army any longer, and after fifty years, they surrendered. The war lasted a long time, but the battles were few and far between, so finally near the end, the defenders decided enough was enough, and went straight for the heart of the Qaralon and Framgar. They managed to finish the war in four awful weeks. The attackers became very desperate near the end, and just before they signaled defeat, took out many ships.

The Humans had lost roughly fifty thousand ships, and many more millions of people during the war. Many more people were lost due to Qaralon raids however, they would take whole families while they slept, and what happened to them, no one knew, or wanted to guess. The Tenarians lost in around the same amount of ships, but not quite so many people, and the other races also lost many. It was a bitter victory, but victory none the less. Captain Casey had retired after nearly thirty years, becoming the most decorated and celebrated war hero, his victories in the war equaled

1

many ships all together. During the war, he married his first officer, and they had six children all together, their oldest, Jonathon Casey, was the only one to also become a ships captain.

Jonathon had learned everything he could about flying a space ship from the many years of growing up on one. He did everything in the ship he was able to do; from cleaning, to helping to repair anything and everything, he did it all. All the children were tutored on board the ship, and Jonathon excelled, he did so well in fact, that by the age of fifteen, he had already graduated. Not only was he a high school graduate, but he was fully qualified to operate his very own ship, there was simply nothing he did not know about them.

At their next stop at home, Jonathon left his family, and his home for the very first time in his life, and headed to school. At university, Jonathon exceeded every expectation, and graduated after almost ten years, at the top of his class, with masters degrees in Child Psychology and Advanced Space Engineering, and more than a few minor degrees in varying areas of medics, space travel, and child behavior.

Once Jonathon left school, he was handed a ship of his own to captain, for what was to be the last ten years of the war, and he got his parents ship, none other than the original Universe Explorer, now dubbed the UE1.

The surrender of the Qaralon was a much celebrated time among all those that had fought. The losses however dampened the spirits, but everyone still celebrated the end of the war, and the final freedom it created. Finally, the rebuilding of the planet could take place. With the war ended, and no more ships being built, and other than a few kept to repair the current ships, every shipbuilder was utilized to rebuild the cities.

It turned out however that a much greater problem had occurred because of the war. Many people were lost, but the children were as protected as they could be, so because of this, there ended up being a great many orphans. As many were adopted by loving parents as could be. The care centers that were built to care for all the children during the war, while the parents were away, turned into orphanages, where the remainder stayed. These children were never forgotten by the governments caring for them, every one of these children had suffered great losses, and because of this, they received the best possible care.

Jonathon of course saw to this, he made sure that every country treated these children with the utmost of respect and care, to help them to grow into fine adults. After working in more than a few orphanages for a few years, and helping the children, he started to get restless with the itch to be in space again. He had never really lived on Earth before, except the years that he was at school, and even then he itched to be in space. An idea started to form, one he hoped would combine his talents. With that idea forming in his mind, he decided to call his parents to see what they thought.

"Hi Mom and Dad, how are you guys doing?" He asked of his parents when they answered their video phone.

"We're doing fine Jonathon, how about you?" Admiral Casey asked. His dad of course got many promotions over the years, and retired an admiral.

"Just missing being in space. I'm thinking of doing something drastic, so would like your opinions." He said, something that hardly surprised them.

"We know how you feel, we've both felt the same many times, that's why sometimes we go for a month or two and fly somewhere. We find it real handy since they retired the Universe Explorer and gave it to us, so now we can use it whenever we want to." His mother, Captain Casey said.

"That's kind of what I was calling about as well. Well you see, I need to get back in the sky, and I want to borrow your ship for a while, a couple years at least I figure, but don't worry, you'd always be welcome aboard." Jonathon grinned.

"You know you're welcome to borrow the ship any time you want, because it really is as much yours as it is ours. I have to ask though, what do you have in mind, since I can't really see you giving up on the kids?" Admiral Casey asked curiously, knowing that the kids were the one and only reason that their son was not still in the sky.

"Definitely not, they're in on this as well. Here's what I have in mind. I want to take twenty kids that we find, preferably right off the streets, and use them to run the ship. I'll teach them everything they need to know, I'll school them, and we'll take on missions the same as everyone else, just like any crew. Because I want to gather the boys right off the streets, ones who are very good at slipping by the police, it could be difficult though."

"Difficult may not be the best word to use. There are a lot of children on the streets, and even with our best efforts to get them into homes, it's been difficult, they're very slippery. Your idea's ambitious, but nice, are you sure you can do it alone though?" His mom asked, she had been trying for years to get all the children into homes as well, but most of the ones still on the street were very well versed in evading capture.

"I'm sure of that, the kids will have very little trust of adults, so the fewer, especially to start, the better. I'm going to call in a few favors, and get the ship outfitted to start taking missions again, of course for the first month or so, we'll probably just stay pretty close to home, so that the kids can learn in relative safety."

"Well, it sounds like you've got everything thought out then. When are you going to announce this all and get the ship?" His father asked.

"I was thinking of finishing out the current month, and start searching for the perfect boys for this mission on my off time. I think I'll be able to get most right from this area alone, if not all. I might try and use some of the kids I know from the orphanage to help, the street kids are more likely to trust them. I'll also check the hospitals for ones who've been injured, and then I'll test them all to see if they'll be able to do this. I hope to be in the sky in less than a month." Jonathon said.

"Sounds good, but if you need any help at all, just ask us, or your brothers and sisters, we're all willing to help wherever possible." Jonathon's mom told him.

"Will do, love you guys, have a good night."

"We love you too Jon, be careful though, those children are very good, and even you could get hurt." His mother admonished one final time before they hung up, knowing of course that it was of very little use, she knew that Jonathon knew of the risks of what he was planning very well.

A few days later found Jonathon in the office of the orphanage director, telling him all about his plans, the conversation went much the same as the one with his parents. The director of course offered what assistance that he could. Jonathon informed the director that, if possible, he would get the boys that he found, that did not meet his criteria, into the orphanage to get them taken care of properly.

CHAPTER 2

THE SEARCH BEGINS

Jonathon's first find, when he started looking a few days later still, was a twelve-year-old boy who had been beaten up by a rival street gang, and was in the hospital. Jonathon had been alerted by one of his contacts at the hospital about the boy, and his supreme attitude problem, and knowing from what Jonathon had told him, that the boy would be perfect.

When he went to the hospital to meet the boy, he found a young thin red haired boy strapped to the bed. He was dirty, more than a little smelly and unkempt would be putting it kindly. He was also wearing a pretty hefty looking leg cast and was still pretty bruised and battered. As soon as he walked in the room, the boy eyed him warily, seeing very clearly that he did not belong in the hospital and wondering what he could possibly want.

"Hello young man, I understand you haven't told anyone your name yet, but that's okay, I understand. I'd like to talk to you for a few minutes please, if I could?" He asked.

"No, I haven't told anyone my name, and I won't either. Who are you, and what ya want?" He asked defiantly.

"That's okay, you don't have to tell me yet, but I'd like to be able to call you something other than young man. So tell me if you have a street or nick name I can use? As for who I am, and what I want. Well, my name's Captain Jonathon Casey, and I'd like to give you a test, it's fairly simple, but will take a little while."

"If I told you what most people call me, it'd make you blush, just call me kid, most others do. Are you related to Admiral Casey, he's awesome? Will the test hurt any? I'm not going anywhere, they have me all tied down, so that I won't try and escape again."

"First of all, I can assure you that nothing you say can or will make me blush. I'm a doctor as well as a captain, and I help children. I'm probably more aware of what you had to do to stay alive on the streets than anyone else. I've helped a lot of you guys out there on the street. Yes, Admiral Casey's my father, and I agree with you. Let me see, what was your next question? Oh yeah, the test won't hurt any, just some questions. Now, tell me, why would you try to run away when you look as beat up as you do? It hardly looks as if you can walk, let alone run, you're one massive bruise. Not to mention the cast on your leg, it goes all the way up!"

"I hate hospitals, and I don't trust them doctors, always trying to get me into an orphanage, or possibly worse." He spat out.

"Well hating hospitals I can understand, not the most pleasant places to have to spend a few days, but would you rather the alternative? I'm told that with the amount of internal bleeding you had, that you would've died within a few hours, had you not been brought in. As for not going to an orphanage, tell me, why would you hate that so much? There are adults there to care for you, other kids to play with, you get to go to school and learn, you wouldn't have to live on the street and freeze every night, or wonder how or where your next meal was going to come from. As well you wouldn't have to do all that I know you've had to do to get that food. Stealing being the least of which. We won't go further into that, it isn't my business, and no one needs to know." Jonathon said softly.

"Well they fixed me up, so now I want to go, that's all. I've just heard bad things about orphanages, some say you're nothing but slaves, and others say that you get no food, and are crowded into tiny rooms with dozens of kids. I'm better off on the streets."

"Yes they patched you up, but you aren't healed yet, far from it in fact. Now orphanages are nothing like that, there are two boys, or two girls per room, you aren't a slave in any way, and you get fed and treated very well. At most you'll have basic chores to help with, like laundry or dishes or helping to cook, little things like that, and it's at most an hour or two a week. Not exactly hard work, but heck, even if it was as bad as all that, it would've been a lot better than living on the street if you ask me. Thankfully though we'd never treat any kid like that. Let's get started with this test then, if that's okay by you?" Jonathon asked softly again, and the young man just nodded.

For the next half hour, Jonathon administered a verbal test to the boy, and he did very well, but not all that surprising really, considering just how smart the kids had to be to evade the enemies that were always after them. He was able to answer almost all the questions that Jonathon asked quickly and correctly, almost without thinking.

"Well kid, you did very well on the test, congratulations. You of course lack the book knowledge, like reading and general math, but you're very bright. You also have the other skills I'm looking for; you're a very fast thinker, but most importantly, you're a survivor. I have a proposition to make."

"What is it?" The boy asked with a bit of curiosity peeking through the tough exterior he tried to show.

"How would you like to be part of the crew on the Universe Explorer One. I'm looking for twenty boys just like you. It'll be kind of like a space school kind of thing. You'd be expected to follow orders, and work very hard, but you'll get so much more out of it than you could ever put into it." Jonathon told the boy quietly, as if he were telling a huge secret, to help pique his interest even more, and by the size of his eyes, it had.

"Are you gonna be the captain?" The boy asked almost excitedly, then clamped down on it to try and stop his feelings from showing.

"Yes. Now could you trust me enough with your name and age, so that I can put you on the crew manifest?"

"My name's Brady, and I think I'm twelve, when do we leave?" He asked excitedly now, no longer even trying to act tough.

"In a few days I'm going to start taking kids up to the ship, but I'm told that you're here for at least five more days anyway, and I'd like for you to try and cooperate, as well as get better! Now, I'd like to give you an official crew communicator, so that if you need me for anything at all, you can call. For now, once this is put on, it won't come off, okay, so that that way no one can try and take it from you. It'll also allow me to teleport you when you're ready to leave. Will this be alright?" He asked Brady, knowing full well the answer by how much Brady was vibrating in excitement now.

"I guess so." He answered and held out his wrist to have the communicator attached. Jonathon took a few minutes to go over the controls and how to contact him.

"Okay Brady, I have to go now, because I only have a short time left to gather all the boys I need for this mission. I'll see you in a few days."

"Okay, thanks. Can I recommend someone to come along? He's my best friend." Brady asked hopefully.

"Tell me where to find him, and I'll find him and give him the test. If he passes, I'll make the offer, but if he doesn't make the cut, then he'll have to stay. Is that okay with you?"

"I guess so. He goes by Raven, and you can usually find him in the alley behind the library. He has very black hair, that's why he's called Raven." He said, telling Jonathon any other information he could.

"I'll go find him right away then. See you in a few days then, and remember to call me if you need anything."

"I will, bye, oh, and thanks."

Jonathon left the hospital and took almost two hours to find who he thought was Raven. He ended up having to chase after him. It had been tough to find the young man, because as with most of the kids on the street after the war, they had become very adept at hiding and sneaking to escape becoming a nice Qaralon meal.

"Raven, if that's you, stop, I was sent by Brady, he asked me to find you." Jonathon yelled out easily as he was running after the boy. The boy stopped and turned, staring at Jonathon for a few moments before speaking.

"Who are you, and how did you get Brady to tell you his name? He tells no one his name, I didn't even know it for almost a year."

He kept his distance, but did not start running again, although he was well prepared to just in case.

"My name's Captain Casey, and he told me his name when I asked him to tell me, after I told him some things, and made the same offer I'll give to you."

"K, I'm listening, but make it quick, 'cause I'm hungry and need to find some food."

8

"Okay then, why don't we make this offer over dinner then, you pick the place, and we can sit in comfort and talk." Jonathon offered.

He figured that with how tough Raven was acting, he would appeal to the one thing that seemed to control young boys universally, their stomachs.

"K, take me to the steak restaurant down the street, and we can talk." Raven said, thinking that such an expensive meal would scare the man off.

"Okay, follow me then." Jonathon said happily, only too happy to give the young boy probably the best meal he would have had in a long time, if ever.

So they walked down the street to the restaurant the boy had mentioned, they were seated and then ordered, all without saying a word to each other. Raven, for his part, never looking at anyone or anything in particular, also looking at all times as if he were ready to make a run for it.

"So what's this grand offer that made Brady give you his name?" Raven asked finally.

"Uh uh uh, not before some other things. First I'd like to give you a test, we can do that during our meal though, and we can take all the time we need, the restaurant won't kick us out. This way we can also be comfortable. Could you answer a couple questions for me first though?"

"Whatever, ask, you're buying, so you can ask what you want, but I won't promise an answer, and I'll give you nothing either, that wasn't agreed upon." Raven said harshly.

"I'd never dream of making you answer something that you didn't want to, but tonight we're just talking, and you get a nice meal out of the deal, nothing more. You have nothing to fear of me, don't worry. I understand that you guys on the street don't normally trust us adults too much, and that's okay, I know why, better than you know. All I wanted to know is; how old are you and what your real name is? If you aren't ready to give it to me yet, that's okay, but if you take my offer, I'll need to know it at that time."

"I'm not ready to tell you yet, we can get started on the test though."

"That's okay. If you want to take the offer, then I'll assume you're ready at that time. We'll wait a few minutes until we get our food, and then start, so let's just talk for now." He said softly, trying to ease the boys tensions.

So for the next few minutes Raven asked questions and Jonathon answered them as best he could. The one that everyone asked though, was whether or not he was related to the admiral, and he of course answered proudly. Their meals came, and they both dug in with gusto. Jonathon started asking the questions of the test, and Raven answered everything quickly and correctly. About half way through the test, Raven finished his meal and asked for seconds, so Jonathon called the waitress over, and she took the order. The two started the test again, before Raven's second helping came, and they finished the test. Once the test was completed, Jonathon offered the boy dessert, and he gladly accepted, so they both ordered a dessert. Once it came, and they were both eating, Jonathon explained what was happening.

"So Raven, you did very well on the test, even better than Brady did, and he did very well. Now, I know you've been curious as to what I'm offering, even though you've hidden it very well, just not well enough to hide it from me. How would you like to become a crew member of the Universe Explorer?" He asked, dangling that bait out there.

"You're kidding right? I'm just a street rat, I couldn't be part of the crew of the most famous ship there is."

"No, I'm being totally honest, and what you were before you came in this restaurant means absolutely nothing to me, because the second you say yes, you become a crew member. Now, before you say yes, you need to know a few things. I'm the captain, and I'll expect to be obeyed. You'll have classes every day, and you'll learn everything there is to know about running and commanding a space ship. But before we can even do that, you need to trust me enough to tell me your name and age?" Jonathon asked gently.

"You really mean it, don't you, but why would you do this? My name's Francis, but please call me Franky, and I'm fourteen. And yes, I'd love to go. So I guess Brady's going?" He said rapidly, Jonathon chuckled.

"I'm doing this because it's my job to help kids that are in trouble, just like you guys, but I'm also a captain, and I miss flying. I'm taking a decommissioned ship on missions, and I need a crew, so what better way to merge my two passions, helping kids and flying. Now, I'm going to give you an official crew communicator, and it'll be temporarily attached permanently, so that no one can take it from you. This way I'll know where to get you when the ship's ready, and we can communicate with each other. You'll also be able to contact and talk to Brady. Give me your arm please if you're ready?"

"Okay, I guess, I'm not sure why I'm letting you do this, but I trust you for some reason." Franky said while holding out his arm nervously.

"I'm glad. I mean, if you can't trust me, you can't trust anyone."

"Normally I don't!" He stated simply while Jonathon was attaching the communicator.

Jonathon then gave Franky a quick run down on all the features of the communicator and how to use it, but asked him not to use any of the features except the communication functions as of yet. He had paused their previous conversation to do this, so continued where he had left off.

"I'll teach you to trust again, don't you worry there. I have to be going now, but I'll contact you in a few days or so, as soon as I get everyone else gathered, because I'm looking for a crew of twenty, and you make number two so far. Make sure you call me if you need anything at all though, okay, even if all you need is something to eat."

"Okay, thanks." He said simply and got up and left.

Jonathon figured he could probably go out and find another boy or two before it got too dark out. He was not that terribly afraid of the things that go bump in the night, because he was well trained in many forms of hand to hand combat, and very little that he would find could harm him.

He went the opposite direction of Franky's alley, ducked into a dimly lit back alley, and soon found a small group of boys huddled around a small fire. He walked up to the boys, as if it was a normal thing to do.

"Good evening gentlemen, mind if I join you for a few minutes." He asked pleasantly.

"Get lost, or we'll all beat you up and rob you blind, in fact, we should do it anyway, just for being stupid enough to come up and ask." The biggest and toughest looking boy said, as big as he could say it.

"No need to be rude, I was being polite. As for you all ganging up on me and beating me up, I've taken on a group of ten Qaralon, and come out with nothing more than a scratch, when one of them tried to take a bite out of me, so I doubt very seriously that a group of five young men such as yourselves, no matter how tough you look, could really do me any damage. Now, I'm going to sit and talk for a few minutes around this cozy fire you have going. If you don't wish to listen, then you may leave, but beware, you may be missing a great opportunity." Jonathon told the boys calmly.

Jonathon could see that the tough boy figured that he was just acting tough, and smiled serenely when the boy decided to make a run at him. Without even moving at all, his hand shot out and hit the boy in a way that made him collapse in a ball on the ground, crying.

"I'm sorry I had to do that to you, but you should never attack someone unless you want to be hit. I didn't hit you very hard, just take a few deep breaths, the feeling will come back, and the pain will go away. I just stunned a nerve in your side, perfectly harmless, but it hurts like hell at first. Now, may I sit and talk with the rest of you, or do you wish to try as well?" He asked just as calmly as if nothing had happened.

"Go ahead, we're not going to stop you." The next biggest boy said in awe, never had any of them seen such a thing before.

"Thank you, my name's Jonathon by the way, but we'll wait another minute or two to find out if your friend over there wants to join us or not." Jonathon said as he sat down near to the warm fire.

A few minutes later the boy on the ground got up, and when he realized that his side was going to stay attached, he stretched a bit and came over.

"What did you do to me? That hurt so bad at first, but I can't even feel it now. What do you want to talk to us for?"

"First, I again apologize for hurting you, it isn't my intention to cause pain to anyone. You had to know, however, that you won't win against me. I could hit you in many ways to cause excruciating pain, without even leaving a mark, and that was the least painful one by the way. Second, I have some questions to ask you guys, the first of which is how would you all feel about taking a test to become crew members of a space ship?"

"You mean that was the least painful way you could've hit me? Man, if I'd known that, I wouldn't have tried to attack you. What kind of test, and what do you mean crew?"

"You would've been smarter yes, but I know the reason you did it. On the street you sometimes have to prove yourself, but please, never believe you need to prove yourself in front of me. As for the test, it's a verbal test, and it takes about half an hour each, so we'll separate to do that, but you aren't obligated to do this. Now a couple things before you decide to take the test, and possibly become crew members. I'll be the captain of the ship, and you'll need to obey me, you'll be schooled every day, and taught every thing you'll need to know about operating and commanding space ships. Also, I'll need to know your real names and ages. I'm fully aware that most of you guys out here won't tell people your real names, but if you agree to join the crew, I need to have it." Jonathon told them, and they all looked more than a little curious, yet still skeptical too.

"Well my name's Jesse, and I'm ten, and I'd love to take the test. I've always wanted to go into space. Can I take the test first?" He said, the only other kid to have talked so far.

"Sure Jesse, come on, let's do this. Let's go over here out of the way. I need you guys to stay here, so that you don't hear the questions, and I'd also ask that you don't tell the others the answers once you've had the test. And just so you know, I read people better than I can hit, so I'll know, please don't try me." He told the boys. They all gulped as one.

As Jesse and Jonathon walked away a bit, the others all burst into chatter, Jonathon distinctly heard, 'wow, this is so incredible' from more than one of the boys.

"So Jesse, what are you normally called out here, I know you probably have a street name?" Jonathon asked the blond haired boy, who was bigger than a ten-year-old should have been, he looked more like thirteen.

"I normally get called Sparky, 'cause my hair's so blond. So what do I do?"

"Not much. Let's sit down and get comfortable, and then I'll start asking you questions."

"Okay"

Jonathon started asking the questions of the test, and Jesse answered them quickly and easily, almost all without thinking. The test was done a full ten minutes earlier than normally expected.

"Very well done Jesse, you answered every question perfectly, you're a very smart young man. You must have went to a very good school."

"No, before the beasts came and killed my mom and sisters, mom used to teach us at home. I was able to fight them off of me, and I killed one, then the others took off, but it was too late, they were all gone. I cried for days, 'til I had to leave to get food. I called the police while I was gone, and told them what had happened, I've never been back." Jesse said while crying.

"I'm very sorry to hear that you had to be there. I know many of the kids on the streets lost their parents in the war, and it's a truly sad thing. Seeing it happen though, has to be worse. Your mom though was a great teacher, she must have been a wonderful lady, was your dad lost in the war as well." Jonathon asked sadly.

"Yeah, she was the greatest. Yes, my dad was killed fighting in the war. I know that Admiral Casey is your dad, you look just like him, I've met him before, he was the one who came and told my mom, because they were old friends. He's very nice." Jesse said, a single solitary tear rolling down his cheek.

"Yes, my dad's the best as well. So I'd like to offer you a position on the ship Jesse, if you'll take it of course."

"I'll only go if all the others get to go as well."

"That's fair, and I figured as much. Let's go tell the others the good news."

They went back and met up with the others.

"Guys, you all have to pass the test, because I did. It was easy, and I get to go, but I said I'd only go if you all did as well." Jesse said excitedly.

"We will." The others all answered, hoping that they were right.

"So, who'd like to be next." Jonathon asked suddenly, to get things going.

"Me please. I'm Jamie and I'm fourteen, but I usually go by Jammer out here. I won't go though, unless we all go too. We're a team, and my little brother is here as well, right over there." Jamie said, pointing at a small boy. Jamie was a pretty good size for fourteen, he had long brown hair, but as with most street kids, he was pretty dirty and skinny.

"Come on over here then Jamie, and let's get this done shall we."

They went over and sat down and started the test. The test took a little over the half hour, but Jamie did very well. Jonathon informed Jamie that he had done very well and that he would be happy to offer him a position on the ship if the others wanted to and were able to as well. They headed back and Jamie excitedly told the others that he had passed, telling them that they had to as well. Jonathon asked for the next volunteer.

"Can I be next please Sir? My name's Kelly and I'm seven, and Jamie's my big brother." A scrawny little boy asked excitedly, he looked exactly like a smaller younger version of his big brother.

"Sure, come on little man, let's do this quickly, because I'm getting tired." Jonathon told the young boy.

He had not wanted to go quite this young, but to get the others, he would happily lower his age requirements by a year. It was not a big deal really, since it was his project after all and he could change anything he saw fit to at any time.

So off they went and did the test. As expected, Kelly did not do quite as well, because this test was designed for the slightly older boys, but he still did pretty good, so Jonathon felt he would be a fine addition. With that done, he then offered Kelly the position if he wanted it as well, and asked the young man what his street name had been, just because he was curious.

"Great, they call me killer, not sure why though, just always have been. My brother and me have been on the streets since before I can remember, he says I was still in diapers when our parents were killed, and we left home." He answered honestly, smiling brightly.

"Well, Kelly the killer, must be because of that killer smile of yours, let's go tell the others the good news."

The next two boys also did very well on the test as well, and were also offered positions. The first boy was named Robert, but went by Bobby. He was one of the few who did not have a nick name, was ten, average size, a bit thin, which was also somewhat normal on the streets, and had somewhat long dirty blond hair. The second was Bradley, or Brad, but went by Racer, because he was really fast, was eleven, with medium length brown hair, and normal size.

"Okay guys, you all did very well, and if you'd like, you all have positions on my crew. If you'd like to join, please stand now, and I'll give you all a communicator and put it on. They'll be permanently attached for the time being, so that it can't be stolen, and so that you can contact me at any time." Jonathon offered, already knowing exactly how many of them would be standing.

Each boy stood almost immediately, all very excited to be part of the crew of a space ship. Jonathon attached their communicators and taught them how to work them.

"So, would you guys like to know what ship you'll be crew on?" Jonathon asked, having not yet told the boys.

"Sure!" They all shouted.

"We'll be crew on the original Universe Explorer, the UE1."

"Really, I thought the government decommissioned that ship and gave it to Admiral Casey?" Jessie asked.

"They did, so I'm borrowing the family space ship. I haven't told you my full name yet, but it's Captain Jonathon Casey, and Admiral and Captain Casey are my parents."

"Now that's pretty cool. When do we leave?" Kelly asked innocently.

"In a few days I hope to have gathered the twenty boys I want for the trip, and including the five of you, I now have seven, but one of them is in the hospital for about five more days. So that of course means I still have a bit of work to do before we can go."

"Could we stay with you 'til then? It'd be really nice to sleep inside, or where it's warm for once." Kelly asked innocently again.

"Kelly, you shouldn't just ask things like that, it isn't nice." Jamie gasped.

"No, it's alright, really, if you'd like to come and stay with me 'til then, you're welcome to, all of you. I only have a pretty small apartment though, and only one bed, so you boys 'll have to curl up on the living room floor. I do have lots of blankets though, so it should be fairly comfortable. I would've offered, but I didn't want to push you guys. I'm sure that even curled up on the living room floor, with lots of nice soft blankets, would be much better than what you're more than likely used to." He told all the boys.

"It sure would be. Can we Jamie, please? It's getting cold at night, and ever since those guys stole most our stuff, we don't have enough blankets. I know you've been giving me most of yours, so you've been very cold!" Kelly pleaded with his brother.

"Are you sure it's okay with you?" Jamie asked to make sure.

"Certainly! I wouldn't have said yes otherwise. Why don't you guys go grab your things, and we can go. It's only a five or so block walk from here, so it won't take long."

CHAPTER 3

HOUSE GUESTS

Without a word, they all took off and grabbed all their belongings from the alley they were standing in. What they grabbed though was not a lot, in fact, it appeared as if it were only enough for one of them, not five.

"Is that it? You've hardly got enough stuff between you all to sustain one of you!" Jonathon asked in amazement.

"Yeah, 'bout a week ago a bunch of older boys stole most of our stuff, so we've been making due as best we could. To tell you quite honestly, if you hadn't come along, I wasn't sure what we were gonna do. I didn't want to have to go and steal things from other kids, and I didn't want to go out and use other methods of getting things again." Jamie said sourly.

"I understand, you're proud and strong, and you guys have done well out here, when many would just curl up and die. I don't blame you for not wanting to steal, unless necessary, and as for the other things you may or may not have had to do to stay alive, you'll never need to do that again, all that life is now behind you." Jonathon told all the boys, they were very happy to hear about that. The things boys on the street had to do, to get what they needed to survive, were never talked about, and were mostly very unpleasant.

"Thank you." Jamie said simply.

"No need to thank me. Follow me, let's get outta here, I'm scared of the dark." Jonathon grinned at the boys, they all chuckled, and followed him home.

It was just a short walk to Jonathon's place, and like he had told the boys, it was not much, just a simple one bedroom apartment. It was a fair size though, and all the boys would easily be comfortable on the floor in the living room. The boys set down their meager belongings, and then just stood there, kind of wondering what to do next.

"Well boys, it's getting a bit late, and I have to go to work in the morning. If you want anything to eat, the fridge is open. I'd also suggest you all grab a shower, because unfortunately you all smell a bit ripe. There's a washer and dryer beside the bathroom, so you can throw all your dirty clothes in the washer as well, and just dry them in the morning."

"Some food would be nice, but showers would be great. We probably do smell a bit, but we try to keep as clean as we possibly can living on the street. Problem is though, we have no clothes to change into." Jamie pointed out.

"Well I have a bunch of pairs of drawstring shorts I can give you guys. They'll be big even on the biggest of you, but it'll keep you covered. Kelly, however, I'm afraid the shorts would fall right off of you, no matter how much we tighten the strings. For you, I think a shirt would be best, kind of like a night gown. You could probably all do that if you wanted, it might be easier." Jonathon offered to the boys.

"Can you bring out both, so that we can decide after we get cleaned up." Jamie asked.

"Sure, give me a minute, I'll be right out."

Jonathon went to his room and grabbed four pairs of shorts and five tee shirts, and brought them back out to the living room.

"Here you go boys. Why don't one of you go grab a shower now, while the others grab a bite to eat, then you can switch off. You won't have to worry about running out of hot water, so have nice long hot showers if you want, and as soon as you finish, just throw your dirty clothes in front of the washer. I'll put them in the washer before I go to bed, or in the morning, depending on how long you all take." Jonathon told the boys.

"If you have to work in the morning, and are tired, why don't you just head to bed now, we can manage I think." Jamie offered.

"Are you sure? I know you guys are used to taking care of yourselves, so having an adult help you out might make you uneasy, but I'm here to help if you want. If not, remember that if you need any help, I can stay up, or you can ask me, because you never need to be afraid to ask for help."

"No, you've helped so much today already, and we can all see that you're tired, go ahead and go to bed. Where's the bedding, and we'll get that all out as well?" Jamie asked.

"Hall closet, across from the bathroom. If you're sure you're okay, I'm gonna go to bed then, so you boys have a good sleep, and I'll see you in the morning."

Jonathon went to his bedroom and got ready for bed in his bathroom, then crawled into bed, and fell asleep quickly after the long day.

"Well guys, Jonathon must either really trust us, or is testing us, but I don't think he's testing us. We could easily rob him blind and leave, and he wouldn't know 'til morning. I don't think that'd be a good idea though, especially since we have these communicators on, so he'd easily find us. Kelly, why don't you go get the first shower, while I make us all something to eat." Jamie told everyone.

"Okay Jammer." Kelly said happily, glad to get to have a hot shower.

Kelly grabbed one of the shirts and scampered off to the bathroom. He started the shower as hot as he could stand it, then climbed in after undressing and just stood there, letting the water cascade over his thin body, soaking up the great feelings of the hot water. He could not remember the last time he had had a hot shower, and he thought it was the best feeling ever. Nearly half an hour later, Kelly climbed out and dried off, using one of the towels on the stack, and then put the over large T-shirt on. It nearly fell right off again, and he had to hold it on with one hand. He picked up his clothes, exited the bathroom, and deposited the clothes by the washer as instructed.

"Shower's free." He called out as he left the bathroom. "This shirt's way too big, can you do something about it Jamie?"

"Jesse, why don't you go next, then Bobby, then Brad and then I'll go last. Come here squirt, let's see if there's anything in the kitchen to help."

Jamie and Kelly went to the kitchen, and Jamie went through all the drawers. He found a couple large safety pins in one of the drawers, so pinned the shirt at the neck, on both sides, so that it would stay on Kelly. It still looked ridiculously large, but it worked.

"Thanks Jammer, you're the best." Kelly said with a loving smile to his big brother. He may have grown up on the street, but he got as much love as his big brother could possibly give to him. Jamie had tried his best to raise his little brother as best he could and loved him a great deal, especially since they were all they had left.

"You're welcome Killer. Grab some food and eat up, there should be lots, we've all eaten already. You took a long time in the shower."

"It just felt so nice, I didn't want to get out. I like it here." He smiled brightly.

"I don't doubt it. It's been way too long since any of us has had a good long hot shower. Come on, eat up, and then we can go figure out the TV, and watch it for a while. I can't even remember the last time I watched TV you know. Actually I know you know, you probably don't remember ever watching TV."

"Nope, I don't . . . . Hey this is pretty good." Kelly said as he was taking his first bite of a nice hot meal, something that was also very rare for the boys.

"It's just macaroni and cheese with fried ground beef, quick and easy, but it sure did taste good to us, especially after some of the trash we've been eating lately." Jamie said with a disgusted look on his face, and meaning trash quite literally.

"Tell me about it. People haven't been throwing much good stuff out lately." Kelly said, also disgusted.

"Hopefully we'll never have to do that again, huh buddy."

"I hope not too. I don't think we will though."

They heard Jesse come out of the bathroom, and Bobby going in, then the shower starting again. Kelly finished his meal a few minutes later, having seconds in the large bowl he had grabbed, then he and Jamie went out to join the others.

"Man, that felt so nice. I was starting to think I'd never feel clean again, now I am. Hey, are there any more of those pins, this shirt's too big on me too?" Jesse asked.

"Yeah, I found these ones easily enough, so there might be more, no idea. They were in the drawer by the fridge."

"Great, thanks." He said and then went to the kitchen to search.

He came back a few minutes later carrying two pins. He handed one to Jamie.

21

"Here, can you put this on please? I couldn't do it myself, I almost stabbed myself." Jesse asked with a chuckle.

"Sure. What did you grab the other one for though?" Jamie asked, because he figured that Jesse would only need one, since the shirt was not quite as big on him.

"Well, I figured Bobby's even smaller than me, so he might need one as well. I didn't see any others, so I hope you guys' shirts fit a bit better." Jesse told him.

"Okay, good idea. Let's watch some TV."

Jamie then told the TV to turn on, it switched on, then he told it to scroll through the channels, it did. They watched for the better part of a minute, until he saw something they would all like, so told it to stop. The boys all decided that what Jamie had chosen was suitable. Bobby came out a short time later in his over sized shirt as well, and Brad went in. He took the offered pin, and Jamie put it in, and then he too sat and watched the TV. Half an hour later, Brad came out, and told Jamie it was his turn.

Jamie went to the bathroom and stripped down, and he too turned on the shower as hot as he could stand it as well, then climbed in. He too, just like every boy had, just stood and soaked up the luxurious feeling for many minutes before washing off. About half an hour later he climbed out and dried off as well. After putting on his shirt and grabbing his clothes, Jamie exited the bathroom, put all the clothes and towels into the washer, added plenty of soap, and turned the machine on. He then went to the linen closet and grabbed a bunch of sheets and blankets.

"Okay guys, TV off, let's go to bed." Jamie said, and as soon as he told it to, the TV turned itself off.

They all got a large nest like bed made up, and not even bothering with the shorts, they all crawled in. After Jamie told the lights to turn off, they all fell asleep, nice and warm and cozy for the first time in a long time. For each and every one of the boys, it had been far too long, in some cases to remember, since the last time they got to sleep where it was warm and safe. Sleeping out on the mean streets, no matter if you were lucky enough to have somewhere almost safe to call home, had always been dangerous, most kids that went missing, went missing while they were sleeping.

Franky though was having not too pleasant a night, and he had been kicking himself for not calling Jonathon as he should have. As with almost all the kids on the street, calling for help never did anything, so he never even bothered, though he should have known better. Some older boys had decided to try and make his life more miserable than it already was, so stole all his things, including the shoes he was wearing, and left him laying on the ground writhing in pain, after the leader punched him in the stomach a few times for resisting. He decided instead, to just wait until morning, so found a nice quiet alcove, deep in a back alley, and went to sleep, cold, sore and alone. Granted, this was not entirely a new sensation for the boy.

The next morning found Jonathon awakened by the smell of cooking food. He crawled out of bed, threw on a robe, and went out to investigate. It was only shortly after five in the morning, not too big a deal, since he normally got up in half an hour anyway. He decided that he may as well get up and get started with the day.

CHAPTER 4

THE SEARCH CONTINUES

When he arrived to the kitchen, Jonathon found all the boys sitting around in there, except Jamie, who was standing at the stove cooking something that smelled pretty good. All the boys were talking softly and laughing as quietly as they could, so that they did not wake up Jonathon. None of the boys had even noticed as he walked in, they were so happy and talking as such. It pleased Jonathon a great deal to hear how much happier they all sounded after just one good nights safe sleep and some good food.

"Good morning gentlemen, how did you all sleep last night?"

"Great, I haven't slept so well in like . . . . well forever!" Bobby answered.

"Me too." The others chorused.

"Glad to hear it. Sleeping in a safe location, while nice and warm and with a nice full belly sure has its benefits. Jamie, what are you cooking, it smells really good?"

"I just fried up some potatoes I found, added some sausage, onions, peppers, and mushrooms. I'll add some eggs and cheese in a few minutes. I hope there's enough for all of us."

"I'm sure there will be, it looks like there's lots there. I'm going to run and put your clothes in the dryer, since I heard you start the washer last night. I hope they're good and clean."

"K, hurry, breakfast 'll be ready in just a few minutes." He said.

Jonathon headed over to the washer, and as soon as he opened the lid, he knew instantly that the clothes needed another round. The smell was still bordering on revolting, so he turned it back on with a double dose of soap, a double dose of washing soda, as well as fabric softener to also help improve the smell.

"Sorry guys, all your clothes still smelled pretty bad. You'll have to throw them in the drier when they finish washing again. I guess that means that you'll all just have to stay in your night shirts a while longer. I have to go to work soon, and you're welcome to stay the day here, or you can leave and do what you wish, I'll just set the door to open to your voices." He told the boys.

"Great, thanks. I think we might just stay in today though, because we don't often get a chance to just lay around and relax, so it might be kinda nice." Jamie answered for the others.

"That's fine, and I can well understand that. You guys just lay around and have fun. There are a few board games in the linen closet, and there are the TV and computer that you're welcome to use as well. You should be all set." Jonathon told everyone, and they were more than happy to hear that.

"Great, sounds nice, breakfast is ready, everyone dig in."

Jonathon let the boys get their fill first, he normally ate just a small breakfast anyway, and they all looked as if they could stand to put on a few extra pounds. They all ate with only the speed that young hungry boys can, and Jonathon more than once shook his head in amazement.

"Jamie, that was very good, thank you. Now, did any of you actually taste that? You all ate so fast I was starting to wonder if you were chewing." Jonathon teased the boys.

"Yep, and it was very good." Kelly said while patting his little belly.

Everyone gave a little laugh.

"Well, I'm gonna go hop in the shower and get ready for work. I don't have tooth brushes for you guys, but the mouth wash I'll grab for you should at least clean your mouths up a bit."

They nodded, so he headed off to get ready for work. He always went in early, so that he could get out early. After getting dressed, he went and found the boys.

"Okay guys, I have to go now. I don't know when I'll be home, but call me if you need anything at all. I'll be stopping at a store on the way home, and I'll also try and find a few more crew members if I can. You can go ahead and help yourselves to the food. Oh and before I forget, come to the door with me, so that I can put your voice prints in the lock."

They followed him and he spent the next few minutes adding their voices to the lock.

"There, now if you want to go out for anything, you can get back in." He told the boys.

"Cool, thanks. Take all the time you need, 'cause the sooner you find everyone, the sooner we can go right." Jesse said.

"To a certain extent, yes. My last day at work is tomorrow, and we need to start getting supplies for the ship, as well as the rest of our crew, so can do nothing 'til at least all that's done. I'm hoping though, that in about five to ten days that we can take off. We'll need to go up to the ship at least a few times to take the supplies up, and get everything organized. A few things need to be done on the ship as well, but nothing major." He told the boys.

"I can't wait to get to go, I've always wanted to go on a real space ship. Can we go up tonight maybe?" Jesse asked excitedly.

"Probably not, but we can try for the day after tomorrow though, because we won't really have time today, okay. You'll all just have to be patient. Now, I have to go, so you guys have a good day."

"Bye." They all said.

Jonathon left and started walking the eight blocks to the orphanage he worked at. As soon as Jonathon left, Jamie turned to his crew.

"Well guys, let's go watch some TV for a while. We can break out a game or two later maybe."

Jonathon arrived to work a short time later, and was met at the door by the director.

"Could I have a word with you before you start." He was asked as soon as he entered the building.

"Sure Jack, what's up?"

"Not much, except the police found a gang of boys and brought them all here. They were all to be your projects for today, but I think they'd all be perfect for your other little project instead. They're all very spirited, smart beyond belief, and won't even talk to us at all. They just start screaming and kicking whenever one of us gets near, and I think the leader needs your special touch." Jack said, referring to the fact that Jonathon had easily brought a number of gangs under control quickly when he dropped their leader in a fraction of a second without a mark.

"Excellent, how many of them are there?" Jonathon asked happily.

"There are ten in there, and if I had to guess, I'd say the oldest is maybe twelve, but he's a tough little bugger. He actually managed to give three police officers injuries, before they were able to subdue him."

"What exactly were the police involved for, they usually just leave the kids up to us?" He asked curiously.

"Well, it seems the police were handling another matter nearby, and the gang of kids decided that while they were busy, they'd try and raid their vehicles for anything they could use. I understand the police have a dim view on that. They got all the kids, and they did so without hurting any of them amazingly, but after the last time you tore a strip off them for hitting a kid, they wouldn't dare hurt another child, no matter what they did." Jack said blandly.

"I'd hope not! Well the kids weren't exactly smart on that account were they? But I guess hunger can cause you to do some pretty stupid things sometimes. Where have you got them stashed?"

"Meeting room one."

"Okay, talk to you later."

So Jonathon went down the hall and soon came to the room the boys were all in. He told the door to unlock, and then entered. As soon as he entered the room, ten pairs of eyes turned and glared at him, every last one of them trying to show the new man that they were the bosses and that he could do nothing. They were all dirty and skinny, and tough looking to be sure, once again, all trademarks of the street. Jonathon just looked at them and smiled warmly before starting to speak.

"Good afternoon gentlemen. I hear you've created quite a stir today."

"We didn't do nuttin." The boy who was obviously the leader said harshly.

"Oh, really, raiding police vehicles for anything you could get, and beating up on police officers, that was nothing? Well in that case, I guess you're free to go." Jonathon said cheerfully, opening up the door.

"Yeah right, you wouldn't just let us walk out of here." The leader said defiantly.

"Actually, I would. You'd have to want to stay here, because this isn't a prison, we just help kids like you guys. I know all the horror stories you guys are told about orphanages, but they simply aren't true. However, for you guys, I have a much better proposition, you'll have to trust me a bit first though." Jonathon said, closing the door, dangling the hook.

"Yeah, right, like we'd trust you!" The leader said stubbornly.

"Whatever, then I let you all go with a warning that the next time the police catch you, it's straight to jail." Jonathon told them.

"And we'll just beat them up even worse next time, but they'll never get us a second time." The leader said.

"Boy, you're not being very smart right now. The only reason you guys did inflict so much damage to the officers, was simply because of the fact that I've instructed them to never hit a child, or they'd have to go a few rounds against me. Next time you may not be so lucky, if they could've restrained you like they normally do, you'd all be very bruised right now for what you tried." Jonathon calmly said.

"Yeah, whatever, they fought us plenty hard, and we almost won. You're nothing though, I could take you in a heartbeat!" The leader said.

"If you wish to believe that, you can, but I assure you, I can cause you a world of hurt, and never even leave a mark." Jonathon said with a warm smile.

The boy did not bother saying a word, just charged. Jonathon quickly sidestepped his straight on approach, and then struck with his hand so fast the boy had no idea what hit him, only that he was on the ground, gasping in pain.

"Young man, you need to know one thing about me, I never lie. If I tell you I can cause serious pain, believe me, I can. Now, take a few deep breaths and relax, the pain will disappear momentarily, and as soon as you stand up, it'll be all gone." Jonathon told the crying child.

It took a few minutes of the boy gasping for breath to work out that he was still alive. The other nine boys in the room just looked on in awe that someone hurt their leader so easily, and quickly. Finally the boy got up.

"Are you ready to listen to me yet?" Jonathon asked softly.

"I guess so. What'd you do to me though? That hurt so bad."

"Good. All I did was hit a nerve in the right way, and it caused lots of pain. Just be thankful that I didn't use one of the other methods I know, because that was the least painful of them, believe me."

They did not respond to that, other than to make a collective gulping sound, especially the leader.

"Okay, now that the messy stuff is all out of the way, why don't we go sit and talk like civilized gentlemen?" Jonathon asked gently, grabbing a chair and sitting down.

They all went and sat at the table, and just as Jonathon was about to start speaking again, his ship communicator beeped at him, signaling an incoming message.

"Oops, sorry, give me a minute please?" Jonathon said and activated his communicator to see Franky.

"Hey Franky, what's up? How can I help you?" Jonathon asked, actually surprised to see him.

"Some older boys beat me up and took all my stuff last night, so I was wondering if you could help me out a bit." Franky asked pitifully. He was not used to asking for help, and he did not particularly care for it either.

"Sure, you can either come to the orphanage, where I'm at right now, or go to my house, where there are a few new crew members already there, so that you can go and get to know them a little, and maybe get some food, and a shower even." Jonathon offered.

"Um, I'd rather not come to the orphanage, they make me uncomfortable. I think I'd prefer your place, how do I get to your house?"

Jonathon gave him quick instructions to get to his apartment, and Franky thanked him. As soon as they disconnected, Jonathon called home and told Jamie what was happening, he said that was fine.

"Sorry about that boys, one of my crew members was in a spot of trouble, as I'm sure you heard. Now, as for the reason I have you all here still."

"That's okay. That sounded like Raven, he's a good kid." The leader said.

"Yes, it was, his real name's Franky though."

"Wow, how'd you ever get his name? Almost no one knows it, and this is the first time I've heard it."

"Because it's a requirement of what I'm about to offer all of you. You have to trust me. Nothing more, nothing less. Well there's a test first, but that's pretty easy."

"Um, okay, what's this grand offer." He asked warily.

"Just to become crew members on the most famous Earth ship there is." Jonathon said to get their attention.

"You're talking about the UE1. How could we become crew of that ship, especially since it was given to Admiral Casey?" The leader asked.

"Time for introductions." So Jonathon told the boys exactly who he was and who his parents were "Now, I'm looking to find a crew of street kids, just like you guys, to teach everything there is to know about flying and commanding a space ship. All I ask, if you accept, and pass the test of course, is to obey me, since I'll be the captain, and learn the best you can." He told the captive audience.

"Wow, what do we need to do?" One of the other boys asked.

"Well, like I said, I'll give you all a test to see if you qualify, however, I'm pretty sure that you'll all pass easily. Now for the really tough part. If you want to come, you can either stay here for the few days it takes for me to get everything ready, or go back out and live on the streets. Either way, once you become crew members, a communicator, just like I wear, will be attached to your wrist."

"We wouldn't have to stay here if we didn't want to?" The leader asked cautiously.

"Nope, you could come and eat and clean up if you wanted, and then go about your normal business, if you wanted. All the orphanages have an open door policy. It'd probably feel real nice to sleep in nice soft warm beds though, I bet it's been a while!"

"Really, that would be kinda nice I guess, we didn't know that though. Okay, can I be first?" The leader asked.

"Yeah, all the orphanages are like that, they aren't prisons, and they don't want to hold you and make you do things you don't want to do. And sure you can go first, but first I need name and age, your real and street names if you please?"

The leader chewed on his lip a few moments, thinking as to whether or not he should trust Jonathon. Finally he decided to trust the rumors that Jonathon was in it to help the kids.

"Okay, I go by Sneak 'cause I can almost always sneak in and out of any place, I'm twelve, but turn thirteen in a couple weeks or so, I think. My real name's Pete." He was a good sturdy boy, with dark blond hair, light blue eyes and strong features.

"Excellent, come with me Pete, and we'll go get this test over and done with. You boys stay here, oh, and one other thing, don't ask about the test, you need to pass it on your own, and don't feel you can hide it from me if you do, because you can't."

Jonathon and Pete went to a smaller meeting room next door, and proceeded to do the test. Once finished, Jonathon congratulated the boy for passing. They went back to the other room, and Pete was smiling.

"Okay, who would like to be next?" Jonathon asked.

The only other boy to have spoken so far put up his hand. Jonathon and he went to the other room and did the test.

One by one Jonathon gave the test to the remainder of the boys. Each and every one of them also passed, one of them did so with almost as much ease as Jesse had. The boys' names are Tony, but goes by Tiny, is nine, has black hair, and is just like his nick name suggested, tiny. Zach, who goes by Sly, is eight, has brown hair, is pretty normal size, and wears glasses. Next is Cullen, who is also eight, has blond hair and freckles, is about average size, and goes by Cull. And then there is Tristan, who is thirteen, with brown hair, and a good size as well, but just goes by his first name. Next is Devon, who goes by Wired, because he was so wiry, and he has red hair. And then Ryan, who goes by Stump, is twelve, has light brown hair, and is pretty short and squat like a stump, but not heavy. Next is Lance, he is really tall and thin, so goes by beanpole, he is twelve, and has brown hair. And then there is Kelvin, he is eleven, has brown hair, and no nick name. Finally there was Marty, and he goes by Smarty, for good reason, because he is real smart. He is nine, about average size, and has blond hair. Finally, after everyone was done, Jonathon took Marty back and gave them all the good news.

As soon as they were back in the room, Jonathon informed all the boys that they were all welcome to join the crew and asked them to come get their communicator if they would like to join. They all stood as one and formed a line. Jonathon first attached the communicators, and then gave a crash course in their usage.

"Well guys, you're free to do as you please now, but I'd recommend though that you all go get a good meal and a shower, and even some good clean clothes. Just drop your clothes in the laundry, and the next person can use them, you pretty much all share the clothes around here, because it's easier that way, and you get clothes that fit you better. I have to go to work now, so I'll find you when it's time to go up to the ship to get it ready." He told the boys happily, because this was going far easier than he had thought it might.

Instead of answering they all cheered, and as soon as Jonathon opened the door, they filed out and followed the arrows on the wall, pointing to the dining hall. Jonathon, once the boys were all gone, headed to the directors office.

With a happy spring in his step, caused from getting far more kids far more quickly than he had dreamed possible only a few short days ago, and with less pain all around involved, he walked toward the offices. When he reached the directors office, he knocked and Jack told him to enter.

"Hey Jack, they all passed and have accepted the offer. Now all I need are three more boys, and I'll be all set."

"Wow, you are good. You've only been in there just over three hours, and I expected them to take you all day, with how stubborn and tough they were. They were your only job today though, so you're free to go if you wish."

"Thanks, and thanks. I'll take you up on that offer, and tomorrow I'll say all my goodbyes as planned, clean my stuff up, and take off early as well."

"Sounds good to me. We'll all miss you around here, that's for sure."

"I'll miss this place as well, and I might be back, you never know. See you tomorrow."

CHAPTER 5

A WELL DESERVED DAY OF REST

The boys in the apartment, for the most part, spent the whole day laying back and watching TV, and other than getting up to go to the washroom, getting food, and Jamie getting up to put the clothes in the dryer, they did not move. They never even got dressed all day. When Franky got there, he went and had a shower, dressed in a shirt like the others, and he too just laid back and watched TV all day. The boys hardly talked at all, they just lazed around all day. Jonathon did call the boys though and told them all about his find at the orphanage, and they were all happy with that, because it put them that much closer to getting to leave.

Jonathon decided to go ahead and see if he could find any more boys before going home, since he seemed to have plenty of time to do so. He went down a well known back alley, and searched for a while for the boys he was looking for. He saw a number of boys, but most ran when they saw him coming, but he did not bother following them. A short while later he found a pair of boys hiding in behind a garbage dumpster, and they appeared to be eating something, that was more than likely recently pilfered from the bin they were behind.

"Good afternoon gentlemen. Please don't be afraid, I mean you no harm." Jonathon quickly and quietly said when the look of fear crossed their faces and they started to move.

"Sorry, didn't mean to startle you. May I join you for a few moments and ask you some questions?" He asked gently.

"No, leave us alone, we didn't do nothing, this food was thrown away." The bigger of the two stated sternly, visibly shaking and obviously scared.

"I don't wish to take away your food, and I don't wish to cause you any trouble. I just have a few questions for you guys, and then we can either separate, or go for some real food."

"Real food, as in hot, and not out of a garbage bin? Ask away." The other boy asked, clearly more hungry at that time than he was wary.

"Yes, exactly. How would you two like to become crew members of a space ship?"

The boys' eyes told him that the answer to that question was a yes.

"What would we have to do, and why do you want us?" The bigger boy asked cautiously.

"Well, you'd be crew members with full crew responsibility, so you'd have to be willing to work hard, listen to orders, and most importantly, learn. As for why I want you, well I'm looking for twenty young men just like you two, and I have three spots left. All I need to start is to give you a test, and you'll have to give me your real names and street names, if you have them, and your ages. Pretty simple actually." Jonathon answered.

"Could we eat first?" The smaller boy asked.

"Sure, why don't we just go to my place! I should have enough room to fit you guys in, I already have a house full anyway. We can just eat there and get everything else done, and you can even have a nice long hot shower." Jonathon told the boys, knowing that food and feeling clean would almost certainly cinch the deal.

"I guess so. You're not going to try anything are you, we don't do anything?" The bigger boy asked cautiously still, his street smarts telling him that he should not be doing this, but his heart told him to trust.

"Never! I'd never do anything to hurt a child, unless they attacked me first, and even then, when such measures are called for, I do so without leaving marks, and no permanent damage. Follow me, you'll be allowed to leave at any time, should you wish to do so." Jonathon told the boys softly, because he could easily feel their uncertainty.

They stood to follow him, and without a further word, Jonathon started walking, letting the decision to follow be up to them, they did follow though, and he walked the whole way home without saying anything, neither did the boys.

"Well boys, here we are. It's not much, but it's home, at least for the next few days. Come on in and meet the others." Jonathon said, waving the boys in.

Jonathon opened the door and was met by the boys all turning their heads to see who it was. When they saw them, they all hopped up and came over to say hi. Jonathon chuckled at their appearances.

"Well, hello guys, I didn't figure that sit back and relax all day meant not even getting dressed. I don't mind though, I'm sure you all deserved it a bit. As I'm sure you've noticed by now, I have a couple possible new recruits with me, and they've requested some decent food. I was going to cook something up while they grabbed showers. Would someone grab them a couple shirts, seeing as how you obviously know where they are?" Jonathon asked, looking at Franky.

"We didn't mean to snoop, Raven just needed something to wear. Hi guys." Jamie said to Jonathon then the boys behind him.

"Don't worry about it, I'm not mad, and I figured something like that would happen. Jamie, would you show the guys where everything is please, while I go get a late lunch started." Jonathon asked.

"Sure, come on guys, follow me. You'll like it here, and I think once we get in space, you'll really love it, I can't wait." Jamie said excitedly, taking the younger boys' hands and leading them toward the bathroom. He was very excited, because he knew that they now needed only one more boy before they could go, so that meant they were even closer to getting to go.

Jonathon called after their retreating backs. "Use both bathrooms to make it go faster, no point in going one at a time."

"K!" Jamie called back. "Let's get you guys some shirts first. We'll see about something to hold them up better later. When you're finished your showers, just put your clothes here." Jamie said, pointing at the small pile left by Franky.

"Okay, thanks." The bigger boy said in disbelief, because he could not believe that this was all happening.

After getting their offered shirts, the boys took a washroom each, stripped down, turned the water on as hot as they could take it, and climbed in. They soaked for quite some time before starting to wash, same as all the previous boys had done. They too both enjoyed getting the chance to get a hot shower and to feel clean once again, for the first time in far too long.

Jonathon and a couple of the boys were making a big lunch, while the boys that were left at the orphanage were just heading off to get some nice hot showers, after having had a nice big lunch themselves.

The two boys came out at almost the same time, and dumped their dirty clothes by the washer, then came to the kitchen and sat down.

"Feel better guys? I hope so, you look a lot cleaner now. Lunch will be ready in a minute." Jonathon said warmly to the two boys that looked a little happier than they had before.

"Much better, and good, I'm starving." The older boy said.

"Hey, can you boys at least tell us your names." Jonathon asked.

"I'm Matty and this is Teddy." The older boy said. Jonathon figured them to be eight and ten, and Matty was about average size, with blond hair, and Teddy was pretty small, with nearly white hair.

"Great, Matty and Teddy, I'm Jonathon. I'll let all the boys introduce themselves after lunch. Let's eat." Jonathon said while dishing out the last of the food.

"Thanks Jonathon." Matty said.

They all sat down to eat, and again Jonathon was amazed at the speed at which the boys ate.

"Okay guys, I have to go out and get some groceries and a few other things, would you all just stay here and clean this up please, and then you can relax more? Matty and Teddy, I'll do your tests when I get back." Jonathon asked once everyone was finished their filling lunch.

Jonathon left, after getting nods of approval from all the boys. He headed to the nearest grocery and department store, and stocked up on some much needed supplies. He then grabbed each of the boys some toothbrushes, and then some pants, underwear, and shirts from the proper departments. He headed back home a short time later. On the way though, he was confronted by a boy of about fourteen, almost as big as he was, but the boy was holding a knife, and was standing in the way in a fighting stance.

"Give me the bags and anything else you have, and you walk away." The boy snarled out, obviously he was hungry and desperate.

"Sorry son, I can't give them to you just because you demand it. I can give you some stuff if you put the knife away and ask politely, if not, and you wish to pursue the matter, I'll be forced to disarm you, without even putting the bags down. What will it be?" Jonathon asked calmly, as if dealing with this type of situation were a daily occurrence.

Sadly, while not exactly a daily occurrence, this had happened to Jonathon more than a few times before, each and every person that did so ended up going to an orphanage or somewhere else for help, because after knocking them down, he always talked to them. The daily muggings though had gotten to be a huge problem throughout virtually every city, the street gangs were making it incredibly unsafe to walk the streets at any time, day or night. Jonathon though had never worried about that, and had gotten many people the help they clearly needed when they pulled the exact same stunt the young man in front of him was currently doing.

"You shoulda just given me the stuff." The boy snarled and rushed Jonathon.

As promised, Jonathon never even dropped a bag, but the boy sure dropped the knife, and then fell from the twin kicks that Jonathon delivered with perfect accuracy. The first right in the boys right armpit, to stun the knife wielding arm, and then the other to his side, to cause him a little pain.

"Now, if you just relax, and take a few deep breaths, the pain will go away quickly. I promise I didn't kill you, and you'll survive, hopefully with a lesson learned." Jonathon said gently.

"It feels like you crushed my ribs, you could've killed me." The boy sobbed out.

"And how would that have been any different than what you were planning for me?"

"Wouldn't have been any different I guess. Do you think I could get some food off you now though." The boy asked pitifully.

"Afraid not, if you wish to have a good hot meal and a shower though, you may follow me. I have an offer to make you though, but I'm afraid I don't just give things away to those who attack me."

"Whatever, I've been with your type before, it don't bother me none any more." He spat.

"No, nothing like that, I promise you no harm will come of you, and you'll never have to do anything like that at all ever again. Right now, the offer is simply a hot shower and meal, and then we can talk." Jonathon told the boy.

"Fine." He said quietly, wondering what was happening.

Jonathon just turned and started walking back to his apartment, and the boy followed after a moment. He too was not sure why he was following the strange man, but he felt that he had to trust a man that he just tried to stab, but only received a slight amount of pain as punishment, and not instant death, because he was well aware, after the kicks, that the man was very good, and that he certainly could have killed him. When they arrived, Jonathon opened the door and walked in, and the boy followed him in. He found a large group of boys already there, and they all looked happy, so he visibly relaxed some.

"Hey everyone, I think I found our last crew member, but he's probably wondering what I'm talking about, as are Matty and Teddy, but you'll find out shortly. I have some clothes here that should fit you guys, do you want to go get changed, or just stay like this."

"I'm just staying as is." Jamie said, and all the others agreed in quick order.

"Okay, well as for you, I'm afraid you kind of smell, so the washroom is right down there. I'll get you some shorts and a shirt, my stuff should probably fit you, and then we can all sit down and have a talk."

The boy did not know what to say or think, so just followed Jonathon's orders quietly, pondering what he had meant about crew member.

"Here you go kiddo, just throw your dirty clothes in the pile in front of the washer when you're finished."

He had a nice long hot shower, then got dressed, and went out to the living room, where everyone was sitting and waiting for him.

"Okay, well Matty and Teddy, I imagine the others told you a bit about what's happening, so this is mostly for you Sir. You're going to be offered the final position as a crew member of our ship. There'll be a total of twenty of you guys as the crew, and I as the captain. If you pass the test, you'll need to agree to a couple things before I'll accept you. First, I need to know your name, age, and your street name as well, if you have one." Jonathon told them.

"What kind of test." The newest boy asked.

"It's a verbal test, it's designed to find out how smart you are, and it takes about half an hour normally. I'll take the three of you, one at a time, for the test, and if you pass, I'll offer the position to you, and if you accept, you'll be given a communicator. That simple." Jonathon told the boys.

"Okay, I go by Muscles, but my name's Donny, I just turned fourteen a few weeks ago."

Jonathon administered the tests to the boys in the kitchen, while the others stayed in the living room, and as expected, they all passed, so he made the offer, and they all accepted. They were all given their personal communicators, and were taught quickly how to use them. Everyone welcomed them to the crew, and they were all excited, because they all knew that this meant that they could go, hopefully very soon. Jonathon of course was asked when they could go up to the ship, so he told them that they would try for day after tomorrow.

CHAPTER 6

GETTING READY TO GO

The next morning found Jonathon telling the boys to have a good day, that he would be home early and he left for work. He walked to work and met up with Jack, they had a coffee and chatted about Jonathon's up and coming trip. Finally Jonathon excused himself and went to his office and started boxing everything up that he wanted to take.

An hour later he was making the rounds and saying his goodbyes to everyone. Many of the farewells were tearful and heartbreaking, since Jonathon had raised more than a few of the kids here for a quite a while, and helped them to work out a lot of the emotional turmoil that losing their families had obviously created. He took more than three hours just saying goodbye to all the kids, and then he went and said his goodbyes to his coworkers.

These goodbyes too were emotional, and many of the people cried, since a good many of them had come from that very orphanage themselves and Jonathon had helped to raise them some. Finally, with his boxes in hand, he went outside and hailed a personal transporter to carry him and his possessions home.

The personal transporters were a great invention of many years ago. They replaced the cars that many people had used for many years, so no one needed to have their own vehicle. They were small to large maglev hover vehicles that could hold anywhere from one to twenty people, depending upon the size of the one you got. They were always parked on the side of the roadways, so if there was one there that you could use, you just got in and told it where you wanted to go, and it would do the rest. If there was not one there, or there was not a suitable one available, it was as simple as keying into the posts how many people you wanted to transport, and as soon as there was one available, it came right to you.

The wait was normally very short. There were posts with the call centers every half a block or so, so there was usually not much walking involved either. The little transports were very fast as well, and in the city they could travel up to a hundred kilometers an hour, but on the highways, they could go as fast as two hundred and fifty. Because they were completely controlled by the computer, and followed maglev lines built into the roads, they were exceptionally safe, and boasted a less than one hundredth of a percent accident rate.

Each transport was powered by Nutronium maglev engine, which allowed them to have the speed necessary to transport people quickly. They were also very strong and durable, made of the same material that their ships were made of, so they lasted nearly forever, and some cities still had the originals that they had made almost a hundred years before, yet they had clocked many millions of kilometers. Most of them were nice and sleek looking, looking somewhat like the bullet trains that had been designed and built in the twentieth century, just they were much smaller.

The insides though were almost totally opposite to the exteriors. Where the exterior was just plain white and sleek, the interiors were often bright and cheery, very inviting. The seats, the number obviously dependent upon the size of the chosen vehicle, were soft and comfortable, could recline, and even had foot rests should you need to really lay back and relax for a longer journey. Each hover vehicle was also equipped with a full computer system that you could use during your travels, which allowed for you to do work or just watch a television show, all while in almost total comfort. As well there were two different sound options for the occupants, good sounding speakers so everyone could hear, or personal headphones for more privacy. Most of the larger units also had multiple computer monitors and or terminals for multiple people, this mostly depended upon the age of the machine and what features it had at that time.

The only time people had their own vehicles now were for recreation. These too were probably the only vehicles that had wheels, because there were still hundreds, if not thousands of back roads that had no maglev lines in them, and there were always signs warning people as such. Of course the computers knew this and stopped the vehicle long before that could happen, and if it were a cross vehicle, meaning it was meant for both on and off road, they had wheels that could be lowered to compensate for this. This too was the only time anyone had to physically drive their vehicles any more, because the computers could not drive on these roads. Many people still had personal off road vehicles; such as four wheelers and dirt bikes, recreational vehicles; such as trailers and motor homes, and many people had boats as well. The major difference with all these new vehicles of course was that they were all fully electric and had small Nutronium power generators in them.

Finally Jonathon made it home and carried his boxes to his apartment. When he entered, all the boys turned to see who it was, and he almost laughed at the fact that they were still all in the same things he had left them in that morning.

"Hey guys, how are you all doing? I see you didn't bother getting dressed again today."

The boys had all just been sitting around playing board games when he arrived. He did not mind in the least that the boys would do this, because he knew that this would have been the very first time in a long time to just kick back and relax, to really forget about their problems.

"Oh hello, we all decided that we should take advantage of being lazy while we could, 'cause we've all heard working a space ship is hard work." Donny said for them all, but they all nodded in agreement.

"Can't say's I blame you. I'd ask that you all get dressed now though, because some of the work is about to start. Now that I'm off work, we have a lot to get done, and I don't want to spend too much time doing it. We have more time than expected to do it though, but that just means we can leave that much sooner if we can swing it."

"Awesome! What are we doing?" Jesse asked excitedly for them all.

"Well, we have to go get supplies, I want to stop at the hospital to visit Brady, see how he's doing, find out when he's getting out, and then I figure we can all go out for dinner. So you guys all go get dressed, and we can head out."

All the boys just grabbed their clothes and started dressing right there, and in minutes they were ready to go. Jonathon just shook his head. He knew that there was very little shame or modesty on the street, so this was probably normal for them.

They all took off a few minutes later, and headed to the hospital first to see Brady.

"Hey there Brady, how are you holding up?"

"Pretty good, getting excited to go though. I was going to call you tonight to see if you could spring me from this place. Who are all these guys, well except Raven, I already know him?"

"I bet you are. From here on out though guys, your street names stay on the street, when in ships company, you use first names, except for me, because once we're on the ship, I'm Sir, or Captain Casey. As for you Brady, I'll see what I can do about getting you out of here. Have you been behaving, and not trying to escape every time they let you go to the washroom?" Jonathon asked with a smile.

"Ever since you made the offer, I haven't tried, and I hadn't tried after the nurses threatened me with diapers, instead of washroom privileges. I decided that they were being serious, so I didn't bother then. I still really want to get out of here though, I hate hospitals." Brady said vehemently, and most of the boys giggled at this.

"Give me a few minutes to see what I can find out, and while I'm gone, you boys can start getting to know each other." Jonathon told the boys and then left the room.

The boys all gave their names to Brady, and they sat around chatting until Jonathon came back.

Jonathon though headed out to the nursing station to find out who the doctor in charge of Brady was at the moment. When he arrived, he asked the nurse there who he was looking for. It took her a moment to find it, but told him that a Doctor Campbell would be who he talked to and that he would have just finished his rounds, so might be found in the lounge. With that information, Jonathon took off to find the doctor.

"Excuse me, are you Doctor Campbell, and is Brady one of your patients." Jonathon asked the only person in the lounge when he arrived.

"Yes, to both questions. You must be Doctor Casey, I've heard a lot about you, and you worked magic on Brady, he hasn't tried to escape once since you came. Well the nurses also stopped some of that I suppose." The doctor said with a chuckle.

"Thanks, and yes they did. It's amazing what treating an independent young man like a baby could do, but he certainly didn't want to try them, for good reason. I don't doubt they would've done it too. I did have a question for you though! When can Brady be released? He'll be released into my custody, since he's officially accepted a position on my ship."

"You're right, they would've in a heartbeat, had he tried them again. And yes, he told me all about it, in fact I haven't heard him talk so much since he's been here, he's been quite excited. I was going to release him tomorrow, but he's probably fine now. All the internal damage is healed now, and the cast can probably come off any day now, because the bone regrowth has pretty much completed. I just like to leave the casts on for a couple days extra to make sure. If you're willing though, he can go right now. I'll give him a couple more medications to take with him for the next few days, I'm sure you know how to use an auto injector."

"That'd be great, and yes, I most certainly do! One of my minor courses was as a med tech, so that I could do most basic medical procedures on board a ship. Will he be able to walk on the cast?"

"Yes, I used a good ultra light, ultra strong casting material, because of how the breaks were. His foot is free and clear, so he can walk easily, if not a bit awkwardly. Do you have the equipment necessary to remove the cast, and how about a scanner to make sure it's healed? The bone re-grower usually only takes two to three days to work, and it's been three now, but I always err on the side of caution, so I was going to leave it for another two or three days."

"Yes and yes, the ship has a fully equipped medical center, and it was upgraded just before it was decommissioned, so it's all up to date too. Actually, thinking of that, I could use some medical supplies though, what kind of deal would the hospital work out for me, maybe on the quiet?"

"I'm sure we could work something out. Go down to shipping and receiving, talk to Joe, he can set you up. They usually charge not much more than what we buy it for, so it's a lot better than elsewhere. Well, I should go start my rounds on the next floor, I'll stop at the nursing station though and sign Brady out."

"Thanks for everything."

The doctor nodded and left. Jonathon headed back to the room and found the boys still talking excitedly about the trip. They all stopped talking as soon as he came in the room, and stared at him, waiting for the answer. Well Jonathon did not intimidate easily, so this did not bother him and it actually got to the boys long before it would have bothered him.

"Oh would you tell us already, what did the doctor say." Brady asked impatiently.

"I'm sorry, the news is grave, he wants you to stay for another three days." Jonathon said with a sad look on his face.

"What, no! He said I was healing nicely, why won't he let me go tomorrow like he was planning?" Brady asked in a near panic.

"Okay, fine, but you can't go tomorrow though." Jonathon said.

"Huh, what do you mean?" Brady asked in confusion.

"Well, because you won't be here, he released you to me night now. Let's get those restraints off you, then you can get dressed. We have a stop to make a purchase before we leave the hospital though, and then we can go."

"Oh great, I was starting to go mad being tied to this bed like some sort of animal."

"Well had you not been acting like one, they wouldn't have had to resort to these methods, now would they? You have to remember that it's your actions, and your actions alone in life, that get you the things you want and need. Sometimes though, the actions you make, get you something you don't want, so you have to be careful and weigh all your options first." Jonathon said softly to all the boys, so that they could think it over.

"I see what you mean, and I guess I kinda did deserve it, didn't I!" Brady said after a few minutes of thought.

"Yes, but now you know for next time. Remember, a day without learning is a wasted day, I think Einstein said, and the day you stop learning, better be the day you die, I say." Jonathon told the boys.

Jonathon had gotten Brady released from his bonds, and he stood up and worked out the kinks for a minute, and when Franky handed him his clothes, he stripped off the hospital gown and quickly got dressed, as if the others were not there.

"Okay boys, let's go see about getting some medical supplies, follow me!" Jonathon said happily.

They walked out of the room and took the elevator down, then got off in the shipping and receiving department. As they entered, someone was walking by, so Jonathon asked him if he could speak to Joe.

"Speaking, how may I help you Sir." Joe asked.

"Doctor Campbell says I should ask you for a quantity of medical supplies to equip a ship. I hope you're the right person to talk to?"

"You have the right person. If you give me a list, I can have it put into a crate, and you can teleport it in an hour or two, just call me. Do you have a list ready yet, and if so, can I have it so I can work out the cost?"

"That'd be great. I don't have a list yet, however, if you give me a pad, I can make a list in just a few minutes."

Joe grabbed a pad and handed it to Jonathon, who took it and started entering the information. Ten minutes later he had the list of everything that could possibly be needed. He handed the pad back to Joe, who took it and worked out the list for the total price. He showed Jonathon the price, and nodded his agreement and put his thumb on the appropriate pad to pay for the supplies.

"Okay, well now that that's all taken care of, what ship will be picking this up, and about when?" Joe asked.

"It'll be the UE1, and sometime tomorrow, I hope."

"Very nice. Can't say I've ever made a deal with the captain of the most famous ship before. I'll have it ready for you by tomorrow for sure. I should get back to work then and get your order ready. Have a good day gentlemen." Joe said and everyone waved.

"Okay guys. Our next stop is WSEC, but remember that you have to stay with me at all times while we're there. You'll be given passes, but if at any time you get separated from me, you're to stop and call me, immediately. This shouldn't happen though, because you're to stay right next to me at all times. They won't tolerate unauthorized personnel running around, and you'll be kicked out immediately, no questions asked."

"Yes Sir! It'll be awesome to go there though, it's the most incredible building on the planet." Zach said excitedly.

The others all nodded their agreement, so with that they were off. Jonathon hailed a personnel transport to take them to the WSEC building. It was about half an hours ride, so they all sat back and enjoyed the ride and chatted. When they arrived, Jonathon signed himself in and then got guest passes for all the boys.

Like Zach had said, the building that housed WSEC was one of, if not the most incredible buildings on the planet at the time. It was huge to start with, easily 200 floors above ground, though the rumors said that there were more than twenty more underground as well. No one at WSEC would confirm this rumor though. The design was also the most unique, looking a lot like a dozen offset blocks had been placed one on top of the other. Right in behind it and connected was another smaller building, though it took up nearly an acre of land, a large domed glass roof was on it, and once again the rumors said it was a garden to rival all others in its beauty and tranquility.

The inside was every bit as nice as the boys figured it was going to be. The main lobby was not only very large, but very grand as well. There was plenty of seating around a large circular fire pit that was not currently going, all the chairs were over stuffed and very comfortable looking. Next to the doors that they had entered was the largest pond and fountain that any of them had ever heard of being inside. There was even a large realistic rock waterfall splashing down into the water, adding easily ten times more water to the pond than any of the fountain heads were. The fountain heads though were all exquisitely designed, all of them statues of varying styles, and the quick counts the boys came up with ranged from twenty five to thirty, but there were twenty eight in total. The reception area in contrast was boring, it was a long counter that had a dozen stations for workers to greet and direct all the traffic that came through, though at the moment there were only five people working. Though boring compared to the rest, it too was very tastefully done and was comfortable as well.

The bank of elevators was just beyond the edge of the counter and in order to get to them, you had to pass through a bank of detectors. All weapons were to be tagged upon entrance and the sensors would verify that all weapons on any persons entering were in fact tagged. It was felt early on that the large amount of military people that came and went through the building meant that surrendering weapons was too hard to do, so you were allowed to keep them, but the sensors would ensure that should any weapon be used, you would not be leaving the building, the entire place was put into lock down the second any weapon was used, so to do so would be incredibly stupid. The sensors would also know instantly who did it, so once again, it was perfectly safe to walk around with weapons.

The boys stayed huddled in a group as Jonathon was at the counter talking to a young blond lady, just looking around at everything that there was to see. There was so much to take in; from the fire pit, to the fountain, to all the artwork, it was the most incredible place they had ever seen. It was comical to watch, because they had been told not to wander around, so they did not, but they just kept turning on the spot, looking at everything from where they stood.

Once cleared, Jonathon led the boys to the Admirals offices to see if anyone he knew was in to arrange supplies. When they arrived, he found that Admiral Kenton was in, so he asked to see him, and was let in a few minutes later.

"Well Jonathon, I see you've brought your crew with you to get your supplies finally. Your father called and told us about your trip, and that we were to put all your supplies on his company tab. It's good to see you again though, and I can't say that I was at all surprised when your father told us of your plans." Admiral Kenton smiled.

"This is only half my crew, and thanks, it's good to see you as well. I'm not really surprised that my dad did that, it's the kind of thing he does for everyone after all. Well, I'm sure that you're busy, so we'll get out of your hair and go get our much needed supplies. We only came up as a common courtesy, to say we were here."

"Nonsense, I was kind of bored for the time being, it's kind of quiet here today, so this is a nice interruption. I think I'll go with you, so that you have no problems. Not that I think you would've had any anyway, everyone here knows you, and they all know that it's to be charged to your fathers account. Let's go." Admiral Kenton said, hopping up to join them for the walk.

"Thanks, that'd be nice. Lead the way Sir."

So they went down to the supply storage warehouse section of the building, and Jonathon started picking out everything that they would need. The warehouse section took up five of the first above ground floors in the building, and it housed everything that any ship could possibly need. He got easily two years worth of food for everyone, plus the food that would be grown on board the ship. He picked out a uniform design and sent it to the machines to make them. He chose the standard design in a deep blue, he ordered one hundred in various sizes. The Uniforms were a simple design, but multi function, and you could choose from dozens of designs and in even more colors, so that every ships crew could be just a bit unique. They were also full space suits, so could be worn in space with the proper boots, helmets and gloves, but they were fairly thin and unobtrusive, so that you still had a full range of motion. They were impact resistant, as well as heat resistant, including fire, and cold resistant, not to mention that your body stayed at a nice even temperature at all times.

While the uniforms were, for the most part, one piece, the top could be detached as well, so that it could be taken off, or for ease of using the bathroom facilities, yet to look at it while being worn, it was almost seamless. They were designed like that so as to be used as space suits as well, since you could not have any leaks. With the use of the helmets, that had a built in two hour oxygen supply, you could easily go out and repair the hull of a ship, or just relax in space tethered behind the ship, Jonathon used to love doing this. With a full oxygen tank system, of which Jonathon picked out sixty, you could go for almost twenty four hours, and were rechargeable on board the ship. Jonathon got all the boots, helmets and gloves next, in plenty of different sizes, and lots of them.

Of course he also picked out a few cases of Nutronium, a full ten years supply, just in case he needed to barter for anything, or just in case of emergency. Next were the weapons. He loaded up with a couple thousand of each of the three sizes of missiles, because he did not care to be caught unarmed, especially not when the Qaralon were still out there, and very mad. He also picked out a few crates of other assorted personal weapons. He picked out a number of things as well, that would either be needed or would come in handy. All the boys mostly just tailed Jonathon as he did all this, because they had no clue as to what he was really doing.

"Well Admiral, I think we have about everything we could possibly need. We'll pick it up tomorrow, unless you think it won't all be ready."

"Should be fine, I'll get the guys to start packing it all right away. The longest one will be the uniforms, but those should only take a few hours to make."

"Great, well thanks, I'll talk to you later."

"Yeah, talk to you later as well. You boys enjoy your trip, and learn everything you can, because there isn't a better teacher out there, except maybe his dad, and he taught me and your captain everything we know." Admiral Kenton told the boys.

As one they all stood at attention and saluted the admiral, and shouted out a 'yes Sir.' It would not have passed inspection, but it was as good as gold. Admiral Kenton returned the salute, nice and sharp, and simply said 'dismissed' with a nice genuine smile.

They left and got back into the carrier that had brought them to WSEC. Jonathon told the machine where to go, and it drove the almost half hour in near silence to the restaurant that Jonathon had picked out.

"Now boys, this is a buffet style restaurant, which means you can eat as much as you want, but please only take what you'll eat, and there's no need to pile a plate ridiculously high. You can always go back for more. I also suggest you try a few new things, and since this restaurant serves a number of Tenarian dishes, as well as Human, you'll get to try a few new things. If you're not sure about something though, only take a small amount, and try it out."

"Yes Sir!" They all said happily, already enjoying the restaurant, because it smelled so good in there.

They waited in the proper area and were seated in about fifteen minutes. When the boys all went up to the serving counters, they did not know which way to go first. Everything looked and smelled so good. Most of the boys opted to just start at one end and try a small bit of each thing. Jonathon had of course known what he wanted, so went and got his meal rather quickly, and a few minutes later the boys met him at their table. Not one of the boys' plates could be seen under the piles of food they all had, but they were not piled high, just well stuffed. They all sat down, and started eating as if someone was going to take their plates away any minute.

"Hey guys, slow down, enjoy the meal. This is one of the things I'll be teaching you, so start now, chew your food at least fifteen times, and enjoy it. It's not a race to see who finishes first, and no one's going to tell us to leave."

They slowed down a bit, but they were still all going up for their second plates before Jonathon finished half of his first. It was at least a start, Jonathon chuckled to himself.

After each of the boys had all put away roughly enough food for three people, they all headed back to the apartment for the evening. They mostly just sat around and watched the TV and talked, but they did all have showers before bed. It was getting a bit crowded in the living room with ten growing boys all curled up on the floor, not that any of them minded in the least, because this was some of the best sleep any of them had had in a long time. The boys were very nearly piled one on top of each other, looking much like a large litter of puppies sleeping, it was almost cute.

CHAPTER 7

ALL ABOARD

The next day, after getting up and everyone having a large breakfast, Jonathon and the half his crew he had, went to the orphanage to pick up the remaining half of the crew. He had called first to make sure they were all there, and he was told that they were, that they were all ready and waiting, if not a bit impatiently. They all walked there and met the boys that were staying there, and they all looked more than a little excited, because they knew that it was almost time to go. Jonathon greeted them as soon as they were within easy talking range.

"Hey guys, how's it going? Enjoying your stay in the lap of luxury I hope?"

"Actually, it's been very nice. We've been able to relax and sleep comfortably, the first time in a long time. We're really ready to go though, are we going up to the ship now?" Jamie said.

"That's good to hear, and yes, so are you guys all ready to go then, because we have a ship to prepare?"

The unanimous reply was of course a resounding yes. So they all gathered up and Jonathon hit the teleport feature on his communicator, and had everyone teleported up to the ship.

"Wow, that feels weird. I've never been teleported before, does it always make you feel that dizzy?" Pete asked, he and a few others nearly fell from the feelings.

They entered into the cargo bay of the ship, and the boys were all amazed by the size, it was the largest room any of the boys had ever seen before, well until they had went to WSEC, but that was a building, they had not expected to have a ship to have such a large space. Their heads were once more swiveling, looking at everything, even as they talked.

"No, after the first couple times it becomes normal to you, so it doesn't affect you like that. You guys go ahead and roam the ship and look around for a while, just meet me in the officers lounge in an hour. I have to go get the ship all ready to go, and then transport our supplies up as well. If you need help finding the lounge, just ask the computer, and it'll tell you how to get there. Oh, and by the way, don't touch anything just yet, you'll soon be taught how to use everything."

"Yippee, come on guys, let's go!" Kelly stated giddily, taking off at high speed.

The boys all ran off and started looking at everything they could. Even with an hour, and the boys practically running the entire time, they would not hope be able to see the entire ship, but would get a good idea of the size, and a few of its amenities.

As soon as the boys took off, they started by just looking into any room that would let them in. There were many locked doors, because the boys did not have the required clearance to enter them, had they have had it though, they would have been allowed in instantly. The halls were long and fairly wide, five boys could easily walk side by side, and the amount of doors leading from the hall were staggering as well. There were also several cross halls that they came across, and when they decided to go down one of them, they found that it led to another parallel hallway just as long as the one previous to it, and when they went back down the same way that they had come, eventually they made it back into the cargo bay once again.

This of course explained to the boys why there were four doors leading from the cargo bay, these however were not the only doors, just the largest, because the rest were not as large. They headed back out, going to the next door and finding that it led to yet another hallway. Every one of the doors that they had come to were all the same, except the cargo bay doors. Every door was a piston actuated sliding door that slid into the wall silently, nothing except a soft whirring sound could be heard as it opened or closed. Ever door that they came to was approximately a meter wide, and the only difference to them and the cargo bay doors were that the cargo bay doors were twice as wide, and were two doors that slid into each side.

The doors themselves were a painted flat metal door, and while most doors were a warm brown colour, some of them were different colors. Almost all the doors that were of different colors would not let them in though, such as the yellow doors and the blue doors. The green ones did let them in, but these were small bathrooms consisting of only a toilet, sink and a shower. The boys were realizing that the doors were color coded. The brown doors were to bedrooms.

The bedrooms that they had come across so far were simple one man rooms, they each had a good sized bed, and the boys guessed correctly that they were queen size, and were furnished with tables on each side, (with a lamp on top of each one,) a good sized dresser, a fair sized wardrobe, and a good sized desk. There was also a small bathroom attached to almost every one of these ones, but not all of them, and in each bathroom that they saw, they were all the same; just a shower, toilet and sink.

While almost every bedroom was the same, they were all different too. All the furniture was almost the same, yet in all of them they were different woods and or done in different finishes. None of the beds had any bedding or pillows on them though, each occupant would get what they needed when they received their room, it was not kept in the bedrooms though, so the boys had no idea what it was like. They guessed correctly that these bedrooms were all the officers and scientists bedrooms. The higher the rank, the better you would expect to get. The ones that they had found on the inside of course had no windows, but nor did they have their own washroom attached. Down these halls were more bathrooms of course. The ones on the outside had the bathrooms but also got windows. The sizes of the windows varied depending upon where exactly that particular bedroom fell in the part of the ship.

Almost every level was the exact same, and when they got to the end where the cargo bay was, they found out where the windows led, because they were able to look down into the cargo bay from the next two decks, which told the boys that the cargo bay was three decks high. All the walls down every hall was painted the same soft warm brown, whereas every bedroom had a different color, from browns to blues and greens to reds, not one room appeared to be the exact same colour as any other room.

They had even found the dining hall, the only purple door that they had come across, and it had let them in, so they looked around in there for a few moments. They found dozens of round tables in there, each with as many as twelve chairs at them. The only long table was the head table, and it was at the end furthest from the kitchen, it too had twelve chairs at it, but they were more comfortable looking and all of them were on one side, so that the occupants of that table could see everyone still. The serving tables were every bit as large as the ones the boys saw in the restaurant, only they were set up in a large ell shape, instead of three long rows as had been at the restaurant.

The boys could tell that the dining hall was at the very front of the ship, because it had windows all the way around it that went floor to ceiling, and the wall was curved to match the curvature of the front of the ship itself. Of course they noticed this too in the fact that there had been no further doors after the purple one and the window in the end of the hall signified that for them as well.

They even ventured behind the serving tables and checked out the impressively large and very nice looking kitchen. None of them had ever truly seen inside a proper five star kitchen before, though they had seen them on TV, and this looked much like that. There were several preparation areas, a huge stove and what appeared to be six ovens. There was an tire wall of refrigerators and freezers, all of them very large, the boys opened up a few of them to check them out too. All the surfaces in the kitchen were done of copper, and it gleamed brilliantly.

They ventured back out into the hall and went up to the next level on the next nearest elevator. There was one in every section of hall in the centre of the ship, so there was always one close by. The elevators had grey doors, were also double wide and of course slid open as well. They did find a few stair wells though but did not venture up them, these too were hidden behind grey doors.

With only sheer luck, the boys realized what time it was, and knew that they had to hurry to make their meeting with the captain, so asked the computer for directions to where they needed to go, and took the fastest route there. When they made it, they found themselves in the most amazing room that they had yet seen. It was smaller than most of the rooms they had seen, except the bedrooms, but it was very well appointed. There were about twenty very comfortable chairs scattered all around the room.

There was even a very nice looking stone fireplace in one corner, but it was not a real one, just used electricity, so that flames did not use more oxygen than needed. The floor was the only one they had yet found with carpet, whereas the rest of the floors they had found yet were just painted metal, and it was thick and soft and a warm taupe color. The walls were painted in a complimentary rich brown colour and there was plenty of nice rich woods used throughout to compliment them even further. Beside every chair was a nice table, and in the opposite corner to the fireplace was a matching bar, where you could get almost anything you wanted to drink, as long as it was not alcoholic. There was none allowed on board, except some wine, for just such an emergency.

When the boys had taken off, Jonathon smiled at their exuberance and went up to the bridge of the ship. He got started on the procedures for powering up all the services of the ship, and warming up the engines, this was pretty easy, it was mostly automated, but did take a while to do. The boys even guesses correctly what it was when it happened, because the entire ship started vibrating for a few seconds as it all came on line and the engines started warming up.

Once that was done, he called the hospital and asked if his supplies were ready. He was told that they were, so he arranged to have them teleported to the ships cargo bay. He then called WSEC, and was given the same answer, so minutes later they teleported the rest of their supplies up. Jonathon then took a few minutes to get a few other systems up and running. By the time everything was finished, Jonathon rushed to meet the boys, because if he did not hurry, he would be late. They all arrived within seconds of each other.

"So Boys, does your new home meet with your approval?" Jonathon asked all the happy looking boys.

"Yeah, this is so incredible. Will we all get separate bedrooms, there are so many, we looked in the few that would let us in?" Devon asked.

"That's one of the things we're going to be going over this afternoon. We have a lot of work to do, so we'll go over that later.

I really don't see any reason to go back down to the planet now, so from here on out, you're to address me as Captain Casey, and you're my crew. You're to show respect to me, to your fellow crew, and most importantly, to yourselves. This trip won't always be easy, and there are going to be times that you're going to hate me. I'm going to push you harder and farther than you ever thought was humanly possible."

"In just a few minutes, I'm going to assign you to your teams. Your team is your family, you eat together, you sleep together, you bathe together, you fail together and you rise together. What that simply means, is that if one of you screws up, you all get punished, if one of you succeeds, you all succeed. You will have a team leader, who at this time will be the oldest person, but can be changed if I deem it necessary. Any questions or comments about what I just said?" Captain Casey asked.

"No." Most everyone said.

"Okay, here's a little pointer, when asked a question, you're to all clearly state your answer, and address me as Captain Casey, or Sir, please remember this. For the first few days I'll be more lenient on this point, but as time goes on, even minor infractions will be punished. Now, let's try it again, any questions gentlemen?" Jonathon asked.

Everyone answered 'No Sir!' except Donny, who said 'Yes Sir!'

"Excellent, never be afraid to say yes or no to a question, or to ask questions when I am telling you something important, or even not important, if you don't understand something, you must let me know. What was your question Donny?" Captain Casey asked.

"I have a couple questions Sir. First, what do you mean when you say we'll all be punished, and second, what kind of punishments do you hand out?"

"Very good questions, ones you should've all been asking. Maybe you were thinking of it, but were afraid to ask. Don't be. You'll never learn anything unless you ask questions, however I'd ask that if we're in an emergency situation, that you just follow orders, and leave the questions 'til later. I trust you're all smart enough to understand the reason for that."

"Now, as for the questions. What I mean for the first question is how it sounds really. If one of your team makes a mistake, your whole team gets punished, you're a team, and you should think that way. You ask your team members first, consult each other, and if all of you together aren't sure, then you ask me. I'm available at all hours."

"The next question though, what's the punishment, well, that'll vary depending upon the reasoning. Usually I'll exercise you near to the point of exhaustion, but if worse punishment is needed, it could be solitary confinement for a time, the amount of time depends upon the severity of the act. Other things could also be done, once again, dependent upon what it is you did or did not do, but exercise is my personal favorite. Does that answer your questions?" Captain Casey asked.

"Yes Sir!" They all answered together.

"Now, you should all know a few of the rules here. There's to be no back talk or swearing at each other, at your team leaders, or myself. There's to be absolutely no fighting or harassment. Yes I understand that there'll be disagreements at times, but you need to learn to work things out with calm words, instead of fists. You're to all do all the work assigned to you each day, every day and as quickly as possible. The first little while will be difficult on everyone, because you first need to learn everything."

"We'll start out pretty slowly at first, and work into everything as we go. Once I feel that you're all competent enough, I won't be pleased to find duties not done if there isn't a valid reason. I'm also aware that you're all young men, and you need your time off to relax and rest, don't worry, you'll get that time, eventually. The first couple weeks you may not get lots, so we'll all have to deal with it. As for me, if you think you're all working hard, I'll probably be doing twice as much as all of you put together, and I'd never ask anyone to do something I myself wouldn't do. There are other rules as well, but those we'll go over in time. Are there any questions about this?" Captain Casey asked.

"No Sir!" They all said.

"Great. Now for your teams. As I call out your team, you're to fall in, in formation, in the order in which I call it out. There'll be four groups of five, these are your new families, remember that. Team one; Franky, you're team leader, with Ryan, Kelvin, Jesse and Tony. Team one line up. Team two; Jamie, you're team leader, with

Brady, Devon, Marty and Teddy. Team two, line up. Team three; Donny's team leader, with Tristan, Matthew, Cullen and Kelly. Team three line up. Finally we have team four; Pete's team leader, and has Lance, Brad, Bobby and Zach. Team four, please line up as well." Captain Casey called out, and they all sort of fell into a formation. It was not perfect, but they would work on that.

"Okay, now to get you all properly lined up. When I call formation, you're to line up just as I'm about to show you, make it perfect. I'll also be teaching you how to salute, so that you can salute officers without embarrassing yourselves." Captain Casey told the boys, and then spent the next half an hour teaching them how to line up, stand at attention, at ease, and finally how to salute, not that they would use it often on board the ship.

"Captain, when do we get our uniforms, and start learning everything?" Jamie asked.

"All in good time Jamie, you need a little patience. As soon as we go and have some lunch, we're going to go and start unloading the supplies. At least I hope we can have some lunch, but I'm sure there are some packaged lunches in the kitchen still. Follow me and let's go eat." Captain Casey said.

They went down to the kitchen and Captain Casey found enough packaged lunches to go around, and handed them all out. Each boy took their offered meal, took them to the re-generators, to make the food edible, and then went and sat down. Captain Casey went to go to his table, and then noticed the boys' seating arrangements.

"Attention!" He barked out, and they all stood at attention. "Exactly what part of eat together as a team did you fail to understand a short while ago. In case you didn't understand the concept, I'll go over it again briefly. You're to sit together as the team you were assigned, there's no argument on this point, please sit in your teams." Captain Casey said firmly.

"Sorry Sir, won't happen again." Franky saluted.

"Thank you. There's really no need to salute though, I only taught you for if you're with higher ranked officials. You guys aren't an actual space crew to the fleet, so it's not completely necessary, now please be seated correctly and enjoy your lunch."

The boys all shuffled to their proper tables and talked in their little groups, and got to know each other better as they ate, and they also did a bit better about speed, but were still finished long before their captain was. Once he was finished, Captain Casey stood and got everyone's attention.

"Okay, you guys go ahead and start cleaning up the dining hall, and meet me in the cargo bay as soon as you can."

"Yes Sir!" They all called out.

Jonathon went to the nearest lift that would take him to the cargo bay, and then relaxed and enjoyed the ride. He got off at the cargo bay and started by opening the crate that said it held all the uniforms. He found his and got suited up. He was just pulling on his boots when the boys all came in.

"Okay gentlemen, fall in, it's time to receive your new uniforms. As I call out your name, you're to come up and receive your new uniforms, and then fall back in." Captain Casey said.

"Yes Sir!" They all said.

One by one, Jonathon pulled out the uniforms, called out the boy they belonged to, handed them to him, and they returned to their positions.

"Now that you have your uniforms, you may all go get changed. There's a change room right through that door. You may leave the rest of your uniforms, as well as your regular clothes in there for now, while we get our supplies all ready." Captain Casey told the boys.

"Um, Captain, a bit of a problem!" Brady said.

"What would that be Brady?"

"Well, how am I supposed to get this uniform over my cast? Getting dressed with loose pants is hard enough as it is."

"The uniform will easily stretch over such a thin cast as that one is, although if you find it difficult to dress yourself, you may either ask a team mate or myself to help."

"Oh, okay then. I'll manage with getting dressed then, I was mostly worried about it fitting."

"Okay, dismissed, come back as soon as you're all presentable, and then fall back in."

The boys all took off and went to get changed. They took about ten minutes or so, and then all came back out, every one of them was fidgeting around, and tugging at the tight material, trying to get used to it. The material was tight fitting and was quite uncomfortable to most at first, something that clearly showed on every one of the boys' faces at the moment.

"Well, now we look like a proper crew. Stop squirming around, you'll get used to the uniforms before too long. I know they feel tight right now, but that's the way they're supposed to be." Captain Casey explained.

"But Sir, they're so tight, and well they show everything, we may as well be naked in these things." Marty said uncomfortably.

"Yes, they're tight, but you'll get used to them. As for showing everything, not really, you'll find though that wearing underwear will help, I recommend you start wearing them." He said and a number of the boys blushed at this.

Captain Casey did not care, he was used to the uniforms, and when they were working, they wore some form of utility belt that helped cover them up a bit more, but most of the time, as they were now, was how they would normally be, not that the belts really covered that much anyway.

"Okay, let's start by unloading all the boxes. Keep everything neat and organized, but if you aren't sure where something should go, just ask your team leader, and if he doesn't know, then ask me."

"Yes Sir!"

For the next few hours the crew got everything out of the crates, and everything was neatly piled in about five different piles to go to the five different places. Once this was done, Captain Casey used the teleporter to get all the supplies to their correct homes.

"Okay guys, off to the infirmary next to get everything stowed there, then the kitchen, and then the engine room. After the kitchen's done, we can stop and make dinner. Today will be group one cooking and group two cleaning, and it'll rotate to the next group every day. Any questions?" Captain Casey asked.

"Yes Sir!" Franky said.

"Yes, what is it Franky?"

"Well, I kind of don't know how to cook. I'm not sure about the others though. What do we do if none of us knows how?"

"Well, don't be afraid, first of all, no one will make fun of you if it doesn't taste that great. If however you give anyone food poisoning, I won't guarantee even that. As for not knowing, you'll learn, and it's really not all that hard. There are a large assortment of cookbooks in the kitchen, as well as you're always welcome to ask me for help. I enjoy cooking, and from time to time I'll probably join a group to cook dinner."

"Thanks Sir!" A relieved Franky said.

"No problem, any time. Now let's go guys, the faster we do this, the faster we can go eat, and I'm getting hungry again." Captain Casey said, because the packaged lunches were far from large or filling.

They all went to the infirmary, it had a deep green door, and started unloading everything. The infirmary was another large room, but it had curtains hung up that could be pulled around each of the four beds that were in there. The walls were painted a bright cheery yellow and the floor was charcoal coloured. On both sides of each bed were numerous medical monitors and equipment. Some were built right into the wall, while some were free standing. The bed itself had a screen on it with hundreds of options for the medic to use, because the bed itself was a piece of medical equipment and could scan the entire body with ease.

Captain Casey ended up having to stand back and direct everyone, because it was just too hard to work, and answer all the questions as to where everything went. In less than an hour they were finished, so they went to the kitchen and started the task of putting everything away there. Captain Casey told team one to break off and start getting dinner ready, so that they could eat as soon as they were finished. Captain Casey was able to more easily help here though once everyone had been told where the basics went. One of the boys in the group must have been able to cook somewhat, because whatever they were making sure was starting to smell good, and by the time everything was put away, the food was ready.

"Boys, this looks and smells really good, but then again, with how hungry I am, I could eat almost anything." Captain Casey complemented the boys with a grin.

"Thanks Sir! Jesse knew how to cook, and a couple of the other guys said they were pretty good as well, so we were fine. So I let them tell me what to do." Frankie said with a bright smile at the compliment.

"That's good, but you'll learn quickly as well." Captain Casey said and they all sat down to eat.

After the meal was completed, they all went about getting the last of the stuff all put away, while team two took care of the cleanup. When they were finished, and it did not take long to do, they joined the rest of the crew. The weapons were interesting, the boys had never even fathomed so many missiles in one location before. The weapons room had been one of the locked doors they had been unable to enter earlier. The personal weapons were stored in the weapons lockers where they belonged, but they stayed in their crates, so the boys did not even see those.

"Well, now that everything's stowed, it's time to show you to your quarters. Lights out will be in one hour, so you'll have enough time to get your racks made up, get cleaned up, and then relax for a few minutes." Captain Casey told the boys.

"Sir, what time will we be getting up in the morning?" Donny asked.

"I'll be waking you all at 0600, which is six am, breakfast will be made by the team that's in charge for that day, and everyone eats at 0700. Also during the time that the team who's cooking is busy, the rest of us will be doing our morning exercises, they'll last for forty five minutes, so that leaves fifteen minutes to get ready for the day. So you have to be up as soon as you're called, get cleaned up, and in your uniforms immediately, or the punishment is an extra hour of exercises following breakfast, should you be late. Exercises will be held in the cargo bay." Captain Casey told the boys.

"Yes Sir!" They all stated.

Captain Casey took the next fifteen minutes to show the boys their quarters. Each room had two sets of bunk beds and a single bed, they had an attached washroom, with a five person shower, and five toilets in their own little cubicle with privacy door, as well as five sinks. The rooms were not extravagant, but were spacious and homey, and were plenty for most people. The walls in these rooms too were all painted differently, same as all the bedrooms they had seen on the lower decks. These bedrooms were actually on an upper deck, and not far from the bridge or the captains suite.

As each group was shown their room, the team leaders all chose the single beds, and the others all called upper or lower bunks, only two did not care for the bed they got, but it was talked out.

Once the boys were all situated, Captain Casey went to his own room. The captains suite was very nice, it was large and spacious. It had a nice sitting area for reading and relaxing, as well it had a large bed and bureau. The bathroom was equally as nice, large spa style tub, which had been upgraded to a sonic bath, as well as a large shower. Captain Casey got himself all ready for bed, and then got his bed ready. As soon as lights out time came, he sent the message out to the four rooms, and instructed the computer to cut the lights. Everyone said their good nights, and they all passed out, from sheer exhaustion, minutes later.

CHAPTER 8

THE TRAINING STARTS

The following morning, Captain Casey woke just before 0600, and as soon as the clock hit 0600, he sent the call out for the boys to all get up to start the day. He went out in the hall outside the rooms and waited for the boys to come out. As each group exited their dorms, he told them to line up beside their doors. The last group out was group three, and they had but thirty seconds to spare.

As soon as they too were lined up, Captain Casey went into each of the boys' rooms to inspect them. As he had not informed them of this little requirement, he was not at all surprised to find that the rooms were all a mess. He went back out and left the boys all standing there for almost a full minute before he spoke, looking at them with no expression on his face, making the boys sweat just a bit.

"I'd hoped that you boys would've thought of this on your own, however, you did not, so now it's a requirement. Before you leave your rooms in the morning, your beds are to be made, and your dirty clothes and towels are to be put in the laundry chute. This ship is equipped with an automated laundry system, so by the end of the day the clothes will be cleaned, folded, and sent back to the room that they came from, it's then your duty to put them away when you get in each evening. I'll inspect every room every morning, and failure to have this done is extra exercises. For now this can stay as is, since we're already late for getting started, so this'll need to be done this evening before bed please." Captain Casey said.

"Yes Sir!" The boys all said.

"Thanks, group two to the kitchen please, have breakfast ready for 0700, and we'll be there by then. You only have half an hour now, so you better hurry. The rest of you, please follow me, we'll do a light jog to get warmed up." Captain Casey said and then started jogging.

Instead of using the lift to go down to the cargo bay though, they jogged all the way down the ten flights of stairs, and down multiple corridors until they reached the cargo bay. Jonathon started them on some good stretches, then spent about fifteen minutes giving them a good workout, and then a five minute cool down. One of the nice things about the uniforms that the boys found, was that they stayed a nice constant temperature, and even with the calisthenics they had done, they did not sweat much at all. Once finished, Captain Casey led the tired boys to the lift to take them up to the dining hall.

"Well guys, you did very well, you kept up, however you all look tired already. We'll be doing this every day, me included, so you'll get used to it very quickly." He said, and the boys all groaned.

"Do we have to do it every day Sir, this'll kill me?" Tristan whined.

"Yes, and unless you want another half an hour of intense workouts, I'd quit whining. Not only do I hate whining, but it's unbecoming of a ships crew, especially mine. Like I said, you'll get used to this very quickly, and as soon as everyone's ready, you'll move up to my pace, which is more intense, and twice a day. This is also very necessary on a ship, because normally you don't get quite as much exercise as you would on the planet, so we have to make sure to stay in good shape."

"What! Are you saying you went easy on us today?" Tristan asked incredulously.

"Afraid so!" He grinned. "You're all in really good shape, but still you get winded easily, because you're not used to real exercise, so as soon as you're ready, we'll move up to once a day intense, and then twice a day, as soon as you're ready for that."

The lift opened across from the dining hall, cutting off any further response, because they all headed into the dining hall. Team two were just setting the tables as they walked in, so they all sat down and started eating.

"Well guys, that was a very good meal. You'll be expected to be back up here no later than 1100 hours to have lunch ready for 1200 hours, and then the same for dinner, here by 1700 and dinner ready for 1800. Team three, it's now your duty to clean up both the kitchen and dining room, and meet us on the bridge in one hour, that should give you plenty of time. If you're early, then come up early. Come on guys, let's go. Time to start cramming those little minds of yours full of powerful knowledge." Captain Casey told the boys happily.

They headed up to the bridge of the ship, and for the next hour, until team three arrived, they just went over some basic things. This was the first time the boys had been on the bridge so far, though they had all seen it on TV before. The bridge too was very large, two decks high, and the entire ceiling was glass, so you could see out it easily. The back wall was flat and square, whereas the rest of the walls curved all around, because the front of the ship was rounded, and it housed four large doors, one leading from each of the four corridors. The windows came down to the top where the first and second levels would have met, had there been a floor there, and then below that were all the electronics that controlled the entire ship. The captains chair was set near the back, where he could see everybody and everything that was happening at any given time.

There were two distinct stations on either side, and while each of the two merged into another, there was a clear line between them as well. Each station was a good two and a half to three meters wide. There was a lot of equipment packed into each one, though the greatest portion of every station was taken up by view screens, so that they could have multiple views of anything at any given time. The very front though was where the massive screen was that could be set to show almost anything that they cared to see at all, and it was easily three meters wide.

Where there were walls that could be painted, they too were painted a bright white that made the whole bridge very bright. So far this had been the only white they had seen inside the entire ship, everything else had been all sorts of colours. The floor was charcoal coloured. Every station was set up for a particular set of activities and there were many screens and control pads to do everything that one could hope to do at these stations. The captains chair housed a universal controller system, so that he could take over any one of the stations at any time should he need to do so. The view screen at the front would be his to use, and he controlled it from there,

there were pads on both arm rests so that they were in easy reach at all times, and the functions changed depending on what station or job he needed to do. Once more the boys just stood there taking in everything.

"Okay guys, now that you're all here, let's get this training started. First you already know, my orders are to be followed as quickly as you can at all times, the reason for this is simple. In an emergency situation, none of us will have time to be slow about things, so make sure everything is done quickly and efficiently, but make sure it's done correctly. Should there ever be a time that you're running something, and you don't know an order I give, ask. Most of the systems in here are highly automated, so there's very little interaction from the crew, you can just tell the computer what you want it to do, and it'll be done. For the time being, until you've proven worthy, the computer has been instructed to ignore any requests for ship operations that you guys give. There are only two reasons at this time that the computer will listen to you, one is that I give it temporary permission, or two, I'm unable to tell it what to do. Our life signs are at all times monitored by the computer, so it'd know. Any questions so far?" Captain Casey asked.

"No Sir!"

"Excellent, it's pretty simple. Now on to the systems. The bridge is broken into five main sections. First and foremost is command, from the command chair, every system can be taken over and controlled if needed. Next is navigation, then weapons, which also incorporates shields, then communications, which also covers teleportation, and finally scanning, both internal and external, but also controls the environmental systems. For the most part, each station only requires one person to man it. For the first little while, a whole team will be running each station, until you're all familiar with the full operation. Once the bridge operations are down, we move on to the engine and power rooms, and do much the same things there, there are four sections in there as well; power and engines of course, but also the inertial compensator and the shield generators. Most bridge operations as well can be handled from there if the need ever arose, which would be very rare, but it can be done. Any questions so far?" Captain Casey asked.

"No Sir!" They all said, except Bobby, who asked, "Except how do we use it?"

"Patience young man, we'll get there eventually. We're not moving this ship an inch until you can all fly it. It might take a couple days, or a couple weeks, depends entirely on how fast you all learn. I expect that with you guys that it'll only take three or four days for you to get everything, because you all seem to be very quick learners."

The boys all nodded to this, thinking that they were not going to be able to learn all that they needed to know to fly a space ship so fast, but they trusted the captain, so said nothing. Jonathon though could see the looks, just chose to ignore them.

"The first lesson today will be the scanning section. Follow me and pay attention, and if at any time I go too fast, or you don't understand something, make sure and ask. You have to remember that every person around you depends upon you to know your job, but if you don't, and an emergency happens, and you freeze at the wrong time, because you don't know something . . . . Well, then I'll leave what can happen up to your imaginations. I'm not trying to scare you, or make you nervous, I'm just trying to make you understand and learn the reasons."

"Yes Sir!" They all said

"We understand." Donny added.

"Excellent, very simple, but sometimes people forget the simple things, or try and over think them. So, with that said, you'll find that the systems are pretty easy really."

So for the next two hours he went over every aspect of the internal and external scanners, how to read the information, how to run the built in diagnostics, and most importantly, how to find the information of the ships around you. The scanners had been upgraded a few times since inception, and they were pretty good by any standards, to the point they could tell what kind of shields a ship was using, and sometimes their armament. He also quickly went over how to work the environmental systems, but that was very simple, so only took a few minutes.

"So, as you can see, it looks pretty simple to use. You have all the screens on the wall and the console, they're all touch screens, so you can just drag and drop what you need to where you want it, or need it. It can even be set to show up as a three dimensional model, but most people find it too distracting, so just rotate the ship on the screen. As I told you before, on all screens, our ship's always the very center, and to rotate any view, just put your finger on the ship and turn it whichever way you want or need. The internal scanners though only show the ship, and you can break it up from the full view, as it shows right now, down to a single room, or show an entire deck, and you can rotate that any way you see fit as well. You can also get full vid feeds to see any area of the ship, except personal areas of course, or just use the sensor information, which sees everything. Either way, you can almost always tell who is where and or doing what at almost any given time."

Finally, after Captain Casey was finished going over the scanning systems, team two headed down to the kitchen to get lunch started. Captain Casey, and the rest of the crew paused the training, until after lunch, and went about cleaning the bridge thoroughly. After lunch was done, everyone, except team three, went back to the bridge. Once they were joined by team three, they started in on the weapons systems.

"Now gentlemen, this is the weapons section. It controls the massive firepower that this ship wields, as well as it encompasses the shield systems that help to protect us. Running this station is of course a huge responsibility, and any slacking in this section, or playing around will result in some of the most severe punishments I can think of, and believe me, I can think up lots. This is to scare you, I'm afraid, and for good reason."

"Now the computer, for the most part, doesn't control this section, for pretty obvious reasons, so it's almost all manually controlled. You touch the screens to choose the target, and then press these three buttons here, here, and here to fire, it's designed to be a safety feature, so that only one button can't be accidentally pressed and destroy someone, or something you don't mean to. You tell the computer what size of weapon you want, and it'll load them automatically. There are sixteen points at which the ship is capable of firing from, but that's fully automated, so all you have to do is target, and it selects the easiest port to fire from for you."

"Shields are also really easy, you just tell the computer, shields up or down, and what percentage you want, it goes up in increments of ten. While in flight though, the shields should always be at ten percent, to help protect the ship from space debris, but to save power they're not normally higher than that, unless needed, because it's not required. The shields also cannot be any higher than twenty percent if someone or something needs to be teleported though. Any questions so far." Captain Casey asked.

"I do Sir!" Kelvin answered.

"Yes, what is it Kelvin?"

"Well, let's just say someone were to accidentally set off a missile, is there any way to stop it?"

"Not really, no. If the target was far enough away, and you had time, you could order the self destruct of the missile. If however the target was too close, you'd never have the time. Our missiles travel at extremely high rates of speed, and will travel more than ten thousand kilometers in one second. So as you can see, don't make a mistake. This is the reason it has a triple fail safe system. It slows the operator down slightly, but it helps to prevent mistakes."

"Even still, I can tell you that at least five ships were damaged due to such friendly fire. For the most part though, even our largest missile won't take out a ship in only one hit, so hopefully the worst that could happen is some damage. However, hit a ship at only ten percent shields, and you'd destroy them instantly, this is why there's to be absolutely no fooling around with this. Does that answer your question?" Captain Casey asked the boy gently, they were all a little ashen faced at this news.

"Yes Sir, but I'd be scared to have control over this section. What if I accidentally targeted the wrong ship, and fired, I could be responsible for killing innocent people." Kelvin asked, looking almost green.

"And keep that fear, it helps you to keep your focus. The good thing is that only the enemy ships fully show up here, friendly ships only show as a light image, the not so friendly ships are bold and red, that's what the scanning department does, and the computers also automatically do this for you. However, even still you can lock onto a friendly target, and fire at it, the rule of thumb here though, is check three times, and fire once."

"Simply put, once you fire, it can't be taken back. Now, like I said before, manning the weapons station is a huge responsibility, so it's not to be taken lightly. You'll all be taught how to use it, and you'll even get a chance to use the weapons, to see just what they can do, against some asteroids in deep space of course. We may all hope that we never have to use them against a ship, however, with the mission we'll be taking on, it may unfortunately happen." Captain Casey informed the boys.

"Thank you Sir for the information." Kelvin said.

"Sir, I have another question please?" Lance asked.

"What is it Lance?"

"What is our mission? You just said that in our mission we may have to use our weapons on another ship, but what are we gonna be doing that could be so dangerous?"

"Well I was going to get to that later, after all the training was done. Seeing as how we're done the weapons for now, until we get to a suitable training ground, I'll tell you. We're going to be taking on search and rescue missions. There are many of our people still lost and presumed alive. There are also still a lot of Qaralon ships out there, picking off too many small ships, again we'll do what we can. At times we'll be joined by other ships doing the same thing, and we can call on help if needed, but only if needed."

"Most of the time though we'll be completely alone out there with no help near by. This is a tough ship, you all know many of the stories of what this ship has gone through, and a great many of them are true. Together we'll go out and do what we can to clean up after the war, there are many years worth of work to be done, and we'll spend at least one year doing this. At the end of the year, we'll evaluate how well this little experiment worked, and move on from there." He said.

"Sounds kinda scary. I never wanted to see another Qaralon in my life, and now I might have to. More than one chased after me, trying to catch me. Most of them said I looked real tasty, and would enjoy having me for dinner." Teddy said.

"Yes, a great deal of people were lost from such raids. It also seems the Qaralon like to torture their captives, sometimes for years. They never hit, oh no, that bruises the meat. We captured ships where humans were nothing but toys to be played around with, some had humans on leashes and were treating them like dogs. Any complaints, and they were shocked. There was also the constant fear that misbehavior would get them put on the dinner table. Kids were also reported to have been purposely fattened up for dinner. Some of the reports as to what happened to the poor captives were so horrible it made many fully grown men burst into tears, and/or lose their lunches. Should we find any such situation, the offending ship will be permanently disabled, and the crew left afloat in space." Captain Casey stated coldly.

"Why not just kill them Sir?" Ryan asked.

"Because we're humans, we're not sick and twisted beasts like the Qaralon. Even during the war we'd only go so far as killing the enemy when all else failed. We killed many, but we disabled huge numbers of ships. Eventually those ships can and will be repaired, whether or not they'll then again pose a threat to us, will remain to be seen. Also, we're not currently at war, so we won't fire upon any ship unless they fire first, and even then, we'll try to talk first."

"What if we know that there are captives aboard Sir, what would we do in that case." Tony asked.

"Again, we would talk first, and demand the release of any captives. Now the tough part. If the Qaralon were to fire upon us, and we're unable to disable them without killing them, we'll fire to kill. Even if there are captives aboard. It's long been the policy that hiding behind captives won't save your lives, and personally, I believe that slavery is worse than death. At all costs though, we'll attempt to get our people back, even by trickery if needed." Captain Casey told the wide eyed boys.

"I'd never want to be one of their slaves, and if it were me, and there was no choice, I'd gladly accept death." Donny said honestly.

"I'm the same. Hopefully no one ever has to be in that position though." Captain Casey said.

"So, when do we start the mission then Sir." Zach asked.

"As soon as I feel you're all comfortable enough on the systems, and even then, for a couple weeks or so, we'll stay mostly in ours or the Tenarian's systems, where we'll be relatively safe. Now, our cooks for the day should be going soon, we'll be up in a little over an hour. The rest of you come with me."

The groups separated and went their ways. Captain Casey and the remainder of his crew went down to the engine rooms. The engine room was another of the rooms with a locked door, the boys understood why that would be of course, but with the captain with them, it opened automatically. This room too was painted bright white and had several work stations all around it.

Like they had been told earlier, everything about the ship could be controlled from that room as well, but there were even more stations than the bridge had, simply because there was far more to do in here of course.

The power generator room was reached through a door to their right as they entered, and they guesses correctly that the door to the right when in the hall also led to there, so you could get to there from either place.

The engine itself is massive, it has large solid pipes leading to and from it in many places, massive cables also come out of it and go up to the ceiling three decks above and run to the generator room. The engine is a little more than two decks high, and more than twice as long and about half that in width. There were access panels all over it, and the work stations were not touching, but were connected via many wires to the engine, each on it's own pedestal.

They could hear the engine, but it was not loud at all, just a low hum was all they heard, and it was almost at the bottom of their hearing. It would be louder, they all assumed, when in flight, and they were correct, but the loudest it ever got was just about normal speaking volume, so even when going as fast as they could, the people in there could still easily have a conversation.

The coolant lines entered and exited in several locations, and the boys could feel the heat radiating from them when they got too close, and every one of them had large yellow lettering on them, warning anyone that they were extremely hot and to not touch, this of course made sense. All of these lines went down into the floor and disappeared. This room was normally kept very cold to compensate for the heat that was generated, but given the engine was barely running at all, it was not hot in there. The heat was of course recycled throughout the ship to keep it nice and warm at all times, and that was where the lines ran to, to the furnace room, any excess heat that could not be used was cooled outside. Once more the boys just looked around but did not touch anything. The captain let them look for several minutes before starting.

"Now, this isn't really a class, because we'll want all of you here for that. What I want is for you to all tell me what, if anything, you know about what you see in here?"

For the next hour the boys all called out various things, and Captain Casey either congratulated them on a good answer, or corrected them on an incorrect, or partially incorrect answer. For the most part though, the boys knew most everything about a space ships engine, and how it worked. There were some fuzzy areas of knowledge, and Captain Casey helped to fill in those blanks, but assured the boys that once their actual classes started, they would learn everything they would need to know. Finally their time was up, so they all headed up for dinner. When they arrived, they all sat down and had an enjoyable meal together, all of them eating well.

"Well guys, now that dinner's over, so are our lessons for the day. You may now relax for the rest of the evening. Lights out is at 2200 hours, and you're to be in your rooms no later than 2100 hours. Now, this ship does have a number of things for you to do in your leisure time. There's the workout room with sonic hot tub and sauna, we don't do our exercises in there, because it's just not big enough for all of us. There's also the theatre, where you can find almost any movie you want. There are the multiple lounges, where you may sit back and watch TV, or play games with your friends."

"I also recommend the observation deck once we get moving, the views are incredible. I, for one, am going to sit in the sauna and the sonic tub for a while after a good workout, only about ten people at a time can use it, so some of you are welcome to join me, if you so desire, if not, feel free to do as you wish. You guys on the cleaning crew, however, have to do that first, so you should get started, the sooner you finish, the sooner you may relax, however, make sure that it's clean." Captain Casey told everyone.

Captain Casey went up to the workout room and started a good stretch, and then a vigorous workout. The room was large and spacious, very bright and well appointed. There was a mixture of weight and cardio machines to use. Due to the nature of the location, any and all weight equipment were of course not of the free weight design, and everything was very well secured to the deck, because the last thing anyone wanted was to have weights falling should the ship lurch for any reason whatsoever. Donny and

Tristan also came and joined Captain Casey in the workout room, minutes after he had started his workout.

"Hey guys, what's up." Captain Casey asked the boys without even stopping his fast paced movements, which appeared to the boys to be some fancy martial arts moves.

"Not much, we figured we'd come check this place out, try out some of the equipment, and definitely try the sonic tub, but the sauna sounds nice as well." Donny answered.

"By all means, don't let me stop you guys, I'm just going through some of my martial arts moves as a workout. This'll be some of the training you'll also receive, eventually, when I feel that you're ready for it." Captain Casey said, again without slowing down, it also did not appear as if the fast movements even bothered him, since he was talking perfectly normal.

"Sir, how can you talk while doing all that, as if you were just walking with someone? I'd be so tired I couldn't speak." Tristan asked.

"I've been exercising like this since I was eight years old, so I've had lots of practice. You too will be able to run a fast pace and keep up a full conversation by the end of the year, I can almost guarantee it."

"If you say so Sir, but just watching you is making me tired, and I can't imagine doing it." Donny said.

"I do say, and you will do, but it'll come slowly, so don't worry. It isn't expected for you to be able to do this overnight, I don't wish to kill you boys. Now, you guys go do what you came here to do, don't worry about me." He smiled.

They went off and started mostly playing on the equipment, and then a short time later moved to the sauna. Jonathon was just starting his cool down when they exited the sauna and climbed into the sonic tub. He joined them a few minutes later. After relaxing in the hot soothing water for a while, they climbed out and hit the shower to rinse and cool off.

The rest of the crew split into two different groups, one group went to the theatre, and another to the main lounge, it had the best games in it. Jonathon, and the two boys with him, joined the others in the lounge, once they were finished cleaning and drying off and finding where the others were. The boys that had gone to the theatre had watched a movie, and when they were finished that, they too joined the rest of their crew and captain in the lounge and played as well.

The theatre was really nice, every bit as nice as any theatre on the planet, with the exception of course that it was smaller. It could hold a total of a hundred people in it though, so it was still a very good size. It had large comfortable chairs arranged in such a way on a sloping floor so that everyone would be able to see the screen, no matter where they sat. The screen itself was huge, though was of course a much more advanced version of what theatres used to use, it was all in one device and required no projector, much like a TV, just huge. The screen was capable of playing any sort of format and the boys all loved the three dimensional capabilities, it looked far more realistic than they had ever heard of, but then most of the boys had never had a theatre experience. The sound system of the theatre was also superb in every way, a real Earth moving experience in sound. The whole thing had been upgraded not long before the ship had been given to Captain Casey's parents, so was still very close to brand new and very high end.

The main games lounge was also impressive, games galore for everyone to enjoy. There were several table style games, such as; billiards, air hockey, table soccer and cards. There were also a great deal of arcade style games, including pinball machines. These had hardly changed any at all in all the years that they had been around, but the video games were incredible. There was even a small bowling alley in there with two lanes for people to play. Given that the ship was designed to hold far more people than it currently had on it, there was always more than enough room for everyone to play and never have to worry. In fact, the boys and the captain could play three or four games at a time if they were able to, and there would still be enough for them all.

They all played in the lounge until it was time to go to their rooms for the night. They all wished each other a good night and they all headed to their rooms for the night. Once there, they all got ready for bed, and when lights out was called, everyone went right to sleep.

The next couple days was much the same as their first day in space. Early morning rising, calisthenics, breakfast, training, lunch, more training, dinner, then relaxation time. They were all kept busy at pretty much every second of every day, with of course the short period of time where they had some free time in the evening to relax. Captain Casey removed the cast off of Brady's leg, and he was very pleased now that he could walk normally, and without so much as a limp, it was fully healed.

On their fourth day in space, Captain Casey felt that the boys were now proficient enough in most of the basic ship operations to get under way. So on September tenth, they started on their journey, and what a journey it would prove to be.

CHAPTER 9

AND THE TROUBLE STARTS

Captain Casey had Team one working navigation today, so he gave the coordinates and the speed he wanted, and they got them going. Slowly at first, gradually increasing the speed as they had been taught, team one got them going. An instantaneous maximum speed jump was hard on the ship, and the body, so as such, was only ever used in extreme cases because of this. It could cause the ship to come apart, and the people inside to get very sick from the very sudden movement. The inertial compensation systems could not keep up with a change that was that drastic. You might not be plastered to a wall behind you, but the force was still more than enough to make you think your stomach was.

The rest of the crews were also on the bridge, each one of them assigned a different station to monitor everything as they were going.

Finally the ship was up to the cruising speed requested, and they were well on their way. Scanning crew, team number two, was busy searching everything around them, making sure nothing snuck up on them. Team three was on communications, not that they would be doing much, and team four was on weapons, they had the shields at the recommended ten percent, otherwise everyone hoped nothing more of their services would be required. Captain Casey would also have each team rotate daily, so that everyone got very familiar with the workings of all the equipment.

As they were going, Captain Casey was drilling the boys on the workings of every piece of equipment on the bridge. He would fire off questions while pointing to one boy, and said boy would then be expected to answer it as quick and with as much detail as he possibly could. When and if one of them got the answer wrong, he would then call everyone over for a brief recap, to make sure that it was explained completely and fully, so that they each understood exactly what they needed to know. As they went of course, they would learn more and more in this area, until each and every one of them was fully proficient in every area.

Every day now would be a few hours of flying, and the rest would be spent on studies Captain Casey had explained to the boys. Most of the boys needed a lot of help in most areas of normal schoolwork, not to mention the new things about the ship they needed to learn. Their only day off was going to be Sunday's, so the rest of the time would be busy days. The first day the crew flew the entire day, to get as close to an asteroid field that was often used as target practice, and by the time the day was closing, they arrived. Tomorrows class would be interesting to say the least, because none of the boys had ever truly seen just what their defensive weaponry was capable of. That night, before going to bed, Captain Casey set the scanners to automatic, so that they would alert him should anything come within a few light years of them. Because they were stationary, the scanners could work at maximum, and pick up anything at all now, even a long range, shielded missile would be seen, that flaw had long ago been fixed. The night proved thankfully quiet, at least from the outside.

The next morning Captain Casey did his morning inspection of the boys' rooms, and found that team three's room was still somewhat messy, and the beds were not made.

"Team three, your dorm's a disaster, team leader, please explain?"

The boys all knew by now that when a specific person was asked, that no one else was to speak. Captain Casey had been very clear and concise on this particular requirement to the boys.

"Well, you see Sir, someone wouldn't get up, and he caused us all to be late." Donny answered, his head held as high as he could force it.

"Team leader, that's not the full answer." Captain Casey stated simply, softly.

"Well Sir, I tried, as did Tristan, but Matthew wouldn't get up, he said he was too tired." Donny answered, now getting a dirty look from the aforementioned boy.

"Thank you. Matthew, please approach me." Captain Casey calmly said.

Matthew walked up, the ten feet looked a kilometer the way he was walking. Captain Casey put his hand up as the boy approached, and Matthew shied away at first, as if he were about to be hit, but he held his ground. The captain felt the boys forehead for a moment.

"Are you sick, you don't have a fever, and your color is good?" Captain Casey asked gently.

"No Sir, just very tired." Matthew answered honestly, knowing that lying would be really bad right now.

"And you feel that the rest of us are not equally as tired, and that we too wouldn't love to sleep in a bit?" Captain Casey asked just as gently.

"Ah no, I guess I never thought of that."

"Please speak up when you talk to me. So the main problem was you didn't think! Why is it you ignored the pleas of your team mates? I'm sure that more than once they warned you as to what would happen if you weren't ready on time." Captain Casey stated gently still.

"They tried Sir, I guess I was just too tired to listen."

"You guess, or you were, maybe tired, or was it stubborn?"

"I'm very tired Sir, I wasn't thinking clearly Sir."

"Well, now as a punishment your entire team gets an extra half an hour of intense exercise after breakfast, as well as you yourself gets to join me in my evening exercises. If you believe that you're tired now, just wait 'til tomorrow morning. As for the rest of you on his team, you aren't to harass him, this of course would bring further punishments."

The entire team groaned as one, but Matthew very nearly started crying. The breakfast crew was dismissed to go start cooking, while the rest of them went to the cargo bay to do their exercises. Jonathon had been steadily working them a bit harder every day, so they were all getting very tired, but the work was also starting to pay off. All the boys were starting to fill out a bit more, both because of the exercise and the three good meals a day, but mostly because of the good food they were getting. They were also becoming more accustomed to the workouts, so their breathing was coming easier, so today he tried adding a new element to the workouts.

"Would anyone tell me why it's so hard to talk while doing exercises?"

"Sir . . . . it's because . . . . we're using . . . . all of our . . . . energy and . . . . breath while exercising." Pete gasped out.

"That's correct. Now tell me, someone else this time, why it is that I can talk very easily while doing this?"

"Because you have more practice Sir." Lance shot out in one very fast breath.

"While that's somewhat correct, there's more to it. You all need to learn how to breath properly, and how to pace yourselves. Right now most of you are trying to match me step for step, you couldn't keep up to me, even if you wanted to. If I were to speed up any more, most of you would collapse. If you need to slow down a bit, do so, don't push yourselves so hard that it starts to hurt, a good burn is all you want. As for breathing, learn to control it, breath in deep and slow through your nose, breath out slowly through your mouth, concentrate on your breathing, not the exercises. For the rest of the exercises, follow me, slow your pace a bit if you need to, and concentrate only on your breathing and the sound of my voice, ignore everything else, even the pain in your body, or how tired you feel. This way you'll be able to properly breath under pressure."

He watched the boys all clamp down on their control, and they tried hard to adjust their breathing patterns. They also all slowed down a bit.

"Okay boys, better, in time it'll get easier, you'll eventually be able to do this without concentrating so hard, and therefore be able to talk normally. Keep it up, and I'll now voice our changes in routine."

For the rest of the forty five minute session, he called out the exercises, and the boys followed as best as they could. Finally he started their cool down period, and then finally stopped.

"Well guys, you did much better today, you aren't all panting like normal at the end of an exercise session. Like I said, in time it'll become easier, almost second nature. Let's go eat a good breakfast."

The boys all followed him to the lift and went to the dining hall. They had a nice breakfast, and then Captain Casey stood.

"Would team three please follow me to the exercise room, the rest of you may go rest for the next half an hour."

They set out and arrived in the exercise room a few minutes later. Captain Casey started a new round of exercises, and the boys all used their new found knowledge, and tried to control their breathing. Twenty five minutes later, he started the boys on their cool down, and as soon as he stopped, the boys dropped.

"Team three, on your feet, you weren't given permission to rest, this is punishment, and while you're being punished, you do nothing unless told to do so, is that understood?" Captain Casey said firmly.

"Yes Sir!" They all said as they stood up shakily.

"That's better, now the reason for being here today, I'm sure you all remember. Things like this can't happen in the future, it damages the glue that holds the team together, causes friction which can tear things apart. Now obviously sometimes there'll be a reason that someone can't get up, that information should be honestly given to the team leader, and if he feels it's a valid reason, he'll then explain it to me. Just refusing to get up though, because you're tired, I'm sorry, that's simply not acceptable. Matthew, you're to meet me here this evening at 2000 hours for the workout of your young life. You'll fall into bed more exhausted than you've ever been. Tomorrow morning you're to get up, and be as cheery as I know you can be. It won't be pleasant, I can guarantee you that, but it wouldn't be punishment if you enjoyed it, now would it? Captain Casey said softly.

"No Sir!" Matthew answered quietly.

"Now we get to go have a bit of fun, and see how well these missiles work, it should also really open your eyes a bit." Captain Casey said cheerily.

He called the rest of the boys on the ships intercom and told them to all meet them on the bridge. They arrived within a few seconds of each other, from a few different doors. The boys not on punishment had decided to hit the games lounge and enjoy their unexpected free time.

"Well boys, I'm sure you remember why it is that we're here today. You will, today, get to see just what our weapons can do. Would someone go over to the scanning station and find the largest asteroid in the field, and then load that information to the defense section please? Just remember, that before you send any and all information to defense, that you scan the entire area around to ensure that there are no friendlies in the way of harm. This would of course be normal in battle that you check to make sure nothing's in the way first, then defense also checks once again, but out here you wouldn't think you'd have to. Don't think that, at any given time, there could be someone close by and you might not know it 'til you do something stupid, like forget to check. Asteroid fields, for instance, are great places to hide and take refuge, and you never know when someone could be hiding behind the asteroid that you're about to blast apart. Just remember that."

Bobby went over and looked for a few minutes and found the largest one he could. He first checked everything around it that he could see, found nothing to be concerned about, targeted it, and manually sent it to the defense section. Once that was done, he went over and joined the others.

"View screen, zoom in on the current target." Captain Casey told the computer.

The view screen automatically brought up the selected asteroid and put it so that the entire thing took up the entire display.

"Now, what team's on defense today." Captain Casey asked.

"We are Sir." Franky answered.

"Excellent! Franky, would you and your team please lock onto the target and fire a maximum yield missile at it? Everyone, please pay close attention to the screen?"

Franky and his team worked a few seconds to make absolutely certain of their target and its surroundings, and then Franky spoke. "Firing in, three, two, one."

A quarter second later, there was a near blinding flash of light, and then it was gone. There was now no asteroid, where seconds ago there had been an asteroid easily as large as the ship had been.

"So boys, what did you think of that?"

Not one of the boys said anything, they were shocked.

"That rock was about the same size as we are, that was our maximum power missile, and that asteroid didn't stand a chance. Would someone else go over and choose another asteroid please?" Captain Casey asked.

Kelly this time went over and looked for a few moments, then picked one and sent it over. He then walked over to join the others as well.

"Team two, please fire a medium yield missile at the selected target?"

Team two went to the defense section and checked everything to make sure it was fine, loaded the requested missile, and then Jamie called it out. "Firing in three, two, one."

A quarter second later the rock again exploded on impact with a blinding flash. Again there was simply nothing left.

"So, now you see what the difference is. Not a whole lot on an unshielded item, that's for sure. Now would someone else please go select another target, and team three, you're up, minimum yield this time please?"

Zach went over and chose another space rock, sent it over, and then joined the others.

"Firing in, three, two, one." Donny said, after getting the asteroid targeted. Another quarter second later, and the asteroid was gone.

"So, there you have it. On an unshielded rock, or ship, it makes no difference which one you use, they'll all destroy virtually anything you throw them at. In most situations, we'll start out with the minimum yield, to show we mean business. If they don't heed the warnings, we bring out the big guns. Now this time, someone go pick out five targets, a fair bit apart, and then team four, you're up next, fire a spread of minimum yield please?"

Tony this time went and chose the targets, he found five large asteroids, roughly a thousand kilometers apart from each other, and sent them over to defense. He went and joined the others. Pete and his team took a few seconds to verify and target everything.

"Firing in, three, two, one." Pete said, and a quarter second later, five very bright flashes all occurred at the same moment, and where there used to be huge rocks, there was now nothing more than space dust.

"With this demonstration, you can see how it's pretty easy to target multiple enemies, and fire at them. In most cases, it's far faster and easier to target your enemies one at a time, but in some cases, you can hit more than one if needed. I hope these little demonstrations have shown you just what you have control of, and why you must respect that power." Captain Casey told all the boys.

"Yes Sir!" They all said.

"Good, now that that's done, let's go to the scanning station and see if any of these asteroids are of any use to us."

The boys all played with the settings of the scanners, trying to find certain things, and for a few hours they searched. They only found a few large rocks that appeared to have any good metals in them. This was not what they were looking for, so they called it a day. From there they headed for a much needed lunch. As usual, everyone enjoyed lunch, and when they were done eating and the cleaning crew were finished, Captain Casey stood and got the boys' attention.

"Okay guys, time for some class work. We need to start in on your reading, as well as your math, science, and even some history. Follow me please to your classroom?"

He led them to what used to be his own classroom many years ago. At that time there had only been ten students in it, but Jonathon had added more desks, and rearranged it so that it was better organized for their needs. The room was large and bright, the one wall was all glass, so they could see out into space at all times. The colors had been chosen specifically to be bright and cheery, so that you would want to learn in there. Each desk in there was a good sized unit with a few drawers and a computer terminal attachment on it, so that the students could just insert their pads and they would be at a more comfortable angle. There were also keyboards and multi use controllers on a sliding tray, so that they could type and move around far faster than when normally using one of the computer pads, which was normally just by use of fingers on the touch screen. The boys had yet to receive theirs, but they would today. Each desk also had a very nice chair for the boys to sit in, so that they could learn in comfort. Captain Casey's desk was pretty much identical, only it was facing the rest of the desks and was slightly larger.

"You'll find that there are four distinct groups here, so each team is to sit in the section with their group number on it, your names are on your desks. Each of you is to work at the pace that you're comfortable with. In your desks you'll find the supplies that you'll require for our courses when we're in here. Our only courses here are the math, language, history and some science, the rest is held in different parts of the ship, for obvious reasons. Now, please be seated at the desk with your name on it?" Captain Casey ordered, and they all shuffled to their desks.

Once at their desks, the boys each got their pad from the drawer, got it situated and turned on, but that only takes a second, and then got themselves comfortable. As soon as they were ready, Captain Casey instructed the boys on how to get to where they needed to be on their programs, then told them the basics of what they were about to do.

Captain Casey had the boys do one hour of each course, and he was roaming the room helping each boy with their work as needed. From time to time he would go up to the board and show a student, or all the students different things, or how to work out particular problems. History was spent with Captain Casey standing at the front of the class the whole time, telling the boys about some of the Earth's most famous people. Once class was over, the daily cooks went to get dinner prepared, while the others went up to the bridge to scan more of the asteroids.

After dinner everyone went and had their free time. Eventually though, it was time for the remainder of Matthew's punishment. Matthew was wearing a light shirt and a pair of loose fitting cotton shorts, he figured that they would be fine, so headed to their workout room for the remainder of his punishment.

"I see you're here right on time, that's good. Let's start with a good warm up, remember to keep your breathing under control, try not to gasp for breath. Follow my lead and keep up with me, I'll slow down if I think you need it, but otherwise, you follow my every move." Captain Casey told him. He too was wearing a pair of loose shorts, but was not wearing a shirt.

"Yes Sir, I'll try my best." Matthew answered. He knew he was going to be hurting by the time his punishment was finished, but he was determined to not let it show.

Captain Casey led the boy through a good warm up. When the warmup ended, Matthew removed his shirt as well, because he was already starting to get hot. He then started a strenuous routine that had the boy burning like he had never felt before, he almost gave up. Captain Casey saw this, and slowed the pace slightly, Matthew felt the change, and it came at the right time, for he was able to push on. Finally, after the poor boy was nearly drooping under his own weight, Captain Casey stopped the exercises, and started on a cool down routine. Matthew followed, glad to finally be slowing down.

Once they stopped, Matthew just slumped down. Captain Casey went over and picked up the boy, carried him over to the sonic tub, and sat him down in the hot bubbling water. He started tenderly massaging the sore muscles in the boys neck and shoulders. Matthew was enjoying the massage so much, he actually fell asleep, and a few moments later Jonathon noticed. He looked to confirm, and found the boy sound asleep. He again picked Matthew up, and just as he was standing up, Matthew threw his arms around Jonathon and hugged him in his sleep. Jonathon smiled, he knew none of the boys had any kind of affection for a long time, so Matthew must have felt very safe at that moment. He carried the sleeping boy to the shower room, turned the water on to a cool setting, and then carried him under the spray. Matthew awoke with a start, and nearly jumped out of the arms that were holding him.

"Hey, that's mean, the water's cold!" Matthew nearly yelled.

"Yes, I guess it's a bit mean, but you needed a shower, and a cool shower after such a strenuous workout always feels good. Hop on down, grab another shower, turn it as cold as you can, and wash up."

He got down and turned on the shower next to the captain, and started to relax under the nearly cold water. He started washing down slightly, and even pulled his shorts out to wash inside, neither of them having taken their shorts off. Captain Casey had felt it would not be right. He was surprised however that Matthew had not. After both were completely cleaned, they dried off and headed up to their rooms. As they reached the area that the rooms were in, they found the others just coming up as well.

"Hey guys, so what were you up to this evening?" Captain Casey asked as they all met up.

"We'd been playing games, and then we went and watched a movie. Matthew of course left half way through the movie. So how was your workout tonight?" Jamie asked.

"It was a bit slower than normal, and I didn't get through the whole routine, but it wasn't too bad. Matthew here, though, I'm sure will be sleeping very well tonight." Captain Casey answered while ruffling Matthew's still wet hair.

"Well that's good, have a good night Sir. Come on guys, let's go." Jamie said to the captain, and then to his team.

"Yes, have a good night boys. I'll see you in the morning." The captain told his crew, and then went into his room as well.

As soon as they entered their bedroom, Donny asked the burning question that they all wanted to know, "So, how bad was it Matthew?"

"Real bad. I thought I was going to pass out at one point, he slowed down enough for me to catch my breath, and I was able to finish. I fell down though as soon as we stopped, so the captain picked me up and took me to the sonic tub, and massaged my shoulders a bit. It felt so nice I actually fell asleep. But what he did next was real mean. He woke me up with a cold shower. It did feel good though after a few minutes, and it sure helped my burning muscles. I sure do hurt though. I can tell you this though, that if that's his light punishment, I never want to see a heavy one. I think it might kill me." Matthew answered honestly.

"Wow. I'll have to remember that. I don't think he'd actually push any of us that far. I think he's too good for that, but he sure has a way of torturing us, doesn't he?" Donny grinned.

"Yeah, that he does. I do feel a lot better though after the workouts he's been giving us, and the way he taught us to breath does make it a lot easier." Tristan said.

"I agree. Well Matthew, we've all agreed that you were punished more than enough for getting us all in trouble, so let's just say that's that. I will say though, that if you don't have a good excuse next time, I'm dumping you out of your bed, and or carrying you straight in to a cold shower. And don't even think I won't." Donny said.

"I won't, don't worry, I don't want to go through that again. If you guys don't mind though, I'm going to bed. I'm almost asleep on my feet."

"Help us clean the room first, and then I think you'll find the rest of us falling into bed at the same time." Donny said.

"Okay, let's make this quick though." Matthew yawned.

They spent maybe five minutes quickly cleaning the room, then they all took care of their night time business, and then crashed into bed.

As soon as team one entered their room, Kelvin said to the rest of his team mates, "Man, did you see how beat Matthew looked? And Captain Casey said that he didn't even go close to full speed. I've seen him do his evening workouts before, and I doubt any of us could survive what he does. I do have to wonder though what he'd do for a major punishment, if that's what he does for something minor!"

"No kidding, poor Matthew did look as if he'd pass out any minute. I bet as soon as he went to his room, he fell into bed and fell asleep right away." Tony said.

"No, Donny probably made him help clean up first or something. They all looked tired, so I think they'll all be going to bed early, but they'd still have to make sure everything was clean before doing so, same as we should be." Franky said.

"Yeah, you're probably right!" Kelvin said.

The rest of the time, before lights out, they sat around and talked for a bit, cleaned the room, and then got ready for bed. The other two rooms had much the same conversations, and they too all wondered about what Captain Casey would do to them if they really did something bad. Captain Casey though was thinking about it as well.

"I hope I wasn't too hard on the poor boy. He was dead." Jonathon muttered to himself. "No, it's better to start out tough, it'll be easier on them in the long run." He said again after a few moments thought.

Jonathon had always felt that with boys especially, that it was easier to appear tough when they needed it, and show compassion when they least expected it, like what he did with the massage and the shower.

"Yeah, that probably helped him more than anything." He said out loud again.

For the rest of the time Jonathon made some logs about the trip. Once time for lights out came, he sent the message and shut out the lights. A few minutes later, he himself was fast asleep.

Chapter 10

Battle Simulated

The next week went by much the same as they started. They started the morning by going somewhere, and then the afternoons in classes. Three days a week were in the classroom, and the other three were hands on with the ships components, learning all about them, how they functioned, how to repair them, everything. During this time of course, they had a day off, as Sundays were supposed to be, and the only things they had to do were their morning calisthenics, and the teams whose turns it were to cook and clean still had that to do. Captain Casey joined the boys that day and they made three huge hearty meals. Otherwise they rested and did nothing all day but play and have fun.

Wednesday of the next week started out like most days, they did their exercises, and then their breakfast, they then flew for the first part of the morning, Captain Casey quizzing them the whole time on the workings of the equipment. They then had lunch, the team on cleaning cleaned up, Captain Casey stood to get the boys' attention, and that was when the day turned sour.

"Okay guys, time for class." Captain Casey said.

"NO, I don't want classes today! They're boring, and I'm not learning anything. I want to go on the mission now, like we're supposed to be doing." Cullen said stubbornly.

"Oh really." Captain Casey asked softly.

The rest of the boys stared on in morbid fascination. Captain Casey could see right away though that Donny, however, was not going through another workout session, so he stepped up.

"Captain, may I deal with this?" Donny asked.

"As team leader it's your duty. Please do so." Captain Casey said with a smile.

Donny took Cullen firmly by the hand and left the dining hall to talk in private, pulling the younger boy with him.

"Cullen, we're going to classes, you know this isn't an option." Donny told him.

"I don't wanna." Cullen whined.

"You're sounding just like a baby, you don't wanna, you're whining, and you know how Captain Casey hates that, but then, so do I. He also told us, when we accepted his offer, that classes and learning were part of the deal, and that it was basically non negotiable right! Now why is it you believe that you shouldn't have to go to class?" Donny asked gently.

Cullen burst into tears and started to sob out something. Donny grabbed the boy and hugged him to himself to try and figure out what was wrong.

"Tell me, what's wrong, why's this upsetting you so much? The classes aren't so bad, Captain Casey's a really good teacher, and I know we've all learned a lot already." Donny asked gently, still hugging Cullen to him.

"I'm stupid, that's why!" Cullen yelled out, pushing himself away.

"I don't think that you're stupid, why do you believe it?"

"Because, I can't read hardly at all, and I can't even add or subtract like all you can, I just can't figure it out. I tell you, I'm stupid, I'll never learn this stuff." Cullen said while still crying.

"Just 'cause you're not as good as we are yet, doesn't mean that you're stupid! Most of us are older than you are, and most of us have been to school, at least some. You never got that did you? You were, what, five when your parents were killed, and you've been on the street since, I think that's what you said. Now, what that tells me is that you really need to start at the beginning, but you tried jumping in and starting where your age group should be, didn't you? Now tell me, if you didn't know how to swim, would you just jump in the deepest section of water right away?" Donny asked logically.

"No, I . . . . I . . . . I . . . . I'd drown." He sobbed and stuttered.

"Well now, then why would you jump right in the deep end of learning? It's impossible to learn like that, like it'd be impossible to swim like that. So why haven't you told the captain this yet, or asked for more help, even from the rest of us? You know we're allowed to help each other."

"'Cause then everyone would've known I was stupid." Cullen said, while still sniffling a bit.

"Just 'cause you don't know this stuff yet, doesn't mean that you're stupid. A lot of the others, that are older than you are, are still in the first levels as well, and they're not stupid, are they? I know for a fact that before we started, Zach couldn't read at all, and now he's reading good. Now take me, I was only in school for a little over two years when I hit the streets. When we started all this training, I knew almost nothing, I read very badly, I could hardly do no math at all, and now I'm doing lots better. Some of the younger kids are way better than me, but I don't feel stupid. Why should I?" Donny asked gently.

"I guess I was acting stupid, wasn't I? Do you think the captain's gonna punish us now?"

"We'll have to see, but do you think you deserve it after that outburst in there?" Donny asked pointedly.

"I'd like to say no, but I guess I do huh?"

"Yes, and if it happens, we'll do it without complaint. Now, when we go inside, you're to look the captain in the eye and apologize, then I'm gonna bring him out and talk to him for a few minutes. Got that!" Donny ordered.

"Yes Sir!" Cullen said and they went back inside.

"Captain, I'm sorry for what I said, I know I shouldn'ta, but I was just being stupid." Cullen said, looking the captain straight in the eye.

Jonathon could tell the boy had been crying, and that he was indeed sorry.

"Apology accepted, are you ready for class now?" He asked, glad to see the boy looking him straight in the eye for a much needed apology.

"Yes Sir!"

"Could I speak to you for a moment first Sir, before we head out?" Donny asked.

"Okay, why don't you boys go ahead and head up there, and we'll meet you there? Start in on your math work please?" Captain Casey asked, the boys all nodded, and headed out. As soon as the rest of the boys were gone, and it was just he and Donny, he turned and said, "Okay Donny, what was that all about?"

"Well it seems that Cullen was feeling very stupid, and more than a bit frustrated, 'cause he was trying to do the work of his age group, when he's never been to school before. He thought that everyone was so much smarter than him, that he never stopped to think about that I suppose. I had to tell him that before starting, Zach couldn't read at all, and I was almost no better, and that most of the others were only in the starter levels as well." Donny told the captain.

"Okay, well that explains that. So what do you believe that we should do about this?" Captain Casey asked.

"Well Sir, I'm not sure a punishment would be needed in this case, I think he needs to be started over, at the level that he's really at, and let him learn properly." Donny said hopefully.

"Could this be because you don't wish to have another exercise session this morning?" Captain Casey asked with a grin.

"Well, there's that too, but can you really blame me, we're all beat." Donny answered truthfully, but smiling.

"I thought as much. I do agree with you though, because I knew this day was coming. He's refused help, and I could tell that he was struggling, I'm actually surprised it took so long. You handled the situation very well I might add. Choking back the fear you must have had at asking me to take over yourself, it had to have been difficult. It's that that makes a good captain, taking hold of your fear, and pushing it aside when you have to do something you believe will hurt no matter what you do." Captain Casey told him.

"You have no idea Sir. I had to hold with all my might to not pee when I asked you if I could deal with the situation. I actually thought you'd get really mad." Donny smiled.

"Never! One of the things you guys are here for, is to learn how to be a captain of a ship, and how to command people. As team leader, it's your duty to deal with minor issues such as this. Why do you think a ship has a command structure, just so that the captain doesn't have to deal with every little thing that comes up! Now, as for getting really mad, have you ever even seen me close to mad before?"

"I never thought of it that way. It makes sense though. No, I guess I've never seen you mad, I can't even say I've seen you angry, you're always so calm and cool. I can tell you're mad or upset though, 'cause your voice goes just a little softer, and you sound almost sad that you have to punish someone."

"You're very perceptive, that's also a very good quality in a captain as well, I can tell you that for sure, you almost have to be able to feel how others are feeling. And in a way, I am sad when I have to punish one of you guys, because it makes me feel as if I've let myself down, but more that I've let you down. When a ships crew hurts, the captain hurts, well a good captain anyway. You should've been on this ship when my parents ran it. Every person on it was like family, and it nearly killed dad any time someone got hurt, or he had to deal with a rotten situation. He always felt that it was his fault that it happened, and that he let the crew down. He punished himself far more than he ever did someone else, I do the same though. I had a nearly full verbal conversation about the punishment I gave Matthew that night, and I almost told myself I was too hard on him. I know I wasn't, and you have no idea how it hurt me to make him work so hard, I almost cried when he slumped down in exhaustion. You see, sometimes being captain is not so easy as it seems."

"I didn't know any of that. Matthew was perfectly fine, if not a bit tired, but he survived it, and he's better 'cause of it. He now outperforms most of us in our morning exercises. Why would it hurt you so much though?"

"Well think of how you'd feel to make someone else hurt for no real reason. I mean, all he did was not get out of bed and help clean, a fairly minor thing right, well what would you feel like?"

"I don't know, I guess maybe mean, like I was being too hard on him. I don't know if I could do it."

"Exactly, but now think of it this way, you all know the rules right, and getting up and making sure your room passes inspection is one of them, right? Well what do you think would happen if I let that slide, even just once, without dealing with it?"

"That maybe we could all get away with it all the time." Donny said, seeing the big picture.

"Exactly! Now you see why you need to deal with these things quickly, even though minor. I was probably a little hard on Matthew, but I never pushed him beyond his limits, but tell me, do you think any of you will do that again?"

"I doubt it. So if you don't deal with an issue right away, it could get out of hand, and it would be harder to control in the future, right Sir?" Donny asked, really starting to understand the captains reasons.

"That's exactly it! You don't have to be a monster and beat someone, nor do you have to go out of proportion in dealing with a situation, but sometimes you have to show a strong hand. Normally with kids I just exercise them, but for a more major transgression, for instance, the session would either be longer, or over several days, I find that's generally sufficient. Rarely have I ever had to go to other measures, and I hope that you boys never try me that far, because I assure you that you won't like what I can be like when I'm angry."

"I understand Sir, and my team will never be the ones to do it, I hope I can guarantee that."

"And that Sir, makes you the best choice for team leader. Now let's go join the class shall we?"

"Yes Sir!" Donny answered happily. They left the dining hall and headed to the classrooms.

"Does anyone have any questions so far?" Captain Casey asked after they walked in, and Donny took his seat.

"No Sir!" They all answered.

"Great! Cullen, would you please come see me for a few minutes?"

Cullen rose slowly and walked to the door, where Captain Casey was still standing, in a slow, almost shy movement, but did not lower his head. As Cullen reached him, Captain Casey turned and exited the room. They walked silently a few doors down, to where they could sit and talk. As soon as they were both seated and comfortable, Captain Casey started.

"So Cullen, do you have something to tell me?"

"Um, I guess so. I don't know how to read or do math, I've been trying, but I just can't figure it out."

"Okay, so that's not such a big deal. You've seen me helping some of the others with simple things, so did you feel that you were any different and could start in the middle?"

"I don't know. I just didn't want anyone to think I was stupid, but I am. Donny said I'm not stupid, just 'cause I don't know nuthin, but I still feel real dumb. I should be able to do all this, just 'cause I'm eight."

"But how could you! You've never been taught the basics right? So how do you think you could learn to do it all on your own, with no help, and starting in the middle no less? Almost every one of you boys here needs a lot of help, to get caught up to be anywhere near where your age group would be in a normal school. I'm hoping that by the end of the year that all of you'll be at that level, or higher, but we have a lot of hard work to do to get there. Now, tell me, if you can, why you've never asked for help? Even when I saw you struggling, and I offered to help, you refused, why?"

"Because I thought I should just know it. I'm eight, so I should be able to do anything other eight-year-old's can do. I didn't want you to know I was so stupid, not to be able to do the work."

"Okay, well now the first thing we're going to do is strike the words stupid and dumb from your vocabulary. They no longer exist to you. You're smart, you'll learn, it might take some time and some patience, but I know you can do it. Now here's the deal. Every time I hear you call yourself dumb or stupid, you get to spend an extra fifteen minutes with me in the exercise room that day. For this mornings outburst, there won't be any additional punishment, but you have to promise me that from now on you'll talk to me when you're frustrated, or on the verge of a nervous break down. What happened this morning can't be allowed to happen again, to do so, no matter the reason, will result in an hour long session in the workout room to make you wish I'd just kill you, am I making myself clear?" Captain Casey asked gently.

"Yes Sir, I promise to talk to you, and I'll try not to call myself those things. Thanks." Cullen said with conviction.

"Good, then we're all good. Now let's go back and get started on some work that is more level appropriate, shall we?" Captain Casey asked all upbeat.

"Okay." Cullen said, thankful that he was not going to be punished.

They got up and went back to the classroom, walking side by side, neither of them speaking. Captain Casey waited for Cullen to be seated, and then got the boys' attention.

"Could you please put down your work pads, we need to talk about a few things." He started out. Once they were all focused on him, he continued. "Thanks. Now, Cullen has been informed of a few things I'm going to share with you now. I know that he's not the only one doing this, so you all need to know it."

"First of all, none of you are stupid, dumb, or any other thing you wish to call yourselves. Almost none of you're at nearly the level at which your age groups would be in if you were in school, nor do I expect you to be. So why would you struggle to do what they've slowly been taught to do, there's really no point? Now, that being said, I'm giving you guys the same warning that I gave to Cullen. Should I hear of any of you calling yourselves, or others for that matter, stupid or dumb, because of something you aren't capable of doing, you'll spend fifteen minutes with me in the workout room, for each time I hear it."

"Name calling of any sort, in fact, will result in this. So think of it this way, if you called someone or multiple people six names throughout the day, you'd spend an hour and a half in the exercise room that evening with me, working harder than you ever imagines possible. You're all doing very well in your morning exercise classes, but do any of you believe you can do my evening class for that long?"

"No Sir!" They all answered.

"I thought not. Now Cullen and his team have not been given any extra punishment, because their team leader stepped up and took charge, and brought forth the information to me. They have however been told that outbursts like that will be punished in the future. If ever, at any time, you feel frustrated or angry, to the point that something like what happened this morning might happen to you, I want you to come and talk to me, or to your team leader. You have to remember, I'm here to help you guys. I know I can be hard on you at times, but remember, I'm just as hard on myself. Now, let's get back to work."

"Yes Sir!" They all said.

They all got back to their work, and Captain Casey went and sat down next to Cullen for a good portion of the class, going over some of the basics. Cullen knew how to read, but barely, he knew his numbers, but nothing else, so he worked from the very beginning. By the end of the class, Cullen was actually feeling a lot better about himself. They ended up skipping the history lesson, but that was fine.

The next couple days went by pretty quick, and on Saturday, Captain Casey decided to treat the boys. They did their morning exercises and had breakfast as normal, but as soon as the cleaning crew was done their chore, he gathered them all together.

"Okay guys, it's been a long, hard couple weeks, so today we get to go play a bit. So you have the weekend off, but of course, morning calisthenics and meal duties still stand as always. So what would everybody think of going outside the ship? It'll be mostly fun, but you'll learn a few things as well."

"That'd be awesome!" "No way!" "When can we go?" Were a few of the excited responses from the boys.

"I thought you guys would like that, so let's get going then. Your helmets and gloves are already in the airlock, and you're in uniform, as you should always be anyway, so we're all set."

They went to the upper airlock and sealed themselves inside the room. They all donned their equipment, as they had been taught during the past couple weeks, and stood by, ready and waiting. Captain Casey handed out some propulsion packs to the boys, so they all put them on. The packs were fairly small and light, so even the smallest of the boys could take them easily, yet with their Nutronium cores, they had more than enough power to move people a great distance and for a surprising amount of time before they had to be refueled. Each pack had more than thirty nozzles on them and an on board computer, so that you could maneuver in almost any way you so desired, yet to look at them, you could not even see the directional nozzles, they were very nearly invisible to the naked eye. The packs were simply white in color and had one controller that the wearer used to control their movement. There was also a plug that connected to the wearers helmet that connected to the helmets heads up display, which gave the wearer important information, fuel amount being one of the more important ones. The captain then went over how to use the packs, they were very simple, and all the boys had the controls down in a few seconds.

"Now for a few rules. You must all stay close by at all times, because these thruster packs have a range of about a thousand kilometers, but you aren't to get anywhere near that far away. If I can't see you at any given time, you'll spend an hour with me this evening, so please don't ruin this. We'll be in full communication at all times, and we're nowhere near anything dangerous, so we're relatively safe, but that doesn't mean that it's totally safe. Now, let's go have some fun." Captain Casey warned the boys.

"Yes Sir!" The boys all said, and as soon as they did, Captain Casey hit the button to open the door.

The airlock itself was only just large enough for all twenty one of them to be in at the same time, and only because half the occupants were quite small. Normally only five or so adults would go into an airlock at a time. Obviously the door leading to the ship was very well sealed, as was the door leading out, and there were controls by both doors with information screens, so that you could enter or exit safely and not damage the ship, or more importantly the people inside the airlock. Clearly it was not at all good for the body to go outside the ship without full and proper space gear, and the computers automatically checked every person in the airlock before it would even open the door, and if it found any problems at all, it informed the occupants as such. The exit door, also, would not open, for instance, until the inner door was sealed and locked, and the display would inform you of this. It also informed you when it was safe to open one or the other door. There were windows in both doors as well, so that should anyone want to go in, they would be able to see immediately if there was anyone in there. The door of course would not open unless it was safe to do so, this was only a backup.

Instantly, as soon as the door opened, all the boys started floating, so they followed the captain out the door, and they just floated around for a bit. Captain Casey started his propulsion pack, and the boys all followed suit. He then took them on an external tour of the ship, explaining everything as he went.

"From time to time boys, something will hit the ship and cause damage, or things can stick to the ship, so at these times someone has to come out and either fix or clean the section. The ship has gone through all the repairs it needs, so there's nothing damaged yet that I can show you how to fix, but the time will come I'm sure. But you see over there, something that's stuck on, just some spacial sludge. Most of the time all it takes is prodding it with your boots to dislodge it, but sometimes you have to actually scrape it off. Why don't a couple of you go ahead and get it off."

Franky and Jesse went over right away and scraped it with their boots, and it came off and floated away lazily.

"Pretty easy huh?" Captain Casey asked.

"Yeah, but really, why bother?" Franky asked.

"Couple reasons actually. First, it just looks bad, and we have more pride in our ships than that, so we keep them clean. Second, and most importantly, is some things can interfere with our shields, and we certainly don't want that, now do we?" Captain Casey asked.

"Definitely not Sir!" They all answered.

"That's right, we need our shields to always be at their best performance. Even if that small amount of sludge caused just a thousandth of a percent of shield loss, it's too much. Too much of it could affect them even more. Well enough of the boring stuff. Let's go explore that asteroid over there. Now remember, asteroids can have gas pockets, and very sharp rocks, so you always have to be careful. We'll stay on the dark side of the asteroid to prevent gas pockets from exploding on us, but make sure you don't catch your suit on sharp rocks. Your uniforms are very strong, so they shouldn't tear, but who wants to take the chance!"

So they propelled themselves over to the nearby asteroid and explored for a while. They all played around for a while, the boys pretty much looking at each and every rock they found excitedly, enjoying being out here exploring. Captain Casey was almost five hundred meters from Donny when the boy called out.

"Hey Captain, can you come here for a minute please?"

"Yes Donny, what is it?" He asked when he arrived.

"Is this what I think it is? It sure looks like Nutronium to me."

"I think you might be right. Let me check."

He grabbed out his scanner and checked the rock. Sure enough, it was pure Nutronium.

"Well young man, looks like you found a rock big enough to provide the ship with power for a few months, and it looks like there are more just laying around. Do you have your teleport tagger handy, to tag all the rocks to teleport later?"

"Yes Sir! You said we should always have them when outside the ship." Donny answered proudly.

"Good, take the scanner, find any that are pure, and tag them please?"

"You got it Captain." Donny said happily, took the offered scanner, and got to work.

Normally Nutronium was buried deep inside the asteroids, and could usually only be reached by mining, but from time to time a gas pocket would explode, sending the Nutronium to the surface. Donny worked for almost an hour, finding all the rocks he could. He ended up finding nearly three years worth Nutronium just scattered around.

"Captain, I think I've finished. Did you guys find anything interesting?" Donny asked, coming up to all the others.

"Yes, Kelly found some precious metals, including some gold, which is quite rare on an asteroid. He tagged them as well. Otherwise we've found nothing much. I think it's time we head back for some lunch though, if we aren't already passed due."

"That's really good. Are you going to tag the whole asteroid to have it mined Sir." Donny asked.

"Yes, and because we're in the Tenarian system, I'll send them the tag ID number, so that they'll be able to find it. It's quite large, and if the amount that we found just laying on the surface is any indication, what it hides inside could be quite a find. But then again, it could literally have blown all it had to the surface, you never can tell." Captain Casey said as they started heading back to the ship.

The kitchen crew took off to the kitchen, as soon as they were released from the airlock, while the others went to the cargo bay. Captain Casey had the teleporter in there lock on to all the tags they had set, and teleported the items to the ship.

"Could a few of you go grab some Nutronium cases please, so that we can get this stuff stored safely? The rest of us will go through the rest of this stuff and get it stored." Captain Casey asked.

"Yes Sir!" They all said.

Franky, Jamie, Pete, and Lance all went and grabbed two cases each, and came back over. They let the others do what they were doing, while they loaded the cases up, and closed and locked them. They were finishing up, just as the others were finishing up as well, so together they all went up to the dining hall to wait for lunch. Team three, who was doing the cooking today, saw that they had arrived about twenty minutes early, so brought a first course out to the guys, so that they could get started. Ten minutes later, the rest was finished, so they brought it all out and served it, then sat down to eat as well. After lunch, team four took on their chore of cleaning up, while the others went to the nearest lounge. Captain Casey had decided to join the boys, and they all sat and watched some TV together and chatted, waiting for the rest of the crew to join them. Soon they did.

"Well, now that the others have joined us, who wants to go watch a movie and eat lots of popcorn?" Captain Casey asked.

"That sounds really good Sir." Donny answered, while the others all just said "Yay."

They all went to the theatre, and it took almost ten minutes for all the boys to agree on a movie, while the captain got a whole lot of popcorn made and lots to drink brought out for them all. Finally, with their choice made from the computer, they all sat and started the movie they had chosen, and laid back and enjoyed it for the next couple hours while enjoying their treats.

"Let's go up to the games room for a while, 'til it's time for dinner, and play some games." Donny said.

"Sounds good to me, come on guys, let's go." Captain Casey said.

For the next couple hours they played. Team three excused themselves when it was time to go make dinner, and the rest headed up to the dining hall when it was time for dinner.

"Dinner was great guys, thanks a lot!" Captain Casey told the boys.

"Thanks Sir." Donny said.

"Team four, you're up, meet us in the games room when you're finished, and we'll continue playing." Captain Casey told the boys.

For the rest of the evening they all played and had fun. Captain Casey excused himself to go do his evening exercises. Donny also excused himself and asked the captain if he minded being accompanied, to which Jonathon said it was not a problem. So together they went to the exercise room, and Donny tried to keep up with the captain, but failed miserably, he did get a good workout though. They sat in the tub for a few minutes and chatted, and then hit the showers. Donny was not shy at all, and stripped right down, but the captain stayed in his shorts while they cleaned up. After getting dried off, they walked amiably up to their rooms. The others were just coming up as well.

"How was your workout guys?" Jesse asked.

"Really good, I tried my best, but couldn't even halfway keep up to the captain. I hurt all over too, but the sonic tub sure helps."

"I bet. I'm not sure why you'd willingly do that, but I bet it'll help you sleep." Jesse laughed.

"I don't know about Donny, but the reason is simple, it's good for the body and the soul. It helps to work your muscles to stay in shape, and it works great to reduce stress. Eventually all of you'll be joining me in the evening as well, but most of you aren't quite ready for that yet. You may however join me as you wish."

"I don't know about the soul part, but it sure makes my body feel good. I don't hurt nearly as much anymore after working out as I used to, but it still burns lots though. Tonight I think I over did it a bit, 'cause I hurt a bit more than normal, but I'm sure I'll be fine by morning."

"You might be a bit sore still, you probably shouldn't have tried to keep up to my pace so much, but it was your choice."

"Yeah, it was, and I'll deal with it, no prob. Well I'm heading to bed, how about you guys?" Donny said to his team, and they all nodded.

"You have a good night guys, I too am heading to my room." Captain Casey said.

"Goodnight Captain." They all said and went into their rooms.

As soon as they entered their room, Donny told the others, "Let's get this room cleaned up quickly, and then I'm going to bed."

"Yes Sir!" They all saluted, mocking their fearless leader.

"I'd beat you senseless, but you're already there. Now get to work you brats." Donny laughed.

A couple of the boys stuck their tongues out at him in good humor, but they got started cleaning the room right away as well. A few minutes later, Donny crawled into bed and fell asleep, while the rest of his team sat around and talked until lights out.

The rest of the rooms, except the captains of course, just sat around after cleaning their rooms and talked. Captain Casey did his daily logs until it was time for bed.

Sunday, as always, was just a day of rest, and the crew sure seemed to appreciate having the two days off, because on Monday morning they were all much happier, and the classes went smoother than normal. The rest of the week passed much the same way. It was also the end of the month, and October was creeping up on the crew. Captain Casey was also starting to believe that his crew was almost ready to get started on their real mission. So during class on the last day of the week, Captain Casey brought it up.

"Well guys, you're all doing very well, your school work's improving a great deal, and while you have much room to grow still, you're well on your way. Your duties on the ship are being handled quickly and efficiently, and your knowledge of the ships systems is becoming close to the point that I believe that our mission may soon start. I want to give it another week, or maybe even two, and if I feel that you're ready, we can leave the relative safety that we've become accustomed to. If at any time, any of you feel that you aren't ready, you may tell me, whether in private, or as a group. I won't take you unless I feel each and every one of you is ready for this." Captain Casey told the boys.

They all looked around at each other for a few minutes, but no one gave an answer, yes or no.

"Well, seeing as how no one else will answer, then I guess I'll answer for all of us. I'm not so sure I'm ready yet, I'd like to have a little more practice, at least another week or two like you said." Donny said.

"Thank you, that was all I needed. Now, eventually we'll have to go out and start our mission, but if we have to wait six months to do it, then so be it. I hope it doesn't take that long though, still, if it does, then oh well, so be it, that's how long it takes. I'll ask the same question in two weeks time then, you have two more weeks at least, but we're going to bump up the training a bit. You'll now be required to join me in the evening for more physical fitness training, and we'll start working on the martial arts and hand to hand combat. Our classes will now only be two hours in class in the evenings, and the entire day, before dinner, will be dedicated solely on ship operations."

"So you'll now only have two hours of actual free time in the evening, except the clean team, who will get one on the days that they're cleaning. Sundays, however, are still free, until we're on our mission, and then it'll rotate that each team will be off one day a week, but not the same for obvious reasons. Now I can see some of your faces falling, but I need to tell you that this isn't punishment for Donny saying what he said, these changes were going to be put in place today anyway, and I wasn't leaving for at least one more week to begin with, so you now just get two weeks to get used to a more difficult schedule. Are there any questions so far."

"I do Sir." Jamie said before anyone else could say a word.

"Yes, what is it Jamie?"

"Well, I was wondering, when we do start the mission, how will we deal with classes and training and all that, oh and meals as well, how will we handle that?"

"Much the same as we'll be doing on the current schedule. Because we don't have a large enough crew, or an actual kitchen staff, we can't run twenty four hours a day as a normal ship would. So at night we find ourselves a nice safe hiding place, set our sensors just as high as we can, and hope we never get waken up by them. We'll however be having emergency preparedness drills in the coming week, again, this is something that was going to happen this week no matter what. During the day we'll fly and help out as needed, and in the evening we'll stop, like I said, and we can do your classes. I'm afraid that the easy life's now almost over. Tomorrow we'll be simulating drills throughout the day, getting each team where they need to be, and as quick as possible. I should probably also tell you before it happens, and you either hit the ceiling or the floor, but in an emergency situation, the lifts will go approximately five times faster, so it's strongly recommended that you hang on. You all know how fast they are at normal speed, so I don't have to tell you what would happen if you weren't prepared for it. Any other questions so far?"

"Actually yes, but it's one of the same ones that Jamie asked. I think you forgot to answer it. What about meals and things?" Brady asked.

"Ah yes, I did forget that, I apologize. The teams who are cooking won't change, they'll cook the meals, and if needed, deliver the meals to where everyone is. The cleaning however may have to be put on hold, should we need the people for more pressing matters. We'll attempt to keep our meals at the same times, but again, in an emergency, eating might just be the last thing on our minds, although to keep our strength up, we still need to eat. During the war, my dad wouldn't let any situation come between his ship and their meals. If everyone had to inhale their food in the middle of a fight, so be it, but he made sure they all ate. We all became used to eating while literally running at times. Hopefully you won't have to do that. Does that answer everything, am I forgetting anything else, or are there any other questions?" Captain Casey smiled.

"I have a question Sir." Kelly asked.

"Yes Kelly, what is it?"

"Well it's about the exercises. I don't know if I can do any more. I can't keep up in the mornings as it is, so I don't know if I can do the nights as well." Kelly said.

"Well, I know you and a few of the others aren't going to be able to keep up with the bigger boys, and none of you can yet keep up to me. I don't expect you to even try. All I expect is that you'll do your best, and learn. If at any time you have to slow down, do so, just don't stop, that's the worst thing to do." Captain Casey told all the boys.

"Okay Sir, I'll try. How long are the evening exercises."

"Same as in the morning. For the first few days I'll go a bit easier on you, until you get more used to it. Mornings are still the aerobics, but the evening will be, like I said, the martial arts and hand to hand combat, so you won't have to do quite so much in the evenings as you fear. A lot of it's just learning the moves, and lots of flexibility and speed maneuvers." Captain Casey told everyone.

"Oh, okay Sir. Thanks."

"You're welcome. Now we're going to be late for lunch, so why don't the kitchen crew go and get us a quick lunch ready, and then we can eat."

Team four got up and left and headed to the kitchen. They talked on the way and figured soup and sandwiches would be the fastest and easiest, so that was what they did. The others joined them at the proper time, so they all sat and ate.

Saturday morning came, and after their exercises, and breakfast was eaten and cleaned up, Captain Casey took everyone to the bridge.

"Today, as promised, we'll be starting emergency preparedness, and doing drills and what not. During all drills, same as in an emergency situation, I'm to be listened to immediately, and remember, no questions, just do it. Remember to save all questions for after the drill is over, and then we can go over the questions together. I'll have the computer play out different scenarios most of the day, then we'll break and talk about the drill, about what we did right and what we did wrong. You'll then be able to ask questions. As always, never be afraid to ask why I gave the order I did. Don't forget, I am in fact human, and as such, do make mistakes, and if I happen to make one, I too need to know it. Most of the time though, my commands will come from experience as to how best to do things. Now, are there any questions before we start?"

"No Sir!" They all said, sounding more than a bit nervous.

"Okay, for the first drill, we'll all be in here as if we were flying around, and I'll have us being attacked by twelve attackers. The rest of the drills though, you won't know what's happening, but for the first drill, we'll make it a bit easier on you by telling you what you're getting into." The captain said while smiling.

"Easier Sir! Are you are saying that knowing about twelve enemies attacking us is any easier than not knowing that two are?" Brad asked incredulously.

"Actually yes, not knowing what you're going to find is a hard thing, and not being prepared is probably ten times worse. That's why whenever we're in space, we treat every moment as if we're about to have an emergency, and to always be prepared for virtually any situation. Let's get this party started shall we." Captain Casey said, and he initiated a pre-programmed attack simulation.

All of a sudden the alarm bells started ringing.

"Everyone at your stations." Captain Casey called out. "Shields to maximum, view screens, show external views. Navigation get us out of here." He started calling out.

All of a sudden the ship lurched as if hit by a large blast.

"Communications, tell these people to get off our tail, or we blast em out of the sky. Weapons, get ready to fire." He called again.

All the boys did what they were supposed to do. A simulation enemy being that none of the boys had ever seen before, was shown to have come on the screen. The simulated being was very generic in appearance, vaguely humanoid, but blocky, meant to look exactly like it was, fake, so that no one could accidentally mistake it for the real thing. It told them to surrender, or be destroyed.

"Never! Target their lead ship, and open fire." Captain Casey said.

Team three, who happened to be on weapons for this simulation, chose the lead ship, and fired three maximum yield missiles at it, they did not destroy it, but a large chunk was missing once they could see it, and with that they were disabled.

"Weapons, lock on to the rest of their ships, but hold your fire, communications, get them back, and instruct them to shut down their engines and weapons, or we open fire, and we won't leave them alive this time." Captain Casey called out.

Team one did as they were asked, as team three was busy locking onto all the remaining ships. A moment later another person came on the screen, said they surrendered, and that they were shutting down.

"Confirm they've shut down?" Captain Casey asked.

"Confirmed, all remaining ships have shut down their engines, and their weapons are now down as well." Brady said.

"Great work boys, simulation complete, computer, shut down simulation." The captain said and the simulation ended, the view screen cleared.

"That's it Sir." Brady asked.

"Yes, for now. That was a basic simulation that was pretty simple. Some fights end that quick, others don't. In real life though, you can never depend on the fact that an enemy will be smart enough to back down. Now, can anyone tell me what we did wrong in this simulation?" Captain Casey asked.

"I thought we did real well Sir, we were only hit once, we disabled their lead ship, and the rest surrendered. What else is there?" Jamie asked.

"You all followed the commands I gave very well, that much is for sure. What I'm looking for is something that we did to the others during the attack, something that maybe wasn't quite fitting. Does anyone know what I'm talking about?" Captain Casey asked gently.

"I still don't see it Sir." Jamie answered, and the others all agreed with him.

"Well it's pretty simple really, but when we targeted the lead ship, we fired three maximum yield missiles at him, that could be considered excessive force. Even though we were outnumbered, we should never do that unless necessary. They only fired one across our bow, as it were, as a warning, and it was a low yield one at that. So, to retaliate by nearly destroying the ship is considered wrong. Only if the rest had have started joining the fight, and firing upon us, would we then consider such a drastic course of action. Can anyone tell me what we should have done in a case such as this?" Captain Casey asked.

The boys all thought for a few minutes and then Donny got it.

"We should have tried to find the power section, or their propulsion system, and fired a lower yield missile at those more sensitive areas. I think that was pretty much what you told us is the way to handle this type of situation, to try to reduce damage, yet get the job done." Donny answered.

"That's right. In this case, with these ships, aiming at the rear end, right between the propulsion pods would have been the most preferable target, because it wouldn't have created nearly as much damage to the ship. The way the ship was damaged, you could assume that many people were killed, not really what we want to do. Again, the only time we shoot to destroy, is when they're trying to do the same to us. This simply was not yet the case here. This scenario can play out that way though. Had we have just returned the warning shot, then maybe they would have all joined in on the fight, and then we would have had a real fight on our hands. Again, in this situation though, pretty much destroying their lead ship could've caused the rest of them to get very angry with us, and just start opening fire upon us. Remember, always err on the side of caution, but be prepared for the worst."

"So, did we fail this simulation then?" Donny asked.

"There's no pass or fail, there's only live or die. We lived, therefore in a way you did pass. However, again, there's no pass or fail, this is simply a learning tool, you only pass if you take as much knowledge from the lessons as you can, and apply it in a real life situation. If I were to mark this like I did a test though, I'd say you had an even chance of passing as failing, you did disable the lead ship, and the others surrendered, but you did so at a great cost."

"Now, the next drill will be in a little while, but I won't tell you when, nor what. I want you to all go about your normal duties. Just remember to hold on in the lifts if you need them. As soon as you enter the bridge, assess the situation, and take your stations. Rotate to the next station, as always, as well please." Captain Casey told the boys.

The boys all left in their teams and went to their dorms, mostly to hit the washrooms and clean up a bit. They all sat in their groups talking over what had just happened.

The next drill came just as team one was heading to the kitchen to get lunch prepared. As previously instructed, they did not vary their destination, the other three teams hit the lifts from wherever they were at the time though.

All the boys, no matter how prepared they thought they were, nearly lost whatever was in their stomachs due to the intense speed at which the lifts went. They arrived in seconds, they all ran from the lifts to the bridge as fast as they could, and found what appeared to be four ships facing them. The captain had yet to show up, so they went to their stations. Team three was now on communications, so they called the ships facing them to find out what they wanted. They came on the screen, and it was the same faceless race as before, just different fake ships, and demanded that they surrender the ship, that they would be boarded.

"Sorry, surrender isn't an option, please back off and surrender, or we'll be forced to defend ourselves." Donny said forcefully.

Captain Casey was just entering the bridge as he heard this, and as he did, the fake ship fired, and their ship lurched. Captain Casey was thrown, he was fine, but he acted like he was knocked out, to see how the rest of the crew would handle things.

"Captain down, return fire, target their lead ships engines." Donny said, taking over, and ran to the command chair.

Team two, now on weapons, did as instructed. The missile missed and the enemies started to open fire. They started getting hit rapidly, and their shield warnings were going off, saying they were losing shields.

"Okay, enough of this, we tried to play nice, now open fire, target the lead ship and destroy them." Donny yelled out.

They did so. Four maximum yield missiles were quickly dispatched to the lead ship. Just as they were being destroyed, the remaining three ships were targeted by two missiles each, and were firmly disabled.

"Tell them they better shut down their engines and power down their weapons, or they'll join their lead ship." Donny yelled out.

They were hit again by two of the ships, the third missed.

"Destroy them." Donny yelled out.

Team two wasted no time in removing the threat. Within only a few minutes, they won the battle soundly. Captain Casey stood up.

"Well done gentlemen." He said, startling a couple of the boys.

"Oh, I actually thought you were really hurt there when you got thrown and didn't get up." Donny said, turning sharply at the voice.

"Nah, it'd take a lot more than that to take me down, but I had to know what you guys would do if I was taken out of the picture, so I took advantage of the situation. I watched and listened to the whole thing though, and you guys did very well. You showed proper restraint, when necessary, and showed you were men of your words, when it was warranted. You did everything just as I would've commanded you to have done it as well. I don't believe that there was anything wrong with that simulation. Computer, end simulation." Captain Casey said, and the emergency alerts shut down.

"Captain, are the people in the simulations always the same?" Cullen asked.

"Yes, they are, it helps to be able to tell the difference between a real life situation, and a drill. Like I said, over the next week, random drills will be done, and even though we're pretty safe where we are, you can never tell when a Qaralon ship might sneak in and attack us. We're a lone ship, just sitting, we don't look like much of a fight. So if something like that were to happen, how would you really be able to tell. Almost no race of people will attack first and talk later, and even if they do fire a warning shot, they'll usually tell you what they want. The Qaralon will usually demand to hand over your ship with all the crew. They like to eat humans remember, so they don't like to destroy their meals. I however have no intention of being someones dinner, so you can bet I'll fight 'til my last breath."

"Oh, okay then. That makes sense." Cullen said.

"Yes it does. Now let's go see how the guys in the kitchen are doing, I hope our meal didn't end up all over the floor as they were making it though. You can almost guarantee though, that the meal won't be hot. Most people aren't really willing to work around a hot stove when they're being thrown around. That also brings up another thing, make sure all knives are secured at all times, many injuries, and even a few fatalities have been caused by just that type of thing. No matter how hard you try though, if the ship is hit and you get thrown, you're probably going to get hurt, hopefully not badly. Even when I was thrown, had I hit anything, I could've been hurt. That's why almost nothing in the ship's made with sharp corners, everything is made to be as safe as possible." Captain Casey said as they all walked to the dining hall.

"Oh, hey guys, how did it go up there." Franky asked.

"It went really well. Captain Casey was the last to make it to the bridge, but he was thrown just as he was entering the bridge, so he pretended to be knocked out, and I took command and we won the battle, it was pretty tough." Donny said excitedly, in almost one long breath.

"Yes, they did a very good job. How did you guys fare?" Captain Casey asked, eying Franky's bandaged arm.

"During one of the hits, I cut myself, 'cause the knife I was using jarred, so I cut my arm a bit, but it's not a big deal. We all decided that using knives was probably not the brightest of ideas, same with the stove." Franky said while holding up the arm that had a makeshift bandage on it.

"Well, I'll take you up to the infirmary then, while the others finish up here, and I'll get you fixed up properly."

"I'll be fine Sir, we can do that after the meal."

"It wasn't a request young man. March."

"Fine Sir, you guys finish up in here, we'll be right back." Franky told his team, and he and the captain headed down to the infirmary. Once there, Captain Casey had Franky hop up onto one of the beds while he gathered anything he might need.

"Okay, let's get that bandage off you." Captain Casey said and proceeded to remove the bloody bandage. "I thought you said you only cut yourself a bit Franky, this is a deep cut, and will require some nerve regeneration, and putting it back together. Do you even feel any pain?" Captain Casey asked in a shocked voice.

"Well it hurts Sir, but not that bad. I couldn't see it really, so I just put a bandage on it and kept going. If it's that bad, why isn't bleeding very much?" Franky asked.

"Not too sure. You must have managed to miss most of the major blood vessels, but it's still bleeding quite a bit, especially after taking off the bandage. I guess this uniform is garbage now, so we'll have to get you a new one. Here, hold tight while I get this cleaned up and mended." Captain Casey said.

Jonathon took a few minutes to clean the wound, after cutting the sleeve of the uniform right off, and giving Franky a pain killer, because the next part was going to hurt, a lot. Then using the hand held nerve re-generator, Jonathon squeezed the skin together a bit, so that it would work better. Once it was saying it was complete, Jonathon switched tools to the hand held dermal re-generator, and quickly mended the cut flesh.

"Okay, you're all done. Go on up to your room and clean up, get into a new uniform, and then come down and join the rest of us for lunch."

"Yes Sir, be right there." Franky said after testing his arm for functionality, then they left.

"How is he Sir, is he okay?" Tony asked as Captain Casey walked back into the kitchen, the boys were just getting ready to set the table.

"I'm afraid he lost his arm, he'll never be the same." Captain Casey said with a sad look.

"What, it was just a little cut though, he said he was fine!" Tony said in shock.

"Oh I'm just teasing you. He's just fine, in the end all that lesson cost him was a new uniform, and the knowledge to not use knives in the kitchen while in battle." Captain Casey said, not able to torture the poor boy further, Tony had looked like he was going to start crying.

"You're mean Sir. I thought you were serious." Tony said while smacking the captain on the arm.

"Ouch, hey, that hurt." Captain Casey said.

"Yeah right, like I could hit you hard enough to hurt you Sir." Tony said, while the others around him were laughing.

"You're right, you didn't hurt me, but believe me, even the youngest and smallest of you could easily hurt me, especially once I start teaching you some things about hand to hand combat. So are we ready to eat then?" He grinned.

"Yes Sir, we were just getting everything ready when you came in." Ryan said.

"Great, let's eat then."

"Yes Sir!" Ryan said, and they all went out and joined the others that were waiting, Franky joining them a few minutes later. They all ate a good hearty cold lunch, the boys talking excitedly about the simulation that they had won.

"Now that lunch is done, I should tell you that we'll be having at least three more drills throughout the day. You won't know when the next one's coming, so be prepared, but enjoy your break. I have some work to do, so won't be joining you boys. You guys go ahead and have some fun, and relax a bit, because I know even drills are tiring."

"Yes Sir, you can definitely say that again. I think I'm more tired after the two training drills, than I am after two workouts and classes." Donny stated seriously.

"That's because of the stress, it's very draining. That's why you'll have at least an hours rest. However, as we get into the drills, sometimes you won't even have that luxury, sometimes I'll do back to back to back drills, to simulate an actual battle." Captain Casey told all the boys. They just nodded and turned and left.

CHAPTER 11

THE TOUGHEST TEST

Captain Casey went to his office to set up a couple more simulations, and when he was done that, he called home.

"Hey Mom and Dad, how are things going at home." He asked once they came on screen.

"Good, things are starting to get done around here, and the story of what you're doing is going around. So how are things going for you guys up there?" Admiral Casey asked.

"That's good, glad to hear it. I'm kind of surprised it hadn't gone around while we were still at home. As for how it's going, it's going really well. In two weeks I take the kids out and really show them what we can do. You should have seen how they handled themselves on only their second drill, they seemed like a veteran crew. I used your favorite one dad, we were hit quite a few times, but they destroyed every one of the attacking ships, plus we received no actual damage, and the shields didn't drop below fifty percent. The guys on navigation had us moving around so much, that they couldn't get a proper lock on us. When I'd entered the bridge, we'd taken a hit and I was thrown, so I made it seem like I was knocked out, and the oldest boy took complete control and did all that, it was pretty good." Jonathon told them.

"That's pretty impressive Jon. How are they taking everything so far though?" Jonathon's mom asked.

"They're doing amazingly well, just a couple minor rough patches, considering none of these boys has ever been in space, and most of them have had little to no schooling. They're all very smart though, it comes with surviving on the street, the really smart ones were able to survive, and these boys survived. I've heard some of the stories, and they don't compare with some of the stories we've heard. Some of the things these boys have lived through is truly amazing. I was wondering if you knew anyone that'd like to act as a cook and a doctor for us though? It's getting a bit tiring doing all the organizing for the kids doing the cooking. I'm also a good med tech, and the nasty gash I dealt with today was easily handled, but then I thought, what would happen if I were to actually get hurt, none of the kids would really know what to do."

"We'll check around. Ashley just finished medical school, so she might be interested, or there's Jim, he's also a med tech, you could ask him. He's pretty busy though, so I don't know if he will, plus he'll want to bring his family I'm sure. Was there any special requests though?" Jonathon's dad asked, Ashley is Jonathon's cousin and Jim is his brother.

"I'd prefer another male, but Ashley might be good, she's really good with troubled kids. That has to be one of the requirements, they have to be really good with troubled kids. I'm not so sure Jim could do it, just because of that, I'm not sure he has the patience. I'd also like someone who can cook really well. The kids are trying, and a couple of them are pretty good, but let's just say you probably won't get fat from eating the food. I think that's about it."

"You might be right about your brother, patience doesn't seem to be one of his strong suits, and I don't think that he's a great cook. As for Ashley, I'm not even certain she can cook. I'll ask around. I assume you'll pay for both aspects?" His mom asked.

"Of course. I'll give the going wages, and a bonus upon finishing one year with us. If we decided to extend the leave, then if the person decided to stay, the same deal would then be given. I'd prefer no families though. At this time, that type of thing could hurt the boys, they've all lost their families, many of them saw them killed right in front of them."

"Okay, I'll get back to you. When were you planning on leaving then, and where are you now?" His mom asked.

"We're just outside the asteroid fields on the outskirts of the Tenarian system, it's only a three day trip home. I was planning on actually going out in about two weeks, once I and the boys feel they're ready. They said they weren't yet, I knew they weren't though." Jonathon told them.

"Okay, I'll see what I can find for you in less than a week. I'm sure I can find someone who's just itching to get out into space." His mom smiled.

"Thanks guys! When we get there, I want you guys to come up and inspect the crew. Getting an official inspection by the most famous admiral in the fleet can only boost moral even more."

"Are you trying to butter me up boy?"

"Nope, just telling the truth, even if you don't like to admit it. You want to know something though? Every one of the boys knows almost every one of your victories, and they're very accurate as well. Meeting you guys will definitely be a real treat to them."

"Okay, we'll come up then and give them an official inspection. Have you got dress uniforms for the boys yet? If I'm going to inspect the crew, I'd better be seeing them in their best." His dad asked.

"No, I didn't even think of that. I have to get a few more uniforms anyway, so I'll get them to make me some dress uniforms as well, just for you dad. See you guys soon. I have to set up another drill now."

"Have fun, but try not to torture those poor boys too much, and at the very least, save impossible one 'til the end, you don't want to discourage them too much. Good night." Admiral Casey said and then signed off after the rest of the pleasantries were taken care of.

Jonathon took a few minutes to set up the chosen simulation, and set it to go off within the next half an hour, then went out to find his young charges.

He only managed to find half the boys before the emergency alarms all started going off. He hit the nearest lift, only two of the boys managed to catch up and jump in as the doors were closing, and they were off like a bullet. The boys were a little more used to the feeling now, and Captain Casey was an old pro by now, so it hardly even bothered him. They jumped out and ran to the bridge just as another group came spilling in to the left of them.

"View screen, display." Captain Casey called out to the computer.

"Everyone to your stations. Find out what these people want, and get those shields up to maximum." Captain Casey told the boys.

"Captain, they're not responding." Teddy yelled out.

"That means they aren't here for a social call, get us moving, weapons targeted on the lead ship, the second you see them fire, I want you to disable the lead." Captain Casey yelled out.

"Yes Sir!" Everyone answered.

All of a sudden they were hit multiple times, so the boys on weapons took fire. They were being heavily targeted, twelve on one was not exactly fair, so the boys decided that this was about the right time to start fighting dirty. The boys on navigation decided to take a head on approach, and went in at ramming speed, while the boys on weapons started firing bursts of everything they had at anything they could hit. Their aim was straight and true, therefore they destroyed everything in their path. As soon as the guys on navigation saw that these attackers were cleared, they switched tactics and came up and started circling the bigger ships, while the guys on weapons just kept firing.

They switched the weapons to low yield, and were now just toying with the enemy, while the guys on navigation kept them moving so fast that the attackers hardly had a chance to fire. Captain Casey was amazed at the tactics the boys were using, all completely non verbal, and he sat there with his mouth open. He had not even said a word since the fight had started, and they were about to win. He also knew exactly what the boys were doing, by using the lower power weapons, they were making the enemy realize that they were about to die, but die slowly, an inch at a time. The attacking ships though never cut their engines or weapons, to signal surrender, so the boys carved them like a thanksgiving turkey, and only minutes later the last of the attackers was destroyed.

"Computer, end simulation. Battle won. You guys realize you may be the only crew that I know of, other than my father, to have beaten this scenario. When we were talking earlier, he told me to leave this one 'til last, so as not to discourage you. I think I was right to throw this one at you. But how did you guys work so well together to do what you did, without even talking to each other?" Captain Casey asked in awe.

"Well, when we started, I figured that team three was good enough to figure out what we were doing, so we just started moving to keep them off of us." Pete said, as his team had automatically went to navigation.

"And we knew that they knew what they were doing, so we just switched automatically when they did." Donny said, he and his team had been on weapons.

"And we just sent them everything." Jamie said, they were on scanning.

"Well that was some of the best teamwork I've ever seen. I didn't even have to command you guys, you just did it. Well I think the rest of the night you guys can have off, I think you've more than deserved it. I'll warn you though, that it might not be tonight, or even tomorrow night, but soon we'll have a night time emergency. I think it's getting about time for dinner. I need to go call someone though, so I'll meet you up there in a few minutes to help you guys cook." Captain Casey said.

"Yes Sir!" They all said, and Captain Casey turned and left the boys, they in turn started talking excitedly.

"I think he's real happy. I've never seen him shocked before, and he said only Admiral Casey has ever beaten that before, so that must mean we did very good." Donny said in shock.

"Yeah, I think so too. It's funny, but if that was the hardest training simulation they have, then we're obviously doing pretty good." Tristan said.

"Uh huh." They all agreed.

"Okay, team three up to the kitchen, I think we all deserve a good meal, so let's get cooking." Franky called out.

"Yes Sir!" They all said, and then saluted him with their tongues pointing at him.

"I should hand you over to the captain for a punishment for that, that's clear insubordination." Franky told his team.

"You wouldn't dare!" Tony teased.

"Oh no, care to try me young man. Well you I can deal with all by myself, I'd just sit on you and tickle you until you give up." Franky warned him.

"Okay okay, you win, let's go guys." Tony said, everyone knew he was seriously ticklish.

They all headed out, team one to the kitchen, while the rest went to the closest lounge to sit back and relax.

Once Captain Casey reached his office, he made a copy of the battle recording, and then called his parents back.

"Mom, Dad, you'll never believe this. I went against your judgment, and gave them the big test."

"You didn't, they can't possibly be ready for that, how bad did they do?" Admiral Casey asked.

"Dad, you're mistaken, this isn't the look of disgust, but the look of shock. They won, and they did so in less than ten minutes. I believe you're the only person to have passed it so far, and you took half an hour to do so. You almost lost the ship, whereas we suffered almost no damage. I didn't even say a word, they just reacted to each others moves like you wouldn't believe, they never even talked to each other, they just reacted to the situation around them." Jonathon told his parents, who were now also registering shocked looks.

"How, they're so young, and they've barely had any training? Do you have the battle recording handy, can you send it to me, I have to see this for myself? I'm also going to send it up to WSEC as well, so that they can analyze it." The admiral asked.

"Yes Dad, I have it right here, I knew you'd ask for it. Uploading now."

"Thanks, give us a few moments to go over it, and then we'll talk more." His mom said.

"Okay, take your time." He said and they turned away to watch the recording on another screen. They ended up watching it twice, because they both thought that they had missed something the first time around.

"I'm not sure what to say Jonathon. Those were some of the most incredible moves I've ever seen performed, and they hardly even made a sound as it was all happening. Well now, the inspection I plan to give went from just being a courtesy, to a full blown honor." Admiral Casey said.

"Now you know why I was so shocked. Here I was thinking that I needed to show them the downside, and show them what could happen, and they beat the most difficult scenario we had. I mean no one but you's ever beaten that one before, and they did even better than you did. I never even thought it was possible, especially not from a group of students. Street kids with no schooling no less. I guess, in a way, they're using the skills they learned on the streets to survive, so in a way it comes as second nature to them."

"I think that I'm going to wait until after your visit to show this little recording though. I don't think the kids are ready for an entire press conference, or for an entire group of admirals and captains to interview them yet. I also have a feeling that you're probably correct about their instincts, they grew up evading and fighting to stay alive. Now, your mom found someone she thinks will be perfect for your trip, though, I'll let her tell you about that." His dad said.

"Thank you, the boys will appreciate that, they aren't used to lots of people, let alone having them pawing all over them, so that'd make them clam right up for sure, I'm willing to bet. Soon they'll have to face it, and I'll tell them this, but I still have to teach them and work with them to be more prepared for it. So who did you find for us Mom, that was real quick?"

"There's a young man right around where you live that just finished his doctorate, and he put himself through school as a chef. He meets all of your criteria, but more importantly, he was an orphan and street kid as well. He lost his parents much like many of your boys did, so I think he'll be perfect. He's said that he'd love the experience, but said that he'll hold off on accepting until you get here, and meets you in person. I of course told him that you'd expect nothing less of him."

"Now, I also took the liberty of making a call into the office, and ordered the uniforms for you. I wasn't sure what sizes to get, so I just ordered two of pretty much every size they could make in the dress uniforms, and five more of the standard uniform style you chose, again in every size. I figured that if this little experiment worked out, that you'd need them anyway."

"Well, okay then. I think that takes care of everything, and thanks Mom. I'll call them as soon as we get into teleporter range, and have them send everything up, and I'll call you as soon as we're in orbit, we'll come home at maximum speed."

"Okay, see you in a few days Jon. Bye and love you." His mom said.

"Bye, love you too." He said and they disconnected.

He went in search of the boys, and found them in the lounge next to the dining hall, so he sat with them silently and watched TV, until it was time for dinner, and they all went and ate. Once the meal was finished, but before team two got up to start cleaning, Captain Casey cleared his throat to get the boys' attention.

"Boys, just before dinner I went and talked with my parents. I gave them a recording of the simulated battle that you guys won, and to say they were amazed would be somewhat of a major understatement. As I told you before, my dad, Admiral Casey, was the only other person to ever beat that scenario. However, you guys made it look like he barely won. You did it in a third the time, took less than half the damage, and destroyed all the attackers. So, because of that, we're heading back to Earth, where we have a bit of a surprise for you. Now I need to warn you, when we actually leave on our mission, that battle recording's going to be handed in to WSEC, so that it can be analyzed, to see if there's anything to learn from what you boys did today."

"The reason that we've decided to wait until after we leave, is so that you guys don't have to go through a full blown press conference, or meet all the political people who'd undoubtedly love to talk to you guys. I know how you feel in crowds, and I didn't want to put you through that, at least not yet. When, and if we come back from our mission, we'll have to surely face it at that time. I'll also tell you that when we get back home, I'm going to be interviewing someone to take over as cook and doctor, he's just out of school to become a doctor, and put himself through school as a chef, so he should be perfect. My mom personally picked him out, so he has only the best of recommendations. This'll help relieve some of the burden on you guys, as well as get us a fully trained doctor, for just in case we need one. Also, due to the incredible performance shown by all of you, I've decided that once we leave home, I think we'll be ready to head out. If you have any objections to that, you need to tell me, either now or in private. Otherwise do any of you have any questions?"

"What's the surprise Sir?" Zach asked.

"Well, if I told you that now, would it be a surprise when the time comes? I don't think so, so don't bother asking again, I'll never tell." Captain Casey grinned brightly.

"How come a whole bunch of people would want to meet us Sir?" Bobby asked.

"Simple. You're a bunch of ex street kids right? Well you bunch of kids just did what no other captain in the fleet has been able to do. Every other captain and crew that has attempted that training simulation, has been blown out of the sky. So you see, you're kind of heroes right now, and everyone will want to meet the boys who managed it. By waiting, that attention will die down some, but when we get back, you'll have to go through with it, so you need to be ready for it. I'll do what I can to help prepare you for it, I'll teach what I can, it may still be difficult, and I hate press conferences myself, but we'll manage just fine, when the time comes."

"So, we won't have to do the cooking and cleaning any more?" Ryan asked, figuring that was the most important thing to them at this minute.

"For the most part, no, I'll have one of you in there helping every day though, and it'll rotate just like it does now." Captain Casey answered.

"I'm not so sure about having to have a big meeting with a bunch of people, even when we do get back home and you've taught us. I'll still feel yucky." Donny said.

"I know how you feel, I hate press conferences, big political meetings and that type of thing, but unfortunately, sometimes they can't always be avoided. When it happens, you'll all survive, I promise you that. I'll also make sure that no one pushes you too much, gets too nosy or anything like that. Your past is no ones business but your own. We all know that what you boys had to do on the streets to survive was just that, survival. No one will hold it against you, but sometimes people will ask anyway. I'll handle those questions though." Captain Casey told all the boys truthfully.

"Thank you Captain, I know we all appreciate it. Now who's this cook, and what do you know about him?" Donny asked.

"Actually, I know nothing about him, not even his name or anything. The only other thing I know, that I forgot to mention earlier, is that he used to be a street kid too, and somehow managed to go to school and make something of himself."

"That's neat, just like us then. He should know lots about how we lived, and what we had to do to survive then." Brad said.

"Yes he will, and that'll make him the perfect choice, if we all like him. Team two, you start getting this cleaned up, the rest of you come up to the bridge with me, I want to get home as quick as we can."

"Yes Sir!" They all said.

The captain and his crew went up to the bridge, and the captain took his seat.

"Navigation, please point us toward home, and put us at maximum speed. Weapons, keep the shields up at cruising level." The captain commanded.

"Yes Sir!" They all said.

In just a few seconds the commands were carried out, and they were on their way.

"Sir, are we going to fly through the night as well, so that we can get home as soon as possible?" Donny asked.

"No, I don't think so. The ship has an auto pilot of course, but unless we're awake, I don't care to use it. We can just get as early a start tomorrow morning as we can." Captain Casey answered.

"Sir, I volunteer my team to pull the night shift and keep us going. If we go to bed now we can get up when you guys go to bed, and we can get someone up in the morning if we're too tired." Donny offered, and the rest of his team nodded their heads in agreement.

"I don't know, are you sure you're ready for that? It's a pretty large responsibility, and I don't want you to do this if you don't think that you're even remotely ready to take it. You'll have very little sleep, but I could stay up 'til midnight, to let you sleep a little longer I suppose if you're sure."

"Yes Sir, I know I'm ready, and I believe my team is as well. As for sleep, we've slept lots more in the last month than any of us are used to, so this'll be a snap. We'll head up now, and you can wake us at midnight then. Goodnight guys." Donny said, and before anyone could say anything further, they were heading to the closest lift.

"Well guys, it looks like we go straight through with no stops then. If we go through the night tomorrow as well, we should make it by the morning after, instead of the next day sometime. Any volunteers for tomorrow night then?"

"We will captain." Franky said for his team.

"Do you all agree?" Captain Casey asked team one.

"Yes Sir!" The whole team answered.

"Then it's settled. Right after dinner tomorrow night, you guys go to bed, and I'll wake you at 2400 hours to take the night shift. I'll tell team three tonight, when I get them up, the same thing I'll tell you now. Absolutely no fooling around, and if there are any problems at all, you call me, instantly. Is that clear?"

"Yes Sir!" They answered.

So the crew settled down and flew through the evening, Captain Casey kept up the quizzing though, asking the boys all questions, ranging from ship operations to math, science, history and language problems. When it was time for the boys to all go to bed, the captain sent them on their way, and told them he would call when it was lights out. They all went without argument. The captain sat back in his chair, and thought about all that they had been through and done, and in such a short time no less. He could not help but wonder when something would go wrong. So far the boys were handling everything amazingly well, and were all getting along great, but he felt that could only last so long. He sent up the lights out command a little later, and then sat and pondered until midnight, when he left the bridge and woke the night crew. He gave them the same warning, and then he headed to bed, while the boys went up to the bridge.

"K guys, each take a station, I have command, and let's make this as smooth as possible." Donny commanded his team. They all took a station and they talked for a while.

A few hours later, the boys were all getting hungry, so Donny got an idea.

"Tristan and Cullen, why don't you guys go get us some food and drinks, and bring it back up here please? We can eat here, and we'll manage just fine while you're gone." Donny asked.

"Okay, be right back." Tristan said.

The boys were back a short time later with some sandwiches and a couple pitchers of juice, and the boys all sat and ate. Once finished eating, they sat back down and continued talking through the rest of the night, and were still going when the captain came in a little early to see how they were all doing.

CHAPTER 12

SOMEONE NEW JOINS THE CREW

Captain Casey had slept well the whole night, not at all worried that the boys that he had entrusted to the ship for the night would not be able to handle it. He had known that they could do it, and was happy to let them take the chance to do so. It would also go a long way to help boost the boys' morale he figured. He did know though that the odds of something happening when so close to home were slim, so that did make it easier. He woke up just a little before his normal time and decided to just get up right away and see how the boys had fared through the night, so headed out right away and got to the bridge quickly.

"Good morning boys, how are you all doing, holding up okay? None of you're asleep, so that's a good sign."

"Good morning Captain. No problems at all. We all got a bit hungry around 0300, so I sent Tristan and Cullen down to the kitchen to get us some food. We sat and ate and talked all night, it was kinda nice." Donny answered.

"Good to hear. We'll go down for our calisthenics in a few minutes, then have breakfast, and then you guys can go to bed for a few hours rest. Team one has volunteered to take the night shift tonight by the way."

"Sounds good to me Sir. Okay guys, let's go." Donny said.

They all headed down to the rooms to wait for the others, once the captain woke them up. They all came out a few minutes later, and Captain Casey went in and gave the rooms a quick inspection.

"Team four, your room isn't up to your normal standards, please make sure it's perfect tomorrow morning, or you'll spend an extra half hour doing exercises tomorrow."

"Yes Sir!" Team four said.

"Let's go then and get some exercise and food, so that team three can get some sleep." Captain Casey said.

"Yes Sir!" They all said.

They headed down to their normal exercise room and did their workout, then headed for breakfast. As soon as breakfast was finished, team three went up to bed, while the others all went to the bridge, or to clean up. Other than talking the morning away, they did not do much. Although Captain Casey did drill the boys on the ships operational equipment, and other such things once more.

Just before lunch was to be served, Captain Casey sent Zach up to wake up team three, and when they arrived, they all sat down to lunch. The rest of the day went by in much the same way, and after dinner, team one went to bed to rest for their night shift. Team one had taken over at midnight, as had been planned, and much the same as the night before, a couple boys were sent down for some food, and the boys sat around much of the night and talked the night away. By early morning they were in orbit over Earth, and by the time the captain woke up, team one had the ship in synchronous orbit over WSEC.

"Good morning boys, I see we're home already. Any problems at all?" Captain Casey asked when he came up to the bridge.

"None at all Sir. We're parked above WSEC now, and in a synchronous orbit, so we should stay put." Franky answered.

"Excellent. Would you boys go down and get the others up, and I'll be down in a minute to do the inspection? Once we get that out of the way, then we can get our morning routine and breakfast over with."

"Yes Sir!" They answered and they left the bridge.

"WSEC, this is Captain Casey of the UE1, you should have a package ready for teleportation, please send it to my cargo bay." Captain Casey said.

"Acknowledged, sending right away Captain, welcome back." The voice on the other end said.

"Thank you, but we're only back for a day or so. UE1 signing off."

"Very well Captain, enjoy your visit, signing off."

Jonathon then called his parents and left a message, telling them that they were home early, because they pushed through the last couple nights, that he would like for them to come up this afternoon, and that he would call them to tell them when.

Jonathon went down to find his charges and give their rooms the inspection.

"Team four, much better, everyone else is good. Let's get going, I'm sure team one wants to get some sleep." Captain Casey said.

"Yes Sir!" They all answered, and headed out on their way.

They got through their morning routine in the same amount of time as usual, and as soon as breakfast was done, team one was sent up to bed to get some rest. Captain Casey got the remainder of the boys' attention.

"Okay, while team one's sleeping, and three's cleaning, two and four can come with me to unpack some stuff."

"Okay Sir."

They all split up from there and the two teams followed the captain to the cargo bay, and started helping him unpack the crates of uniforms.

"Sir, why did we get so many more uniforms, and what are the new ones in the packages?" Teddy asked.

"My mom ordered them for us, because uniforms get worn out very quickly, and I barely got enough to last most of you six months. As for the others, that's part of the surprise for this afternoon, so you'll have to wait patiently."

"Nuts. I hate waiting." Teddy pouted.

"Come on you, you'll have to wait no matter what, so let's get this finished up, because we're almost done."

So they finished up and put the new uniforms in storage, but Captain Casey teleported the dress uniforms to his room. He would hand them out once team one was up, and after they all got cleaned up.

A few hours later, just as lunch was about to be served, Teddy was asked to go get the others up, but told him to tell them to not bother getting into clean uniforms for now.

They came down just as lunch was being served, so they sat down and they all ate.

"Okay guys, change of plans. We're all going to help clean up, so that we can get it done right away, and then we'll have to go up and get cleaned up. As soon as you've had your showers, and are all clean and presentable, don't get dressed, line up in the hall in just your towels, and I'll hand out what you're to wear."

"Okay Sir." They all said, but were clearly puzzled.

So within only a few minutes, they were able to clean up the dining hall and the kitchen, and were off to their rooms to get cleaned up. Captain Casey got the dress uniforms out, got the correct sizes for all the boys, then went and had a real quick shower himself, and then did his hair. He wrapped himself in a towel and took the bundles out to the boys. They were all out in the hall and waiting already, so he handed the packages out.

"Okay boys, these are dress uniforms, you're to go get dressed up, and then meet me on the bridge as soon as you can. Check each other and make sure there's nothing out of order, that your clothes are all straight, and you're all neat and tidy. See you in a few minutes." He said, and then they all disappeared back to their rooms to get dressed.

Captain Casey got himself dressed in his dress uniform as well. He had always hated getting dressed up, but no matter how much you hated getting dressed up, getting into a full naval dress uniform always made you feel better. The uniform had hardly changed looks in a couple hundred years or more, but it was made of newer materials now that would never shrink, wrinkle, bur or snag, so the uniform that Captain Casey had, was from when he was nineteen, and it still looked brand new.

The design for these uniforms came from the American naval dress uniform, theirs had been chosen to represent the space fleet as being the nicest looking. White crisp and clean was how most saw it, and with high collar, ranks and decorations, shiny black shoes, gold buttons, white gloves and of course the hat, it did dress up almost anyone. As soon as he was dressed, Jonathon made the call to his parents. He told them that he and his crew would be ready in just a few minutes and that he would teleport them up to the ship once everyone was ready. They were good with that, so it was arranged.

His parents were already in their dress uniforms Jonathon noted when he called, and his dads chest could barely be seen for the various medals and commendations he had received, his moms was almost as full. Jonathon already had a few, but nothing like what either of his parents were adorned with.

Jonathon waited in his room for a few minutes longer, purposely waiting to make sure the boys would be waiting on the bridge when he arrived. He asked the computer to confirm they were all there, and it said that they were, so he headed out.

"Captain on deck, please form up for inspection." Captain Casey said as he entered the bridge.

The boys took a few seconds to line up as they had been taught. Captain Casey then spent a few minutes to inspect the boys, and they were all perfect.

"Excellent, you guys all look perfect. In a few minutes you're going to be inspected again by a pair of high level WSEC authorities, so please stand at perfect attention, and only speak when spoken to."

The communication center pinged, but instead of going over to answer, Captain Casey went to the teleporter station, which is part of the communications station anyway, and hit the teleport button. Within a couple seconds, Admiral and Captain Casey were on the bridge.

"Admiral on board, welcome Admiral." Jonathon saluted his father.

"Good afternoon Captain, may we inspect the crew." Admiral Casey asked.

"It would be my pleasure Sir." Captain Casey said.

Admiral and Captains Casey took about ten minutes to inspect the twenty young men, who were all very nervous, but stood at absolute perfect attention for the inspection by the most revered admiral they knew.

"Your crew's in excellent shape, you should be very proud. At ease gentlemen." Admiral Casey said.

The boys automatically relaxed a little, and went to the at ease stance.

"So, I hear you boys kicked my butt on the hardest battle simulation we currently have?" Admiral Casey asked with a smile.

The boys all stayed silent, not really knowing if an answer was required or not. Finally Donny figured he should say something.

"I guess we kinda did Sir, at least that's what Captain Casey told us. We had no idea that it was the hardest one there was, or that you'd been the only one to beat it, up 'til then of course. We just did what we were supposed to do Sir." He said, in a voice that was clear and as strong as he could make it.

"Kind of. Boy, had that been an actual test, I would have scored a ten and you guys would've scored an easy hundred. You soundly stomped my crew, and you should be more than proud of yourselves. I knew at some point that someone else would beat it, I just never figured it would be a group of young men in training to do it. I don't have words of high enough praise to tell you how that makes me feel, and I know your captain feels even better. You're a remarkable group of young men, and if you can stay working together, as well and as smooth as you've done so far, you'll surely go far in this world." Admiral Casey proudly told the assembled boys.

"Thank you Sir, your kind words are more than enough for any of us. You're the most famous person in the entire war, and to have you feel proud of us, I know for me, makes me feel better than I've ever felt in my life." Donny again said, but this time with a tear in his eyes.

"You're most assuredly welcome, all of you. Now let's go inspect the rest of the ship, you gentlemen get to lead the inspection."

So for the next couple hours, the boys led them through the ship and they inspected everything. They all chatted back and forth the whole time.

"Jonathon, could I talk to you for a minute." His mom asked.

"Sure Mom, what's up." He asked when they stepped away a little bit from the others.

"Nothing much. I just wanted to tell you that your crew is an amazing group, and you've done very well with them. I also wanted to tell you that the young man, who I'm sure will be your new doctor, is awaiting your call, so you should call this evening or tomorrow morning."

"Thanks Mom, for everything."

"You're welcome, it's nothing much really, it's the the least I could do to help. Your dad 'll have a bit of a surprise in a few minutes I'm sure." She said cryptically, but he just ignored that, being more than a little used to it.

The two went and joined up with the rest of the inspection for the last few minutes.

"Well boys, you've treated my old ship very well, and it looks very nice." Admiral Casey said.

"Thank you Sir." They all said.

"No, thank you. In fact, my wife and I'd love to treat all of you, and your captain to a very nice fancy dinner. We've already made arrangements, we've booked an entire five star restaurant for our dinner tonight. Anyone feel like getting royally spoiled?" Admiral Casey asked.

They were all silent. No one knew what to think about that, none of them had ever been anywhere fancy before, and it kind of scared most of them.

"Um Sir, I think we'd all like that, but I don't think anyone's ever had a dinner like that before. What do we do?" Jamie asked.

"Well, just eat of course. No one would expect you to know what fork or spoon to use, in fact I still don't, and you couldn't make me care either. All I ask is that you're polite and courteous of course." Admiral Casey said with a smile.

"Okay then Sir, we'd like that very much." Jamie said for everyone.

"Well then Jonathon, get us to the ground, just outside WSEC, and we can walk the block to the restaurant." Admiral Casey commanded.

"Yes Sir!" Jonathon said and saluted his father.

"Enough of that you brat. I'm no longer officially an officer, and I hated it even when I was." Admiral Casey said.

"I know, why do you think I love doing that to you when I can." Jonathon said with a grin.

Before his dad could comment, Jonathon programmed the teleporter and got them outside the front doors to WSEC. A few people noticed all the people dressed in their best, but what they noticed most was all the boys dressed in the dress uniforms. Admiral Casey led the way to the restaurant, and when they all entered, the gentleman at the door welcomed the crew, then closed and locked the door.

As the man led them to their tables, the boys were enjoying all the sights and scents that the restaurant had to offer. It smelled so good in there that every last one of their mouths started to water, thinking that if the food smelled that good already, then they could not wait to taste it as well. Then there were the sights, it was a fairly small restaurant, capable of seating maybe fifty to sixty people at most, which helped to make the place very cozy. There was a large stone fireplace in one corner that was burning, giving the whole place a very homy feel, as well as suffusing the air with a hint of smokiness that only added to the delicious smells. Each table itself was capable of seating up to four people, but all the tables that they saw only had two chairs at them, they figured correctly that more chairs were brought out when and if needed. The chairs were upholstery covered antique looking wood chairs that were very intricately carved, more like art pieces than seats to be used. The floor was done in a very dark brown wood that was polished and gleamed brilliantly, all the boys felt that they should have taken their shoes off before walking on it. The walls were done in rich colors with some wood paneling that set off the whole cozy feeling perfectly.

He then showed the group to a large circle of tables close to the fireplace, and a group of waiters and waitresses seated the lady and all the gentlemen. Everyone was given a menu by one person, while another was pouring a small glass of champagne for the boys, and a full glass for the adults. They were also asked what they would like to drink, so everyone gave their personal server their request. They left and were quickly back with the requested drinks. Everyone took almost ten minutes to decided what they wanted for their starter course and their meal. Their orders taken, the admiral stood up, champagne flute in hand.

"I'd like to propose a toast to my son, the captain of the Universe Explorer. You've got a fine crew and you're doing a fantastic job. We wish you all the best of luck on your missions to come." Admiral Casey said and raised his glass.

Everyone raised their glasses to the toast and had a sip of the champagne.

"Next I'd like to toast the newest crew of the Universe Explorer. You may be the youngest crew the ship has ever seen, or the fleet for that matter, but you may be the most capable it, or they've ever seen. To you we wish the best of luck in your up and coming missions, and life, and ask you to watch over our son, and bring him home in one piece." Admiral Casey toasted.

Again everyone raised their glasses to the toast. They all sat down to a nice conversation, and enjoyed their meal slowly as it came out to them. None of the boys had ever experienced such an exquisite meal before, nor had they ever had a meal served so slowly. None the less, everyone enjoyed the meal to the fullest, but the desserts were not to be compared. Once the meal was all cleaned up, they all sat back and chatted for quite some time, before Admiral Casey called it a night.

"Mom and Dad, thank you very much for the lovely evening." Jonathon told his parents.

"Yes Sir and Ma'am, we too thank you very much for the wonderful dinner." Donny said as graciously as he knew how.

"You're all very welcome. Well have a good night you guys. Keep in touch okay." Jonathon's mom said.

"We will." Jonathon said.

They parted ways, and Jonathon teleported the boys and himself back up to the ship as soon as they were able to.

"Well guys, how did you like your surprises today?" Captain Casey asked once they were back on their own bridge.

"That was incredible. Admiral Casey personally inspecting us and complementing us. I was so nervous during the inspection, I almost peed my pants though, well that and I almost passed out 'cause I forgot to breath while he was inspecting me." Donny said with a blush.

"Me too." Almost everyone stated as well.

"Yeah, I always felt the same while being inspected by an admiral, or other high end officials. Be thankful you didn't though, one of the guys actually did when we were being inspected once. He was so embarrassed, but absolutely no one laughed though, because we all felt the same, and I'm equally certain he wasn't the first either. Well it's been a long day, so let's all go get changed and go sit back, relax, and maybe watch a movie or two, even if we go past lights out. You may of course go to bed when you're ready."

"Sounds good to me Sir, and I'm sure the others will agree." Donny said, and the others all nodded their heads in agreement.

"Good, let's go then."

They all headed to their rooms and got out of their dress uniforms; they all threw the uniforms in the laundry chute to get cleaned. They would put them back in their protective coverings in the morning, once they got them back. Once everyone was more comfortable, they met at the theatre. As with the last time, Captain Casey sat back and let the boys choose the movie, then sat with the boys and enjoyed the movie they chose. After that movie ended, they all chose another one, it was started, and they sat back and watched it as well. All of team one had fallen asleep, as well as Kelly, Cullen and Zach.

"I can grab both Franky and Ryan, if the rest of you bigger boys want to grab the others." Captain Casey said, when it was pointed out to him by Donny.

"Okay Sir." Donny said.

It was harder than Jonathon had thought. He was able to lift the weight no problem, but it was different when the weight was asleep and very limp. Donny ended up having to help get Ryan into the captains arm, the one that Franky was not currently occupying, and he carried both boys, while Donny grabbed Kevin, Jamie carried Jesse, Pete carried Tony, and the three younger boys were taken by Lance, Tristan and Brady.

They carried the boys up to their respective dorms, and laid them down on their beds. Captain Casey figured it was just easier to leave them dressed, other than removing their shoes, so after covering them up, he left the boys to sleep. It kind of amazed him that not even one of the boys had waken up while being carried to bed.

He bade the others a good night, and he too went to bed and fell asleep very quickly. First thing Wednesday morning, after their morning routines were finished, Captain Casey called the doctor who would hopefully be joining them.

"Hello, my name is Captain Jonathon Casey, my mother has been talking to you about a possible position on my ship!" He asked as soon as the person answered.

"Oh yes, hello Captain Casey. My name's Warren, and I hear you're looking for someone to cook for you, and act as doctor when needed, and that you'd pay for both positions. Your mom also tells me that the term will be one year, that may or may not be extended."

"Yes. You'd be required to cook and clean the kitchen, and one of my crew would be assigned every day to help you. And yes, you'd also be the ships doctor as well. I'm a fully trained med tech, and can take care of almost anything, but then I thought, what if I was injured, or what if there was a situation I couldn't handle, it could prove fatal. I'd like to prevent that at any cost. I'd like for you to come up, and we can sit and talk for a bit, and then if I think you'll fit in, then I'll let you meet the boys."

"That sounds fine. I can come now if you'd like."

"Okay, I'll bring you up now. One moment."

He then got the teleporter on Warren, and brought him right to his office. Captain Casey stood and shook Warren's hand. Warren is just a little under 2 meters tall, a very good strong build, dark brown, nearly black hair, hazel eyes, prominent nose and chin and was wearing blue jeans and a tee shirt.

"Welcome to the UE1 Warren. Please have a seat."

"Thank you for having me Sir." He said, and then sat down.

For the next hour they sat and talked. Jonathon got a real good feel for Warren, and felt that he would definitely be a great addition to the crew. He found out that Warren had been on the street from the time he was six, with his big brother, after his parents and three other siblings were all killed in the war. He found out that Warren and his brother had been captured when Warren was twelve, his brother had been killed, but he managed to kill two of his captors and escape. He had then lived on the street all by himself, until he was sixteen, when he got really sick and landed in the hospital, and then was convinced to stay in an orphanage and go to school. Warren said that he had poured everything into his school work, and ended up graduating only a year after his peers had. He then got a job and went to university, and paid for it by cooking. There he worked his way up to be a fully trained chef. Now at the age of thirty, he was a doctor and a chef.

137

"Well Warren, I can tell you that I believe that you'd be a perfect addition to our crew. You know even more than I do about what these boys went through, since they're all street kids as well, some with stories just like yours, and one I've heard so far, even worse."

"Even worse than that Sir, and I thought my story was bad. May I ask what happened to that boy."

"I don't know all the details yet, but his family was murdered right in front of him, because he fought them. They then captured him and held him captive, and then they raped, tortured and electrocuted him repeatedly. He has such a hatred of the Qaralon, that it makes the rest of us look like we like them. I have no idea how long they had him captive, nor how long they tortured him, but I think it was about a year. I still have no idea how he escaped. I suspect that he killed his way out, much like you did. Now, I'd like to take you to meet the boys, they're still in the lounge, I hope, but it's getting close to lunch, so the team responsible for cooking today may have already gone up to make it. Follow me please." Captain Casey said, and Warren looked disturbed by the story.

"Yes Sir!" Warren said after a minute.

They headed to the lounge down the hall from where they were, Captain Casey had asked them to stay there, and they entered just as team three was getting up to start lunch.

"Why don't you guys hold up. You can stay here and talk with Warren for a while, while I go up and start lunch. Join me in about thirty minutes to help okay." Captain Casey said.

"Yes Sir!" They said and the captain headed out.

"Hey guys, as Captain Casey said, my name's Warren, and he wants me to be the doctor and cook, but only if you guys all agree. So as I understand it, you were all street kids when the captain found you, and he's training you. I also understand from his mom, that you guys are doing exceptionally well."

"Thanks." They all said.

"I should tell you that I too was a street kid. My parents and brothers and sisters were all killed, except my big brother, when I was six. Then when I was twelve we were captured by a couple Qaralon, and when we fought to get away, they killed my brother, right in front of me. I managed to get a hold of a weapon, and I killed them and escaped, I took my brother with me, so that he wouldn't get eaten, and then I buried him."

"I was very angry after that for so long, I hated the Qaralon so much, I wanted nothing more than to find and kill every last one of them. When I was sixteen, I got really sick, and I somehow got to the hospital, where eventually I got better. A very nice nurse there convinced me to go to the orphanage, so that I could keep from getting sick, and so that I could go to school. As they say, I never looked back, so now here I am. So now you know all about me. You never have to feel that you have to tell me your stories, same as I'm sure the captain said. But I'd like to hear them."

"Well my name's Matthew and I'm ten. My family was all killed in front of me as well. They tried to kill me first, 'cause I was the youngest, but I managed to stab one of them with a knife from the kitchen, where we were when they attacked. I was hit very hard, and then restrained and forced to watch as one by one my entire family was killed in front of me, I was seven. We were then all teleported up to their ship, and they kept me in nothing more than a closet and force fed me, 'cause I refused to eat. I'm even pretty sure I know what they were feeding me, but I can't force myself to say it. I was repeatedly raped and shocked and beaten for hurting their leader."

"I was there for so long, I'm not even sure. All I know is I was seven when I was taken, but that I was about eight when I escaped, and it was about the same time of year again, so I was there for about a year. I managed to escape, when I killed one of the Qaralon, using the gun he was wearing, while he was raping and zapping me. I then ran for my life, and killed I have no idea how many more, until I found a teleporter console, and got out of there, still naked and carrying the gun I had used to escape."

"I was lucky that we were even close to Earth at the time and that I was within teleporter range, but the monster that was torturing me at the time said they were there to get more nice tender meat, they loved our kids, they said that we tasted the best. That was when I decided I had to do something, even if it got me killed. Of course I was in real bad shape from the torturing and everything else, and I got hit a few times really hard while trying to escape, but they all regretted not trying to kill me, because I killed them instead. So yeah, I got to the planet, I had no idea where I was going, nor did I care, I just teleported and landed pretty much where Captain Casey found me. Some of the kids here found me, and helped me. They fixed me up, and even they didn't know the whole story 'til now. I don't know what I'd do if I saw another Qaralon now. I feel like I'd kill every one of them in sight, but I also feel like I'd either throw up or run and hide like a baby." Matthew said, almost emotionless.

"I'm so sorry to hear that. Captain Casey told me that one of you boys had a story worse than mine, he had a little of it, and he told me what little he knew. I know how you feel though. I'm not sure what I'd do now if I saw another Qaralon as well. I have a feeling though, that sooner, rather than later, we'll all have to find out. But all of us together, helping each other through it, will be just fine. I know you guys obviously love and trust the captain, probably even more than he knows, I can tell just the way you all look at him."

"Yes, but please don't tell him that. He rescued and saved all of us, and we trust him like no other person. I know that we all love him like a father, but I don't think he feels the same way about us." Donny said.

"I think you're wrong there. From what his mom told me, you guys have only been in space a month, but she says he thinks the world of you guys already, and trusts you with his life, as you guys trust your lives with him. Have any of you actually gone and told him any of your stories, you know he's a therapist, and could help you guys a lot!" Warren told the boys.

"I've thought of it a few times, 'cause no one really knows what happened to me, except me, but I didn't want to put that on him as well, he's got enough to worry about with all of us as it is." Donny said.

"I bet that he'd love to hear the stories. You know he used to work in an orphanage, and he helped a lot of kids who went through what we did. Someone just like him helped me when I got to the orphanage, and you have no idea how much easier it was to deal with it all after that. I still get the nightmares sometimes, and sometimes they're still really bad, but now I can deal with them, instead of breaking down completely for a week or so. You can also come to me at any time. I'm not a therapist, and I won't be able to help sooth the pain like he'll be able to, but I listen real well, and

I know what you all went through, all of it, I did it myself too to survive. But please talk to the captain, he's your best chance at a normal life." Warren warmly told the boys.

"We'll think about it, really we will. My team should be going though to help make lunch, come with the others at 1200 hours, and eat with us please?" Donny asked.

"I hope you do, and I will, thank you." Warren said.

For the rest of the time Warren sat and talked with the boys about nothing much, but they got to know each other a lot, and all the boys really liked him. Warren was really starting to like the boys as well though.

"Hey guys, so what do you think of Warren, do you think he'd make a good addition to our crew?" Captain Casey asked when the boys entered the kitchen.

"I really like him. He told us about what happened to him, and Matthew told all of us what happened to him as well. I think he'd be really good." Tristan answered.

"That's good to hear, I'm glad that you all like him and that he told you all what he went through."

Captain Casey noticed that Donny was being very quiet, and looked as if he were a light-year away. He went over to the boy, put his arm around the young mans shoulder, and gave him a squeeze.

"Hey Donny, is there something wrong, is there anything I can help you with, or maybe even just sit down and talk for a while?"

"I don't know, I'm just thinking about something Warren said. He seems real nice by the way."

"And what did he say that has you so quiet?"

"Well, he told us that we should all tell you our stories, that you could help. I'd thought a few times about telling you, but I didn't want to burden you any further than you already are. Taking care of all of us can't be easy as it is." Donny said quietly.

"I'd never say that you have to tell me, but I certainly invite you to do so, because, like Warren said, I can help you. Do you have problems with what happened to you that you'd like to talk to me about? You never have to worry about that by the way, you guys telling me your stories, when you're ready, is no burden to me at all. It'll help you lighten your burden, which in turn, might reduce mine. Do you think I don't know you all have nightmares during the night, that some of you wet the bed some nights from the nightmares and or cry yourselves to sleep? I wanted you to all come to me when you were ready, but I was starting to think I was going to have to come to you." Captain Casey told him.

"How did you know, are the rooms monitored or something?" Donny asked, looking shocked.

"No, but I check in on you guys from time to time, and I can hear you as well, especially when you scream in your sleep. I'm up two or three times a night, and I've had to come rub your back and get you back to sleep more than once."

"I never knew Sir. I think I should tell you then that we all really love you a lot, like you're our father or something, I can't explain it, not sure I want to." Donny said with tears now pouring out his eyes and he swung his arms around the captain and hugged him tight.

"I hope you all know I feel the same way about you. And from now on, when you have problems, I want you to come and talk to me, you aren't alone, and I can help." Captain Casey told all the boys, and they all came and hugged him. They had all been standing there and listening, but not saying anything.

"Okay guys, we should get lunch finished, because the others will be here soon." Captain Casey said.

"Okay Sir. Thanks." Donny said quietly while wiping his eyes.

"You're welcome." Captain Casey said softly.

They got everything finished up for the lunch that Jonathon had started, and were setting it out just as everyone was coming in.

"Warren, please come sit with me at the head table?"

"Yes Sir!"

They all went and sat down and got started on their lunch. The captain turned to Warren as they were eating.

"So warren, I hear you had a good chat with the boys, and Matthew even told you his story. Donny also tells me that you told them that they should come talk with me about their histories, because I can help."

"Yes Sir I did, I hope I wasn't out of place, but I felt they needed to know, because when I asked them if they'd told you yet, they all said no. They also have a great deal of love and respect for you, however they didn't want me to tell you that for some reason. I think they have a hard time loving and respecting someone, for fear that they'll be killed as well. I know I felt that way for a long time."

"No, you weren't out of line at all. I was actually going to move from letting them come to me when they were ready, to actively going to them, because they weren't coming to me as I'd hoped they would. Yes, I knew they loved me and respected me as well, but I knew they were trying to hide it, and I suspect that that's the reason as well. I've seen the same thing from so many kids before, it's really so very common, and even understandable. So far the outlook is good for you joining us, so what do you think so far?"

"I think I'd really like to join the crew, if you'll all have me of course."

"Well let's finish eating, and then see about making it official."

"Yes Sir!"

The boys had of course already started eating, and had not been paying attention to the adults at the head table. Soon everyone was finished their meals, and Captain Casey stood and got everyone's attention.

"Okay guys, I want to put this to a vote. All in favor of Warren joining our crew, raise your hands?"

Without a second thought, every one of the boys raised their hands.

"Well there you have it, you already had my vote, so if you want it, the position is yours Warren."

"I'd be honored to Sir. I'll just teleport my belongings up to the ship, and then as soon as you want to, we can leave."

The boys all cheered.

"I do have to make a call first, but that'll only take a minute. We'll leave as soon as you get all your things, do you need to go home to pack any of it?"

"No, I actually packed all the things I wanted, in case I got the position. There really isn't much, only two small boxes, and they've even been tagged already." Warren grinned.

"An optimist, rare these days." Captain Casey smiled.

"No, a realist. I knew, by what your mom had told me, that I was almost exactly what you were looking for, and I knew I was perfect for the position. I would've been a bit surprised had I not got it, to tell you the truth." Warren said with a grin.

"My mom's so good at picking the right people, I had no doubt either, to tell you the truth, so I too would've been surprised. Well, welcome to the crew. Seeing as how this is your first day on the job, we'll all help you clean the kitchen and dining hall, and then we'll show you the infirmary and then your room, which is of course right next door to it."

"Sounds good to me Sir."

"So what do you like to be called anyway, do you give out your last name, I know many of the street kids won't, and I haven't even asked the boys for theirs, so should we call you Warren or Dr. Warren?" Captain Casey asked curiously.

"I still don't like to give my last name no, too many bad memories there, so I just go by Warren whenever possible."

"Then Warren it is. You guys heard us, so let's get cleaning." The captain said to the boys who were gathered around them.

They spent a few minutes cleaning up, and then they all took Warren to his office, and then to his quarters. He was very pleased with the setup of the infirmary, and he loved his room as well. From his room, Warren teleported his belongings up, and set the boxes aside to go through later.

"Well Warren, we're going to get underway then, seeing as how you're ready to go. I'm going to go call my parents quickly, to tell them that we're on our way, and then we'll head out. I'll be in class with the boys 'til just before dinner, and someone will be up an hour before to help you out." Captain Casey said.

"Will do Sir, I'm just going to explore the ship for now then. I'll call if I need any help."

"Sounds good. Come on boys, our class will be held on the bridge today, so grab your pads and meet me up there."

"Yes Sir!" They all said.

CHAPTER 13

FIRST RESCUE MISSION

For the next couple weeks the crew settled into a nice slow pace of flying during the day, and classes during the evening. They never even went above twenty five LYS, since the captain said they were in no rush to get anywhere, and they would not be called upon for some time to come yet. Mornings still consisted of their calisthenics, and then breakfast, followed by ship operations and flying. The evenings were filled with the various classes. From time to time Captain Casey had a pair of boys out on the hull of the ship inspecting it, they all enjoyed this task, because it felt very free, and was kind of fun. There had yet to be any damage, so none of the boys had yet to be taught how to repair any kind of damage.

The last Sunday, Captain Casey sat with a few of the boys from groups two and three, and the boys all told their stories to him. They all cried most of the time they sat together, and the captain told them all that nothing that happened to them was their fault, but that they were all strong enough to have survived this long, and that they would continue to be strong enough to stay alive and live full lives. He of course told them much much more than just that, and they did all feel a lot better after getting all the pain and hurt and distrust off their young shoulders. Each of the boys, who sat with the captain, left and mostly went straight to bed, because they were exhausted afterward from the emotional purge that they went through.

It was coming up on the second weekend of their journey and they were no longer within the relatively safe confines of the Human or Tenarian solar systems, they were now into the wild universe, somewhere that no human had ever gone before, that they were aware of. As usual, there was always someone on scanning, and today it seems they found something.

"Sir, I think I've got something on the scanners, but I can't tell what it is though." Tony said, sounding a little frustrated.

"Let's take a look, and see if we can't figure it out together then." Captain Casey said, and went to see what the frustrated boy was looking at.

The captain, and a few of the others on the bridge, gathered around the scanning station to look at the display.

"It looks like it could be a debris field from something, but I'm not sure what that thing is, it looks as if it's intact though. If I had to guess, I'd say that it's some kind of an escape pod, but it's of no sort I've ever seen before. Kelly, would you try putting a call out to it, and see if anyone answers?"

The object that they found in the centre of the debris field was spherical in shape, approximately three meters across, and as they got closer and better images, they could even pick out a door. There was clear and obvious damage to the thing though, black scorch marks, more dents and scratches than they could count, and there was a small bit of its armored plating blown clean off. There were no obvious forms of propulsion or power generation, so it was more than likely intended only as an escape pod, but once out, you would be forced to be rescued, which was why the Earth ships escape pods had small engines and power generators of their own.

"Yes Sir!" He said and spun around and did as he was asked.

"Sir, there's a very weak signal coming from it, but it seems to be either in a language we've got no information on, or it's too weak to get anything from." Kelly answered.

"Well talk to them, and see if they can understand us." Captain Casey said.

"Unknown escape pod, can you hear or understand us, this is the Earth ship, Universe Explorer One." Kelly said as clearly as he could manage in his small treble voice.

A small crackling sound came back, but it was not enough to get anything, whether it was English or another language.

"Well boys, we may just have our first rescue mission. Navigation, get us there as quick as you can, and scanning look out for anything that could be attempting to set a trap for us." Captain Casey said.

"Yes Sir!" The boys said.

They went about their business. At the time there were only five boys on the bridge, while the rest were taking care of other business throughout the ship.

"Franky and Jamie, wherever you are at this time, please meet me in airlock one, we have a possible rescue mission. Donny, I need you to come take over the bridge." Captain Casey said into his communicator.

"Yes Sir!" All three boys answered.

A few seconds later Donny came up and went over to the captain to be briefed.

"Donny, we're coming up on what might be an escape pod, but it isn't of any style that we're familiar with. Frankie, Jamie and I are going out to it to see if we can find anything out about it, and I want you to take over the bridge. I have the boys doing scans to make sure there's nothing out there setting a trap for us, but if something happens, get as far away from us as you can, deal with the situation, and then come back for us. Boys, Donny has the bridge, you listen to him as if I were giving the orders."

"Yes Sir!" The boys all said.

The captain left the bridge to go meet with the boys, he made one detour, and that was to grab three guns, for just in case.

"Hi Franky and Jamie. I have some guns here for you, I'm sure I don't have to tell you to be careful with these. The safety is here, and right now it's set to stun, just leave it there, unless I tell you otherwise. You have your scanners I see, so that's good. Let's get suited up." He said and they all did so.

"Are we almost at the pod Donny, and have you guys been able to get better contact yet?" Captain Casey asked a few minutes later, when he and the boys were all suited up.

"We're almost there, about another thirty seconds or so Sir, but the message is still pretty garbled, we still can't even tell if it's English, or what it is. We have the computer trying to clean it up, but I think the signal's just too weak. My guess is that their power is so low, that even their communications don't have enough power to run. I don't think you'll find anything alive though, if that's the case Captain."

"If you're right about the power, then you're right about the other probably, but we have to check. There's nothing out there other than the pod though, right!"

"No Sir, there's almost nowhere for someone to hide anywhere near by. We have scanners running at maximum though, and as soon as you're clear, the shields will be raised to maximum. We're also going to move away a bit, just in case, but we'll keep in contact at all times though. We've just come to a complete stop, so you're clear to go Sir, good luck." Donny said.

"Will do, and you too."

The captain and the boys exited the ship and started toward the pod. As soon as Donny saw that they were clear, he moved away a couple hundred kilometers. Captain Casey was first to arrive to the pod, because the boys had fallen behind and beside, to provide cover. He searched the pod and found the airlock, and hit the communications button. He was more than a little surprised when someone answered, and in perfect English no less.

"Hello, is this the UE1 rescue crew." A young male voice asked.

"Yes, this is Captain Casey of the UE1. Can we be of any assistance?"

"Yes please, we've been floating out here for a few weeks or more now, and we're running low on supplies. The external transmission antennae were apparently damaged so badly you couldn't hear us, even though we could hear you." The voice said.

"Please have all your people come to the air lock, so that we may see that this is no trick?" Captain Casey asked.

"Of course Captain." The voice said.

A moment later three human boys came into sight, the oldest maybe fifteen, and all were in ragged clothes that made them look like they were more naked than dressed.

"Are you boys all that are in there?"

"Yes Sir!" The oldest boy said.

"Do you have space suits in there?" Captain Casey asked.

"No Sir, all we have is what you see, we also have maybe one days worth of food left, and not much more power, so if you hadn't come along, we would've been dead by tomorrow night."

"Okay, I'm going to have the ship move back, and we'll get you brought into the cargo bay of the ship. We can't scan this thing at all for some reason, so we won't be able to teleport you out."

"Okay Sir, thank you very much." The boy said, the other two nodding.

"Donny, bring the ship back around and lower the shields please? Get us as near to the cargo bay as you can, and have the cargo doors open and ready for us as well please?" Captain Casey asked.

"Yes Sir, be right there."

"Okay guys, the ship will be right here, and we'll get you into the cargo bay right away, so that we can get you out of there. Are any of you hurt?"

"No Sir, just hungry, because we've been trying to make what little food we had last." The boy said.

"Okay, we'll get that taken care of soon enough." Captain Casey said.

A couple seconds later the ship was in position, and the cargo doors were open and waiting. Using the tractor beam in the cargo bay, Captain Casey pulled the pod inside, and then closed the doors. As soon as the bay was pressurized, the crew removed their helmets and gloves.

"You boys can come out now!" Captain Casey said.

The door opened and the three boys exited. The oldest about fifteen, then the next at about twelve, and the youngest at about ten. The boys all looked like they were on the verge of starvation, and their clothes now looked even worse than they had through the thick slightly tinted glass of the pod. None of them appeared to be injured or in bad shape, other than being very thin, so the captain decided that the boys needed food more than anything and told them so, and then they would head to the infirmary to have them all checked out. All three of them were good with this and very happy to hear food. When the captain called Warren to let him know what was needed, Warren claimed to already be way ahead of him and the food was ready to be eaten as they spoke.

"Come boys, follow me, and we'll get some food into you." Captain Casey said.

The three hungry boys, as well as the other two who had rescued them, followed the captain to the dining hall.

Half way there, Jonathon was pinged by Donny, so he answered. "Captain, would you like us to get back under way?"

"Yes Donny, that'd be good, same direction as before should be good."

"Yes Sir, consider it done."

By this time the six people were walking into the dining hall, and Warren was just setting out the food. The three hungry boys pretty much attacked the food, and after their third helping each, said they were done.

"Now guys, some questions for you. Just how long have you been floating out here, how did you get out here, and exactly what kind of escape pod was that? Oh and of course, last but not least, what are your names and how old are you?" Captain Casey asked the boys.

"First of all I'm Will, and I'm fourteen. Then there's Dillon, he's twelve, and then Alex at ten. We're brothers. Our ship was captured a couple years ago by the Qaralon, and then my family, and a few of the other crew were soon handed over to the Framgar as prisoners. That's whose escape pod it was by the way. Well about a month ago, the adults worked out a plan to escape. We were smuggled into the escape pod for our safety, and they attempted to take over the ship. All of a sudden we were launched from the main ship, and we watched it explode. We were still too close though, because we ended up getting thrown around a lot, and the pod got some damage. The way I figure it, the Framgar somehow got wind of it, so the adults had to fight, and then someone blew up the ship, but launched us first to save us. Probably our dad, he always told us that in a case like that, that they'd gladly sacrifice themselves to save us. Personally I hate him for doing it, they could've figured something else out, even if we had've been prisoners for another year or two, who would've cared." Will said sourly.

"I'm sorry to hear all that, and while I understand where you're coming from, I also understand where your parents were coming from. It's a tough decision to make, and your parents believed that in this case, you were better off this way, than being prisoners with the possibility of death, this way they tried to give you life. It almost failed, but how were they to know that. So now it's time for you to see our doctor, to make sure you're all in good condition." Captain Casey said gently.

"I know Sir, and yes Sir, but it still hurts. Alex hardly even talks any more, and Dillon almost refused to eat, saying he was the smallest and weakest, so we should eat the most so we could survive." Will said, nearly crying.

"It'll take time to heal, but you will, and you'll find every member of my crew has stories just as bad, if not worse than yours. You may ask, but if someone tells you no, then please respect their wishes. Not everyone is ready to tell yet." Captain Casey told them as he was leading the boys to the infirmary.

"Yes Sir, we all understand." Will said.

"Good, you should also know that you're all welcome to come talk to me at any time about how you feel. Not only am I the captain, but I'm a child psychologist as well, so I can probably help. Here we are. I'm going to leave you in the capable hands of Warren, while I go get you some clothes."

"Thanks Sir. Hey, weren't you the cook as well?" Will asked Warren.

"Yes I am. I do double duties here, since I'm not always needed as a doctor. Captain, you and the boys may now leave, I'll take care of the rest, and I'll call you when I'm done." Warren said.

"Okay, I'll have some clothes for them when I get back. If you would, let them have a shower after you finish?"

"Sure Sir." Warren said and the rest left the room.

"Okay boys, back to your duties, and I'll join you in a few minutes." Captain Casey said, and the two boys still with him, just nodded and headed off.

"Will, Dillon and Alex right?" Warren asked.

"Yes Sir!" Will said.

"Okay, I'd like you to all go in the bathroom right over there, get out of those clothes and throw them out, get cleaned up, then put on these robes here, and then I'll give you a full checkup?" Warren asked.

"Okay Sir." Will said.

Will took the offered robes and led his brothers to the washroom, and they all got cleaned up, Will helping his brothers. They put the robes on and exited the room.

"Could you each hop up onto a table, and I'll run an auto scan on each of you, it'll only take about two minutes, and then I'll do the manual stuff?"

Each boy got on a table, Will in the middle, and his brothers on each side. Warren started the three scanners he needed, and they each did their work. Two minutes later the scans came up on the screens. Warren took a few minutes to look at each one, and then grabbed a few things, and starting with Alex, started the rest of the checkup. It took almost an hour for him to do so, but he thoroughly checked out each boy to make sure everything was good.

"Well guys, other than being a little on the thin side, you're all in pretty good shape." Warren told the boys.

"The Framgar never beat us or anything, we were treated pretty good, but we weren't allowed to move at all, we had to stay in the tiny room they gave all of us. We had no idea what was going to happen to us, but they threatened to kill us if we made any fuss at all, but that if we were good, we'd live." Will said.

"Yes, I've heard of such things from them before, but never what happened once the prisoners reached wherever it was that they were going. Okay, I'm going to call the captain now, you're all free to go." Warren said.

"Thanks." Will said.

"Captain, the boys are ready now." Warren said into his communicator.

"Okay, I'll be right there."

A few minutes later the captain entered.

"Hello boys, you clean up nicely. So Doc, what's the verdict?" Captain Casey smiled.

"Hello." The boys all answered, the two youngest barely audible again, but the captain heard them none the less.

"They're all in excellent condition, if not a bit on the thin side, but we'll get that taken care of though easily enough."

"Great, thanks. Here are some clothes for you guys. They're ships uniforms, but it's pretty much all we have, I just hope these and the underwear I brought you fits. Go on in and get dressed, and then we're going to go for a nice long talk." Captain Casey said, handing the boys each a garment.

CHAPTER 14

GETTING SETTLED

The boys each took the offered uniforms and went into the washroom again to get changed. Warren and Captain Casey just stood there and waited for the boys, not saying anything.

"Captain Casey Sir, these uniforms are too tight, they're a bit uncomfortable." Will said as they came out of the washroom a few minutes later, all three of them tugging and pulling at the tight material.

"That's how they're supposed to fit, and they all look as if they fit about right. Don't worry, you'll get used to it in a day or so. All the other boys on the ship got used to them in one to two days, and you will as well. Let's go to my office so we can talk."

"Okay Sir." Will said.

Captain Casey noted that all the boys looked amazingly alike with brown hair and eyes, Will was a bit taller, whereas both the younger boys were a bit shorter than normal. Will was almost as tall as the captain was, while the other two only came up to his chest, Alex just a little shorter of the two of course. The captain had been unable to tell exactly what the boys had looked like before because they had been so dirty and ragged looking, so he got a good look now. They all walked out of the infirmary, and Captain Casey led them to his office.

"Pull up some seats boys and get comfortable." Captain Casey said, and waited for the boys to be seated. "Okay, that's better. Now, do you know if you have any family left that you can go to?" Captain Casey asked.

"Not that I know of Sir. As far as I know, we're the last after our parents died." Will answered.

"Okay, then if you wish, you may become part of our crew, or we can get you back to Earth and get you into an orphanage. If you choose to stay on board, you'll be required to learn just as the others do. If you choose to leave, the first chance to get you onto a ship heading back to the planet, we'll get you there, if we can't do so, we'll take you home in a few months. What would you like to do?"

"Just a minute, let me ask my brothers."

"No hurry, take your time, but if you need to, you may even take a few days to do so." Captain Casey said, and Will just nodded.

The boys huddled together and whispered between themselves for a couple minutes, and then they turned back to the captain.

"Sir, if we decide to stay with you guys, what would be expected of us, and where are all the other adult crew members? So far all we've seen is you and the doctor, and a few kids our ages?" Will asked.

"Well, if you decide to stay, you'll be part of the crew, and would have all standard crew duties. You'd be under my command, and you'll listen and learn, or there'll be punishment just like on any ship. As for the adults, who you've seen so far, are all there is. This is a special training mission. I have a group of twenty young men, collected from the streets, and trained by myself, to operate a space ship." Captain Casey answered.

"Oh, I see. What do you mean by punish?" Will asked, and his brothers nodded.

"It would of course depend upon the reason for needing punishment, but normally punishments are that I exercise you 'til you want to drop, and then I push you just a little further. Morning and evening there are calisthenics to keep us all in shape, and you'll be expected to join, but not to keep up, especially at first. The other boys have all had well over a month to get used to the routine, and are all doing great, but none of them can keep up to me yet." Captain Casey answered.

"Okay, that's not too bad, just as long as we won't be beaten or anything like that. Our parents were really strict about schoolwork and things like that, but they never beat us, and I'd refuse if that were the case." Will said.

"Oh no, I'd never beat someone, unless they first attacked me, and even then I try and use other methods, I find that they usually work quite well. So how good is your school work then, because you sound as if you're quite well educated?" Captain Casey asked.

"My brothers are both at least three years ahead of where they should be, and I'm now in the university levels Sir. My parents had said that as soon as they got us out of there, they were taking me back home to get me into a good university, so that I could be whatever I wanted to be. I want to be a doctor."

"Wow, you're even younger than I was when I went, very good! Well I have a couple propositions to make then. You take over doing some of my classes, so you teach the others, I'll teach all of you everything I know about running a space ship, and I'll get Warren to teach you what he can about being a doctor. This is of course if you all accept the offer to be part of the crew?" Captain Casey asked.

"That sounds very good Sir. How do classes work?" Will asked.

"Normally I held the classes in the evening, while during the days we flew, and did other things. The boys are all doing pretty good, so maybe we can change things up a bit. Would you be willing to teach about four hours a day, six days a week, and the remaining time work with Warren? I think if we do it this way, I can give half the crew classes, while the other half is helping out on the ship, they can switch off, and we all get Sunday's off." Captain Casey said.

"I think that'd work Sir." Will answered.

"Great! Now Dillon and Alex, so far you've let your brother do all the talking, and I know you've been through a lot and don't talk much, but on this crew we all talk, so you'll have to start answering for yourselves as well. Do you think that you can do that for me please?" Captain Casey asked.

"Yes Sir!" Both boys answered, in what was barely a whisper.

"I'm sorry, I didn't really hear you. Could you try again, but louder this time?" Captain Casey asked gently.

"Yes Sir!" They again answered, this time in an audible sound, still quiet, but loud enough for now.

"Thank you. Now, do either of you boys have any questions so far?"

"Um, I do Sir, are we all gonna get to stay together?" Dillon asked.

"For tonight, yes, but once I figure a couple things out, you'll all become members of a team. Up until you arrived, I had four teams of five, but now that clearly won't work. Each of the dorms is designed for five, so I have to figure out how to work this all out. You'll be on separate teams though, but you'll of course get lots of time together as well." Captain Casey answered.

"But s-s-s-Sir, we'll be s-s-s-scared." Alex stuttered out.

"You'll still have your team with you, and you can talk with your brothers all you want, well unless of course you're supposed to be sleeping, or working on something important, such as school work, the normal stuff really. Once on your teams, you'll find that they're just like family, in fact they're your family on board, or at least your extended family. You'll also find that no matter how scared you are, that someone will be just as scared as you, and that you can all comfort each other. Almost everyone wakes at nights to nightmares, not everyone every night, but enough, and no matter if someone cries themselves to sleep, or wakes up crying, or even wet their bed because of it, they all comfort each other and help each other out."

"Okay Sir." The two younger boys answered, still quietly, but loud enough to be heard.

"Well, it's almost time for lunch! Now I know you just ate, but I'd like for you to join us, and you may eat again if you're hungry again. I'll then introduce you to all of our crew, and explain a few things. I'd also ask that you remember to call on me at any time if you have any questions, or even if you just want to sit and talk about things, any thing. If you're scared, or sad, or just feeling down, come see me okay."

"Yes Sir!" They all said.

Captain Casey led the boys back to the dining hall, and they were the first to arrive, other than Warren and his daily helper of course, so they all sat down at the head table and waited for the others to meet them. Captain Casey felt the ship slow to a stop, and then a few minutes later the boys all joined them. They were all bustling with chatter as they came in, but they all stopped to say hi to the captain and his guests. They all of course knew as much as Jamie and Franky had known. Once seated, Warren started serving the food, then went and sat next to the captain, and they all ate. Will, Dillon, and Alex did have a little more to eat, but not lots.

Finally, once everyone was finished eating, Captain Casey stood and got everyone's attention.

"Well, as I'm sure you all know by now, or at least I'd hope you've noticed, we have a few extra people on board with us at the moment. I'm happy to say that they've all agreed to join us on our mission. The oldest here is Will, he's fourteen, and he's agreed to take on the position of teacher, since he's graduated already, and was in the midst of taking some university courses. I'll still join the classes as well, especially for the first while. The changes will take place on Monday, so tomorrow is your last day of my classes, and then of course on Sunday we rest. These are Will's younger brothers, Dillon's twelve and Alex is ten. For tonight they'll be staying together in the dorm next to team fours, and tomorrow I'll be mixing things up a bit, and reorganizing. Any questions?"

"How are you going to reorganize Sir? We don't have enough space in the dorms, and there aren't enough people to make a full team." Franky asked.

"I haven't yet decided, but I have a few ideas. I'll share these with you once I have it all figured out myself, but that'll probably have to wait 'til tomorrow morning." Captain Casey answered with a grin, knowing full well it drove the boys crazy not to be told things.

"Fine Sir!" Franky said in a fake pout, Captain Casey just chuckled and shook his head.

"Team one and three, please go back up to the bridge, and find a nice quiet location to hide us out for a few days, while we get things settled here? Teams two and four, please go get the engine and power rooms cleaned and restocked? You three follow me please?" Captain Casey ordered.

"Yes Sir!" Everyone answered.

The teams all went their separate ways, and Captain Casey led his three newest charges to their bedroom for the night.

"This won't be your regular room, so don't get too comfortable, I just wanted to show you where you'd be for tonight. If you're tired, I'll leave you now, so that you may rest until dinner. You may either stay here or wander the ship and look around. I'll call you either way once dinner's ready."

"Thank you Sir." Will said and his brothers nodded.

Captain Casey left the boys then and went back up to his office to figure out how things should work out. He emerged a couple hours later with the results of his brainstorming. He first headed up to the bridge to see how it was going. He knew that they had stopped quite some time ago, and he could see an asteroid field out his window, but that was about all he knew.

"Good afternoon Captain. We found a nice dense asteroid field, so are tucked into it, and our shields are at maximum, just in case. I've also had the guys running the scanners at maximum since we parked, to see if there's anything worth looking into closer. We've found two asteroids near by that look promising." Donny said as he stood from the captains chair.

"Very good. I think we can go out and explore this evening, instead of normal classes then. What system are we in anyway?"

"According to the computer Sir, we're in the Racin section, which borders the Framgar system. It's not populated, since there don't seem to be any habitable planets, but it's mined heavily by many races." Tristan answered.

"Very good answer, I like detail, you're learning. I've never been here before, but we have to be careful. I've heard that space pirates love to pick on people out here, saying places like this are their area to mine, and stuff like that, so make sure to keep the sensors and shields at full all the while we're here."

"Already planned on it Sir, because I found the same information. We figured it was worth the risk though, to get some good supplies. We're well hidden though, so no one should see us, unless they watched us come in, and we certainly never saw anyone. They'd have to practically sit on top of us to see us in here, it seems a lot of the asteroids are metallic in nature, so picking only us out of the rocks should be next to impossible Sir." Tristan again offered.

"You're absolutely correct. We can't rule out however, that we weren't watched coming in, so it's wise to already make sure to keep scanners and shields at maximum. I'm going to go check on the others then, you guys keep up the great work." Captain Casey said.

Tristan told Donny, "See, told you he'd like it too." He said with a smile.

"I knew he would, and you know it, I just wanted to point out to you there were safer places to hide."

"Yep, but now we get to go exploring again." Tristan grinned.

"I guess you were right about that though."

"I'm always right, you should know that by now." Tristan taunted, and had to dodge a smack to the side of his head by Donny.

Captain Casey walked into the engine room a few minutes later to find all the boys standing around talking.

"Hello Captain. The engine has been put through two diagnostic tests, and everything's working well within the guidelines. The power systems have been restocked with Nutronium, and fully cleaned, as were the engines. We ran diagnostics on the power systems, and found a minor fault in one of the sub systems, but have already replaced it, then reran the scans, and they came up clean this time. I think we've gotten everything, did I miss anything guys?" Jamie asked the others.

"No, that was it." They answered.

"Very good. When did you get finished?"

"We finished just a few moments before you came in Sir. We were just figuring out what we should do next, since it's an hour 'til dinner time. We were going to go out onto the hull, after telling you of course, and make sure that it was good and clean." Pete answered.

"Okay, go ahead and get suited up then, don't let me stop you. You should know though that we're in a possibly hostile location, we're well hidden though, so should be out of danger. Remember to stay within sight of each other, and call if you need anything. Oh and after dinner, instead of regular classes, we're going exploring on the asteroids for a while. Make sure to grab your scanners and taggers."

"Yes Sir!" They all said happily.

"Oh and Sir, you still haven't taken the gun back." Franky said.

"Okay, keep it for now, soon you'll all be provided with them anyway. They'll all be set to stun, as yours is now, and they'll be locked at that setting, unless I give them the command to do otherwise."

"Okay Sir. Thanks." Franky answered.

The boys went on their way to clean the hull off. After getting suited up, they went outside and started the search. They cleaned off a few patches, but actually found a small damaged portion.

"Captain, we found some damage to the hull of the ship." Pete said after calling him.

"Okay, I'll show all of you together this evening how to repair it when we go out. How is everything else otherwise?" Captain Casey asked.

"Good, it's all cleaned, so we're coming in now." Pete answered.

"Okay, dinner should be ready in a few minutes so come in as soon as you can."

"Yes Sir!" They all answered.

A few minutes later the boys were back inside the ship and getting out of their gear, then headed to the dining hall.

Will, Dillon and Alex had all decided to lay back and rest for a bit, because they were tired. They did not sleep, but they relaxed somewhat. Finally after an hour or two, they had had enough, so got up.

"Well guys, let's go explore our new home." Will said.

"Okay!" They both said almost excitedly, the excitement starting to set in already.

So for the next couple hours the boys explored the ship. They met a few of the boys on the way and learned their names, but they were always on their way somewhere, so could not stay and chat. They had ended up on the bridge at one point, and stood and watched the other boys all working together. They did stop and chat a few times, but they were too busy watching screens and relaying information back and forth, that the boys soon felt in the way.

"Well those guys work well together, but I was starting to feel like I was in the way." Will told his brothers.

"Me too." They both said.

"Oh well, I'm sure that soon enough we'll be right in there with them." Will said.

"I don't know if I can learn all that!" Alex said.

"I bet you can. The youngest boy in there was about eight or nine and he was working just like everyone else in there, and we both know how smart you are. And besides, they haven't been out here that long, so they can't have been doing this for too long, the captain said they're all ex street kids."

"I still don't know." Alex reiterated.

They continued searching and exploring and talking to each other, and to whomever they came across during their travels. Soon though Captain Casey was calling them to dinner.

Everyone entered the dining hall and took their seats, then Warren and Kelly got everything served, and they ate together. Once they were all done, the captain stood and got everyone's attention.

"Okay guys, a couple things for you. We're going to go out and explore an asteroid or two this evening and see if we can find anything useful. Second I've decided on the new team alignments. Donny and Franky won't belong to a specific team any longer, nor will Will. Will has taken the position of teacher to teach all of you, and Donny and Franky will be Senior Team Leaders. Jamie and Pete, I understand that this leaves you out a bit, but have no fear, you'll also get other opportunities, as time goes by, to prove yourselves to me, same as all of you, even though you've all proven much to me already, more than I could've hoped. The teams are now as such. Team one, Brady's team leader with Tony, Jesse, Kelvin, and Alex. Team two, Jamie's still team leader with Marty, Dillon, Teddy, and Devon. Team three, Tristan's team leader with Ryan, Matthew, Cullen, and Kelly. And finally team four, there are no changes, so it's Pete as team leader, with Lance, Bobby, Brad, and Zach. Are there any questions about the team alignments so far?"

"Yes, will my brothers and I get to stay together tonight as you said we would." Will asked.

"Yes, it's too late to change everything around tonight, and we have something more important and fun to do than moving rooms around tonight. We'll do all that in the morning. I'll also have a surprise at that time for you." Captain Casey said cryptically.

"What's the surprise Sir." Will asked, the others groaned, knowing the response.

"If I told you that, it wouldn't be a surprise, now would it? So you'll just have to wait. The others have all finally learned this, I tell nothing 'til it's time." Captain Casey said with a grin.

"Okay Sir." Will said, not seeming to be bothered by this.

"So everyone come with me then, and we can go learn how to repair hull damage first, and then go exploring. Everyone remember to bring your scanners and taggers, I'll get you three yours in a few minutes." Captain Casey said to all the seasoned crew, and added to his three new crew.

The boys all got up and followed the captain. He made one quick stop at a supply locker, and got the three new boys their scanners, taggers, helmets and gloves, and then they were off. They reached the nearest airlock and all piled in, they barely fit now with the added three people and they all kept bashing elbows. They all got into their gear, then grabbed the propulsion packs, and they headed out, after giving the three new boys instructions. This was done quickly, since Captain Casey did not have to do it by himself, because Donny and Franky helped as well.

"This is really neat Sir. Our parents never let us go outside the ship, even though we all had suits, we still weren't allowed, they said it was too dangerous." Will said.

"And it is. I have some very strict rules about this, and I'll tell you three in a minute. I however am not like most parents, I'm not one of course, but I believe that even children should be allowed to try anything that an adult does, at their own pace. And really, this is no more dangerous than almost anything else we can do in space. Now for the rules. You're to stay in contact at all times, you're to stay within sight of me at all times, and you're not to come out by yourself at any time, unless it's an emergency, or you have my permission first, no matter what. Any questions on that?"

"No, none Sir, since it makes perfect sense, right Dillon and Alex?"

"Yes Sir!" The two boys answered.

"Good! Now Pete, where was this massive damage you were telling me about?" Captain Casey asked.

"Sir, you know I told it was minor damage. Grownups, they just never listen to us kids!" Pete said all huffy, but could not hold it and laughed, everyone else followed.

"Sorry, what was that, I wasn't paying attention?" Captain Casey laughed. "Glad you still have a sense of humor. So, show me to it please?"

Pete led everyone to where the damage was, near the nose of the ship.

"Pretty minor damage yes, but see how it's peeling, that could cause major damage, if not repaired. In this case the metal is still all intact see, so using this tool we can reshape and weld the seam back together. In more extreme cases, a new piece of hull plating might be required to finish it off, if that's the case, you ask, and we can teleport the required piece out to you. Gather round and I'll show you how this works, it's pretty self explanatory though."

Captain Casey worked for maybe a minute and repaired the minor damage, showing the boys exactly how the hand held device worked all the time he was working, and explaining everything as he went.

"So, that's all there is to it! From here on out, this tool is a required item on at least one person while inspecting the hull. Let's go explore an asteroid now. Which one was the most promising Tristan?"

"Should be that one right there, second one to the right and back a ways, it's about two hundred kilometers from us, so only a minute or two away."

"Okay, lead the way Tristan."

Tristan quickly led the others over to the asteroid, and when they landed on the dark side, Franky immediately noticed something of interest. He went over to look at it, scanned it, and sure enough, he found a huge rock of Nutronium.

"Sir, I found a huge rock of almost pure Nutronium over here, it's massive." Franky said with excitement.

"Yes, you did and yes, it's big. Good find. Tag it and keep looking. Any precious metals or Nutronium, tag it, and we'll teleport it later. Everyone make sure and call me if you need any help." Captain Casey said.

For the next two hours the boys and their captain all searched the asteroid. It was one of the best finds they had, or ever would find. It had so many metal laden rocks and Nutronium rocks that almost all the boys ran out of tags.

"Well guys, it's going to take the better part of the morning tomorrow just to teleport all this, and then to sort through it all, but this is an awesome find. We have enough Nutronium just in that first rock to power a city for almost a month. We also have probably enough metals in these rocks to reinforce the whole ship if we wanted to. Let's get back home." Captain Casey said happily.

They flew back to the ship, and as soon as they were safely inside, they all got their space gear off. Captain Casey decided to just get all the stuff inside right away, so led the boys to the cargo bay, programmed the teleporter to grab all the tagged items, and hit the button to get all the new rocks inside. The bay was almost filled by the time the teleporter got all the various rocks. It was a good thing that the teleporter had almost no weight limit for that one big rock, because it would probably have exceeded it. Captain Casey was wondering what he was going to do with it, because he did not have the equipment in stock to cut it, and it was so large that it would be impossible to store, but he also could not leave it, since it was such an incredible find.

"Well, it looks like our exercise room is filled up. Now don't get your hopes up, we're going to do our calisthenics in the dining hall for this evening and tomorrow morning, until we get this all cleaned up. So come on. And remember, you don't have to keep up with me, just do what I do at your own pace."

Almost an hour later, the boys all exited the dining hall tired and sore, but not so much as the three new boys were, they had never done anything anywhere near that much exercise before, and even Kelly was able to out pace Will.

"Well gentlemen, it's getting late already, so up to your rooms, clean up, and then it's lights out in an hour and a half." Captain Casey commanded.

"Yes Sir!" They all said.

They all headed up to their rooms for the night, and as they all entered their rooms, they started talking.

"Man, did you see those poor boys! Did we really look that bad when we started?" Tristan asked.

"If not worse. I seem to remember most of us barely walked out of our first few sessions, boy are they going to be tired in the morning though." Donny chuckled.

"Yeah, they will be. Are you excited about becoming a senior team leader?" Tristan asked Donny.

"Kind of yes, but kind of no. I have no idea what I'll have to be doing. How about you, are you excited about becoming a team leader?" Donny asked Tristan.

"Same, I know what's required, well sort of, you guys don't really have to do a whole lot, other than make sure we're all doing what we're supposed to be doing." Tristan answered.

"It's not so easy as it seems. You guys are really easy to get along with, so it's pretty easy most of the time. Just remember though, that the captain expects you to handle most of the minor things, and they're to listen to you. I don't think you'll have a problem."

"Thanks. Let's go get washed up, then I'm going to bed early." Tristan said.

"Yeah me too, after we clean up that is." Donny said.

Meanwhile, in the room where the new team members were spending the night.

"Oh man, I hurt so bad, the others looked as if it was no big deal." Dillon said.

"Yeah, me too. I think they've been doing this a lot longer though, so they must be more used to it. The captain though, man is he ever good. I also have no idea how they can continue to have a conversation while working like that." Will said.

"No idea. I want a nice long hot shower, and then I'm going to bed." Dillon said.

"Me too." Alex said.

"Me three." Will said.

The three boys stripped down and went in to the shower, and stood under the hot water for a long time before washing off. Barely getting dry, the boys all fell into bed naked, and were fast asleep without even turning off the lights.

Captain Casey sat at his desk in his office and did up the logs for the day, and sent a notice to WSEC and his parents, saying they had rescued three young men, who have accepted positions on his ship. After making sure that everything was set for the evening, he too went and had his shower. He laid back and relaxed and read some before calling lights out, and then went to bed himself, once everyone's lights went off.

Saturday morning after their morning exercises and breakfast, Captain Casey led all the boys down to the cargo bay to start the tedious task of sorting through their finds from yesterday.

"Sir, I have a problem." Dillon said.

"What's that Dillon?" Captain Casey asked, suspecting what the problem was.

"I can barely move, I hurt so bad."

"I know, but the best thing to do is to keep moving, take it easy, don't strain yourself, but just keep moving. Take care of the smaller things, you and your brothers, we'll get the rest, but try to keep moving. If you were to stop, it'd make it worse. Once we finish, you three can go up for a nice cool shower, I promise that'll help."

"Yes Sir, I'll try." Dillon said, and his brothers nodded as well.

"Good." Captain Casey smiled warmly.

For the next few hours, they slowly worked through all the various rocks, first sorting them as to what they were and then getting them stored in the various locations. All the Nutronium was unable to fit in the storage cases that they had, so the rest, as well as the large rock, was left in the cargo bay, but was protected by a portable shield, to protect it from getting hit by anything that could cause it to explode, because that would be a very bad thing indeed.

They still had an hour until lunch, so Captain Casey sent the brothers up to their room to get a nice cool shower.

"Tonight you guys will all be in your new teams, and the senior team leaders in their new rooms, so we have to get a few things moved around, and I think that we can do that while Will and his brothers are getting cleaned up. Those who have to move, grab your things, and move it to the new room that you'll be in. The teams will stay in the same rooms. Those who don't have to do any moving, help those who do. While you're doing that, I'm going to go get the new rooms ready. Just call when you're ready."

"What do we do with our things Captain?" Donny asked.

"Just bring them out into the hall and set them down for now." Donny and Franky nodded, and went to help out.

The boys all went to take care of what they were told. They were wondering why they had to go through all that though, since they had hardly any belongings at all, just a few uniforms, one change of civilian clothes, and they figured their blankets and pillows as well.

166

It took them maybe two minutes to get everything, and they all met out in the hall. The boys who were switching rooms went to their new rooms, and their new team mates followed them, and helped them to put their things away.

Donny and Franky waited for a couple minutes, before Captain Casey showed up out of one of the rooms across the hall.

"Okay guys, Donny, you're in here, and Franky the one next door, and then Will will be right next to you. Go check out your new rooms."

"You mean we get our own rooms?" Franky asked in shock.

"Yes, but remember that with them comes more responsibility, and now that you are higher up, that means you have more to lose if you fail, so don't fail yourselves." Captain Casey warned.

"Speaking of which Sir, what exactly are our new responsibilities?" Donny asked.

"Mainly what you're doing now, except the team leaders come to you first, and if you can't deal with something, then you come to me. Consider yourselves links in the chain of command. There'll be other duties from time to time, but for now that's it." Captain Casey said.

"Okay, thanks Sir." Franky said.

The boys both went into their new rooms and found virtually identical rooms. There was a single queen sized bed, a dresser, a desk, a wardrobe, all of it in nice woods and a nice sized bathroom, with tub and shower. Both boys were equally happy with their new rooms. They spent many minutes looking at their new homes, and then went out to the hall, both boys almost at the same time.

"Will they be suitable?" Captain Casey asked.

"Yes Sir!" They both stated emphatically.

"Good."

The boys had all come out of their rooms, and asked to see the new senior team leaders rooms, so the boys proudly showed the others their rooms, half in each. They were jealous of course, but knew they deserved them, even Jamie knew the other two boys were better suited to the positions than he was. Will, Dillon and Alex came out a few minutes later, looking a lot better than they had.

"So, do you feel any better?" Captain Casey asked.

167

"Yes Sir, lots better, thanks. I'm still sore, but no longer like my legs are going to fall off any minute." Will answered with a smile, the other two just agreed with him.

"Good, it's almost time for lunch, but let's get you boys situated in your new rooms first. Go get your things, and we can get you in your new homes."

The boys turned around and headed back into the room that they had been using, picked their things up, and came back out. Captain Casey led Will to his room, while Brady took Alex, and Jamie took Dillon to their rooms.

"This is a very nice room Sir." Will said after looking it over for a few minutes.

"Yes, these are all nice rooms. These are the officers suites and they're much nicer than the dorm style rooms across the hall. Mine is across the hall, but it's a larger suite than these are. It's of course on the end, so I get some nice windows, whereas most of these rooms don't have any windows, but the captains suite of course is always the nicest. Well, let's go get the others and go eat, since lunch should be about ready." Captain Casey said.

"Sounds good Sir." Will said.

The captain and Will left the room, found the others waiting for them, so they all headed down to the dining hall for lunch. They all sat and ate their lunch. The senior team leaders and Will, as well as Warren, were now at the head table.

"So Warren, I have a question for you. Would you mind taking on an apprentice and teach him all you know of being a doctor? Will here is university level already, and he wants to be a doctor, so I was wondering if you'd help him out." Captain Casey asked once they were finished lunch.

"Sure, it'd give me something to do when I'm bored, I've got almost nothing to do other than cooking most of the time, so it'll be nice. How often we talking here."

"I was thinking three to four hours a day six days a week. Between lunch and dinner would be about perfect." Captain Casey answered.

"Sounds good to me Sir. So Will, you're really university level already, that's really impressive?"

"Yes Sir, my parents believed in very good schooling, and no fooling around. Even while we were in captivity, they continued to do our schooling, since we were at least allowed to use computers still. My brothers are both at least three years ahead of their peers already, and Dillon will be ready for university by age fifteen, or sixteen at the latest. I look forward to working with you. When do we get to start Captain?"

"I think Monday is a good enough time to start, I think tonight we're all going to take a break and watch some movies, and Sundays are always our day of rest anyway, unless an emergency arises of course." Captain Casey answered.

"Okay Sir." Will answered.

"Warren, are you going to join us for movies this evening?" Captain Casey asked.

"Yes, I probably will, after I get everything cleaned up of course."

"Okay, see you there. Okay guys, let's go watch some movies." Captain Casey said.

The boys were all happy about this, so followed the captain to the theatre, and everyone let the three newest crew members pick out the first movie of the night. Once it was queued up, they all took their seats around the captain, and watched the movie. About half way through the first movie, Warren showed up, sat next to the captain and joined the others in the movie. They enjoyed their movies immensely, and half way through the third movie of the night, half the crew was asleep. It was difficult, but all the bigger boys grabbed all the smaller boys and carried them to their rooms, the captain and Warren each grabbing one each as well. After tucking the boys in, the adults wished the remaining boys a good night, then went to their bedrooms, and they too headed straight to bed.

The next few days went by pretty quickly for the guys. Sunday was a slow day, and other than their morning and evening exercises, they did nothing. Monday they got back under way, and the new schedule was in place. So half the crew were in class, and the other half the crew were manning the ship. The first day Will was a bit nervous, but he did very well. Captain Casey would sit in on his class for a little while, to make sure everything was going fine, and then slip back out. In the afternoons, after lunch, Will would spend the rest of the afternoon with Warren, while he taught Will everything about being a doctor. They started on the basics, and worked quickly up from there, Warren was surprised by how much the boy already knew. By Thursday, a pattern was already set, and everyone was getting used to it. The boys liked it a lot more, because this way it seemed to allow them just a bit more free time in the evenings.

CHAPTER 15

A SMALL TASTE OF BATTLE

Everyone was just getting onto the swing of things again, and even the new boys were starting to feel as part of the group. Every day they had some sort of emergency preparedness drill as well, and they were all doing very well, and though everyone truly hoped that they would never have to use the skills that they were getting very good at, each and every one of them on the ship knew that eventually their skills would in fact be called upon. It just so happened though, as fate always seems to want, things come at you when you least expect it, and whether you think you are ready for it or not. On this particular morning, they started out just as every other does, and just shortly after breakfast, their communications terminal pinged with an emergency request.

"UE1, this is WSEC, we have a bit of an emergency we'd like for you to help us with." The voice asked.

"On screen." Said Captain Casey, and the screen was activated. "What is it WSEC?" Captain Casey asked once the image of Admiral Daily appeared.

"Well Captain Casey and crew, we have a ship about ten light years from you that was hit pretty hard by a Qaralon war ship, they won, but they're in pretty rough condition. We'd like for you to go render aid. Are you fully supplied, and is your crew ready for this, because they're in Qaralon space. They were searching for a ship said to have captives on it."

"We're certainly ready Sir, and we're fully supplied for a situation such as this. Give my crew the coordinates, and we'll be there as soon as possible. What ship is it by the way?"

"Great, after seeing the playbacks of the battle simulation, I figured there was little doubt, but I always ask. It's the UE10, I've sent the coordinates to your people, they should have them now."

"We do Sir." Matthew said.

"Thanks Matthew. As you heard Admiral, we have it, tell them we're on our way. We'll get in contact with them as soon as we're able to do so." Captain Casey said.

They signed off after saying their goodbyes.

"Navigation, you know the coordinates, get us there as quick as you can!" Captain Casey commanded.

"Yes Sir!" Dillon answered.

"Thanks, how long will it take guys." Captain Casey asked.

"Just a second Sir, working that out now . . . . It should take roughly six hours Sir, we have to go around a couple stars." Jamie answered.

"Okay, Donny, you have the bridge. Call me if you need anything please." Captain Casey said.

"Yes Sir!" Donny said.

Jonathon went first to the infirmary to notify Warren.

"Okay Doc, looks like you're about to earn your extravagant paycheck. We have a ship in trouble, so you and your supplies may be needed, so pack up and be ready in approximately six hours, make sure to bring Will with you, fully loaded as well of course." Captain Casey said.

"Will do Captain." Warren answered, already working to be ready to go before Captain Casey even finished talking.

The captain turned and left and headed to the classroom next.

"Hello Captain, can we help you with something?" Will asked.

"Actually, yes you can, in a few hours though. I'm just coming up to tell you guys that we have a mission. Finish your class first, you have the time. We have to rescue a ship that's in hostile territory, they got beat pretty hard, so as soon as class is over, find me boys, and I'll have work for you all to do, Will, you find Warren as soon as you're finished as well."

"Yes Sir!" They all said.

Captain Casey then went to his office and called the UE10 up.

"Captain Casey, good to see you. I hear we're going to be rescued by a bunch of kids." The captain of the UE10 said.

"You bet, the best trained there are, they have me as a captain, what would you expect." Captain Casey grinned to his old friend. "So how bad are you Evan."

"You always were full of crap. However, after seeing your boys beat the snot out of that simulation, I'd have to agree with you. We're pretty bad though, there's a hole where our engines used to be, so we're barely limping along on auxiliary power, and we haven't a rock of Nutronium left."

"Ouch, that had to hurt. How about your crew?" Jonathon asked gently.

"There are injured all over the place, even I myself have a broken arm I'm sure. We lost no less than ten, when the engine room pretty much disappeared. I have no idea though how much, because the scanners are down. The only good thing is, we do have a spare engine, and it's fine, but I have no one to put it in, everyone's either gone or injured." Evan said, trying to keep his spirits up.

"Sorry about that, you had a top notch crew, and that's saying a lot. Good thing WSEC insists on us carrying spare engines and power systems. My crew will be able to help, they've been fully trained on how to replace an engine, and I have so much Nutronium, it's overflowing into my cargo hold, so we'd be happy to share."

"That's good to hear. So, how far out are you?"

"We should be there in six hours or less, hold in there. How are your weapons holding out, are you going to be okay if they come back?"

"We have weapons, but no scanners, so it could be a little tough to target. We can do it manually, if we have to, but honestly, if they spot us, and we're sitting ducks right now, we're probably dead meat, so just get here as quick as you can please?" Evan asked, not liking his position any.

"If we can squeeze any more speed out of this old lady, we will. We'll be there as soon as we can, and at least feel good in knowing that we'll leave no stone unturned looking for you, if you're feared captured." Jonathon said.

"Thanks. If we get surrounded I'll surrender then, and we'll try and leave some form of crumb trail for you. See you in a bit, we're going to do what we can here while we wait, but like I said, most of us are injured, including our doctor, and our nurse was in the engine room helping someone who was burned, so you know where she is."

"Hold in there, we'll be as fast as we can, so see you in a bit." Jonathon said and signed off.

Everyone, except Donny, met down in the dining hall an hour later and had a real quick lunch.

"Okay, give me Donny's lunch, and everyone come up to the bridge with me. Don't worry about cleaning right now Warren, we don't have time for that." Captain Casey said.

"No problem Sir, I got the food though." Warren said.

They all followed the captain up to the bridge, and as soon as the captain walked in, Donny rose out of the captains chair, and took a seat in his chair. Warren handed him his food, and he started to eat as the captain spoke.

"Captain Evan Arthurs and his crew of the UE10 are pretty banged up, and we're on our way there to give aid. Many of his crew are injured, and at least ten were lost when the engine room was blown out of the ship. Everyone is to provide aid where they're best suited to do so. You all know your strong and your weak points, so go where you're needed most. Their ship is nearly identical to ours, so finding your way around should be easy enough to do. In a few moments, each and every one of you is going to be given a gun, they'll be on the stun setting, and only myself, or the senior team leaders will be able to tell them to go to maximum setting, which will kill most any being. We should be there in a little over four hours now."

"Three now Sir, I was able to find a slightly faster route, and shaved nearly an hour off the times." Donny interjected.

"Better yet, a little over three hours then. We need to get whatever supplies ready that we'll need to help the UE10. Franky, you and team two are to stay here and protect us if necessary. So you guys stay here and get this ship ready for battle, just in case it's needed, so the rest of you come with me. Warren and Will, you go get what you need, and get it to the cargo bay, so that as soon as we're in teleportation range, we can get in there with all our gear and get to work." Captain Casey said.

"Yes Sir!" Everyone said.

For the next two hours, everyone worked feverishly to get everything ready. Warren and Will were done their stuff first, so helped the others as best they could. In the cargo bay they had all the Nutronium, that was not yet packed, ready to go, except the huge rock, all the medical supplies needed were ready and waiting, and as much of the metal as they could spare was there as well. Hopefully the UE10 had some good metal on board, but if not, they would fabricate what they needed from the collected metals, if they had to. It was a large pile for sure, but it was organized for ease of sorting later. They had a little over half an hour left to wait before they could teleport in. Captain Casey decided to call to see if they were still there.

"Hey Evan, good to see you're still there. How's everything going so far." Captain Casey asked.

"We were able to get scanners on line a couple hours ago, and I hate to tell you this, but it's going to be a photo finish. There are three Qaralon ships headed our way, and they're about as far away as you are. We'll start lobbing everything at them we can, even if we have to get out on the hull and start throwing things at them. I hope your boys are ready for this." Evan warned.

"You wait and see what these boys are made of, I think they'll even surprise you. We'll teleport our supplies in, and then as soon as we get there, we'll come in as well, and we'll let my crew take care of the Qaralon." Jonathon told him.

"I hope you're right. This could get real messy, real quick." Evan said, sounding almost sick.

"I am, have you ever known me to be anything but right." Jonathon said with a smile.

"I'm glad you're in such a good mood, but I guess you're a lot more confident than I am." Evan said.

"You haven't seen these boys in action, I have, you have little to worry about. I'd say that I bet they had them beat within ten minutes, but I wouldn't want to steal your money." Jonathon grinned.

"No, I wouldn't want you to steal my money either. See you in a few, and it looks like you just might get here before they do, you're quite a bit faster than they are, thankfully." Evan said.

"Okay, stay well." Jonathon said, and then they signed off.

Captain Casey went up to the bridge to go tell everyone the news.

"Guys, I don't know if you've noticed yet or not, though I hope you have, but there are three Qaralon ships headed for the UE10, but we should get there first, so be prepared for battle. From now until we're clear, we're in full battle mode."

"Yes Sir, Dillon pointed it out as soon as it came up on the screen, and we have everything prepared. Are you guys all prepared down there?" Franky asked.

"Yes, in twenty minutes we teleport everything over, and then we follow about five minutes later. Are you all ready, you have the bridge, so I need to know if even one of you doesn't think you're ready for this."

"I'm not sure Sir. I hardly know how to use the systems, and I feel in the way while these guys are rushing around me doing things." Dillon said honestly.

"I didn't figure you'd be ready for this yet, you haven't had quite enough training on the ship operations yet, thank you for admitting it though. Donny, I need another good man up here, who do you recommend?"

"Ryan Sir." Donny answered without a thought.

"Okay, Ryan, you and Dillon will be trading places today. Dillon you stick with Donny, Alex, you're with me, the rest of you know what to do. Let's go to the cargo bay and wait there. Franky, you have the ship."

"Yes Sir!" Everyone said.

Fifteen minutes later the captain teleported the supplies over, and then five minutes later they followed. Evan was there to meet them.

"Captain Arthurs, good to see you again. I wish it was under better circumstances, but so be it. My guys will go where they're needed, and do what they can. How much metal do you have to patch the hole, we sent what we could, but I don't think it's going to be enough, given how large that hole is?" Captain Casey asked.

"Yes, it's really good to see you as well, and right on time too. We have lots, hopefully enough to patch it up. I fear though that it won't be an easy chore, as most of the floors and walls around it

are totaled as well. My people will help as best they can though."
Captain Arthurs said.

By now the captains were the only ones in the cargo bay, and
they decided they should be doing other things as well.

"I'm going to go to the infirmary and help out, because I'm a
med tech, so I think that's where I'm needed the most."

"I need to go there as well, I need to get this looked at and fixed
up, and then I have to get to the engine room to help there."

"We'll get you done first then, and I can take care of that
myself."

The two captains took off as quick as, they could to the ships
medical center. Meanwhile, on the UE1, the boys were battle ready
and raring to go.

"Okay guys, let's go meet the Qaralon, and tell them we're the
line they can't hope to cross. I don't want them on screen, voice
only, we might do something we probably won't regret if any of us
actually sees them." Franky said.

"Yes Sir!" They all said, and in total agreement.

"Qaralon ships, this is the UE1, don't come any closer. If you
have any captives on board, drop your shields, and we'll teleport
them over immediately. Failure to comply will result in your
ships being permanently disabled." Teddy said firmly into the
communications system.

"Little girl, we not here play games, for insult us, we capture you
ship as well." The voice said.

"Your loss, but for your information, I'm a boy. This is your
final warning, come any closer, and we open fire. Kill your engines
and drop your shields, immediately." Teddy again said, even more
firmly this time, gritting his teeth the entire time.

"No, we get others later, they go nowhere, you to surrender you
ship, or be destroy." The voice said.

"What, and harm such nice young tender meat, we're all young
on this ship, and I bet we'd taste so good. You should try and
capture us, or are you to weak?" Teddy taunted.

"We enjoy feasting on you, surrender now, and we promise kill
you fast." The voice said.

"You surrender now, or we promise to kill you slow." Teddy said,
enjoying himself just a bit too much.

They did not say another word, they just fired a warning shot.

"Well, we tried to tell you, now you're toast." Teddy said, almost giddily and killed the communications.

"Open fire, disable them only, low yield." Franky yelled out.

The boys worked their magic, and flew circles around the Qaralon, firing at every vulnerable spot they could find. Not one of the missiles fired at the UE1 even came close to hitting, whereas almost every missile the boys fired hit the ship that it was intended for, and one even hit a ship when it was destined for another. They purposely kept drawing the fight away from the UE10, to make sure that nothing missed and went their way, and inside of seven minutes, the Qaralon ships were sitting dead in space, their engines and power systems disabled, probably permanently.

From the outside looking in, it had appeared to have been a seriously lopsided battle to start, but within seconds, the reality of it could not have been more stark. The boys in control of the ship were dancing in and around the three enemy ships with speed and grace, hitting them just enough to tell them that they had no hope of winning, but never once did they go for the kill, even though there were several opportunities to do so. The Qaralon ships tried to keep moving, but with the amount that the boys kept the UE1 moving, it looked as if the Qaralon were standing still. Once the last ship was downed, but not dropped, the boys backed off slightly and they opened up communications.

"We warned you to surrender, now, we're only going to ask this once, do you have prisoners aboard your ships." Teddy asked meanly.

"What you going do us?" The voice asked fearfully.

"Answer the question, and we might think of telling you."

"We have no captives." The voice said, clearly defeated.

"If I scan your ships and find you're lying to me, I'll cut your ships into pieces, now answer me truthfully." Teddy hissed, very angry, since he already knew there was, because they had already found them.

"You not dare. If had captives, you killing them." The voice said in challenge.

"Ask them for yourselves, if it meant the destruction of a waste species such as you, they'd gladly die. I dare you, go. And before you deny it, I know each of your ships has at least four captives, now, don't try lying to me again, because I can and will destroy you. Just look at our ship, do we have any damage, now, look at yours, and tell me who do you think will win?" Teddy hissed in anger.

"Fine, we release them, you transport them out here." The voice said.

"Wise decision. Now, we're going to be here for at the very least a few days working on the ship that your people tried to destroy, there's to be no calling for help, we'll be monitoring everything, and if there's so much as one stray signal coming from any of your ships, we'll destroy you on the spot, am I making myself perfectly clear." Teddy snapped.

"Do we have choice." The voice asked sullenly.

"Oh you always have a choice. The choices are; believe me and do what I demand, or try me and find out what I'm like when I'm mad." Teddy said happily.

"Fine, as long you not destroy us. You prisoners ready be teleported over." It said.

"Good, teleporting now." Teddy said.

All of a sudden sixteen people were on the bridge of the UE1. They looked around for a minute, and then looked onto the view screen, and saw what they wanted to know.

"Where's the captain, where are all the adults, and who's in charge here." Asked the person who apparently was the senior person.

"Sir, my name's Franky, the captain is aboard the UE10 helping out. I'm in charge while he's gone, and there are only two adults on the entire crew anyway, because this is a training mission. We're the ones who rescued you." Franky answered softly, already disliking the posture of the man.

"Boy, don't you dare lie to me, who beat down the Qaralon." He said with a bit of a bite.

"Sir, if you don't believe me, you're welcome to ask, however don't ever call me a liar. It was this ship, and this crew you're looking at, that rescued all of you. I can play back the battle recordings if you'd like, I think you'll find the only people on board are in fact the six of us, and we're the ones who did the fighting." Franky said gently.

"I'm taking command of this ship, this is ludicrous." He said.

"Sir, if you even think of attempting to do so, I'll be forced to shoot you where you stand, we're all armed, you aren't, and we're all a very good aim as well. If you insist on trying us, so be it." Franky said, and they all pulled their weapons.

"This is insubordination, I'm a captain, and I have full rights to take over an unfit crew." He said.

"No Sir, you aren't the captain of this ship, and you have no rights at all upon it. This isn't a military ship, it's a private ship, did you notice which one it is. It's the UE1, owned by Admiral Casey, and is currently being used by Captain Casey as a training ship, now stand down, immediately." Franky hissed out.

"I want to speak to your captain!" The captain spat out.

"He's indisposed at this moment, they're busy fixing that ship to get it flight ready again. You'll now be shown to some quarters, so that you may clean up, and get properly dressed and rested, however, you aren't to leave those quarters unless asked to do so." Franky answered.

"You wouldn't dare put me under house arrest." The captain said dangerously.

"Actually, I would. Now if you had've come in here acting more civil and rational, and maybe even a bit thankful, we would've offered you comfortable rooms and lounges. It's your actions, and your actions alone, that got you all into this, and I hope that the others are all very displeased with you. And they look it too." Franky snarled.

They did not look too happy at all, but he was the most senior captain of the bunch, so he had the say. The boys pointed them all out the corridor, not wanting to get in a lift with them, and took them to the nearest quarters. They were all shown into four rooms and the doors were closed and locked.

"Well, that was enjoyable. First we save their necks, and then we have to put up with his pig headed attitude. I think he's ashamed that he was saved by a bunch of kids. Well he should be grateful." Franky steamed.

"No kidding." The others said as one.

The boys all headed back to the bridge, Franky still muttering under his breath about the idiot, as he kept calling the captain. Back on the UE10, work was getting done, and the captains had both made it to the infirmary.

"So, let's see how this arm of yours is."

Captain Arthurs sat in a chair that was available, and Jonathon grabbed his scanner and took a look.

"It only appears to be cracked, you're lucky. I'll give you the bone mender, and it should be okay in a few hours or so. Just keep wearing the sling." Jonathon told Evan.

"Thanks." Evan said.

"Warren, how's everything in here." Captain Casey asked.

"Doing fine. I've already sent a few people on their way, with some minor repairs. There are a few concussions, one of these guys has a broken leg, and another a broken arm. There are a few other people I haven't even checked out yet. I had to make some room, so got the real quick ones out of here first. Now that you're here, and the captain's good to go, let's get busy, we have lots of work to do, and not enough time to do it."

"I can agree with that, you guys get my people working again, and call me if you need any help." Captain Arthurs said.

"Will do. Where is your doctor by the way, I forgot to ask the people in here." Warren asked.

"Good question. Oh there he is over there. He's the one on the floor, apparently passed out." Captain Arthurs answered.

"Thanks, I'll get him going next." Warren said.

"Thanks again Doctor and Captain Casey, I'll get out of the way. If I see anyone with injuries, I'll send them up so they can get a number." Captain Arthurs said.

"Okay, thanks. And you're welcome." Warren said.

About ten minutes later, the captain started wondering how his crew was holding up.

"UE1, this is Captain Casey, as soon as you get this message, and are able to answer, please contact me." Captain Casey said into his communicator.

"What would you like captain." Teddy answered right away.

"Oh hi, I didn't expect you to be able to answer. Are you guys busy?"

"No Sir, the Qaralon have been disabled, and we got sixteen prisoners of war from them, and they promptly insulted us completely, so they're under house arrest, until you get here to listen to the conversation, and decide what to do with them." Teddy answered.

"Oh really, who are they?" Captain Casey asked.

"Not a clue Sir, after the captain had words with Franky, we weren't in the mood to talk to them and go into pleasantries, the guy was a real jerk, and called us all liars. I actually thought the guy was going to attack us, we all had our guns ready though." Teddy answered.

"Okay then, I'll tear a strip off of whomever it is later then." Captain Casey said, also a little upset at the news.

"We'll keep an eye out on everything, and we have no fear of the Qaralon we disabled calling for help, I scared them so bad they think that if they even breath, we'll slaughter them where they sit." Teddy said with a smile.

"Good boy." Captain Casey said, and then signed off.

"He's right, you were good, you sounded downright nasty while talking to the Qaralon, I think you should be our com man from here on out, no one 'll mess with you." Franky said.

"Yeah well, I kind of meant it, but to tell you quite honestly, I didn't really like it all that much. I think I'll let someone else do that from now on if I can. I liked how you dealt with the supposed captain as well." Teddy smiled.

"Yeah, well, I kind of meant it too. He really was arrogant. If you didn't care for having to do that, I'm sure someone else would be happy to do it next time. Well let's get on those scanners and make sure nothing else is coming in. Oh, and keep watch on those ships, I don't think they're really smart enough to be nearly as afraid of us as they should be." Franky laughed.

The boys did so, watching and waiting, making absolutely certain that nothing could possibly sneak up on them. On the other ship, things were getting done, albeit slowly, but at least a whole lot faster than anyone thought it could have gone, given how bad they had been before.

CHAPTER 16

5 AGAINST 1,
PRETTY GOOD ODDS

As soon as Captain Casey turned from speaking to Teddy, he got started on someone else, trying to get them fixed up. As he did so, Warren asked, "So how's it going on the ship Sir?"

"Really well. They disabled the Qaralon ships already, they also have sixteen humans that were captured, but the lead captain really insulted the boys, so they put the POW's on house arrest. I can't wait to get back to see this." Captain Casey said with a grin.

"But Sir, there were three ships coming in, and we've been here, what maybe twenty minutes. They can't possibly have disabled all three ships already, can they?" Warren asked in awe.

"No, you're right, they probably did it in less than ten, longer if they decided to play with them a bit." Captain Casey said with an evil grin.

"You're not joking, are you Sir?" Warren asked warily.

"Nope, those boys are good. Why do you think I had no problems leaving them to take care of three possibly hostile ships? I wouldn't have done so if I wasn't absolutely confident, we also wouldn't be out here for the same reason." Captain Casey answered with pride.

Meanwhile Donny and a few of the crew were in the engine room helping the captain of the ship, and all who could help, to rebuild it enough to put the engine in, and get it working. Some of the rest of the crew were in working on the power systems by themselves, a couple of the ships crew offered to help, but they were told that they had it under control, and to help with the bigger issue, the engine room. They were not sure what to make of it, but left them to their work, especially after their captain told them to listen to the boys.

It was mostly team four working in the power room, and they only asked for help once, and that was just to help move a large fallen beam out of the way. They ended up finishing up and restoring full power to the ship within an hour. They then went and helped the others in the engine room. Another two hours later, the engine room was closed up enough, to the point that with a portable shield put up, they could travel home at a maximum of fifty LYS. They then worked another hour, getting the engine put into place, with the help of the teleporter of course, that was now thankfully working again with the renewal of the power.

Captain Casey had joined the engine room work crew, after working in the infirmary for a few hours helping to get everyone patched up, and as each one was patched, up they were dispatched to the engine room as well. So with all the man power, they did get the engine installed and powered up. They then tried the shields, but as it turned out, they were still inoperable. The shield generator had taken a glancing blow they had not noticed before, due to all the other damage.

"Well Captain, I think this is too much to do tonight, we're all working on pure adrenalin now, and we all need to eat. We've done far more than we ever expected to get done this fast. Come on over to my ship and we'll all eat over there. You may also sleep there as well, no point in putting everyone in danger if we get attacked." Captain Casey said.

"I think we'll take you up on that offer. You're right though, we've done a lot more than I thought possible. Your boys are very good, every bit as good as you brag they are. We can work good and strong tomorrow, and see if we can't get a bit more strength added to the exterior of the engine room as well, while we see how good your boys are on shield generators." Captain Arthurs smiled appreciatively.

"Every bit as good as power systems and engine installations. Come on, let's get everyone else and get back." Captain Casey said.

It was coming up on 2000 hours, and everyone was getting very hungry and tired, so they all gladly accepted the offer to go eat and get some rest. People had of course been cooking and handing out food all day, but it was just not enough with the speed at which everyone was working. Inside half an hour everyone was on board the UE1, and both captains, both senior team leaders, Warren, Will, and the three UE10 cooks were in the kitchen cooking whatever they could to feed the large crew. There were nearly a hundred and fifty people on board now, so it was a lot to cook. Once everyone was fed, they were assigned rooms, and they all went to bed, tired and sore. Captain Casey had thought to himself briefly that he really should go talk to their guests, but he figured that they could wait until morning.

The following morning all that were in the kitchen the night before, were again there, but this time cooking up huge batches of breakfast foods. They all ate as the food was ready for them, all having a large filling breakfast.

"Evan, you and my people go ahead and go back to your ship, and do what you can, I'll be there shortly, I have something to deal with. Donny and team four you have the bridge today." Captain Casey said.

"Okay Captain, you got it. Men and women, you heard the man, let's get going." Captain Arthurs said.

"Yes Sir!" They all said.

In short order, they teleported back to the UE10. Captain Casey went to his office, and played back the battle recordings, and then the bridge recordings after the fight. He was astonished with the performance of the boys yet again. He especially loved how Teddy had handled the beasts, and taunted them so much. He was seeing red however when he heard the conversation between Franky and the supposed captain, 'well not any more, not after I get through with him,' thought Jonathon. He quickly fired copies of both recordings to his mom and dad, and said they would know what to do with them. He then went in search of the captain.

"It's about time you came to see us, this is absurd, making us wait this long." The captain said.

"And who are you to say that it's absurd to make you wait this long to talk to me, when it's you who's an arrogant self centered little man who must think he's more important than anyone else. For the way you treated my third in command, and the people under his command at the time, you're lucky I'm not throwing you out an airlock right now, without a helmet. Instead I've sent the bridge recording to WSEC, and they can deal with you. However you got to be a captain is beyond me. Now what do you have to say for yourself!" Captain Casey spat out dangerously.

"I'm a captain and I have my rights. I demanded to take over the ship, since the crew was unfit to run the ship, and when they told me they were the ones to disable the Qaralon ships, I knew they were lying, and told them so. The brats then pulled guns on us, and stuffed us in these rooms. They also put me by myself, they said that they figured that the others would kill me if I were with them. Furthermore I don't appreciate being called childish names by the likes of you." The captain spat out again.

"Oh really, you thought my crew was unfit. You also feel that the boys were lying to you, because they said they disabled the ships by themselves. And I bet that you'll call me a liar as well, when I tell you that they most certainly did. Now tell me, why is it the boys pulled guns on you, was it because you both insulted and threatened them on their own ship, or was it some other fancy reason I've yet to see. As for calling you names, I'll call you anything I wish on board my own private ship, and you'll like it." Captain Casey said smoothly.

"I was of absolutely no threat to those children, and this isn't their ship, it belongs to the government, not you. If you believe what the kids told you, then you're either really stupid, or not all there. I'm taking command of this ship, you aren't fit to command it either."

"Exactly how long have you been in captivity?" Captain Casey asked curiously.

"That's none of your business." The man said dangerously.

"Oh, but it is, again, you're on my ship, and my rules on this ship say you'll answer me, or I'll toss you out an airlock." Captain Casey said smoothly.

"You wouldn't dare. I'm Captain White, one of the most decorated captains in the fleet, and what I say, goes." Captain White said.

"Oh really, now I know who you are, and how long you've been in captivity. You were feared lost about five years ago now. I see you're still as insane today as you were then. If I remember correctly, the only reason you were ever handed a ship in the first place, was because your uncle was an admiral, and even he didn't want to do it. You alone went through more crew members than all other captains, put together, due to them not being able to deal with your attitude. As for being the most decorated, yeah, right, now there's a laugh and a half, how many times have you been demoted now, oh yeah, three times. The last time they put you back in command, they said you'd never fly again if you pulled another stupid stunt again. Not sure why, even in a bloody war, that they gave you another ship, because I wouldn't let you chauffeur my car. As for daring me, you really shouldn't. This is my ship, my rules. I'm going to take you on a little trip, but if you try anything, I'll stun you faster than you can even think, so don't try me." Captain Casey said.

"I'm far more sane than you obviously are, but seeing as how you've got the gun, and I don't, I guess I have no options." Captain White snarled.

"You're correct, you don't have any options, but it wasn't a request." Captain Casey said politely.

Captain Casey led the captain to his office and had him sit in the guest chair.

"Now, the first thing you need to know is, the war's over, we beat the Qaralon, so now we're cleaning up the mess, and finding as many people as we can to bring them home, though many won't care that I found you I bet. This ship was retired, as pride of the fleet, but as it was still in good condition, it was given to Admiral Casey, my father. I believe you know him, he had a few run ins with you, in fact, wasn't he the one to tell you that if you ever did anything so stupid again, you'd never fly. I understand you don't like him much, well the feeling's more than mutual, and you've now added me to that list. Now, because you were claimed as dead, any and all rank you had was removed, until proven otherwise, and then can be reinstated by an Admiral, or other high government official, so you obviously aren't allowed to boss me around. Given that we're the same rank anyway, that would work as well as you fighting me hand to hand, you'd lose in a heartbeat." Captain Casey said sweetly.

"You're nothing, I could take you easily." Captain White interrupted.

"Sir, and I say that loosely, you're what, twenty years older than me, fifty pounds or more heavier than me, and you've been in a cell for five years? Do you honestly believe that you could take me on and win. Now, as I was trying to say . . . ." Captain Casey started to say, but was rudely interrupted.

"I could take you any time, anywhere, you little piss ant, now quit telling me what to do, and let me get this ship underway, I have to get home." Captain White almost yelled.

"Okay, now you're just being rude. I don't stand for rudeness on my ship, one more outburst, and I'll lock you back in your room until you learn to be a decent human being. Although you should be careful, I forgot to feed the last person who called me a piss ant on my own ship. Now, as I was trying to say, I have a couple videos to show you." Captain Casey said smoothly, as if he were not just interrupted and or insulted.

Captain White obviously realized he was either in a losing fight, or just did not have a comeback, so he just curtly nodded. Captain Casey queued up the first recording of the battle the boys just won. It played all the way through.

"So as you can clearly see, the boys that you insulted, did in fact win the fight, all by themselves. Next video is even more informative, I believe you know this one, you failed three times in less than two minutes each time, did you not." Captain Casey said while queuing up the impossible battle simulation, and they watched it all the way through.

"So, that also shows you that these boys are good, they're in fact the only crew to have beaten this, other than my own father, and they did so in a better time, with less damage. They were personally congratulated by my father, and treated to a large fancy dinner for it. Next is another video, I'm sure you'll recognize." Said Captain Casey icily.

The video of the captain insulting the boys on the bridge played through.

"Now, do you see why the boys might have been just a little mad, you insulted them plain and simple, and you threatened them. They had no choice but to pull weapons on you, you were a threat. Now, I'm taking you back to your room for a while, and you're going to be good right!" Captain Casey said smoothly.

"Whatever, I think it's all fabricated anyway." Captain white said stubbornly.

"Fine! Believe what you will, you're too damned stubborn to believe anything your own mind doesn't tell you. As soon as the UE10 is fixed up, you'll be transported to their ship to be taken home, where a court marshal will surely await you."

"For what, I've done nothing wrong." Captain White demanded in a screeching high voice.

"For anything we can think to charge you for. At the very least it'll keep you from getting your commission back, and if you ever get a ship again, it'll be too soon."

Captain White lunged at Captain Casey, trying to grab the gun. Captain Casey just laughed at the stupid man, as he took one quick swing, and hit the captain in the side. He crumpled to the ground in pain, crying like a child, in fact more so than the two kids he recently had to do this to.

"Oh quit your crying you baby, it isn't becoming of an officer, and I hardly hit you. If you sit up and take a few deep breaths, the pain 'll go away quickly. Now do you believe me, I told you what would happen, and I don't lie. Next time you pull a stunt like that, I'll stun you, assuming of course I don't accidentally have it at maximum setting, in which case it might just kill you." Captain Casey taunted him.

Eventually the captain got to his feet on shaking legs, and decided to go where Captain Casey told him to go. Once the captain was locked back inside his room, Captain Casey went to the other three rooms, and talked to the others. Some were from Captain Whites last crew, while others were from other ships, they were all nice and genuine when they said that they did not like Captain White, but he had held rank, so they were unable to do anything. Captain Casey offered to let them out, and to come over to the UE10 to help rebuild it, and they all readily agreed.

"I brought a few extra people to help out, I hope you don't mind." Captain Casey told Captain Arthurs when they arrived.

"Mind, man you're brilliant! These must be the people that were rescued from the Qaralon ships! Wait, I thought there were supposed to be sixteen!" Captain Arthurs asked after doing a very quick head count.

"There was. Do you happen to remember a Captain White?" Captain Casey asked sourly.

"Yeah, he was presumed dead, and his crew lost." Captain Arthurs answered, also with a sour look.

"Yeah, well he's not. And five years in captivity seemed to have made him more arrogant and overbearing than he was before, so I kept him on house arrest. I actually was getting mad enough to pop the little, well you know what in the mouth. He actually tried to rush me, so I tapped him in the side and made him see my point of view. He actually had the nerve to insult my crew and myself, as well as call us all liars. Just talking about it makes me want to hit him. Well let's get back to work and let me get rid of some of this anger before the first person that pisses me off gets hit instead. Come on men and women, there's lots to do, the engine room being the biggest portion of it." Captain Casey said, and Captain Arthurs just shook his head in amazement.

"Yes Sir!" They all said.

"Come on, let's get going before someone does really get to you, and you rip them limb from limb." Captain Arthurs laughed, because he could see just how angry Jonathon was, and he knew that was a bad thing, since Jonathon had won awards for his hand to hand combat skills. Fortunately it took far more than Captain White to really make him mad.

Jonathon just nodded and they headed toward the engine room together. When they got there, they found as many people as could fit, stuffed in there and working. Half his crew was notably missing though, and the rest were working in the engine room, or the shield generator room.

"Tristan, where's the rest of our crew?" Captain Casey asked.

"Sir, they're on the hull of the ship, with about twenty of the others from this crew, trying to get the outside to a somewhat normal appearance, as well as strong enough so that they should be able to get home at maximum speed. We're working in here doing the same. We decided to salvage from other sections of the ship, to get this part as close to perfect as we could. We're doing good though, and we might even be finished by the end of the day if all goes well. The outside might take a bit longer though." Tristan said.

"We decided, young man! It was you who told us to start salvaging from non essential sections, so that we could do this, and when someone said that that was a bad idea, it was you who stared them down, and told them that bedrooms were lowest priority, and that getting home in one piece, and as fast as possible, was the most important. I of course agreed." Said one of the workers.

"And you were right. Good idea as well, this way we'll have enough materials to finish the outside, and the interior essential areas as well. Well, let's get back to work then." Captain Casey said.

The rest of the day went by fast for everyone, because they were so busy working, and other than stopping to eat, when food was delivered, no one rested. Captain Arthurs and his crew said they would stay on their ship tonight, and Captain Casey and his crew, as well as the rescued crew, went back to the UE1 to sleep for the night. After a brief shower to wash off and relax a bit, every member of the crew fell into bed exhausted.

The following morning, Captain Casey left Franky and team one on the ship, but traded Alex for Lance, and the rest of them went back over to the UE10 to continue repairs. The shields were now fully operable, the engine was tested and working, the hull was coming together nicely, and the engine room almost looked like an engine room again. Everyone figured that about another four to six hours should get it done.

"Good morning captain. The crew of the UE1, reporting for repairs. We'll all go out onto the hull today and help out out there. The rest of my guys need to learn how to do this as well. These guys you can get them to help where you need it." Captain Casey said, pointing to the rescued crew members.

"Sounds good to me. We have plenty of extra capacity air tanks, so you didn't have to bring yours." Captain Arthurs said.

"Nothing to worry about. We brought them just in case, but we'll go ahead and use them anyway. Could I get you to teleport a selection of hull plates out to us as soon as we get out there please?" Captain Casey asked.

"Sure thing." Captain Arthurs said.

A few minutes later, Captain Casey and his crew were on the hull of the ship above the engine room. You could tell it had been patched together, but it was looking more and more complete, and

Jonathon figured they could get it done in just a couple hours or so. Well, had they not been interrupted that is. Nearly two hours into their work, Captain Casey got a page.

"Captain, five Qaralon ships are about an hour out, and they're heading right for us. I don't think it's a social call either. The three ships didn't call them either, they haven't transmitted anything. You better get back in the ship, and I'd get everything powered up if I were you." Franky said.

"I think you might be right, would you like us to come back, or have you got everything under control over there?" Captain Casey asked, pretty sure he knew the answer though.

"Nah, we should be just fine. Do we have any handcuffs though?"

"Yeah, in the supply closet. Wait, what do you need handcuffs for?" Captain Casey asked, suddenly realizing what he had been asked.

"Well, that jerk's still on the ship, and he called me a liar. I may be many things, but I'm not a liar. I'm going to cuff him to a chair in here, and let him see for himself, so maybe this way he can see we're the ones who actually rescued him."

"You don't have to do that, he isn't worth it. You may if you wish though, I won't stop you." Captain Casey said with a smile.

"Thanks Sir."

"Guys, we need to get back in the ship, right now!" Captain Casey said.

"Yes Sir, we caught it as well." Donny said, and they all headed into the ship and found Captain Arthurs as quickly as they could.

"I trust you've seen the ships coming right for us by now." Captain Casey asked Captain Arthurs as soon as he made it to the bridge, where Captain Arthurs was at the time.

"Actually, we hadn't, 'til your ship called us and told us, Franky told us he told you to come in. He also told us to stand back, that we're in no shape to fight, and that he'd handle it." Captain Arthurs said.

"I hope you aren't insulted!"

"No, he's right, we aren't ready yet, a good hit to the hull near the engines, and all our work will be for nothing, and we'll probably be a pretty nice big field of space dust as well. We can stand back and offer support. Aren't you going to your ship though?" Captain Arthurs asked incredulously.

"No, Franky said they had everything under control, plus he wants to teach Captain White a little lesson."

"You sure do trust these boys a lot, I'd never let my ship go into battle without my being on it."

"I do trust them. If I feel they need me, I'll teleport over in an instant, but I doubt I'll need to."

"Well, let's get this ship as ready as we can make it for battle!" Captain Arthurs called out.

On the UE1, the boys were getting ready for battle once again. All the systems were checked, and when they were ready for it, they got down to what they knew they needed to do.

"Come on guys, let's move away from the others a bit, so that they aren't forced into the battle." Franky told the others.

"Already on it Sir." Everyone said.

"I'll be right back, I want to go get our guest of honor." Franky said with an evil grin plastered on his face.

Franky left the bridge and headed to the supply room, he grabbed a couple pairs of handcuffs on his way, and then went to find Captain White.

"Come on Sir, you have front row seats in a show, your appearance is mandatory, please slip into your show attire." Franky said with a smile, while twirling a pair of handcuffs on his finger.

"I'll do no such thing you vile little brat." Captain White spat out.

"Oh, you really don't want to make me more angry at you than I already am. I told you that attendance is mandatory, if you don't come now, I'll stun you, drag you to the bridge, and then revive you. Because I'm not inclined to be very nice to you right now, you might end up bruised a bit if you force me to do that. Like I said, you're coming, now!" Franky said as coldly as he could.

Captain White just held out his hands and Franky snapped the cuffs onto his wrists, and the electronic lock beeped to tell him that they were firmly attached. Franky nodded and pointed for the captain to lead the way. They arrived on the bridge moments later. Franky pointed at a chair and the captain sat down grumpily. Franky unlocked the hand cuffs on one side and attached it to the chair, then attached the other handcuffs he had to the captains now loose arm, and then to the back of the chair as well.

"Now captain, we have to keep concentration, so if you so much as utter a sound, I will strip off my sweaty dirty underwear and stuff them in your mouth. If I'm making myself perfectly clear, nod your head?" Franky asked in as polite and friendly tone as he could manage.

The captain nodded, possibly one of the smarter things he had done so far.

"Good, now that we understand each other, things will go much easier. Brady, how far out are they now, and how far away are we from the UE10?"

"We're just stopping now, ten minutes away from the ship, and they're about thirty minutes away. We were just about to tell them to not come any closer." Brady answered.

"Good, don't let me stop you. Are you sure you can handle this Kelly?" Franky answered.

"Oh yeah." Kelly grinned evilly, and then turned back to the communications center and put through the call. "Qaralon war ships, we know you're coming for us, don't come any closer."

"You destroy three our ships, we coming get them, and invite you to dinner, you be most honored guests." The voice said.

"If we'd destroyed them, they'd all be dead, and their ships nothing but space dust. They're simply disabled, and told to stay put, or we'd destroy them. However, if you come any closer, you'll be destroyed nice and slow. As for being invited to dinner, I'm afraid you'd find we wouldn't be much of a meal, we're nothing but a bunch of skinny little kids." Kelly taunted.

The UE10 was watching and listening to the whole thing. Captain Casey and the rest of his crew, as well as Captain Arthurs, and as many of his crew as would fit, were stuffed into the bridge to watch.

"Then you kept as prisoners and fatten up, you provide nice tasty meal later, I do personally enjoy snacking on you. Surrender now, I promise kill you fast." The voice said.

"Ha, you'd first have to catch us, and I bet you'll be just as easy to disable as the last three were. In fact, I bet you're easier, you sound weaker than the last one was. Oh, and you surrender, or I promise to kill you slow, bit by bit." Kelly said happily, really starting to enjoy this.

"I best captain there be, you nothing to me. I capture and destroy many your puny little ships. We be there ten minutes, I can't wait eat you." The beast said.

"I look forward to the meeting. Remember, when you get here though, that you'll be destroyed."

Kelly cut the communications, so that they could not comment.

"Nice talking Kelly. I think you got them nice and mad, which makes them easier to deal with." Franky said.

"Thanks, so are we going to play with them a bit, and then leave them disabled, or just destroy them like I promised?" Kelly said.

"We'll have to wait and see. We can play a bit first though. You guys buzz around them like an angry swarm of bees, and you guys go ahead and just keep pelting them with the small missiles for now. If we get hit three times, switch to the big guns, and take them out." Franky said.

"You got it." Everyone said.

Ten minutes later the ships were in range. With Brady and Kelvin on navigation, and the others on scanners and weapons, they started the attack. The Qaralon were throwing everything they could at them, and they were getting more angry by the second as the boys dodged in and out of everything they shot. Once again the dance was spectacular as the boys proved to everyone around them just how good they really were. Nearly every missile the boys launched though was a good hit, which also proved how good they were. They kept hitting every vulnerable area they could get at, and in less than fifteen minutes the ships were floating in space, no longer of their own power.

"I thought you say you destroy us." The voice said angrily.

"So sue me, I changed my mind, I decided to play with you a bit. Now you're just floating space junk, and you can stay here floating for forever for all I care. Now, I'll ask this only once, do you have any captives on board, because if we have to scan for them, or if you lie to us and we find them, we'll destroy one of your ships. It'll be your choice." Kelly threatened.

"We no captives, you not dare." The voice said.

"I think you're lying to me. Do they have any prisoners guys?" Kelly asked.

"Yes they do. The ship you're talking to has three, and the others have anywhere from two to ten." Jesse answered.

"Now why did you go and lie to me. Now pick the ship you want destroyed." Kelly snapped.

"We defenseless, you not destroy us, it against you so call morals." The voice said smugly.

"Hey, I'm seven years old, I can't be expected to have proper morals, now pick the ship." Kelly grinned, then muted himself from the Qaralon and looked to the rest of his team. "Get our people out of there right now, and then teleport everyone from the lead ship to the one behind it." He said, smiling to the others.

A few seconds later it was done and the nod was given, and then two maximum yield missiles blew the ship to nothing.

"I told you I'd destroy the ship, and as for my morals, I do have them, I wouldn't kill you unless necessary, but I never said anything about you, now did I." Kelly giggled.

"More our ships will come destroy you." The voice said threateningly.

"We've now permanently disabled eight of your ships, do you think we care. By the time your people get here, we'll be long gone. Now, because I'm such a nice guy, I'm going to put all of you onto one ship and destroy the rest, we're sick of you attacking us."

"You no dare, we get revenge." The beast snarled.

"You people really should learn not to dare us, now I'm going to do it just for fun." Kelly said, and then cut the communications.

Weapons got the nod almost a minute later, and then they destroyed the other three ships.

"Tell your people never to attack us again, or the same thing will happen to them." Kelly said to the beasts and then closed communications again before they could respond.

They then headed back to the others. On their way back, Captain Casey pinged them, and as soon as he was put on screen, he started talking.

"Boys, you were amazing, as always. How's your guest?"

"Thanks, but I forgot all about him." Franky answered.

"Go ahead Franky, you deserve this one." Captain Casey smiled.

"Thanks Sir." Franky said and then turned to the captain. "So, I'm a liar am I? Even you can't deny that one, you saw, heard, and felt it with your very own senses. Now, I want a nice genuine apology."

"Could you please remove the handcuffs?" The captain asked pitifully.

"That wasn't even part of the bargain, however, seeing as how you asked politely, something of which I might add you haven't shown yet, I'll do it." Franky said and removed the cuffs.

The captain stood and put out his hand. It took a moment for Franky to realize what he was doing, and then stuck out his hand, the captain shook it firmly.

"I apologize for my mistake, you're an able captain, and an able crew. Your captain should be proud. Now, if you'll excuse me, I'd like to go back to what I guess are my quarters." The captain said.

"You are excused, but please remember that you don't have free run of the ship, and if you need anything, call and ask, it'll be brought to you as quick as we can arrange it."

"Thanks Sir." The captain said meekly.

"Good job guys." Franky told the rest of the crew.

"Thanks." They all said.

A few moments later they were once again back in their spot, guarding the UE10 and the boys got to work on cleaning up and restocking anything that needed to be restocked. They then got themselves cleaned up, because even such a short battle had left them all sweaty and grimy feeling.

CHAPTER 17

THE REPAIRS ARE DONE, LET'S GET YOU GUYS HOME

On the UE10, the captain and crew of that ship were still standing in awe at what they had witnessed. Captain Casey and his crew were just standing there with happy smiles on their faces, proud to call the crew theirs. Finally Captain Arthurs found his voice.

"Well, I see why you trust them so much. I've never seen flying like that, or heard of tactics anywhere like that. Everything they do I hope is being transmitted back to WSEC to be studied, so that everyone can learn these moves and tricks."

"Told ya so. And yes, they are. I have a few things to send them now. Boy, here I thought I'd be training them, and here they are teaching everyone else. They still have much to learn, but I think that they have much more to teach."

"I'll say, and no need to rub it in man. Well, let's get back to work, and then you can escort us back to safe space." Captain Arthurs said.

Captain Casey nodded, and everyone on the bridge wordlessly disappeared to where they needed to be to get the rest of the repairs completed. There was still much to do, but far less than they thought they would still have by this time. Everyone was glad that they only seemed to have a few hours of work left before they were ready to go.

Once the boys on the EU1 were cleaned and ready to continue, they were once again back on the bridge of the ship.

"Well, I'm going to go greet our guests. You put them in the main lounge correct?" Franky asked.

"Yeah. Hopefully these ones will be more grateful than the last bunch." Jesse said.

"Me too." He said, then headed out for the short ride and walk.

"Hello folks, as I am sure you've noticed already, you're finally free. You're aboard the UE1." Franky said.

The ranking captain stood to greet him.

"And we thank you. Who are you though, and why has the Captain not come to see us instead of sending, who I could only assume is his son." The captain asked.

"I'll get to that in a moment Sir, who are you please, and would any of you like anything, there's a fully stocked kitchen right next door?"

"I'm Captain Pol, some of these folks are my crew, and others are from other ships, we've been talking for a while since we got here. We're fine for right now, but as soon as we get some information, we may take you up on that offer." Captain Pol said kindly.

"That's fine Sir, you may wish to take a seat however. A question though, how long have you been captive?"

"Only just a few weeks myself, and the longest here is a year."

"Okay, then you know the war's of course over, and you should recognize the fact that the UE1 is no longer a government vessel."

"Yes, I knew that, and it never even dawned on me when you said what ship this was. Why is it way out here then?"

"That's part of the explanation. Well, this is a training mission, and Captain Casey's in charge. He however isn't aboard right now, he's aboard the UE10 helping with repairs, because they were hit real hard. I'm in charge of the ship right now, and it was myself and five others that won the little skirmish back there, and got you back to safety."

"That's right, I remember hearing something of the experiment Jonathan was running with a bunch of street kids. That would be you then? Now as for that little skirmish, as you called it, we were made to watch, and I'd say that five on one isn't little. That's a major victory. And you say that only six young men, such as yourself, did all that?"

"Yes Sir, that's all correct." Franky stated simply.

"Well then, I and every person in here owes the lot of you our lives, and we're indeed grateful to you. I'll personally see to it that every person on this ship receives a commendation, you can count on that."

"Thank you Sir, but that won't be necessary, we're just doing our duty to help out, nothing more, nothing less." Franky said, kind of blushing.

"Nonsense. In my eyes you're a hero."

"Hear hear." Everyone else said.

"I need to get back to the bridge, please feel free to get what food you'd like." Franky said, feeling more than a bit uncomfortable. He felt better with someone screaming at him and calling him a liar.

"Thank you, we'll do that for sure. I'd like to come visit the bridge though, and meet the rest of your crew? I can tell this is making you uncomfortable, so I'll come alone." Captain Pol asked.

"You're welcome, and I guess so Sir." Franky answered quietly.

"No, thank you, go ahead, I know you have work to do, and we're all hungry."

Franky headed up to the bridge and relayed the information back to the others, they were all happy too, but a bit uncomfortable as well. They still were not used to praise and kind words. The twenty people now on the ship all headed to the kitchen and grabbed some good food and ate. As soon as the captain was finished, he headed up to the bridge.

Once he made it back to the bridge, Franky asked Kelly to get Captain Casey for him, so Kelly did so right away, and moments later, he was on screen.

"Captain, we're back now, and there are no immediate threats out there. I see you're back to work finally, you were probably all sitting around and resting while we were out here working I bet." He teased.

"You're one to talk, now that you're back, you're going to rest while we work. Good to see you back though, and with not even a scratch. So were there any people on those ships to rescue?" Captain Casey teased back.

"Hey, we've deserved it, and yes, twenty of them. The ranking captain was Captain Pol, and he was very happy, and said he was going to personally give us all commendations. I hate to say it, but that makes me more uncomfortable than Captain White yelling at me and calling me a liar." Franky told the captain.

"Yes, and you know why that is as well, and you also know that when we get home, the press conference is going to be massive. It'll be hard on all of you, but you deserve it. We'll work more on that later, right now isn't the time." Captain Casey said.

"Yes Sir, I know. It's funny though, that someone commending me feels worse than someone berating me. I'm getting used to it from you though. Thanks Sir." Franky said softly.

"Yeah, thanks Sir." The others all voiced.

"You're all welcome." Captain Casey said, just as Captain Pol came on the bridge.

"Oh, hello Jonathon, long time no see. I hear I have you and your amazing crew to thank for my life, and the lives of many crew members." He said happily.

"Good to see you too Wesley, and I had nothing to do with that battle, we watched from the sidelines, here to offer support only if needed, but this ship isn't really battle ready yet."

"Well, you trained them, and from what we saw aboard the Qaralon ship, I might say damned well at that."

"Actually, I only taught them how to run everything, the moves are theirs, they're teaching us all a lot. WSEC is getting a load of data from all of this, and they're implementing it into their training."

"Well then . . . . So when are we heading home then?" Captain Pol asked, not really knowing what to say to that.

"You and all those rescued will be transferred to this ship, and then you can all go home from here, because we'll be continuing on our mission. We're going to escort all of you to safety first, and maybe even call for an escort back home. The ship should be able to fight, but it's still not up to it if it can be avoided. We have maybe an hours worth of repairs left, before you can all leave."

"Oh, I was hoping you'd take us home!"

"No, I'm afraid not. The boys aren't ready for what awaits them at home yet. We planned to be gone for a year, so that'll be soon enough for you to give them the thanks I know you want to give them."

"I understand. I look forward to meeting you in person again. I'll get out of the boys' hair then, and let you all get back to work." Captain Pol said.

"Thanks, and see you soon." Captain Casey said, and then signed off.

"Well boys, I'll let you get back to work."

"Before you go Sir, I have a favor to ask of you. Captain White was also rescued, and he just had a major blow to his pride. He needs some guidance from a strong adult, and you outrank him, so he might even listen to you. Would you get him from his room and take him with you back to the lounge." Franky asked.

"Sure, can't say as I like the man any, he's been gone for, what, five years now, let's see if he's changed any. Where is he?"

"Deck ten, room fifty three." Franky answered.

"Okay, you got it."

Two hours later the ship repairs were done, and everyone was invited over to the UE10 to have celebratory late lunch. Many thanks were given to the crew of the UE1, and toasts were handed out generously. The boys all blushed lots, and looked down, but their captain made them face their complementer and say thanks. He told them that they needed to learn this, and this was as good a time as any. Another two hours later, the crew and their captain were back aboard their ship. Once everyone was ready, Kelly was asked to go ahead and bring up the UE10, so he did so. As soon as Captain Arthurs was on screen, Captain Casey started.

"Well Evan, you lead the way and we'll follow and provide backup if needed. If we get attacked, move out of the action, and we'll take over. I'm going to call for a ship to escort you back home as well."

"Will do, thanks." Captain Arthurs said sincerely.

As soon as they were all underway, Captain Casey headed to his office, telling the boys that they had the bridge. When he made it there, he cleaned himself up real quick, and then put a call through to WSEC to ask for an escort ship to be sent out, asking for them to send replacement supplies for them as well, since they had used lots of things that they needed. He got through to Admiral Daily and almost immediately got through the pleasantries and asked for what he wanted.

"Glad to hear from you Captain Casey, how did it go?"

"It went very well thanks, we got the ship patched back up, and I'm happy to report that when the Qaralon attacked on two separate occasions, we weren't even scratched, and their ships were either destroyed or disabled. The most important thing though, is that there are thirty six men and women that were rescued from those eight ships. I have the battle recordings, as well as the detailed reports as to what happened during the mission, it could prove interesting. You should also note I wasn't even on board the ship during either battle." Captain Casey said with a smile.

"Huh, what! You weren't even on board, and your crew did all that by themselves?" Admiral Daily asked in shock.

"That's correct Sir. There were only six of the boys both times."

"And they rescued thirty six people?"

"That's correct Sir, and as best we know, not even one life was lost."

"Wait a minute, I thought you said that all eight ships were either disabled or destroyed. How can you say you don't believe there were no lives lost?" Admiral Daily asked a moment later, clearly confused.

"Well that's a surprise Sir, and you're going to have to wait for the reports." Captain Casey grinned.

"Pardon me. Did you just tell me to wait son?" Admiral Daily asked.

"Yep, sending the information now, and don't bother trying to order it out of me, you know it won't work Sir."

"Fine, you know I should court marshal you right!"

"Yes, and you know just as well as I do that you'd never do that to your chief trouble maker, I make your days fun."

"Oh fine, be that way, bye then." Admiral Daily said, and then signed off.

Captain Casey laughed to himself, and then left his office and headed to the bridge.

"Hi guys, how's it going here?" Captain Casey asked as soon as he entered.

"Just fine Sir, nothing to report." Donny answered.

"Good." Captain Casey answered, and then hit his communicator. "Would everyone come up to the bridge please?" Captain Casey asked, everyone gave their affirmative responses and headed there. They waited a few minutes for everyone to be on the bridge.

"Now that you're all here, we need to work something out. Captain Arthurs is gonna wanna go straight through the night, so I need a team to pull night shifts for the next few nights? I think it'll be easier if it's the same crew, so that you can all get the sleep you need. We're at least three, if not four days from Tenarian space at maximum speed, but that's assuming of course that the UE10 can hold up under the stress that that speed puts a ship under."

"I'd like to volunteer our team Sir." Brady offered.

"Is your whole team willing?" Captain Casey asked.

"One moment Sir." Brady said. He pulled the rest of his group aside and talked to them quietly for a moment. He then came back. "Yes Sir, we have no problems. We'd like to get to bed after we have a quick bite to eat then Sir."

"Okay, we have our night crew, you're dismissed, go get something to eat. You'll join us in the morning for calisthenics as normal, and then the morning is yours, in bed by 1200 hours and your shift is 2200 hours to 0600 hours. I know tomorrow is Sunday, but our day of rest will just have to wait until the UE10 is safe in the hands of their next escort."

"Yes Sir!" Everyone said.

Team one headed out right away, as did Warren and Will to go get the boys some food.

"Donny or Franky, which of you'd like to man the night shift with the boys?"

"I will Sir." Donny answered first.

"Okay, you head out with them then."

"Will do Sir, thanks." Donny smiled and ran after the others.

The rest stayed around and chatted for a few moments with the captain, before dispersing and going about their daily business.

It took four days to get to Tenarian space, and it went off without a problem. They waited for almost twelve hours at their rendezvous point for the UE152 to arrive, to escort the UE10 back home. Before too long, the captain and crew of the UE1 were ready to head out once again. Before they left though, all the captains and many of the crew appeared on the screen.

"To the Captain and the crew of the UE1, we owe you a debt of gratitude that we'll hopefully never be able to repay. If you're ever in need of help, call, and we'll be there as quick as we possibly can be.

Again we thank you all from the bottom of all our hearts, and look forward to seeing you again when you all get home." Captain Pol said.

"You're very welcome, and hopefully we don't need to call for help, but we will if we need to. Captain Sands, do you have the replacement supplies I requested?" Captain Casey asked.

"Yes I do, teleporting now." Captain Sands said.

"Thanks, have a good safe trip home guys, and see you in a few months." Captain Casey said.

"You're welcome, see you then." He answered.

"Point us somewhere boys and hit the gas!" Captain Casey said.

Cullen, who was on navigation, picked a direction, and put them to maximum speed as quick as he could get away with.

CHAPTER 18

MEETING OF A NEW SPECIES

The next month flew by for everyone, they had been so busy working and learning, that they barely even realized that they were now in the beginning of November. All of the boys were getting further along in their school work, and even the newest boys were getting comfortable with the ship controls, and were learning lots from the more experienced boys on the handling of the ship. None of the boys were having any problems keeping up with the captain during their twice daily calisthenics either, albeit still a bit slower. Nothing really exciting had happened though since the rescue mission, and none of the boys minded that all that much. Captain Casey was also enjoying his time, and had been sending training reports back home every week, but there was nothing of any real interest in it. They had of course done many more training simulations, even two during the middle of the night, as the captain had promised, albeit late. It was the fifth day of November when their near boredom was broken. Donny was on the bridge at the time and called the captain right away.

"Captain, we have an odd ship coming upon us, they're still a few hours away, but they're heading straight for us. It's an odd design though, and one the computer doesn't recognize."

"Okay, I'll be right there."

A few moments later, he was on the bridge.

"Let's see this mysterious ship!" He said as he came on to the bridge.

"On the view screen now Sir." Matthew said.

Once the screen was up, they all saw the ship that they were heading toward. The ship was huge, somewhere around five times the size of theirs was they figured, and it was kind of rounded, almost bird like, but with short wings and bottom mounted propulsion pods. It was painted in bright vivid colors as well, something that was surprising, because Earth did not paint their ships at all.

"I certainly don't recognize it either. They're heading straight for us you said?"

"Yes, in about two hours or so, we should be nearly crashing into each other Sir." Donny answered.

"Okay, keep on the same course, put the shields up, and keep at alert. We don't want to assume they're attacking us, but at the same time, we can't assume that they're friendly either, we'll take the wait and see approach."

"Already done Sir. We figured we'd stay at the same speed and just let them come, because if we were to slow down, it'd show weakness, or that we're scared of them, of which we're not." Donny said firmly.

"I never thought of it that way, but I guess you're right. Have you put through a call to them yet?" Captain Casey asked.

"Not yet Sir. I wanted to see what your thoughts were on this first." Donny said.

"Okay, what was your first thought, what do you think we should do?"

"I was thinking that we should wait until we're closer, let's say an hour or so away, before we did anything like that, unless they contact us first." Donny answered.

"I'd say about the same, that way our scanners will be able to see them more clearly, and also this way there's less chance for interference."

"That's what I thought as well Sir."

For the next hour everyone sat around chatting, but kept a close eye on the approaching ship. Once they felt they were close enough, Captain Casey nodded to communications, and Cullen pinged the other ship.

"Unknown vessel, this is the Earth ship Universe Explorer One, please respond?" Cullen asked politely.

"Earth ship, this is the Drandarian ship, Drandaria 1245, please explain the reason you enter our space without permission!" The voice said, it was polite, but not exactly friendly.

"We apologize Sir, we weren't aware that this space was occupied or restricted. If you'd like, and you'd give us the coordinates of your space, we'll gladly leave and go around. We're simply exploring, so we don't have to go through your space. However, a meeting with your people would be preferable, we'd like to meet all the new people we see that we're able to. If this can be arranged, I'd like to bring my captain and you on screen so that you may speak." Cullen said as friendly as he could.

"That could be agreeable, bring us up." The person said.

A few seconds later Cullen had the conference set up, and the Drandarian captain came up on the screen. He looked almost bird like, but with arms instead of wings, and there was less of a beak than a normal bird would have. He had a plumage of vivid reds and blues, and looked quite amazing to the boys. All the Drandarians on the screen wore simple loose fitting, cotton like clothing, it looked very soft and comfortable. A few of them were just wearing plain white, but many of the others wore bright colors of virtually every shade.

"Hello Sir, I'm Captain Casey, and I'd like to invite you to our ship, so that we may meet. If this is not to your liking, we could come to your ship, or just talk like this." Captain Casey offered.

"I'll accept the offer to come to your ship, but I'll bring my security officers with me though."

"That would be acceptable, you may bring whomever you wish with you, and we look forward to meeting with you." Captain Casey said, and then the screen went blank.

"Hmm, friendly enough, but kind of skittish though, aren't they. I hope I didn't insult it calling it a Sir though, I couldn't tell if it was male or female." Captain Casey chuckled.

"I think it was a he Sir, and he didn't look insulted." Cullen said.

"What makes you think that?" Captain Casey asked.

"I saw a few others in the background, and there were what I figured to be females, they were smaller and not quite as brightly colored, many of the birds I saw on Earth were much the same way for males and females Sir."

"Yeah, I guess you're right about that, at least with some anyway. I know almost nothing about birds though, so I'll have to take your word for it." Captain Casey said with a grin.

"Should we go get into our dress uniforms Captain?" Donny asked.

"Sure, sounds good, you tell everyone, then we can all go get changed." Captain Casey answered.

"Yes Sir!" Donny said.

He went and told everyone through his communicator, and then everyone went and got changed. Shortly thereafter they were parked next to each other, and the Drandarian people were coming aboard.

"Welcome aboard the UE1, I'm Captain Casey, please follow us, and we'll go sit and talk in comfort." Captain Casey said.

"Thank you for your offer to come aboard. I'm Captain Cloudburst, we apologize for seeming rude. You're a new species to us, and we don't like people coming inside our boundaries." The captain apologized.

"No need to apologize, we understand completely." Captain Casey said politely, and they walked the rest of the way in silence.

"Here we are, please have a seat." Captain Casey said a few minutes later as they entered the nearest lounge.

"Thank you. The reason we don't normally like outsiders in our space, is because of the Qaralon people. We seem to please their appetite, so they like to raid our space. Ah, I can see from the looks on the faces of all the young people with you, that you're familiar with them." Captain Cloudburst said dryly.

"Sadly yes. We've just barely ended a fifty year long war with them, and although they retreated, we're still dealing with them. They too seem to have a taste for us, but our friends the Tenarians, are a bit luckier, the Qaralon don't like them, they say they're too bitter." Captain Casey laughed.

"Ah yes, the Tenarians, a good people, don't see them that often this far out though, they mostly stay in their own space. The war you just had would explain the lack of raids on our people for the last many years. I can say it was a nice change, but am sorry it had to come on the backs of your people, and had we known you were at war with them, we would have sent aid." Said Captain Cloudburst humbly.

"We had lots of help from the Tenarians, as well as a few of the other races who were also sick of having their children taken in the night for food. I'm glad though that the war stopped the raids on your people." Captain Casey said.

"Thank you for that, and I'm happy that you did have plenty of help as well."

"Anyway, we're on a training mission, and are exploring the universe, what would you say in the area around here is interesting? Our people have never been out this way, so we don't know the area." Captain Casey asked.

"We have a black star a few light years away, that's what we call it anyway. A star imploded many years ago now, and is now just a hole in space, but don't get too close to it though, it seems to eat anything that gets too close to it. We also have a very interesting ring of planets and moons around a star that's on the edge of our system, it's inhabitable though, due to the light the star gives off."

"Thanks, we've seen a few black holes, or black stars as you call them, and they're interesting to research, and we'll certainly check out the planets. What of your planet, would your people mind if we visited?" Captain Casey asked.

"Sorry, we don't allow outsiders on our planet." Captain Cloudburst said solemnly.

"That's fine, we understand. Earth almost said the same thing, but decided against it, because we have many allies and friends who visit frequently, so it wouldn't work for us. Do you have any close neighbors then?" Captain Casey asked.

"No, the closest are the Qaralon, and those are neighbors we could easily do without." Captain Cloudburst said dryly.

"I can see where you might think that. Would you and your people like to stay and have lunch with us?" Captain Casey asked.

"We'd like that, but you should know that we don't eat meat." Captain Cloudburst replied.

"Then, let us tour our ship, and then we'll have lunch. Just let me go tell my kitchen staff of the guests for lunch, and I'll be right back."

Donny and Franky, as well as a couple of the others, had been sitting and chatting pleasantly with a few of the visitors, while the captains had been talking, and they all seemed to like each other. They mostly talked about their ships and what they could do, and that type of thing, but they had fun.

"Warren and Will, as I'm sure you're aware, we have guests. I've invited them for lunch, so I'm glad to have caught you before you started cooking, because they're vegetarian. Could you make an entirely vegetarian meal for all of us please?" Captain Casey asked a few minutes later when he entered the kitchen.

"No problem Sir, we were just about to start cooking, but were trying to wait until you told us whether or not they were staying. I saw them as you were passing by us, and I guessed then that serving poultry probably wouldn't have been well received." Warren said with a chuckle.

"You're probably right. See you in an hour then." Captain Casey said with a smile and a chuckle as well.

"Sorry that took so long, if you'd like, we can take a tour of our ship while we wait for lunch. It's not quite so large and grand as your ship looks, but it's home, and it's tougher than it looks." Captain Casey said with pride.

"It's a very nice ship so far from what we've seen, how fast is it?" Captain Cloudburst asked.

"Thank you. We can go a maximum of one hundred LYS, and we have almost full maneuverability at that speed as well, due to our smaller size. That was why we decided to keep our ships smaller, as compared to the Tenarians, who lose maneuverability when they're going so fast." Captain Casey said.

"Too true, we too have to slow down when we have to make a sharp turn. I'm surprised however that your inertia systems can compensate for that kind of movement, ours would never allow that, and would likely throw us across the bridge if we forced it to do so." Captain Cloudburst admitted.

"Oh, well we sure do feel it when we do a sharp turn or movement, and we can't jump straight to a hundred LYS, because of that. We can do so if needed, but you'd certainly need to hold on. Also, if you aren't used to it, you'll undoubtedly lose your last meal, not to mention the stress it puts on the ship. Obviously we try not to do either, unless necessary, and when we're fighting, we're not normally going near that fast anyway, unless of course we're trying to escape."

"That's truly amazing, we'd never be able to do it at all. I doubt our computers would even allow it." Captain Cloudburst said.

"Thanks. Well this is our engine room, and our other systems are kept right next door; the power, shield and inertia generators." Captain Casey said as they entered.

For the next half an hour they looked at the engine and utility room, and Captain Casey and the boys explained everything to their guests. They then toured a few other parts of the ship, until it was time for lunch. Captain Casey steered them to the dining hall, and they took their seats. The captains and the rest of the normal head table sat down, while each team invited a couple of the visitors to their tables.

"That was a very nice meal, I thank you, as does my crew. I'd like to invite you to my ship this evening to share a meal with us, and you may tour our ship as well." Captain Cloudburst offered.

"We'd gladly accept your generous offer." Captain Casey smiled warmly.

"So tell me, why is it your entire crew is young, except you and your cook?" Captain Cloudburst asked.

"Well, as I said earlier, we're on a training mission, and all the children on board are orphans of the war, and many were living on the streets when I rescued them for this little experiment. I must say, it's been very rewarding. Due to the nature of the boys, it was felt by myself that the fewer adults around, the better, because they tended to not trust adults. Our cook is actually our doctor, and he too used to be a street kid, he was found by my mom especially for this mission. And if you knew how good these boys were, it would surprise you." Captain Casey said with pride.

"Well that's some experiment. Tell me, how good are they?" Captain Cloudburst asked.

"Well, while in training we have battle simulations to let us learn without being harmed, these boys are one of only two crews to have beaten the most difficult one we have, and they did so in a far better time than the other crew did. Then on two separate occasions, they took on Qaralon attackers and beat them soundly, once against three, and the other against five. They were also the only ones in the fight, as well both of those times I wasn't even on the ship at the time. Now, if they were old enough, this would be considered an actual crew, since they have well proven their worth. Our government's taking much of what these boys have done, and is training our people in their methods, they're that good." Captain Casey answered proudly.

"I'm not sure how to respond to that. It's amazing, to say the least. How long have these boys been training?" Captain Cloudburst asked.

"A little over two months now. I figure in another two, I'll have taught them all I can. They still have much work to do in their school work however, but they're going just as fast and strong in that aspect as well. You should see these boys repair a ship as well, they do excellent work. And I'm proud to call them my crew."

"I'd be more than proud. I can honestly say that I'm glad that we're on the same side, because I wouldn't like to go against your boys, just from what you've told me."

"Thanks, I'll take that as a compliment."

"And you should. We'll leave you to your day, and we'd like to invite you to dinner at 1900 hours."

"Thank you, we'll see you at that time then." Captain Casey said, and walked the Drandarians to the airlock to show them out.

The next few hours went by without much being done, the crew mostly just sat around and chatted about the visit.

Finally 1900 hours came, and Captain Casey called and said they were coming over now and they were told to come over. Franky stayed aboard, he had offered to keep the ship manned, as it should be at all times.

The crew entered the Drandarian ship, and were met by Captain Cloudburst and a few of his crew. The hall was large and brightly lit, and was a very nice blue in color, the captains stepped forth.

"Welcome to our ship, this is one of our smaller designs, in case you'd like to know." Captain Cloudburst said.

"This is your smaller design, how many people can this one hold?" Captain Casey asked in awe.

"About twelve hundred people, where our largest could take nearly twice that number." Captain Cloudburst said.

"Wow, why so many people on one ship though, it can't possibly take that many people to operate even your largest ship." Captain Casey asked while they were walking.

"Not really sure, our ships never have anywhere near their capacity in people, but they're designed to hold crew and their families as well. I personally believe that smaller ships such as yours are a smarter way to go, but our people decided to go larger instead of more. At least they went all out on these ships, and they're very comfortable, including a holographic suite and pool so that we can relax." Captain Cloudburst said.

"A holographic suite would be very nice, but tell me, how do you have a pool on your ship? We have a sonic tub, and every time we make any sudden movements, it loses half its water if we forget to put the lid on it." Captain Casey asked.

"It's protected by a very nifty shield, the only thing it stops is the water, you can jump in and out, and you'd never even know it's there." Captain Cloudburst answered.

"Is it just your regular shield with a modification, and can you tell me how your holograph suite works?" Captain Casey asked as they walked into the dining hall.

"Please have a seat with myself and my second in command, and I'll answer those questions once we finish our meal. The rest of you, please feel free to sit wherever you wish."

"Yes Sir!" Everyone answered.

As they sat down, the meal was served and they started eating. They chatted amiably between mouthfuls, and as promised, once they were finished dinner, Captain Cloudburst answered the questions that he had been asked before dinner.

"The shield is just a modification of our regular shields yes, I don't know if your shields are the same as ours are though, so I'm uncertain as to whether or not the same modification could be used. I'd be happy to look at it for you though, and show you how to do it if you wish. As for the holograph suites, I'd like to make a trade with you if I could. You give us the specifications for your inertial compensation systems, and I'll give you the specifications for the holographic suites?" Captain Cloudburst asked with what Captain Casey could only assume was a grin.

"Well, I couldn't refuse such an offer. As for our shields, they're the same basic design as the Tenarians use, so if you know if theirs are capable, then ours probably are as well." Captain Casey remarked.

"Yes, we use a similar design as theirs, so that should be fine, we can show you that later. For now, let's go ahead and give you a tour of our ship."

"Sounds good to me, lead the way."

For over the next hour they toured the ship. Everyone was impressed with the pool, and were astonished with the holographic room. It was just like being out on a sandy beach somewhere, they could smell the salt water breeze, and feel it on their skin, everything about it looked and felt so realistic that they could have sworn they were actually there, but knew they could not be. They headed to the engine and power rooms next and found that they were nearly identical to their own though. The bridge of the ship was also quite impressive, large comfy chairs for everyone, and everything was laid out nicely. In many ways, it was much like their own, still broken up into the same basic sections, just everything was larger and more spread out, far more comfortable and relaxed looking. Like nearly everything else on the ship they noticed, on the bridge, everything was painted bright cheery colors. About the only place that was not painted was the engine room, though they had no idea why, and did not feel it important enough to bother asking. Over all, the ship was very impressive in its grandness, but was really almost identical to their own ship in how it ran and was set up. Though they did have more creature comforts, that was soon to be remedied.

"I must say Captain Cloudburst, that your ship is certainly impressive in that it is very grand and the colors and comfort that it affords, but I'm surprised just how much alike our ships really are once you start looking at them."

"Yes, in so many ways, they really are the same, and really, other than yours being considerably smaller, there's no real differences. A few yes, but really minor, and only comfort things, things I think we can maybe share very nicely between each other."

"I agree, and that would be very nice. Let me just call my boy on the ship and have him send over a pad with the specifications for our inertial compensation systems for you, I assure you, it makes maneuvering far easier to have a good one installed."

"I can't wait, that'll be really nice, and while you're doing that, I can get the schematics for the shield and holographic suite as well, I'll be right back." Captain Cloudburst said happily.

Captain Casey made the call and a few minutes later he had the pad, and Captain Cloudburst came back holding a similar pad. They traded pads and looked over the information.

"This is great, thank you very much." Captain Casey said.

"And thank you. This should make traveling a bit more comfortable now." Captain Cloudburst said back as well.

"Likewise. Well it's getting late, we should let you guys get on with your evening, and we need to go do our evening exercises before bed."

"Well then, have a good night." Captain Cloudburst said and showed them out.

Captain Casey and crew headed back into their ship for the night, all of them heading to their rooms to get changed into some more comfortable clothes.

Chapter 19

A Fair Trade

Once everyone changed, they all headed to the cargo bay to do their evening exercises, and almost as soon as they entered, Donny cornered the captain.

"So Sir, where are we going to put the pool and holograph room?" He asked excitedly.

"Who says we'll put either one on this ship?"

"Well, we have to know if they really work of course Sir, and I know you'd love to put them in."

"Well the shield we can easily test on the sonic tub, and the holograph room I guess we can try it in an unused room. It'd be kind of neat to have, and the design seems pretty simple, but I don't think we have all the necessary components to build it."

"Well, we have a tonne of Nutronium, almost literally too, we could trade maybe to get the required parts to do it, and maybe even a pool."

"You're right, we have enough to trade for sure, and it's not a bad idea really. Obviously the Drandarians have no problem with the bartering system." Captain Casey said while thinking it over.

"We can talk about it in the morning with Captain Cloudburst, I'm sure he'd be happy with it." Donny said confidently.

"Yeah, let's get some exercise."

So for the rest of their evening, captain and crew did their regular routine before all going to bed and having a half way decent sleep. The next morning, they were all up and at it at their regular time, had breakfast, got their morning exercises out of the way, and the boys whose turn it was to be in class were in class. The remainder of the crew were taking care of all their regular ship duties. They were not long into said duties when they were pinged by Captain Cloudburst.

"Good morning, I trust your sleep was peaceful!" Captain Cloudburst said in way of greeting.

"Good morning, yes it was. I hope yours was as well? How may we help you this morning?" Captain Casey asked.

"Well my engineer was working on the compensator this morning, and he ran into a problem. We don't have a component that's needed, and I was hoping that you might have one so that we can install it. We'll have to give the designs to our people on the planet, so that they can make this one, since it's not something we've ever seen. Everything else we have though."

"Which component is it?" Captain Casey asked curiously.

Captain Cloudburst held up the diagram of the component, and Jonathon recognized it right away.

"Yes, we carry those on board, we use it is a power stabilizer, it's what makes the whole thing work so well really. We'd be happy to give you one. I do however have a question for you though, and I was just about to call you, when you called us. I was wondering if you'd be willing to trade some of the pieces needed to make a pool and holograph room for some Nutronium. We know that you too use Nutronium as a power source, and we have a lot extra, so were hoping that you might wish to trade."

"We might have most of the stuff on board to do it, but probably not all. If you wanted to come home with us, I'm sure we could work something out. This way it would also give us a chance to test out the new compensator's under the supervision of those who know how to use them, as well as you can see some of the things outsiders rarely get to see."

"I see no downsides. I'll send over the two power stabilizers you'll need, and if you need any help, I'm happy to come over as well and help in any way I can."

"I think once we have the parts, my people will manage just fine, but we'll call if we need you. I'm pretty sure we have everything you'd need to make the pool, and modifying your shields you should need nothing for, so we can send over what you'll need for that as well right now, just tell us how big you want it."

"Great, let's do it then. Let's go about the same size as your pool, I'm pretty sure we have more than enough room for it. We'll have all the metal needed from tearing out the few walls needed, so we won't need that, but everything else we'll need. How much Nutronium do you want for that?" Captain Casey asked.

"Does a hundred kilograms sound fair?"

"Sure, we'll send it at the same time."

A short time later the transfers were made, and the captain and many of the boys went down to look at the parts. With the instructions the Drandarians gave them, it would be a fairly simple chore to make everything needed to heat, filter, and pump the pool water. They were all excited about the prospects, both would be amazing to have to be sure.

"So Captain, have you figured out where to put it, and how to build the pool yet?" Franky asked.

"Well I was figuring the lower decks in some of the unused rooms. We'll have to seal them up, remove the floor from up above, and make that the actual pool room, it should work fine. I think next door to that can be the holographic room, and we can expand it by taking up two or three rooms if we need to. I don't really know how it works yet, I have to go over all the specifications still. We have lots of time to worry about all that though."

"Yes, it'll probably only take a few days to do, and we can take our time to do it, but it sure would be nice to swim again. It might be interesting to try teaching some of the others to swim though, I don't think most of us can. I really can't wait for the holographic room though." Franky said.

"Yeah, you're right, it could be interesting to see just how many of you boys can swim, we can teach them though. If I can teach you to fly a star ship, then swimming should be simple." Captain Casey laughed.

"True, but somehow I don't think swimming's as easy."

"To you maybe, but to most they'd think flying one of these was far harder."

A few hours later the Drandarians called and said they were finished installing the inertial compensator, and would like to give it a test, then they could head into their system to get the rest of the parts. Captain Casey agreed to all this and told them to be careful until they knew the full effects of the compensation system in their ships, because with their ship being so much larger, it would still not have quite the maneuverability as a smaller ship would have. They agreed with that, saying they would take it slow and easy until they knew how it handled and work up from there. So the Drandarian ship spent almost an hour doing high speed maneuvers and testing the newly installed system, going progressively faster and tighter, all on board amazed at how much smoother and easier the ship handled because of it.

"So how does it handle?" Captain Casey asked when they finally came to a stop.

"It handles so much better than it ever has, it's an incredible improvement. We can now go nearly twice the speed as we did before, before we even start to feel it. Your engineers are very good. We're ready to go now, try and stay close to us, I've already called ahead and told them that we're bringing visitors, so there shouldn't be a problem."

"I'm glad that the new compensator works well for you. We're ready to go, and we'll stay close, so, by all means, lead the way."

The Drandarian ship took off and the UE1 kept close behind it. They flew through the night, Donny and team three taking the night shift. It was mostly uneventful, just a regular day for them all really, but that was good too, because a regular day is one without danger.

They arrived the next morning and were orbiting high above the Drandarian home planet, and it was huge. The planet is easily as large as Saturn is, it has sparkling blue waters, and large land masses dotted all over where they could see. There were no truly large continents, as there were on Earth, but hundreds of smaller island style continents, so many in fact that they could not count them all. Many of them were right around the size of Australia, or slightly larger, most considerably smaller though. Captain Casey noticed that as soon as they arrived, a large group of massive ships started moving toward their location.

"Well boys, looks like they're sending the whole fleet to greet us. We should probably go get dressed up real quick." Captain Casey said.

"Yes Sir!" They all said and they quickly rushed down to their rooms to get into their dress uniforms, then rushed back up to the bridge.

As soon as they made it back to the bridge, and they were almost all there at the exact same time, they found the communications system pinging them, so Captain Casey told the computer to bring up the communication.

"Yes Captain Cloudburst, we're here."

"Ah, there you are. It seems that many of our high officials have heard much about you and your race, and were delighted that you were coming, so have come to meet you. I see you must have noticed and went and got changed." Captain Cloudburst said with a laugh that sounded suspiciously like a chirp.

"Yes, we noticed, and decided that it would be prudent to dress up a bit." Captain Casey laughed as well.

Their communication system pinged once again, so Kelly went over and answered, and said he would bring everyone on as a conference. No sooner had he said that, when there were twelve people on the screen.

"Hello Captain, I'm Prime Minister Raindrop, and we've heard much of your people and you, as well as your mission especially. I must say it's a very interesting mission you've taken on. Captain Cloudburst has also informed us that you've graciously shared a piece of technology that makes our ships handle a considerable amount better, and in return he has shared with you a couple items of pure relaxation. I however don't see why it was you also gave him some Nutronium, for I would've seen that as a fair trade just as that." Prime Minister Raindrop said.

"First of all, thank you for coming to see us personally, and hello. As I'm sure you've heard, I'm Captain Casey and this is my crew. As for the trade, I felt it was a fair trade, and the amount of Nutronium traded was a very small amount of what I have on board. I assure you we don't feel short handed on this deal at all. Forgive me for asking though, but how is it you seem to know a great deal about us, yet we know absolutely nothing of you?" Captain Casey asked curiously.

"If you're pleased with the deal, then we are as well. As for how we know so much. Well, we watch everything. We have Tenarian friends who keep us informed of most things, but it's mostly kept at a government level, not even most of our ships captains were aware of the war you had with the Qaralon. Had they have known, they would've wanted to go help. I must apologize for not doing so however. We simply didn't have the means to fight a war of that scale. We're also a private species, so we asked that the Tenarians not tell you about us, but most of them actually don't know we're here. The Qaralon sadly do know we're here, and we've regretted them finding us for hundreds of years." Prime Minister Raindrop said.

"I won't fault you for not going to war when you were little prepared to do so. Now that we know you, I hope that we can be called friends, and should at any time you need assistance, you have but to call on us, and we'll come and help as best we can. Humans are a more social race, and we like to meet new people. However, if you'd rather we not tell the general population, we also won't, our government will be informed however, if they don't already know of course."

"Thank you, I'm not aware that your people know of us, and we'd appreciate it if you didn't tell them. I'd like to invite you and your crew to my ship to have our midday meal with myself and the captains, and some of our people?"

"We'd be honored to share a meal with you Sir." Captain Casey accepted graciously.

"It would be I that would be honored. If you'd like to come over in an hour, we can sit and talk, and then have our meal. We were also informed of your need for a few parts, so they were brought up, and if you tell us where you want them, we can teleport them over to you right now." Prime Minister Raindrop added.

"That would be nice Sir, and if you'd just send the parts to my cargo bay, that would be great. If that's all, we'll see you in an hour."

"No, anything else we can talk about later. I look forward to having you aboard, we'll see you in an hour."

The screen went blank and all the people were gone.

"So boys, let's go see all those parts, and see what we can make of them?" Captain Casey said happily.

"Okay." They all said.

They all went down and started going through the parts, and Jonathon realized there were easily enough parts to build at least three holographic suites. Finally the hour passed, and they headed over to the prime ministers ship. They were greeted by the captains of the ships, as well as a few of the high government officials, and then finally the prime minister.

"Welcome to my ship, please come with us, and we'll go sit and talk." Prime Minister Raindrop offered.

They all followed the prime minister to a cozy, but large lounge with comfortable chairs, and they all sat around and talked for a while, until it was time for lunch. Captain Casey had been asked to join the prime minister at his table with a couple of the government officials of course, and it was a very nice affair. The boys were all at different tables with different captains or government people, they too talked with all the people, and they all had a nice lunch. An hour later the lunch was finished, so they returned back to the lounge, where they continued talking for quite some time. It was almost 1600 hours by the time Captain Casey and his crew excused themselves, saying that they should get back on their way, that they very much appreciated the generous offers that had been made, and for the wonderful lunch as well. They too were thanked for their offers, and told that they were welcome back at any time.

"Let's get going guys, we can stop and see some of the sights on the way, but we should be going." Captain Casey said once they were back on board, and changed from their good clothes.

"Yes Sir! I'd like to go see the black hole though, I've never seen one of those before." Jamie asked.

"Well then, you get to get us there, go to it." Captain Casey said, and Jamie smiled and ran ahead to the bridge to get them going.

While Jamie and the rest of his team were on the bridge, the rest of the crew was downstairs starting construction of the pool. They started by removing all the walls that would be in the way, and sealing all the gaps as they went. By the time they reached the black hole, some four hours later, they had gotten most of that done. Because they had had such a big lunch, no one had more than a light snack for dinner, and that was long ago done. They were now parked at a safe distance from the black hole, so that they could see it well and get great information from it, but it would not be strong enough at that distance to pull them in, which they were sure would be the last thing they ever did.

"Let's go to the observation deck and really get a good look at this, and the computers in there will get us some good telemetry on it as well." Captain Casey said.

Instead of answering, the boys led the way at a quick pace to the observation deck at the top of the ship. They climbed the stairs in the room to look out the dome at the huge black hole. According to the computer, it was a massive black hole as well, easily twice as large as any that any person from Earth had ever seen before. Captain Casey decided to stay here and let the computer gather every bit of data about it as it could, so that the Drandarians would not have to worry about a scientific vessel wanting to come out and see it as well. After almost half an hour, the boys said that they had had their fill, so for the rest of the evening before bed, they went back down and worked on their new pool. They started working on the pools deck on the upper level, and got that nearly completed before Captain Casey called bed time. He had figured the boys had worked up enough of a sweat, working on this, that there was no point in doing their exercises.

They ended up spending a total of two days at the black hole, while the computer slowly gathered every bit of information about the hole that it could, and in that time the guys got their new pool nearly finished. All that would be left to do was install the pools pump, heater and filter assembly, as well as make the shield for the pool, and then fill it with water. Captain Casey figured that for that he would just go back to the Drandarian planet, and request them to teleport the water in for him. It would not take much time, and while they were flying, they could easily get the rest of the equipment installed. Captain Casey called the prime minister as they were leaving, to ask if that would be okay, he was told that this was not a problem, and that they had some springs with the most delightful water in the universe that they would be happy to give them.

So about four hours later, with the last of the pool equipment installed, they were above Drandaria, and their pool was being filled. It took maybe five minutes before the pool was completely full, and the boys all wanted to jump in right then and there. The prime minister was thanked, and they were off to search out the other space wonders they had been told about in the area, a few more had been added by the prime minister himself.

They spent almost a week looking at all the sights in the area, while constructing the holographic room. They had not even tried out the pool yet, because they wanted to get the holograph room done first. Captain Casey had to go over the schematics of the room a few times to understand some of the things about the room, but eventually he felt that he understood it all. This had been something that Earth scientists had never really gotten into, so he had known almost nothing about it. After four days, three large rooms had been rebuilt into one even larger room, and the holographic suite was now finished.

They did have to bring in an independent computer system for this room, and program it with the programs that the Drandarians had given to them as well. They were told that by simply telling the computer what they wanted, or program into it what they wanted, they could see or do just about anything, but to remember to be careful, because if you died in there, you died for good. They were told that things like guns, and animals, and vehicles that were generated by the program, could not do harm, but fall off a mountain while climbing, and you would probably not survive. Captain Casey, to test the system, had the computer make up a hockey rink with all the gear, and all the boys played on the ice for a couple hours.

"Wow Sir, this is incredible. I think we should do our exercises in here from now on, so we can exercise almost anywhere we want. Not to mention, with this thing you can go almost anywhere and do almost anything you want." Alex said excitedly.

"I agree with you on both points, so I too think that from now on we'll do our exercises here. You have to remember though, that nothing in here is real. Now there'll of course be limits to the amount each person can use this room, and there'll be no fights. You may use it as a group, which would be the best use of it, but on occasion you may use it alone as well. Of course use will be limited to your off times." Captain Casey warned all the boys.

"Sir, could we maybe go swimming now, I haven't been swimming in forever?" Dillon asked.

"I don't see any reason why not. Seeing as how it's Sunday anyway, we're supposed to be relaxing and having some fun. Now the problem is, not everyone has shorts, so you'll have to swim in your underwear if you don't have any."

"Okay." They all said as they started running to their rooms to change.

Captain Casey followed them and went and got changed himself, and then went down and joined the boys. This was certainly a first for him, swimming on a spaceship, and there would be some very surprised people when he showed them the new toys. He decided to hold off on telling anyone though, because this would be easier to show them. They swam and played and had fun for quite a while, and the boys who could not swim, for the most part just stayed in the shallow end, and just splashed and played, and they only stopped to have dinner.

After dinner, Captain Casey challenged the boys to a war game match, using old fashioned paint ball guns in the holographic room. Captain Casey programmed the computer with a nicely wooded terrain, and they played for a few hours, running and dodging, shooting at each other and getting hit. They had all had a lot of fun, and were happy, but very tired, because they had been going almost nonstop all day.

For the last couple weeks of the month of November the crew of the UE1 spent looking around in and outside the Drandarians solar system, and they saw many sights. They were just about to leave the system when they received a distress call.

CHAPTER 20

DISTRESSING NEWS

The couple weeks since the Universe Explorer left the planet had been fairly quiet for the Drandarians, but as with all things, there always seems to be a calm before the storm. The Drandarians, like most races, kept strict watch on long range scanners deployed around their planets to watch out for threats that might try and sneak in and harm them. It was early afternoon when one of the watchers saw something on his screen that he wished he did not see, but informed his superiors right away. Within half an hour of the viewing, a distress call was being placed.

"Captain Casey, we have a bit of a problem. Some Qaralon and Framgar ships are coming in, but there are too many of them for us to battle. We've called the Tenarians as well, and have requested help, but you're closer. They're a couple days out still, but we could really use your help if you're willing to give it." Prime Minister Raindrop asked softly, pleadingly, looking about as scared as a bird-like looking humanoid can look.

"How many of them are there Sir?" Captain Casey asked.

"There are about fifty that we can see. We're a peaceful race, and as such, aren't equipped to fight a battle such as this. I know you're well equipped for this, and I hate to ask, but how soon can you be here?" The prime minister asked desperately.

"We're about two to three days away, we'll push as hard and fast as we can. We've only just left your system, it's however very large, and we're at the furthest point from you, so it'll take us some time. If you aren't equipped to fight, try and hold them off as long as possible, do what you can, and we'll be there as soon as possible." Captain Casey instructed.

"Thank you." He said simply and disconnected.

"Okay boys, looks like we go into another fight. This time we go against numbers the likes of which I'd hoped to never see again. The Framgar are ferocious fighters, and they're very well trained. You'll find that one Framgar ship will be about the same as fighting five to six Qaralon ships, and they'll swarm you, we'll be put to the test on this one I'm afraid. Tell me now if you don't feel that you're ready for this!" Captain Casey said.

"We're ready Sir, let's go." Donny said after looking around to get confirmation.

"Okay, we'll need a night crew, we'll be going through the nights again. Navigation, get us going, and as fast as you can." Captain Casey said.

"Yes Sir!" They all said.

"My team will take the night shift Sir." Pete said quickly before anyone else could.

"Team four, is this okay with all of you?"

"Yes Sir!" They all stated quickly and firmly.

"Okay then. After lunch you guys can head to bed to get some sleep."

"Yes Sir!" They said.

"Franky, would you like to take the night shift this time?"

"Definitely."

"Then you can head up for some sleep after lunch as well."

"You got it Sir."

"Sir, we have a call coming in from Captain Cloudburst." Alex said.

"Put him on Alex."

"Captain Casey, good to see you again. I wish, however, that it wasn't because we were calling you for help. We seem to be in over our heads though. Even with only fifty ships, they have our entire fleet matched in power, but they're much better than we are. I'm afraid that after you guys forced them to surrender, that they're trying to regroup and beat up on an easier target to save some dignity."

"It's good to see you again as well, but we'll be there as soon as we can, and hopefully we can all hold them at bay until the Tenarians arrive, we'll do our best to not allow them to win. I'd have to agree with you on what their motives are though. Personally I think their world isn't large enough, and or they can't provide enough food to support themselves any longer, so they're getting desperate. It's the only reason I can come up with to explain this."

"I have a feeling that you're correct. I thank you again, and I hope that you get here before they do, and I hope to see you then."

"We'll be there as quickly as we can be, and we'll help you to defeat them. See you in a couple days. If they get there before we do though, do whatever you have to to hold them off." Captain Casey instructed again.

"We will." Captain Cloudburst said and then disconnected.

"Sir, we're getting another call in, this one from a Tenarian ship, a Captain Bloth." Alex said not even five minutes later.

"It's going to be a long couple days I think. Go ahead and put him through!" Captain Casey said with a sigh.

"Hello Captain Casey, it's good to see you again, and in good health. I hear from some very reliable sources that you and your crew are doing very well. I, as well as a few others have been asked to come aid the Drandarians along with you. The problem is though, that we're at least five to six days out. Will you be able to hold them off until then?" Captain Bloth asked politely.

"Captain, it's good to see you too, and I see you've been talking to my mom again. We're doing real well though, thanks. We should hopefully arrive before, or at the worst, at the same time as the attackers, and we should be fine, get here as quick as you can though, just in case there are more on the way, because you can never tell."

"How else can I keep up with what you're up to. We'll meet with you as quick as we can make it there though."

"Okay, thanks." Captain Casey said and they disconnected.

It was almost exactly two days later that they made it to where the Drandarian ships were waiting in a line, and they could see that the Qaralon attack fleet was only maybe two hours away. Lance, who was on navigation at the time, set them at the front of the Drandarian ships as the head of the battle. Kelly, who was once again at communications, since he really enjoyed it, put a call through to the Drandarian fleet as soon as they were parked.

"Drandarian fleet, this is the UE1, we're in battle mode, act as backup, don't let anything surround us, otherwise try not to get too close, we wouldn't want to accidentally hit you."

"Yes Sir!" Was the reply from all the ships.

"Well guys, should we go meet them, or wait for them?" Captain Casey asked.

"I say we give them a warning they can't refuse, and if they do, we go and meet them in one hour Sir." Kelly said.

"Sounds good to me, would I be correct when I say you'll be the one giving said warning!" Captain Casey asked.

"Oh yes Sir, I wouldn't miss this for the world." Kelly said with a grin.

"Well go for it, I know you enjoy this part." Captain Casey said with a warm smile.

"Qaralon attack fleet, this is the UE1, we recommended you turn your fleet around now, and leave this space and never come back, failure to comply will result in the destruction of all your ships." Kelly said as politely as he could.

"UE1, you're no match for us, the whole Drandarian fleet together is no match for us. Surrender now, and we'll promise to kill you quickly." A voice they could only assume was Framgar said, it was a little less course and a lot better spoken.

"We're sorry, that's not an option, it's in your best interest though to back down, again, we'll destroy all your ships if you come any closer." Kelly warned sweetly.

"If you don't surrender now, we'll gladly kill you slowly, and feed you to your friends." The voice said menacingly.

"I'm sorry, was that a threat, you should know we don't take threats lightly." Kelly said warningly.

"It wasn't a threat, we'll do that, and we'll do it gladly." The voice said.

"Oh, okay, I thought you were threatening me. I told you, that wasn't a good idea. Now you get no further warnings, when we meet you, you'll be slaughtered without concern, thank you very much." Kelly said and killed the connection.

"There we go captain, that should rile them up a bit." Kelly said with a grin.

"Yes, I bet it will. A little snot nosed brat like you telling them off, I bet that would tick them off a bit." Captain Casey said grinning.

"Hey, I'm not little." Kelly said while puffing himself up just as large as he could make himself look. Everyone laughed at this.

"Captain, I've been thinking. I have an idea, but I don't know if the Drandarians would like it or not!" Donny said.

"Let's hear it?"

"Well, they say they aren't very good at fighting, what if Franky and I, and two teams take over two of their ships, with them on board of course, and this way we have three ships to do the fighting. I'd say two of their smaller ships, because they'd be more maneuverable."

"It's a good idea, but it's your job to ask then, since it's your idea."

"Okay, Kelly, call up Captain Cloudburst for me please?" Donny asked, Kelly nodded and did as he was asked, and moments later, Captain Cloudburst was on screen.

"Hello Captain Cloudburst. I have a question for you?" Donny said.

"Yes, Donny wasn't it?"

"That's right Sir."

"What can I do for you?"

"Well, remember how you said that you weren't really equipped to fight a battle such as this! I know your ships are capable, but your people really aren't, since you don't fight unless absolutely necessary. Well, would it be an insult if two of our teams were to pretty much take over the bridge of two of your ships, so that we have an even higher chance of winning this fight?" Donny asked gently.

"You're right, the equipment is capable, even more so after your modifications, but our people really aren't. I wouldn't consider it an insult, and would be honored to be able to watch one of your teams in action, so would gladly invite you to my ship. I could ask for a volunteer from one of the others, I'm sure they won't have any problems with it. Doesn't your ship require you though?" Captain Cloudburst asked curiously.

"No, one to two teams can easily manage the bridge of our ship, and everything in the ship can be controlled from the bridge, so unless we get structural damage, we need never leave the bridge. If you'd like to arrange it, Franky and I, as well as two of our teams will teleport as soon as the arrangements are made. I'd like to ask that it's one of your smaller ships though as well, due to their increased maneuverability."

"Okay, give me just a few minutes and I'll make the arrangements." Captain Cloudburst said and then disconnected.

"Very well done Donny, the way you did it made it seem like less of an insult." Captain Casey said.

"Thanks Sir. Which two teams want to stay and which two want to go?" Donny asked.

"We'll stay." Jamie said.

"We'll go." Brady said.

"We'll go." Tristan said.

"And I guess we'll stay then, which was my choice anyway." Pete smiled.

"Good, we have our teams. Team one, you're with me, and Team three, you're with Franky. Everyone make sure you have your weapons and your scanners, we'll be setting them to maximum, so be very careful, and don't shoot unless you're absolutely certain of your target." Donny called out.

"Yes Sir!" Everyone answered.

"Good call. Come on everyone, we better get ready. In ten minutes we head out." Captain Casey ordered.

"Yes Sir!" Everyone said.

"Warren, walk with me please?" Captain Casey asked.

He started heading for the supply closet to get his weapon and scanner, as were everyone else.

"Warren, you and Will will need to be ready down there, any injured will be teleported directly to you. We might get some injuries in this fight, because as you already know, this is a pretty uneven fight we're going into. We'll come out of it alive, I have no fear about that, but can we make it out unscathed, probably not." Captain Casey said.

"We'll be ready, Will's doing amazingly well, and could probably soon pass every test to be a nurse or a med tech such as yourself. This'll be a good test for him. We need to go now as well, good luck up there." Warren said, and started rushing off.

"Thanks, we may need it." Captain Casey called after him.

Not even five minutes later, everyone was gathered on the bridge again, and were waiting for the call to come in from Captain Cloudburst. Finally it did.

"Okay guys, sorry about the wait. I knew it wasn't going to be a problem, but they all wanted one of your teams to come to their ship. Finally I had to pull rank and pick a ship. You may teleport to our ships at any time, I just sent the codes of the ships, and mine is the first on the list." Captain Cloudburst said.

"Okay, is everyone ready for this . . . . Yes, good. Let's go. Marty, would you please do the honors and send us to our ships please?" Donny asked.

A few seconds later the boys were gone.

"Okay boys, are we all ready?" Captain Casey asked his two external teams a few moments later.

"Give us a few minutes Sir to learn these controls, they're slightly different than ours, but at least we can read them, so that makes it easier." Donny answered.

"Same here Sir." Franky added.

"Okay, tell me when you're ready, and then we head out. The rest of you stand back and provide support as was earlier arranged. I'll be directing the battle from here, I hope you don't mind us taking over guys, but I know this isn't your area of expertise." Captain Casey said.

"Please take over, we'd only get us into more trouble." One of the other captains said.

"Okay Captain, we're ready." Franky said.

"As are we." Donny said.

"Lock and load, let's go." Captain Casey ordered.

"Yes Sir!" Everyone said, even the Drandarians.

"Let's go meet them boys." Captain Casey said to his crew.

"Already on it Sir." Dillon said.

And they started heading toward the Qaralon and Framgar ships, they would meet in about twenty minutes. The rest of the Drandarian fleet followed behind, but kept their distance, as they had been asked.

Franky and Donny were flanking their captain, and kept right with them. The three ships had kept all communications open though, so that they could hear absolutely everything that was going on between all three of them.

"When we start the battle, you'll want to make sure that you're always holding on, because we'll pull some pretty high "G" stunts and moves, and if you aren't ready for it, you'll get thrown around. Is there a way to move these chairs though? We aren't used to sitting while fighting, and they might get in the way." Donny asked.

"You got it, and yes, we can remove them for you." Captain Cloudburst said, and he instructed everyone on board the ship as per the instructions.

The same basic conversation had been held by Franky and the captain of his ship, and within a few seconds, both bridges were cleared of the large comfy chairs. Both boys gave their crews other instructions as they went out to meet the attackers. Soon though, they were in the midst of a battle worth telling for years to come.

All three ships worked together, as if they were being directed by someone, yet none of the three ships had even spoken since they left. It was looking like a beautifully choreographed dance number of many dancers, the captain and his boys all working together to deal with the large threat all around them. It had looked like an incredibly lopsided fight with three ships going at roughly fifty, and only the fifty or so ships of the Drandarians well behind them to act as backup, as well to make sure none of the attacking ships slipped through.

The battle was lopsided, but not quite how the Drandarians had thought, nor the attackers for that matter. Everyone watching the fight were amazed at the speeds and maneuvers that the three ships were using in order to negate the large disadvantage that facing fifty some ships posed. All three ships had decided that maximum yield weapons was the only way to go for a battle this size, so they were pelting the attackers in every direction with everything they had. Often times each of the three ships were firing on anywhere from two to ten opposing ships at any given time, yet not once did it look like they were truly out-numbered.

Captain Casey and his current crew decided to move in behind the attackers, and let the other two ships face the front, in this way they started working them even more. They were buzzing in and out of the Qaralon and Framgar ships, and hitting them at every chance. Often times the Qaralon and Framgar ships were hit before they even knew they were under attack, the three ships they were fighting were going so fast and furious, they really should have just backed off when they saw this happening.

Nearly an hour into the fight, the three ships had only been hit maybe once each, and of those, only one was a direct hit, and it had not affected them any, yet the attackers numbers had fallen to almost half already. Of the twenty three ships that had been removed from the fight, only two had been outright destroyed, the others had just been completely disabled.

The Drandarian backup ships sat mostly in the sidelines watching the incredible show in front of them, and only twice, at the prompting of Captain Casey, did they act. On both times, one of their ships had been surrounded, and were at risk of getting hit, so they would rush forward and disable a couple of the ships, and then when it was evened out again, they backed off again. It was in this way that at least one of the ships was destroyed.

With fewer numbers of attacking ships now, the fight started to go easier. The Framgar had the most amount of ships left, as they had proven to be pretty good fighters as well, but even they had started to lose ships. The three ships still being nearly untouched, started circling around the attackers now, and forcing them into a smaller circle, tighter to each other, which meant that they did not have as much room to move, and they risked shooting each other. Captain Casey, Donny and Franky used this to their advantage though. This was the reason why the boys loved this move, it was great for picking off your prey, and they could hardly fire at you. The attackers tried many times, unsuccessfully, to get out of the trap that they all knew that they had been moved into, but each time they they did, they were asked to get back in place, and not too nicely either.

It was less than an hour later when all the attacking ships were disabled. In roughly two hours, three ships had completely removed the threat that the fifty two ships had posed, and they were all scattered over a five minute space. Captain Casey called all the Drandarian ships forward to surround the ships, so they moved into place, and then Captain Casey told Kelly to take the honors, because this was his favorite part. So from the Drandarian ship, Kelly made the call.

"We're going to destroy all your ships now, one by one and your people are to never come back, ever, is that clear." Kelly snapped out.

"We're unarmed, that's not your style, you wouldn't destroy us now." A Framgar captain said smugly.

"Oh, really, watch us. Captain Casey, do it!" Kelly said.

The UE1 started teleporting everyone to the largest ship, and less than five minutes later, all the ships were empty except one. Amazingly enough, they had no captives on board any of their ships.

"Drandarian ships, we give you the honor of destroying all the ships, except the populated one." Kelly said gleefully.

Within five minutes, the Framgar and Qaralon people watched from the ship they were now stuffed into, as their ships were all destroyed by the people they had intended to attack with ease.

"You'll now be allowed to leave this space, and you won't be followed, tell your people that in the future we won't be so kind, leave now." Kelly snapped.

They said nothing, but started to leave the solar system on the limited power that they had, and as soon as they were far enough away, Captain Casey led the Drandarians back to their planet. The prime minister teleported to the lead Drandarian ship as soon as he was able to, and everyone was invited to come over. All the boys came back to the UE1 and got changed, and then headed over to celebrate.

"Captain Casey and crew, we watched the battle from the ground, and I must say that that was possibly the most incredible thing we've ever seen before. You were quick and agile, and beat them without being brutal. Any time that we've ever had to fight the Qaralon, it was a fight just to stay alive. We've never gone against more than four ships at a time, and we usually ended up in losing at least one. My people owe you more than we can ever hope to repay you, yet I have a question for you." Prime Minister Raindrop said in the utmost thanks.

"Thank you Prime Minister, it wasn't a particularly hard battle, and we came out with nothing more than a few bruises, of which we're abundantly thankful. Had your people not been willing to accept a couple teams to have virtually taken over your ships, it may not have gone so well, so we thank them as well. As for the question you have, I believe I know what it will be. You'd like my people to train your people how to fly like we do, am I correct?"

"Yes, you certainly are correct. I'm not certain as to what we can give to you to pay for all the help you've given to us already, let alone if you help us with this, but we'll do whatever we can."

"We won't accept payment for such things anyway, this is simply friends helping and teaching friends, not to mention it'll be my boys to teach your people, which will teach them much as well. All of this interacting with your people and the others they've met has helped their self confidence, and their inherent distrust of people a great deal, far more than I could've done by myself. So you see, it' not as one sided as you thought." Captain Casey said with a smile.

"Well, one way or another, we'll pay you back, whether you want it or not. As I told you before, we're a peaceful people, but this battle has opened many of our eyes, we need to be prepared. I'm not sure what would've happened if you either couldn't come, or didn't make it in time, but I'm sure it would've been disastrous. We may have already collapsed by the time you arrived. What you gave to my people, is far more than you can imagine."

"We'll help your people learn how to fight better, we'll teach them techniques and tricks, and then they can teach others as you need to. However I'd recommend something to your ship builders."

"Thank you, and what's that recommendation please?" The prime minister asked.

"To make smaller ships. The large comfortable ships, while nice for traveling, aren't really practical for fighting, and that was the reason we borrowed two of your smaller ships. As you probably noticed though, even those smaller ships were unable to move quite as quickly as we were able to. Give the ships the same amount of power and shields, as well as increase the firepower, and once your people know how to fly them, you'll no longer need help, although you should ask if needed, because even we too ask for help in the face of large numbers."

"I had definitely noticed how much more agile your ship was in comparison to ours. We built our ships more for the comfort, and built in the protection systems more as an afterthought. I'll definitely tell our shipyards to go with a smaller design with those recommendations in mind though."

"Don't get me wrong, you don't have to sacrifice comfort when building your ships. We now have the pool and the holographic room, as well as many other amenities; including games rooms and a theatre, but if you make them smaller, it just makes them better. Our ship, as it stands right now, after removing some of the rooms to build the pool and holographic room, would lodge about a hundred and fifty comfortably. I understand the largest of your ships could take a considerable amount more than that, really, there's no real need for that. Even though our ship could hold that amount, it almost never has that in it, because there's no point even to have that many. If this ship were to be destroyed, it'd only lose needless lives, and they'd just be sitting around most of the time doing nothing anyway. It's better to have a smaller ship properly manned. I'd also make it so that all systems can be controlled from the bridge for greater control, and it'd also reduce the amount of people needed to operate your ships. In this way you can have a greater amount of ships, with the same, or less people running them. Now I don't recommend you run with only twenty two people as we are now, a normal compliment would be about a hundred, but we don't fly around the clock either, unless we need to."

"That's all very good information. Would you and your people also be willing to sit with our ship builders, and help them plan a ship, this way we can all brainstorm and come up with some good ideas?"

"We'd love to. I know my boys would all have some very good ideas, because they've all suggested changes to be made to our ship as well." Captain Casey said.

"Well then, at the same time we'll redesign your ship with any changes your boys and yourself see fit, and we'll do that first, call it a small amount of payback." The prime minister offered happily.

"We'd all be happy to accept that offer Sir." Captain Casey smiled.

"Thank you, for everything. By now my people on the planet have hopefully had time to make a feast fit for your deed, and we invite you down to our planet to eat?" Prime Minister Raindrop invited.

"Thank you Sir, we'd like that very much."

Communications were shut down and everyone started teleporting down to the planet as soon as they were in range, which took less than thirty minutes.

CHAPTER 21

A HERO'S WELCOME

Everyone was teleported to the surface of the planet, and they found themselves in a very nice outdoor dining area. They were above the sea on a high cliff. They were surrounded by tall carved stone pillars, with streamers blowing in the breeze from the tops of the pillars. Each streamer was a different brightly colored cloth, each of them upwards of three meters long, the brisk breeze whipped them around, causing snaps every few seconds.

The pillars were roughly four meters high, each of them beautifully carved out of what appeared to be a solid round chunk of marble, all the carvings were of various animals that none of them had ever seen before. Every scene though appeared to be very peaceful. Some of the animals appeared quite small, but most were quite large, many of them were bird like, some with feathers, some without, but many too were almost cat like in their appearances. Nothing looked anything like what the captain or the boys had ever seen before, and the carvings intrigued them.

The smell of the sea air and the food though was tantalizing to all the battle weary men and women. The sights were incredible to the captain and his crew, because it was possibly the most beautiful setting they had ever seen. Everyone was shown to tables, five people per table, and they all sat. Captains Casey and Cloudburst were seated with the prime minister, as well as two other people, one who was introduced as the prime ministers wife, and the other was his personal adviser.

Shortly thereafter, a long string of waiters and waitresses came out of the kitchen building, carrying trays ladened with mounds of food, and on each tray a different food. Four of these trays were brought over to the table that Captain Casey was seated at, and everyone took a small amount of each of the four foods. Moments later more trays were brought, these either had bowls neatly stacked on them, with a delicious smelling soup inside, and another had goblets with drinks in them. Again each person at the table took some of what was being served, and then the people moved off.

Once everyone had their plates filled, the waiters and waitresses moved off to the sides, and waited to be called upon if needed. Captain Casey and all the boys enjoyed the food a great deal, and all the boys ate slow and politely, as the captain had been teaching them, and they all talked with the people at the tables with them. Not one of the boys from the crew was seated with another crew member, they were on their own, and they were doing fine. Captain Casey looked around, and was pleased that all his boys were handling the situation well, they were all talking politely with the people at their tables.

Once the meals were complete, the dishes were quickly removed, and the waiters and waitresses came back out with even more trays loaded up, this time with many different types of desserts. None of the boys, nor even the captain, knew where to start, because everything looked so good. They all ended up choosing two or three different ones, as all the other people at the tables were doing. The desserts, if it were possible, were even better than the meal itself had been, and that was saying a lot, and nearly everyone called the waiters and waitresses back to get even more. The boys sure did not mind this, but no one was hungry by the end of such a fine meal, that was for sure. Once everyone was finished eating, the prime minister stood up and all went silent.

"This meal is in honor of our friends, Captain Casey and your crew, please stand. We, the people of Drandaria, thank you for all the help that you have provided to us, and have offered to give to us. There isn't enough that we could offer to pay you back, so we won't try, however, we'll treat you like heroes the entire time that you're here, and at any time should you want or need anything, you have only to ask. As I'm sure you're aware, you're the first people to have been invited to our planet in more years than anyone alive can remember, but for you, you're welcome anytime. We welcome you to visit our many lush forests, lakes and rivers, and sample our many amenities, including our spas. You may either stay on your ship, or at one of our many resorts or spas." Prime Minister Raindrop offered graciously.

"We'd love to take you up on your hospitality Sir and stay at a local spa or resort, whichever will be able to hold all of us. We'll visit our ship, if and when we need to, and I can have all communications routed directly to me from the ship." Captain Casey said, accepting the kind offer.

"I'm certain that the spa on the cliff can accept all of you easily. I'll make the arrangements personally. In the meantime, I'd have Captain Cloudburst give you a tour of our fine city, and show you the many sights it holds. By the time you get back, everything will be arranged. If you go into any shops, feel free to get what you need, and have them bill it to me."

"Thank you Sir, that would be very nice." Captain Casey smiled warmly.

"No, thank you. I should be going, but I'll see you soon. Captain Cloudburst, I leave our guests in your more than capable hands."

"Follow me please gentlemen. I'll show you some of our most pleasant sights in and around the city. I have a transport already waiting for us." Captain Cloudburst said happily.

"Thank you, lead the way Sir."

All the boys were bustling excitedly as they left the dining pavilion. They climbed on the hover transporter, and then they were off. Captain Cloudburst had called it a city, yet by almost any Earth standards, this would be a small village. All the streets were small, barely two lanes, only just enough for the vehicles, and they were all paved with intricately designed interlocking paving stones in many different colours. It was very quaint and quiet, all the homes and store fronts were in rich and deep colors, yet accented with contrasting bright colours as well, and blended well with their surroundings. There was brilliant detail in everything they saw, from the designs of the buildings, to the vivid artwork that adorned nearly every wall, to the many statues that surrounded them. Captain Cloudburst kept a rolling dialog as to what they were seeing and where they were. It was a very pleasant tour, and none of them could wait to see where they would be staying, if the city was this nice.

"Captain Cloudburst. Would it be too much trouble to find a shop that has clothes? We have nothing but our uniforms, and for this place, I think they'd feel uncomfortable." Donny asked.

"Yes, we can find a shop, I'm sure, where you can find clothing that'll be much more comfortable."

"Thank you Sir." Everyone said.

A while later the captain stopped in front of a small store with a large bright sign above it. It was a clothing store, and they all went in. They all looked and found the clothing to be of a very simple cotton like soft material, and in very simple loose designs, just like they had seen every other Drandarian so far wearing. The colors varied from light airy colours, like whites, to very bold and bright colors in the blues and purples, and even oranges, yellows and reds. Everyone picked out a set of pants and shirts in a couple different colours each, as well as a couple pairs of shorts in the same soft material. Captain Cloudburst talked to the owner of the shop, and she took note of everything, and then thanked everyone for visiting and for helping. They thanked her and then they left. As they were leaving the shop, Captain Cloudburst received a call, and he did not even say more than hi, before putting his communicator away.

"That was the Prime Minister, he says your lodgings are ready, and that I'm to take you there now." Captain Cloudburst offered in way of explanation.

"Thank you." Captain Casey said.

They arrived to the place that they would be staying at a few minutes later, and all jumped out of the vehicle. The place looked very calm and peaceful from the outside, and they were relaxed just looking at it. It appeared to be in a style similar to a clay adobe, done in soft earth tones. The roof was a clay tile of some sort, and once again, like much that they had seen so far, was done in many different colors, but this was done instead in a beautiful mosaic, so the roof was a gigantic picture of a very beautiful sunset. There were many windows and doors, all of them large and inviting, with soft round tops and most of them were open, letting their simple white curtains blow in the breeze coming up off the cliff. They all felt that they could stay outside and enjoy the beautiful exterior for hours. Then they went inside. The warmth that flowed from the place made the crew feel as if they had never known peace before, everything was so simple and nice, but very elegant. The entry way was large and stunning. There were stone statues all over, but the most beautiful of them were splashing water into a very simple looking round fountain. They were almost swan looking birds, only they had been painted in the most amazing colours any of them had ever seen before. There were six of these large statues, each half a meter from the other, all spraying water out of their highly arched mouths. The water beams met in the centre and splashed down into the pool. When they looked into the water, not only was it the cleanest and clearest water they had ever seen, but there were fish swimming in it that made even the painted swan like birds seem dull. They were roughly the size of a large gold fish, there were probably a hundred or more of them in there, and their colors varied greatly, it seemed not one was like another in any way, other than their body shape, otherwise their colours and patterns were entirely different. Someone came up to them as they were enjoying the pond, bowed, and welcomed them to his humble abode, and looked forward to serving them for as long as they wished to stay. Captain Cloudburst took his leave, saying he would see everyone tomorrow.

"Follow me please, and I'll show you to your rooms. You boys will need to share, two boys to a room, I hope that won't be an inconvenience." The man asked.

"No Sir, that won't be a problem." Donny answered for them all.

"Then here are your rooms, please feel free to choose which ones you want, there are fifteen rooms, and the whole place is just for you." The man offered, waving them toward their rooms.

"Thank you Sir, that's very generous. What's your name please?" Captain Casey asked.

"I'm called Flowing Sea Sir, and you're Captain Casey, correct?"

"Jonathon please, Jonathon Casey." Captain Casey offered.

"Jonathon then. I invite you all to visit our many amenities while you stay here, our tubs have the most refreshing waters, and my people give the most relaxing massages, I welcome you to try everything." Flowing Sea offered, and then left the men to their stay.

"Okay boys, Warren and I have a room each, as will Donny, Franky and Will. The rest of you may choose your room partner.

Let's go get changed, and check this place out. While we're here, we're on vacation, and you may address me as Jonathon, okay."

"Yes Sir!" They all said happily, Jonathon just shook his head.

All the boys quickly paired off and picked a room, and then went in and got changed into their new clothes. The rooms were all very nice simple rooms, decorated in very tranquil colors and artworks. There was a small bathroom attached, and they too were very nice and simple. The rooms each had only one bed, so the boys would have to share, but they did not mind that. Every last one of them though felt the beds, and as they suspected, they were incredibly soft and luxurious. Then there was the bedding on them, they made silk feel like sixty grit sandpaper they were so soft. They all exited their rooms at much the same time. Some of the boys had chosen the softer colors, while others chose the bold or bright, yet even the brightest yellow looked very nice on the boys.

"Well, we all look comfortable. Let's go look around and see what they have to offer." Captain Casey commented when he exited his room to find all the others there already, waiting for him.

They walked together and saw many people there, and they called out what services they were offering, and once everyone knew what there was, they went back to whatever they wanted to do first. Jonathon and Donny both went for a massage, while Warren and a few of the others went to sit in the large mud baths. Still yet a few went to the sauna, and some went for manicures and pedicures, while the rest went to the bubbling spas. They spent the better part of the afternoon just laying around and relaxing, taking full advantage of all the services that the spa offered.

They went out for dinner at a small roadside restaurant that Flowing Sea referred them to, and they all had a nice light meal. After the very large lunch they had had, this was much appreciated. Once back, they spent the rest of the evening again relaxing, but this time in the large pool. The pool was very grand and beautiful, it had a large rock waterfall feeding it, and had statues of various Drandarian animals spouting water into the pool. These statues were every bit as nice as the ones inside had been, only they were not painted, just left as natural rock. Many of these same creatures they were seeing now they had seen earlier carved into the pillars where they had dined earlier in the day, they all thought that they looked even nicer in this form. The waterfall though was truly spectacular, so very realistic looking, that no one was certain as to whether it was a real waterfall or not.

The following morning, after a rest that none had ever felt before, they got up and met out in the hall, dressed in their other new outfit.

"Man, I don't think I've ever slept so well in my life before. The beds are so comfortable, I felt like I was laying on a cloud all night." Jamie said first, saying it best.

"Yeah, I felt the same way." Jonathon said.

"Me too." Everyone else added.

"Let's go find a place to eat breakfast!" Jonathon said.

They walked outside and were met with a cool morning breeze, and the smell of the sweet salty air. They strolled down the street and found a small bistro style restaurant with plenty of tables outside, so they all took a seat, and then ordered their breakfast. They sat around talking with the many locals that were either sitting and enjoying their food, or the people who were passing by. They enjoyed a very nice meal, and then went and walked the town. They stopped and talked to dozens of Drandarians as they toured, all of them were very pleased to meet the captain and his crew, all of them thanking them, all of them very polite and friendly, and more than a few times they stood and talked for at least a few minutes. The captain and the boys all got to know several people in this way. They had been walking and looking around for more than an hour, when Captain Casey's communicator pinged him, when he looked, he saw the prime minister, so he answered right away.

"Captain Casey, how are you this morning?"

"Very well, thank you Prime Minister, and you?"

"Also very well. I'd like to invite your people to our engineering center, so that we can do up the designs of your ship? We did a full scan on it last night, so have the full schematics for it already ready to go."

"Sure Sir, where is it, and how do we get there from where we currently are? We'll walk though, since it seems that nothing is far from anything here." He asked.

"It's just under a kilometer from your current location, just keep heading the same direction as you're going now. It's the only building that's three stories high, you can't miss it." Prime Minister Raindrop informed them.

"Thanks Sir, we'll be there very soon."

"Thanks, see you soon." He replied and disconnected.

"Well boys, let's get a good jog going, at a fast pace, we should make it in just a few minutes." Captain Casey said, and then set the pace.

They jogged the almost one kilometer to the engineering building, all of them easily keeping up with their captain now. When they had arrived to the building they were told to go to, they found it to be an impressive building. They had seen it from a bit of a distance the day before, but did not get a really good look at it. As they were told, it was three stories high, and it was of a very nice design, very natural looking. It was of the colors of the surroundings, and incorporated as much natural materials as they could use. The building itself was an incredibly beautiful log structure, but many of the supports were made of huge carved stone pillars, also carved with animals in them, similar once again to the pillars at the dining pavilion the day before. This was one of only a handful of buildings that they had come across that did not have any painting done to it, nor was the roof done in any sort of pattern, it was just a nice simple red clay tiled roof. They went up to the large main entrance, that was enshrouded almost entirely in glass, as well there was a very large statue guarding either side of the large entrance. Each statue was at least four meters tall, and as with all the other statues they had seen so far, they were very intricately carved. These ones were of a bear like animal, only it was lean like a cat, far more muscular, and if the carving showed it correctly, far furrier as well. All the boys stared at them, whispering to each other that there was no way they wanted to meet one of them in the wild, especially if they were that big in real life. They entered the building, and were met in the wide reception area by the Prime Minister himself.

"Welcome to our most advanced engineering center on the planet, it's here that we'll do most of our work."

"Thank you for the welcome Sir, this is a very beautiful building, very well designed I might add." Captain Casey said.

"Thank you, but please follow me, we have a meeting room all set up with the hologram of your ship, so that we can go make any desired changes to it."

"Will you be there helping as well Sir?" Captain Casey asked curiously.

"Yes, I'm an engineer first and foremost, and love to design ships. I haven't had much time to do so in the past few years, being a politician and all, but I still draw when I get a chance." He answered with a nice smile.

For the next two hours, the crew, as well as the prime minister and a few Drandarian engineers, tore the ship down and rebuilt it back up, making hundreds of small changes, but nothing very major. The main changes they went with; was an increase in shield generators, and extra strength added into key areas of the ship. There were a few modifications to the bridge of the ship as well, but mostly for comfort, like redesigning the way the stations felt. Once they were finished, the ship still looked exactly like what they were used to, but there were some nice changes that would help a lot.

"Well Prime Minister, why don't we go for lunch, and then we can come back and do up a design, using much of what we just put into our ship, into yours." Captain Casey asked.

"Sounds like a great idea. Let me just send this plan to our shipyard, and let them get to work on your ship, they already have it at the shipyard, and are ready to go as soon as I give them the plans."

They went for lunch in the cafeteria and had a very good meal, especially considering it was in fact a cafeteria, and everyone knew how bad cafeteria food usually was. They all sat and chatted away while they ate, mostly about the design changes that they had made. Just as they were heading back to the conference room, Captain Casey's communicator paged him. The others continued on without him.

"Good to see you're still alive, we can't see any action, yet we can see the planet now, we're almost there, and should be there in about twelve hours." Captain Bloth greeted the captain.

"Oh crap, sorry Captain, I should've called you guys off. We've been so busy, that I completely forgot. We took care of the problem in about two hours, and the attacking fleet is limping home in one ship. We dumped all the survivors into one ship and destroyed the rest. They probably aren't very happy with us, but we told them the next time they come, we destroy instead of disable, so hopefully they'll think twice next time." Captain Casey said.

"Sorry, did you say you took care of them in two hours?" Captain Bloth asked incredulously.

"Yes I did. We borrowed the use of two of the Drandarian ships, two of my teams manned them, and then with our ship, we were able to over power them, even though we were outnumbered, fifty two to three." Captain Casey said.

"There was only three of you, what about the other Drandarian ships, didn't they join in?" Captain Bloth asked, still clearly in shock.

"No, we told them to offer backup only, and they helped twice during the fight, but nothing too major. They were happy to do it that way as well, they aren't really fighters. We are however going to change that a bit. I've agreed to teach them how to fight, and we're designing some new ships for them, so it'll be easier."

"Wow, that is good. Well then, we'll just stay in the area for a bit then, and offer help if it's needed, for just in case they decide to come back. Remember the Qaralon are not really the smartest beings there are."

"Okay, I'm sure that won't be a problem. We're staying on the planet for a bit while helping them redesign the ships, and then we'll come back into space once our ship is finished."

"What happened to it, did you almost get destroyed in the fight?" Captain Bloth asked in a panic.

"No no, nothing like that. We were hit twice, and received nothing more than a few scratches. We sat down and did some design changes, and the Drandarians are going to rebuild it for us to the new specifications. They wanted to do at least something to pay us back, and we couldn't refuse." Captain Casey smiled.

"Very nice. I look forward to seeing it when it's done then. Well, I'll let you get back to what you were doing then, and we'll just keep watch and explore a bit then." Captain Bloth said.

"Okay, talk to you later then." Captain Casey said and disconnected.

Captain Casey entered the room with the rest and explained to them the conversation that he had just had, and they all chuckled that they had got caught up with everything and had forgot to call them off. They did all feel that it was prudent though to stay there for the time being though, because, like Captain Bloth had said, the Qaralon were not too terribly bright.

"No problem. We've already gotten started, and the boys have been firing off ideas since we got in here. We've added a few as well, and we already have a preliminary design. We like the design that we already use on our ships, so we're staying with that, but we've cut its size down to about an eighth of what it was. Come take a look, and see what you think?" Prime Minister Raindrop asked, sounding almost as giddy as a bird could sound.

"Much better, if you don't mind my saying of course. I think you have nearly everything already, so I won't add anything more. I see you went with our idea of increasing the size of the structure around the engine and power rooms, and the dual shield generators. I hope it helps the performance like I think it will." Captain Casey said.

"I'm sure it will Sir. I've run it through the simulators here, four times, and the shields should nearly triple in strength, just by doubling them, and the structural changes decrease susceptibility in that area, like what happened on the UE10, by two hundred percent almost." Donny said.

"Very good, that's what I was hoping to hear. Can you run what would happen if we added another inertial stabilizer to the ship, would that actually help any?" Captain Casey asked curiously.

"Good idea Sir, let me run it." Donny said, and he spent about five minutes programming the computer with the information. When he got the results, after another four tests to confirm, he gave a smile.

"Yes Sir, it looks like adding another, or doubling the power, either way, we could get almost complete compensation. I'd go with a second unit, of the same size, just for the backup factor." Donny answered with a satisfied look.

"Great, we'll have that added as well then. Prime Minister, you might want to add that to yours as well." Captain Casey said.

"Good thinking. Adding now. I'll also call the shipyard, and have that added to the plans for your ship."

"Thanks a lot Sir."

By dinner time, everyone was ready to go. The ship was fully designed, and it was ready to go, the shipyards would get the designs after dinner. Everyone went to a local restaurant and had a nice meal, and it was during the after dinner drinks, that Franky had an idea.

"Sir, what do you think about a small four or five man ship that could be stored in our cargo bay. They could add incredible firepower to the ship, and if we put the same engine, power, shield and weapons as a full sized ship, it'd be next to impossible to catch or beat us." He asked.

"I love the idea." Prime Minister Raindrop said.

"I too like the idea, we can go very basic on the setup, just a bridge, with simple sleeping and restroom facilities, and a small kitchenette, for in case you need to be out for any length of time. We'd have to build it extra strong though, to stand up to the stresses that that large an engine would put on such a small frame. We could cut the engine power in half though, and keep the same speed more than likely, and still keep all the performance and maneuverability you seek. If we're quick, we can make another change to the ship, and increase the size of the cargo bay and put two of them in, depending on the size of the shuttles." Captain Casey said, really liking that idea. They had shuttles in their fleet already, but nothing quite like what Franky was suggesting, because he was almost making a tiny war ship.

"That sounds good, we can design them in the morning, and make the other change to the ship as well, I think we'll do the same to ours as well, but we can do all that tomorrow. Once we're done that, we can have them start construction on two of them Why don't we all meet back at the office at 0700 hours tomorrow, and we can get it done." Prime minister Raindrop offered happily again. He was very happy to be able to do this for the people that were giving so much.

"Yes Sir!" Franky said excitedly, they all nodded as well, and then everyone headed out.

Captain Casey and his crew headed back to the spa, and they sat around in the pool, enjoying the peaceful surroundings, and chatting for the rest of the evening.

The next morning they headed to the office after having an early breakfast, they found that the prime minister and the other engineers were already there and working. They already had a good preliminary design for the shuttles, one that everyone liked.

"We ran some simulations, and found that by cutting the engine size in half, we actually increased performance of the overall design, and it uses less power. We can still only go the normal maximum of a hundred LYS, no matter what, so that's what we're doing." The head engineer said.

"Great, let me see." Franky said excitedly, and then went and looked over what he had thought about. "It's perfect, it's almost exactly how I imagined it. You have the dual shield generators and inertial compensator's, and the engine should be even a bit too large for the design, so we should have incredible handling." Franky said excitedly still, when he took a minute to look it over.

"Yeah, I admit it looks really good. Let's go with this then, and let's quickly modify our cargo bay so that we can hold a couple of these little beasts." Captain Casey said, meaning the comment about the beasts, because that was exactly what they were going to turn out to be.

"I already took care of that before you got here. I've been here since 0500 hours, and got started right away. The changes have been made to our ships as well to hold two to three of them, depending on the size of the cargo bay and the shuttle." Prime Minister Raindrop said.

"Well then, let's get the full design version done then, and get it up to your shipyards so that they can get started." Captain Casey said, almost as excited as Franky and Prime Minister Raindrop were.

Within a few hours the full technical schematics of the shuttle were completed, and they went for an early lunch. After lunch was completed, Captain Casey was able to get from the prime minister a map to some very nice hiking trails, so he and his crew spent the better part of five hours hiking some of the nicest trails that they had ever been on. After the long hike, everyone ate a nice big dinner at a street side cafe, and then went back to the spa and sat in the hot bubbling waters of one of the sonic saltwater tubs.

They spent the next eight days just doing nothing but enjoying the spas services, and the planets beautiful scenery, including swimming in the warm, clear ocean water, but before long, everyone was itching to get back onto the ship, and get back into action. It had been a very pleasant break, but as with all vacations, eventually you want to go home. And the ship was home, to them all. Now that the ship was finished its upgrades and modifications, they were told they could go home any time.

When they got on the bridge of their ship, they were pleasantly surprised that the shipyard had done a very nice job, and even gave everything a nice new coat of paint to brighten it up. They toured the ship and checked out the other changes that were made, and they were all surprised by the size of their cargo bay now. It was still empty, because the new shuttles would not be ready for at least another two weeks.

"So, how do you guys like it." Prime Minister Raindrop asked as he snuck up behind everyone.

"I didn't know you were on board Sir. It looks very nice though, your shipyards did a very nice job. So are your people ready for the training of their lives?" Captain Casey asked with an almost evil grin.

"Yes, I came on board to see how everything was, but just what do you mean exactly?" The prime minister asked cautiously.

"Well, how many of your people have ever been trained by kids? It should be an experience for them."

"Yes, I guess you have that right, none of them would have been, but they all respect your boys a great deal, so they'll learn everything they can from the boys." Prime Minister Raindrop smiled.

Shortly after that, the prime minister returned to the planet, while Captain Casey and the boys went about making sure that the ship was spotlessly cleaned and stocked, but found that the Drandarians had taken care of that all for them already. For the rest of the day, they played and watched movies, did their daily exercises, just had a nice day at home for the first time in a while.

CHAPTER 22

THE STUDENT BECOMES
THE TEACHER

The next morning found all the captains gathered on the bridge of the largest Drandarian ship, and the boys were talking to each other quietly, trying to figure out how best to go about doing this. Finally they separated, and Kelly was voted the spokesman, since he was such a good little speaker, even if he was still real small.

"Okay guys gather round please?" He called out.

A few seconds later all the captains were gathered around the group of kids, and they were all quiet, waiting for the training.

"The first thing we need to do is get you guys working together as a team, as one, we've devised a few things to help you to do this. You need to be able to think as a team in order to win a fight, if none of you're working together, then you can't control the outcome." He said clearly.

"Yes Sir!" They all said. Kelly giggled.

"Guys, I'm not even eight years old yet, please don't call me Sir, leave that for the old guys, like Donny and Franky and Jamie." Kelly said while laughing

"We aren't old." Jamie said.

"Twice as old as me, so you're old. To me anyway." Kelly said and stuck out his tongue.

Everyone laughed at the boys' antics, but then the boys got serious again, so so did everyone else.

"Anyway, we're going to break up into groups of three captains to one of us, and we're going to try and work with you to develop some of these skills with you. Each of us will now choose at random three of you."

A few minutes later each boy picked the three captains that they were going to work with. Once this was done, they all teleported to a ship to work in. Donny, Franky, Will, Warren and Captain Casey did not take any trainees, since they were to be the overseers for the lessons, they each teleported between the ships and watched to make sure everything was going well.

For the rest of the day, the boys worked in their little groups, going over the things that Captain Casey had taught them about teamwork. The boys had already known a lot about teamwork, but oddly enough, it sure seemed that it was a totally foreign concept to the Drandarians. They went strictly on a command base, and if they were not told directly to do something, they did not even think of doing it. To the captains though, there was an even larger foreign concept, to let their crew think and react for themselves. Even they themselves normally just followed their orders to the letter, but they had to control more in the ship, and they relied solely on their crew listening to them for their orders. Obviously in a situation where speed counts, this was not the best way, and this was all being taught to the captains. They were also being told to learn the techniques that were being used to teach them, so that they could teach their people as well. It was long and hard work, because everyone had to, in a sense, erase years and years of training, and start from scratch, something everyone was finding difficult. Like the boys told them, they had to be in command, yet they had to trust their people and let them do what they had to do to do what needed to be done.

By the end of the day, everyone was satisfied that they had a good start, but they all admitted, even the captains themselves, that they still needed a lot of work.

"Boys, you all did a very good job today with the teachings that you gave. The Drandarians are getting a lot of information out of you guys, but you're getting more out of it than they are. The next few days will be hard on everyone, but you guys more so." Captain Casey said.

"We know Sir, they're difficult to teach, because teamwork doesn't seem to be anything they've ever thought of before. It's kind of strange really, but I guess not every race is the same. In some ways we're far smarter than they are, and in other ways they're smarter than we are." Brady commented.

"That's correct, not every race, or even every person for that matter, knows everything, and we all know that not one person on this ship knows everything. For something, like teamwork, that we take for granted as being such a simple thing, that should really require no thought, may be a completely new concept to some. That's why you need to be very patient, which I'm happy to say you've all been very much so. You wouldn't want them to feel stupid, or anything like that, that wouldn't help them learn any faster." Captain Casey applauded the boys' efforts.

"No problems there Sir, they're pretty easy going, and are willing to learn, which does make it easier." Jamie said.

"Come on, let's go do our evening exercises on a nice sandy beach tonight." Captain Casey said, and the boys agreed that this sounded nice.

They all went down to the holographic room, after all heading up and throwing on their nice shorts, but no shirts. Captain Casey set the computer, and they started doing their evening workout on a nice warm sandy beach.

The next few days went much the same way as the first day had. The Drandarians were coming along a great deal, and were starting to understand just how much better they could work together, by using the simple techniques that the boys were teaching them. Their confidence was also rising as they were learning the methods more and better. Each day that the boys were with the captains, they switched, so that everyone got different points of view, and were working with different people.

Finally on the fifth day, all the captains were again brought together on the one bridge of the largest ship. Once again Kelly was elected to start the speaking.

"Today we have some things for you to see, that'll show you just how much teamwork can help you win a fight."

Captain Casey queued up a few of the recorded battles that the boys had been through, and everyone sat and watched and listened to the battles. They spent roughly two hours watching the recordings. As soon as they were all done, Kelly stood back up once again and got everyone's attention.

"Those were a few of the battles that we've recently been through. You'll all recognize the last one, but almost none of you saw it from that perspective. Now, can anyone tell me what you noticed about those battles?" He asked.

One of the captains raised his hand.

"Yes Captain Wind Dance." Kelly asked.

"I noticed that none of you hardly said anything at all. How is that?" Captain Wind Dance asked.

"We'll get to the how in a few minutes. Anyone else?"

Another captain raised his hand.

"Yes Captain Rainy Night?"

"No one was directing you." Captain Rainy Night said.

"That's right, any one else?"

No one raised their hands this time.

"No one, any ideas. None at all. Okay, we didn't question a move."

"I don't understand, why would that be a good or bad thing? Shouldn't you question someone so that you learn from it?" Captain Wind Dance asked.

"Yes, you should, however, questions, such as that, deserve to be asked in a forum like this, after the fact. Mistakes will be made, and moves may be wrong, but to question them in the heat of a battle, isn't the right time to question them. You simply don't have the time to analyze the situation properly while you're in it." Kelly answered, nearly verbatim to what Captain Casey had told the boys at one time.

"Okay, that makes sense, but what about the other things, how is it you can work without talking, or getting direction from your captain?" Captain Rainy night asked this time.

"I'll answer the second question first. In most battles you're moving too quickly to really give or take any direction. The captain should only be there to watch over everything, and catch the things the crew misses, kind of a second set of eyes. With a newer crew, he may have to give quick instructions, but the longer a crew works together, the better they'll become. As for the first question, we work very well together, because we trust each other. We trust each other to know what their job is, and to do it. If someone falls, we trust that someone will take over immediately. Trust is a huge part of teamwork, and it's the hardest part about it. We all knew what teamwork was when we started, yet we had a lack of trust.

We first had to learn to trust each other before we could work so well together, it helps to have a good teacher in this aspect. Trust, however, can't be given, it has to be earned. For instance, your people now trusts us, we had to earn that right, we also trust you, because you've earned that right as well. If we'd just met, we wouldn't trust each other, so we'd be unable to work together near as well as we could now right, like we have been." Kelly said.

"Yes Sir!" They all answered. Kelly did not bother, he had told them all repeatedly over the last many days, but they still insisted on calling him sir.

"So, now you know all about how and why teamwork works. You've built some of the trust you need for teamwork to work. Now, however, you're going to put it into action. We're now going to break you up into teams of five, and you're going to do a simulated battle. Captain Casey's already installed the same program that we use to do simulations into all of your ships, so that we can do this. We'll now pick our teams and go to the ship we'll be using, and then we'll start the simulated battle."

Because there were sixty captains, they ended up with twelve teams, so nearly every team had two bridge advisers or trainers with them. They teleported to the different ships, and they all took stations in quick order.

Donny and Kelly ended up taking five Captains who neither had worked with yet. Once everyone was set, Donny started the simulated battle that had been chosen for all of them. It was the same one that Captain Casey had first given to the kids. It was a simple scenario, and twelve somewhat tame ships attacked, sending a shot across their bow, to warn them that this was not a game.

"Attacking ships, cease fire." One of the captains said through the communications system.

"Surrender or we blow you out of the sky." The attackers said.

"You surrender or we'll blow you out of the sky."

"We're twelve, you're one, who do you think will win!"

"We will, because we're smarter and better trained, again, surrender or be destroyed." The captain said, and then cut the communications link.

Again a shot was fired across the bow of the ship, and the captain on weapons just opened fire with maximum yield weapons and started disintegrating the ships. Navigation was doing his best to keep them moving and out of reach, but he just did not seem to have the feel for the ship, and kept moving them in the way, instead of out of the way. Scanning actually highlighted an innocent with the scanners, and sent it over to weapons, and without looking, the captain at weapons actually fired on a friendly. They had not even started working together, when they were exploded.

"Simulation over, we lost guys. Better luck next time." Kelly said, trying not to let his anger show at the fact that they did not use anything they had learned. He figured rightly that you cannot undo years of wrong teachings in just a few days.

All the teams, now finished their battles, were conferenced in together, because they would be staying on the ships for the time being. Some of the teams won, some lost, some used their training, if even a little, others did not. None had done that well, but everyone remembered that they had not done well their first time out either, and the Drandarians did reasonably well considering.

"Okay, that was the first battle simulation, that was one of the easier ones. There were some good points and some bad points. Next we'll do another more difficult and longer attack scenario, and then tomorrow we'll go over the two battles all together, down on the planet and pick each and every one of them apart, and find what was done right, and what was done wrong, and what you can do to make it even better." Kelly said to all the captains.

The communication was cut, and the next battle simulation started. The captains had each taken a different station this time, so they were all ready to go. This time there were only six attackers, but they were faster and better, they were also toying with them a bit. Donny and Kelly stood back and watched as everything unfolded.

"Scum ship, shut down your engines or face extermination." The enemy said roughly.

"Sorry, not an option, you're the ones who'll shut down or be destroyed." The captain said.

"We warned you, there's no other offer, you'll be destroyed." The voice growled, and then disconnected.

The battle started almost immediately, with three of the six ships firing direct shots at them. Navigation was able to get them out of the way enough, where when the missiles exploded, they were only rocked. Their shield warning went off, saying that they were losing shield power though. Scanning started sending information right away and weapons started firing away. Problem was he was not waiting until he had good clean shots and was just firing and was missing three out of every five that he sent. In this fashion though he was able to destroy one of the ships and disable another. The attacking ships however started a deadly dance around them, and would sacrifice one, and then sneak in from behind, and hit them. They were using only their low yield weapons, so that they would not be destroyed quickly, but the ship never stopped being jarred, and one of the captains was actually thrown with one of the hits, he got up, shook it off and went back to his station at communications, and they continued. Nearly fifteen minutes later they were destroyed. Their aim had gotten worse as their morale dropped, and navigation was hardly moving at all. When the signal came to say that they had been destroyed, all the captains slumped into the chairs near to them, and put their heads in their hands. One of them was heard to say, 'we're really bad at this.' It was only just loud enough that Donny heard it, because he was close enough.

"No, you're not real bad at this, you just need more practice, and to learn to work as a team more, it'll come in time, it isn't an instantaneous thing. Be patient and work with it, or you'll never achieve your goals." Donny said warmly.

"Thank you. Your kind words help, if even only a little." The captain said.

"You're welcome. Now, everyone go home tonight and don't think about what we did today. The next couple days as we pick apart the battles will be hard, but you'll learn a lot from them. We'll call you with the meeting location as soon as we know where it'll be."

Within a few minutes the captains from the bridge were gone. Once all the simulations were over, everyone teleported back to the bridge of the UE1.

"I don't know about you guys, but we still have lots of work to do from what we saw on our team today." Donny said.

"Yeah, our team was actually their own worst enemy in both fights, even though they managed to win the first." Marty said.

"Ours too. I'm not sure how they scraped a win on either one, but they did. We sure got hit lots though, and our shields collapsed just as the last ship was disabled." Matthew said.

"That's enough boys. We all knew this would be tough. Yes, they need lots more help, but they've come a long way already. The next couple days will be hard on them, as they realize their mistakes." Captain Casey said.

"Yes Sir! Do we have a location for the next couple days to do the reviews though Sir? I told the captains on my team that we'd let them know in the morning." Donny asked.

"Yes, the prime minister has given us the use of an auditorium for this purpose." Captain Casey said.

"That should work out well." Donny said.

"I don't know about you guys, but I could go for a nice swim!" Captain Casey said.

"Sounds good to me Sir." Franky said before anyone else could, so the others all just nodded.

Warren and Will joined them for a while, and then excused themselves an hour before dinnertime to go get the food prepared. After dinner, everyone sat back and watched a movie at an old fashioned drive in movie theatre in the holographic room, everyone thought it was kind of neat. After that though, everyone went to bed and passed out.

The next morning, Captain Casey and his crew got their morning routine out of the way and had teleported to the surface to meet the prime minister. After a brief discussion, they headed to the auditorium. Once everyone was there and seated, they got started, Kelly standing at the front as usual.

"Good morning everyone. I'm glad you're all here. I know many of you think that you're doing very badly, but remember, you have years of training to undo before you can truly get the hang of the new things that we're teaching you. That's what we're here for today, and probably tomorrow as well. Now, we're going to go through each and every simulation, one at a time, and critique it. Everyone's expected to be involved in the discussions, and ask questions as well, it's the only way that you can expect to learn."

As Kelly was up there speaking to everyone, Captain Casey could not help but admire how well Kelly was doing. Not all that long ago, he would have run and hid instead of being anywhere near so many people, now here he was, standing in front of dozens of people, speaking and commanding them as if they were younger than he was. Captain Casey smiled to himself, hoping that the others could learn to do the same as well

All of a sudden Kelly started the first of the many simulations that would be played out today. It happened to be the first battle that his team had done. As the simulation played, you could actually hear the groans of the crew as they saw the mistakes that they had made. By the time the simulation had ended, not one of the five captains looked as if they were feeling very good. By the end of the day though each and every captain would be feeling the same way.

"Okay, can anyone tell me what was right about this simulation?" Kelly asked.

It took quite a few minutes before anyone raised their hand, and it happened to be the captain who had been on weapons at the time of this particular battle.

"Yes Running Water, what do you feel was right about this?" Kelly asked.

"The only thing I can see good about this, was that we died quickly Sir." Running Water said.

"Wrong. Yes you did die quickly, but that's a bad thing. There are many number of things you did right. Can anyone else tell me something that this crew did right, I could count at least twelve?"

A full five minutes passed, before Kelly shook his head and spoke up.

"You're all so focused on what you did wrong, that you aren't seeing the things that you did right. Here are a few; first is that you gave a good warning, and spoke your intentions clearly, this is a must. Second, you kept yourself moving around. Third, you reacted quickly to the actions going on around you. Fourth, you did in fact take out a few of them before you managed to get beaten. Like I said there are others, but I'll let you think about that. Remember, you need to learn how to see all that was positive as well as all that was negative, by doing so, you can improve faster and better. Now for the part I'm sure you're all not wanting to get to, tell me what you saw wrong." Kelly said.

Answers started being called out all at once, and finally Kelly had to shout out to all of them to stop, and tell him one at a time. He had a marker in one hand and was waiting at the board.

"Okay, now let's try that again, one at a time so that I can write them down."

The answers that were called out were all good ones, and he ended up with a list thirty items long, and could have gone longer, but Kelly called a stop, because his hand was killing him. The list included, but were not limited to; killing an ally, losing, missing nearly every shot, not paying attention to what was around them, not looking at the whole picture, and the list went on and on.

"Well that's a good sized list, and it's all good information. There's one thing though that you all failed to see, the most important thing, communication. They didn't talk at all." Kelly said.

"But you guys don't need to talk." Captain Cool Breeze said.

"That's right, we don't, we're able to do that, because we trust each other to know what we're doing. You don't yet have that trust, it needs to be built up first. Once you all get more comfortable with the controls, and working with each other, then yes you may be able to do as we do. We're unique though in the fact that we're very good at this for some reason, we all have good instincts our captain tells us, it probably comes from us surviving on the streets for so long. You may not have that yet, maybe you never will, and you'll always have to talk to understand each other. Don't try to be us, be yourselves, work together and get comfortable with each other. Remember it isn't really going to be you guys doing this, you have to teach this, so you have to understand it even more than your crews do. As time passes, it'll come easier for you, however, you may always have to work at it. Now, we're going to go through this list of things that were done wrong, and find out ways that you could have done it differently." Kelly said.

For the next hour they went over this list of things, and some of the items on the list were easy to fix, others they had to brainstorm, and even a couple they actually had to ask when they could not figure out a way.

The rest of the day went like this and they managed to only get ten of the simulations done, the rest would have to wait until the following day, or two if needed. The captain and his crew were informed that the spa was still free and waiting for them, if they wanted to stay on the planet tonight, and they were all happy to say yes. Kelly did not even go to his room first, he went right to the first person offering a massage, and laid down after stripping off all his clothes and enjoyed a nice long soothing massage. After the long massage, Kelly slipped into a hot bath, and nearly fell asleep, and it was only Captain Casey coming to get him into bed that kept him from falling asleep.

"You've done a very good job these past couple days. Tomorrow though you can take a break, and someone else can take over. I know you're very tired." Captain Casey said gently.

"I can do it Sir, I'll be fine." Kelly said quietly.

"I know you could do it, but you have to admit that you're tired. We should also get some of the other boys up there and get their fears of talking to large crowds out of the way. You've come a very long way in such a short time, and will be able to handle any crowd, but some of the others still need help." Captain Casey said soothingly.

"Yeah, I'm tired, and I guess you're right, the others do need to learn as well I guess."

"Good boy. Let's get you into bed." Captain Casey said as he gently steered the tired boy by the shoulder to his bedroom.

No sooner had Captain Casey helped Kelly into his bed, after helping him to get changed, did Kelly start snoring softly, sound asleep, almost as soon as his head hit the pillow.

The following day was a long day for all. They still had fourteen recordings to go through, but this day went by much more smoothly, because all the captains now were actively searching for what they did right, as well as what they did wrong. The discussions became more detailed as to what could be done to change and improve their performance. Because of the more detailed, therefore more lengthy discussions, they were not able to complete all the recordings though, and the last three spilled over into the following day. Again everybody fell into bed. This time it was Cullen nearly falling asleep in the hot bubbling water after a nice soothing massage, since he was the one who had led the class. Everyone could tell that at first he was very nervous, but by the end of the day, they all thought that he had done this a hundred times before, because of how well he was doing.

Bobby was voted to direct day three, and with only three discussions left to have, it went by pretty quick and smooth. Finally the discussions were over and everyone stood and thanked their teachers. Bobby raised his hand to get everyone's attention and they went silent.

"Now, we're going to go back to the ships to do another simulation. This time you're all to use all the skills you learned in this exercise."

Bobby grabbed Will to be with him today, they picked out five captains and they teleported to a ship. Once everyone was ready, the simulations were started. This was the tough one. Will and Bobby stood to the side and watched silently as the crew of captains did their best.

The four very hostile ships came at them and demanded them to lower their shields and be boarded.

"Absolutely not, you attempt to get on this ship, and we'll destroy you where you sit." The captain on communications said.

They were not answered, well not in the normal sense anyway. They were targeted and then they hit them with a direct hit. The team started calling out moves and targets. They did a very good job, and were fighting very well. They lasted well over half an hour, before the destruction warning came up, and the simulation was over. All of the captains slumped down.

"What did we do wrong that time?" Captain Cloudburst asked, he had been on weapons.

"You guys did very well. Your teamwork was almost seamless, you used almost every skill we've been trying to teach you, and you lasted very well against an enemy nearly no one defeats, in fact there've only been two crews to do so. Most ships are destroyed inside of ten minutes on this simulation, because the attackers are designed to be very good and very brutal. You didn't do too bad at all." Bobby told everyone.

"You mean you have an impossible scenario as a training simulation, and only two crews have won against it?" Captain Cloudburst asked incredulously.

"That's right. They made this to test the limits of everyone. We have yet to come across an enemy that's this good and this brutal though, but if we don't train against it, how will we ever win against a truly tough opponent."

"I guess that makes sense. Hey, I recognize some of the moves and the way they attacked, isn't that the one you guys showed us of you? I think it was the first or the second recording you showed" Captain Cloudburst asked.

"I was wondering if any of you'd recognize it. Yes, that was us, and yes we're one of only two crews to have beaten this simulation." Bobby answered proudly.

"Then I don't feel so bad now. What did we do wrong on this one?" Captain Cloudburst asked.

"Not gonna tell you. You'll analyze it tomorrow at the same time you do all the others, same as the past few days. The rest of your time today is free time. You may go now." Bobby said, dismissing the captains.

Bobby and Will were the last ones to make it to the bridge of the UE1, seems their team lasted the longest.

"So how did everyone else do? Our team used almost everything that we taught them, and they did very well, still got destroyed mind you, but that's not a surprise." Bobby asked everyone once they arrived.

"Pretty good." Was the general response.

"We can discuss all of this tomorrow guys, for now, let's go get some lunch, and then go have some fun." Franky said.

"Sounds good to me." Captain Casey said.

Instead of cooking for themselves, they teleported back to the planet and had lunch at one of the many street side restaurants. After lunch they went back up to their ship and played in the holographic room for the rest of the day, stopping only to have a light dinner.

CHAPTER 23

THE BEASTS WITHIN

The next morning found everyone gathered in the auditorium for one of their last visits together. Once everyone was seated, Devon got the group discussion started.

"Everyone did a great deal better yesterday. Going over all the good and bad points over the past few days has really helped you to see what you were doing wrong. I'm glad to say that everyone seems to have learned from those mistakes very well. So, we're going to put on the first recording and I want you to pay very close attention for anything that was right and wrong, and then we'll get the lists together and then discuss them at the end today." Devon told them all.

With that, he started the first of the twelve recordings. Once it was finished, he called out for the things that were done right, and then half an hour later the things that were done wrong. This time the lists were opposite, and there were only three things that anyone could pick out, but they missed probably twenty things they did wrong, and Devon pointed this out to them. The rest of the day went much the same way, and by the end of the day, they still only had a list of twenty things that had been done wrong, and a list of well over a hundred things that had been done right. Many of the things were repeated in each recording, but they were called out anyway. It was firmly decided though, that the teamwork had finally started to pay off.

"We've decided that phase two for your training, is to start training your people. Each of you'll go to your normal ship, and bring back your standard bridge crew, and start training them in the ways we've trained you. We'll be going between ships and watching for a bit to see how things are going, as well as answer questions.

You'll find it a little easier to go over each battle after you finish it. We only had to go to the auditorium, since there were too many of you to do it on the ship. For now, concentrate on only one of your bridge teams, you have lots of time to work at this and train the rest of them."

"Yes Sir!" All the captains said.

A few minutes later, all the captains went back to their ships and called all their first crews up. On every ship, each of the captains was explaining to them the training that they had received, and that now it was time for them to teach their crews, so here they were.

Captain Casey and crew had stayed behind, letting everyone go to where they needed to be. Once they were alone, Captain Casey spoke.

"Well boys, you've done very well. They're well on their way to being able to hold their own against almost any enemy. Let's go and see how everyone is doing. Warren and Will, are you coming as well?"

"No, I don't think so Sir, we can help you guys out a bit, but actually being any help to them, I don't think we can do that. We don't know as much as you guys do, well when it comes to this stuff anyway." Warren answered and Will agreed.

"Okay, you guys have fun today, and we'll see you later then." Captain Casey said, and within a few seconds, everyone teleported to a different ship.

Captain Casey stayed behind for a little bit, because he wanted to do up some reports and send them in, as well as call his parents to say hi and get them up to date, and Captain Bloth to tell him that they could head on home. Jonathon felt that the boys could handle the ships for a while. He spent almost two hours doing up the reports, and then when he was done, he sent them off. Once that was done, he called his parents.

"Hello mom and dad, how are things going back home." He asked when they came on screen.

"We're very good. Captain Bloth called us and told us all about your little battle and what you were doing. Were you too busy or something to call us sooner?" His mom asked, trying to sound hurt.

"Oh quit trying to give me the guilt trip, and get that pout off your face, it hasn't worked since I was a child." Jonathon said with a smile.

"Hey, I'm your mother, and I'm allowed to try and mess with you." She smiled.

"And you try so hard too. As for your question, yes, we've been working very hard recently. After the battle was won, we agreed to teach the people of this world how to fight. They're a very peaceful and shy species, and really didn't know how to fight. It's been a lot of work, but they're coming along. The boys are all out watching, while the students start their next phase, teaching a new group of students. Would I be correct in guessing that you'd like a copy of the battle recordings?" Jonathon asked.

"Yes please. So the boys are all doing very well then I guess? Have there been any problems?" His mom asked.

"I'll send them in a few minutes then. No, we haven't had any problems at all. I've been half expecting problems to have crept up by now, but they're all adjusting very well. They're loving being the teachers right now, and they're all doing very well. Any other kid would be peeing his or her pants to have to stand up in front of sixty captains, and a prime minister at times, and talk and teach, but so far, those who've done it, have done very well. They were all a little nervous at first, but the nerves quickly wore off. I'm starting to see that the boys are becoming very well adjusted, so I shouldn't start having any problems, at least I hope."

"That's good to hear, and you could still have minor problems, but that's normal with any children. They love and respect you a great deal, so I doubt that you'll ever have any major issues, but with all that you've given to them, I don't think any adult will ever be able to push them around. Even the last time we saw them, they were very self confident, and I doubt that they'd have taken any actual orders, even from me, at least not yet." His dad said.

"Yes, once they grow up a bit more, and become adults themselves, they'll be able to take orders from others, but not yet, for now that's fine though. I'd already realized that, and had even foreseen it a bit. Well I should let you go. I'm going to call Captain Bloth next, and tell him he can go ahead and head back home."

"Okay, talk to you soon." Jonathon's parents said and then they disconnected. As soon as he disconnected as well, he called up Captain Bloth.

"Hey Jonathon, how's it going with the training and everything?"

"Hi, good thanks. I think they're getting the hang of it, and soon should be able to hold their own. Once their new ships are built, they should be quite respectable fighters, should anyone decide to attack them. Anyway, I was calling to tell you, I think that we have everything under control here now, and that you guys may as well head on home if you want to."

"Okay then, if you think you guys can handle the rest of it, then we'll see you later, have fun, and good luck on the rest of your trip."

"Thanks, you too." Jonathon said and then disconnected.

Jonathon then went and toured the ships with the boys to make sure the Drandarian captains were doing okay, teaching their crews what all they were only just taught themselves. They all spent the better part of three days doing just this. Everyone was asked lots of questions, and the boys answered them as best they could, but Captain Casey never answered anything, because he wanted the boys to handle all this, he only just stood back and observed.

Finally, on the fourth day after the captains started training their crew, they started the battle simulations. The first few were a fiasco, to say the least, but they started getting better, just as their captains had. None of them had managed to pass the hardest test, but there was little surprise there, seeing as how almost no one had done so before. The Drandarian crews spent four days running through simulations and marking them as to what they had done right or wrong. As the days wore on, the amount that they did wrong, was greatly reduced, still some minor and stupid mistakes were being made, but that happened. With time and training, they would be fine. On the final day of training, the prime minister came aboard the largest ship to greet everyone.

"So, I understand my people are now ready to go off on their own!" Prime Minister Rain Drop asked.

"Yes Prime Minister. They still have much to learn, but little that we can actually teach them. I've given to your people the training simulators, as well as some training information, so that your people can continue to learn. You'll find that in time it'll become easier, and your people will do even better yet. As it sits right now though, your ships have every means necessary to win almost any fight, and once your new ships are done, you'll be a formidable force, but remember, you're a small people, with a very small force, call for help when and if you need it. We'll come as quickly as possible, however, you'll still need to hold your own for as long as possible until help arrives." Captain Casey informed.

"Captain, my people and I couldn't even begin to thank you for all that you've done for us, we do, however, have a small token of thanks to give to you. The two new shuttles that you designed are ready, and are on their way here as we speak. If you'd open your cargo bay doors, they can park them for you?"

"You consider two brand new shuttles a small token of thanks? We spent what, two weeks helping your people, that's more than enough thanks, and we couldn't ask for more. Not to mention all the upgrades you did to my ship, as well as what you don't see. You've helped my boys in ways that you can't even imagine. If anything, it's we who owe you." Captain Casey tried.

"Yes, we did do all that, but you're forgetting a few things. First you became a very good friend, then you helped us in a fight you had no need to join in on, and won it with next to no help from my people, then you teach my people the ways to protect themselves in the future. No, you've given us far far more than you can ever imagine, you gave us life. While it's true that we're a peaceful people, we'd never truly seen that sometimes you need to fight to stay alive. Unfortunately, due to all the raids in the past, our population has been in a steady decline, because we don't breed as fast as many of the other races do. Each couple may be able to have one baby every ten years or so, and of those, only forty percent survive. So you see what your help means to us."

"Then Prime Minister, we thank you for the generous gifts you've given to us, and we hope that your people have many blessed years of having babies." Captain Casey said with a bow.

"Thank you, and we too hope your crew has many happy years ahead of you. Your new shuttles should be there by now, so why don't we go take a look at them. I haven't even seen the finished product yet."

"Thank you, let's go." Captain Casey said.

They teleported to the UE1, and the boys joyfully led the way to the new shuttles, and were looking at the outsides of both of them and chattering happily when they arrived. The shuttles were very nice and sleek looking. They had almost no angles on them at all, and everything was smooth and rounded. They only just barely fit in the newly enlarged cargo bay, length wise, since they were quite large. The propulsion pods on the bottom also acted as the landing gear, so the crafts were raised off the floor almost half a meter, and other than those, there was nothing external to the ship.

Just as Captain Casey reached the door to the closest ship, it opened, splitting in half, the bottom half becoming the entrance ramp, and out came one of the engineers that had helped to design it.

"Here you go captain, it's all yours, and it flies like a dream." Whistling Breeze said.

"Thank you Whistling Breeze, they look incredible, and we couldn't have gotten a better fit had we tried." Captain Casey said.

"You're most welcome Sir. We made them to fit, and we used every last millimeter of space we had available to us. You should be quite pleased with the interior as well, please come in and look. Only about ten people can fit inside comfortably, so I'd ask that only six or seven come in at a time. The other shuttle will open as well when you tell it to open, we have all of your voices already programmed into the locks."

"Thanks Sir. You boys go look at the other one, and we'll look this one over." Captain Casey said.

They did not even stay to answer, the entire crew, except Warren and Will went to the other ship. Warren and Will had of course come to look as well, and they went into the new ship with the captain and the Drandarians.

The new ship was very nice inside, and it was a lot larger than the exterior had suggested. In the rear there were five beds, two on one side with storage underneath the bottom bunk, and three more on the opposite side. There was a small washroom next to the three bunk beds, and there was a small kitchenette, that had everything that they would ever need, right across from the bathroom. And then there was the engine room at the very back, it was accessed by a door behind the beds. The engine room also housed everything else that made the ship work; the power systems, the inertial compensator's and the shield generators. It was a very full room, every space was well used. Then at the front were the helm controls, and a few seats scattered around. The weapons were stored in compartments in an upper compartment in the roof, and that was also where they were launched from. Due to the small design, it could only hold about fifty of the largest missiles, but that was good enough for what the ship was intended. They did however design right into the system, the ability to be able to teleport more weapons in, should the need ever arise. The shuttles were small and comfortable, designed for short missions, but the way they were built, they were very sturdy.

"It turned out very nice. I like the colors that you chose, and the materials you used as well. It makes it seem so much larger than it really is, and much more comfortable as well. Thank you very much." Captain Casey said.

"You're very welcome. We've now started making ours, and since these turned out so well, we're going to use the exact same design. Our new ships for the shuttles should be ready in just a few more weeks, at least the first few. We only have three shipyards, so it'll be a slow process, but one of the shipyards is being dedicated just to these little guys, because we want at least two for every ship, but most there'll be four. So in a few years, you never know, maybe we'll come visit you." Whistling Breeze smiled.

"I'm glad you too also like the design. We should be going soon, because we still have much to see and do before we begin our journey home."

"If you must go, then you must go, however, I'd like to invite you to a farewell feast this evening? I assure you that you won't want to miss this feast, it'll be even more splendid than the welcome feast we had for you, because this'll be under the stars, and the food will be even more delicious."

"We wouldn't turn down such an offer Sir, and we might just come and spend the day on the planet as well. What time would you like us there?"

"Well, after your boys take their new toys out for a spin I'm sure." Prime Minister Rain Drop smiled. "Dinner will be served at

2000 hours this evening though, and you're welcome to come to the planet and enjoy it, until the next time you come back."

"Yeah, you're probably right, there'll be little chance that we get to go anywhere until we've tested these little beasts out. We'll see you this evening then. Will it be at the same pavilion as the lunch was?"

"Yes, it will be, so we'll see you tonight then."

Moments later the prime minister and Whistling Breeze teleported back to the planet with the others that had come with them, while Warren, Will and Captain Casey were left to admire the new ship. After a few minutes, they went over to the other ship to see how the others were doing.

"So, who wants to go for a test run?" Captain Casey asked.

"ME!" Was the resounding response from every single boy.

"Teams one and two get to go first, Franky and Donny you each take a ship, and you may be gone for as long as half an hour. When you get back, Warren, Will and I'll go with teams three and four." Captain Casey said.

"Yes Sir!" They all said happily.

Within a few seconds the two teams were set and ready to go, and the rest who were not protected by a ship, exited the cargo bay, so as not to get caught outside without proper equipment. The power systems were brought on line, and then the engines, inertial compensation systems and shields were all brought up, once the power was at maximum. Team one backed out of their spot first, and then team two followed. The rest of the crew went up to the bridge to watch as the boys played around, and they were talking to both ships non stop to make sure everything worked well. Both ships were having a huge amount of fun flying the very small and extremely agile little ships, doing all sorts of flips and stunts, and pulling very tight corners to test the systems fully. It was a comical sight actually to watch the boys in the two ships, because they were flipping and rolling all over the place, making some aerial acrobats look almost lame.

"Okay Boys, you've had your fun, come on back, and let the rest of us go and have some fun." Captain Casey called out once the boys' time was up.

"Are you sure Sir, it doesn't feel like half an hour yet?" Donny asked, clearly having just as much fun as the others.

"Of course I'm sure, now get your butts back here." Captain Casey said with a grin.

"Fine Sir, be right there." Donny said with a fake pout.

Captain Casey just shook his head, and then he and the rest of the crew went down to wait for the boys to get back, and for the cargo doors to close. When the light went on, saying they could enter, everyone spilled into the cargo bay, and met the boys who were coming out of the new ships.

"So how was it?" Everyone asked.

"They're incredible. Same speed as the ship, but so small you can move like nothing else, and with the two compensator's in such a small space, you hardly even feel a thing. I can't wait to try these things out in a battle." Donny said giddily.

"I bet they're good, but we should be hoping that we never have to try these out in a battle." Captain Casey commented.

"True Sir, but given how long we've been out here, and how many battles we've already seen, I doubt there's much hope of that." Donny said thoughtfully.

"Yes, we've been more unfortunate in that way than I'd hoped, but then again, it's taught you boys a great deal. Okay teams one and two, get out of here, and let us go have some fun now." Captain Casey ordered with a happy smile, for he too wanted to go out and play.

They left, and teams three and four each chose a ship. Captain Casey went with team three, and Warren and Will went with team four. As soon as they were ready, they backed out the door, and they were off. Captain Casey decided to just let the boys have their fun and play with the shuttles, so he sat back and enjoyed the ride, while watching the young men handle the ship as if they were born to it. Had he not known, he would have thought that the boys had been born on a ship, as he had been, and learned everything about flying space ships since the day they were born. All of a sudden, Tristan pulled a hairpin turn while doing a hundred LYS, and other than feeling a bit of a pull, they hardly felt anything.

"Tristan, you shouldn't do such sharp turns in a ship, not until you're more comfortable with it." Captain Casey said gently.

"Sorry Sir, had no choice, there was a comet coming straight at us, and I figured that it was better to test that, rather than how much a comet half our size, at only half shields would do to us. I'm not sure why it didn't show up on the scanners sooner, but it didn't." Tristan said as if nothing happened.

"Oh, okay, I didn't see it either. Well, I guess this way we know the ship will do it if you have to. I think that our time's about up, so call the others and tell them to come on back as well." Captain Casey said.

"Ah, do we haveta." Tristan said in his best whine.

"Yes, and what have I told you about whining!" Captain Casey barked out, but he was grinning.

"I know, I know, but we were having so much fun." Tristan said as he was turning them back toward the ship, the other shuttle was called, and they too were saddened to hear that their playtime was over.

A few minutes later they were docking in the cargo bay, and team four was right behind them. Once cleared, they exited the shuttle and went up to the bridge to find the others, because Jonathon had figured they had watched their flights as well from there.

"What was that sharp turn for Captain?" Donny asked as soon as they walked in.

"There was a comet that the scanners didn't catch coming straight for us, so I decided that that was safer than testing the ship with an impact of that size." Tristan answered.

"What comet, there was no comet!"

"What do you mean? The scanners showed it only a couple seconds before we were to hit it."

"Just what I said. We saw nothing from here, maybe we should run both ships' scanners through diagnostics, one of them might be wrong."

"Good idea, it could have been a ghost image or something like that, more than likely on the shuttle. Did you actually see the comet Tristan?" Captain Casey asked.

"No Sir! I saw it on the scanner, and that it was too close, so I just reacted to save us. I just didn't have time to look."

"Okay, you aren't at fault, and like I said, at least we found out that the ship could do that sharp a turn at that speed, so it wasn't a complete waste of time."

"Okay Sir, thanks, I'll go to the shuttle and run the diagnostics myself right now then. I'll run full diagnostics on both shuttles in fact, just in case." Tristan offered.

"Good idea, take your team, you can all do it, but call if you need help." Captain Casey said.

"Yes Sir!" He answered, and he and his team headed out.

The rest of the crew spent the next half an hour getting the ship ready to go that evening after dinner, restocking the Nutronium and doing diagnostics on the main ship as well, seeing as how it had been a few weeks since it was run anyway. Half an hour later team three came back up to the bridge to find Captain Casey.

"Sir, we found the problem. It was a loose chip on one of the boards, and it seems to have caused the ghost image. Other than that, both ships now have a clean bill of health. It must have pulled loose during the previous flight or something. Good thing it only showed something that wasn't actually there, instead of the other way around." Tristan said.

"Good, I'm glad you found the problem, and that it was such a minor thing, but you're certainly right about that. That's the very reason the diagnostic tests are so important. I hope that teaches everyone a valuable lesson. We run the tests at least once every couple weeks, just for that very reason. We haven't done them recently, since we weren't moving, but even still, they should've been done, because you never know when a circuit might fail."

"Yes Sir!" Everyone said.

"Good. Now we've been invited to dinner tonight at 2000 hours, so we still have a few hours to kill, and I was thinking we should go back down to the planet and visit the spa and relax a bit, or we can go swim in the ocean. We'll come back right before dinner to clean up and change for dinner. So what should we do then?"

"Swimming Sir." Everyone said.

"Swimming it is then."

CHAPTER 24

FAREWELL

Everyone scattered from the bridge and went to their rooms to get changed, and as soon as they were in their shorts, they met in the hall and followed the captain to the nearest point they could teleport from. Within a few seconds, they were on the softest, sandiest beach they had ever felt, and were splashing in the warmest, sweetest smelling ocean water they had ever heard of. They played and splashed in the warm water for nearly two hours, before they all crawled out and laid down on the soft warm sand, and relaxed for a few minutes before they had to go to get cleaned up and dressed. They teleported back up, and in half an hour everyone had gotten clean, were dressed in their dress uniforms, and were ready to go. They all teleported down to the banquet area, and the prime minister was there to meet them.

"Welcome once again, please follow me." Prime Minister Rain Drop greeted.

"Thank you Sir, please lead the way." Captain Casey smiled.

He showed them in, and he showed them to a large central table, big enough for them to all sit at. The pavilion was even more beautiful than it had been before. With the starlight now glowing, and the many small lights that were illuminating the area, it looked very nice. They were seated, and then the prime minister went to his table and sat with his wife and his staff. Once everyone was in and seated, the prime minister stood.

"We are gathered together, this glorious evening, to thank our friends, and to wish them a safe trip, as they wish to be going back on their mission of learning. Please rise and say thanks to our friends, the captain and crew of the Earth ship, Universe Explorer One." Prime Minister Rain Drop said happily.

Everyone stood and said their many thanks, wished all the best to the crew, and then they all sat again, except the prime minister, who stayed standing.

"To the captain and crew of the UE1, I give personal thanks, and offer to you the chance to visit our planet any time that you wish, and I hope that you come back soon. Let the feast begin." The prime minister said, and with that, the same amount of waiters and waitresses as the last time came pouring out of the kitchens, all carrying large trays loaded with food and drink.

They all came to the table that the captain and the crew were sitting at, and they were given the chance to try the foods first. Everything looked amazingly good, and everyone loaded their plates near to the point of overflowing, even the captain. It was understandable though, the waiters and waitresses kept saying, 'you should try this, it's wonderful', or 'try this, you won't believe it.' So they tried a tiny bit of almost everything. Once everyone else was served, the captain and crew started eating, along with the others, out of politeness. Same as last time, the food was marvelous, and they were amply stuffed, but then the desserts came out. The dessert trays were stuffed to the maximum with nearly every variety of sweets they could imagine, and it all looked so good that they wanted to try a little of everything. They ate even more than any of them even thought possible, and would leave the table considerably heavier than they had come. Once the meal was finished, and it was nearing time to leave, the prime minister again stood.

"I understand that you'll want to be heading out now, we won't keep you any longer, so again, we thank you for all the help that you've given to us."

"Yes, we should be going. It's been a great pleasure to work with your people, and to sample some of your wonderful planet, as well your hospitality is second to none. If ever any of you should wish to visit Earth, please contact me, and I'll see to it that you have the best time that we can possibly show you. Also, if I'm available, I'll do so personally."

"We'd enjoy that a great deal, and will hopefully soon be able to take you up on that offer. It's with great sadness to see you leave, however, we know your home is in the sky, so please leave with all our blessings, and stay safe." Prime Minister Rain Drop said humbly, with the deepest of bows to their guests.

"And same to you, everyone, you have all our blessings, and we'll see you soon. In the meantime, I hope that your people continue to learn all that we have taught you, but now we must be on our way." Captain Casey bowed back, the boys also doing so, and with that, he teleported them up to their home.

When everyone arrived back to the ship, it was decided, that after changing, that they would lay back and watch a movie or two before bed, and then leave first thing in the morning.

CHAPTER 25

A VERY MERRY CHRISTMAS

It had been almost three weeks since they had started helping the Drandarians, so it was now almost Christmas time. Captain Casey had figured that most of the boys had not had a nice Christmas in more than a few years, and although they would not have any actual presents, they could at least share a nice holiday together. It was only a few days away, so Captain Casey figured he should get to work on planning it. He would have Warren help him, even though he was sure that Warren himself probably had not had much of a Christmas for a long time either. The morning after leaving the Drandarian world, they headed out on their journey, and just headed further out to explore.

Captain Casey had left Donny in charge of the bridge, and went down and talked to Warren, but he had to kick Will out, to tell him of his plans.

"Hi Warren, now that Will's gone, I have a plan forming, and I need your help. Christmas is in just a few days. I know that almost none of you guys has had that much of a Christmas these last few years. Even if some of the boys' families didn't believe in Christmas per say, they would've at least had a nice quiet family time. We won't really have any gifts, or a tree to decorate, but we can certainly have the feast and the get together. So that's where I need you to come in and help. How does that sound?"

"Very nice Sir. My family was one of those that didn't celebrate Christmas, but we certainly had our holiday traditions, so I'd be happy to help. I'm sure all the boys would appreciate it greatly."

"Good." Captain Casey said, and then they got down to planning.

Will, when he was unceremoniously kicked out of his own infirmary, just went up to the bridge to find the others.

"Hey guys, how's it going up here?" He asked.

"Good, you?" Alex asked happily, giving his brother a brotherly hug.

"Good. I just came to tell you guys that I think that the captain and Warren are planning something for Christmas, because the captain kicked me out of the infirmary and were talking. There's nothing except Christmas coming, so I think that's what it is. Don't tell them we know though. I was wondering, what can we do for the captain though, to thank him for all that he's done for us?"

"Wow, that'd be so nice. When was the last time we had a nice holiday?" Alex asked.

"No idea, too long ago. So what do the rest of you think?"

"I think had we thought of it on Drandaria, we could've gotten the captain something really nice, but we'll have to figure something else out. We'll need to find a way to get the captain out of our hair for a couple hours, and then we can figure something out together." Donny said.

"Yeah, but did anyone else even realize it was December twenty second already, I didn't?" Jesse asked.

"Nope." They all responded.

"Well, how do we all get together without the captain. He usually leaves us alone for the most part, but when we're all together, he likes to be with us, and I can't think of any way to do it without alerting him, you know how perceptive he is. I know, who hasn't told him their story yet?" Donny asked all of a sudden.

"I haven't." Tony answered first without thinking.

"Would you be willing to do that this evening during our free time, so we can all get together. Just tell him you're still having nightmares, and you hate them." Donny said.

"I guess so. I am, so I guess it might not be such a bad idea." Tony said slowly, not really liking the idea too much, but agreeing to it, because he knew they were right, and most of the others were doing a lot better after talking it all out with the captain.

"Good, everyone else meet in the games lounge then right after dinner. Will, you'll need to take care of Warren. If you can figure out a way without him figuring it out, then you can come as well." Donny said.

"Not a problem, I'll just tell him I want some alone time with my brothers, and he'll let me go freely." Will said with a smile.

"Good, then it's all planned."

That evening, just after dinner, all the boys, except Tony, met in the games lounge, the word had of course been passed along. Tony had told the captain right before dinner that he would like to talk after dinner, and the captain had said of course.

"Okay guys, has anybody got any ideas?" Franky asked.

"No." Everyone said.

"Why can't we just make something in the holographic room and give it to the captain?" Zach asked.

"Simple. Anything made in the holographic room will disappear as soon as you leave the room. It only exists in there remember. We could try and make something for him though. Hey, I know, we have lots of metals, including gold right. What if we made a program for the holographic room for a jewelers shop, and had them make a nice ring or something from the gold, do you think we could do that?" Jesse asked.

"I have no idea, but right now it's the best we have, so let's go give it a try. I'll go get one of the larger rocks with gold in it, and I'll meet you guys there. Jesse, you get to program the computer, since it was your idea. You might need to program a forge capable of extracting the gold as well, I doubt a jeweler can do it." Donny instructed.

"Good idea, meet you there in a few minutes." Jesse said, and he and the others all took off right away.

Donny went to the storage area where the precious metals were being stored, and grabbed the largest rock containing the most amount of gold, he also grabbed a few of the other precious metals as well, and then went and met the others in the holographic room.

"Hey guys, this looks cool. Will he be able to do it?" Donny asked when he entered a forge.

"He says he can do it no problem." Jesse said.

Donny handed the rocks over, and the person took it and it said to come back in a couple hours. The boys all went back to the games lounge, after Donny locked the program to stay running after exiting. Just before everyone was to head up to their rooms, and the captain and Tony came down, Donny said he was going to go get the ring started. He passed Captain Casey and Tony in the hall.

"Hi Sir." Donny said as he was passing.

"Hi Donny, where you heading in such a hurry?"

"Nowhere really, just have to take care of something before bed is all, don't worry, nothing's wrong."

"Okay, good to hear, bed in thirty minutes."

"Okay." Donny answered and headed off.

Once in the holographic room, he found the forge worker finished. He handed Donny four small bars of metals. Two of gold, one of platinum, and one of titanium. Donny went over to the jewelers shop, which was programmed to be next door, and entered. He handed over the four bars and told the jeweler what he was looking for, and that he wanted the ring to be laser inscribed with all the names of the crew. The jeweler said it would be ready in the morning. Donny then headed out and met the others in the lounge, just as they were heading up to go to bed.

"Everything alright Donny?" Captain Casey asked.

"Oh yes Sir! Like I said before, there's nothing wrong. I just forgot to do something earlier that I wanted to do, but it was nothing major. So, you all heading up to bed now?" He asked, effectively changing the subject.

"Yeah we were, so you may as well head up as well." Captain Casey answered, noticing the change, suspecting something, but left it at that.

The next morning, before everyone else got up, Donny crept down to the holograph room to collect the completed ring. He had nearly forgotten that they always do their morning exercises in the room, and Captain Casey would have noticed immediately the program that was running, would wonder why, and possibly ask questions none of the boys cared to answer. He entered the room and went to the jewelers shop, was met by the person in there, and was handed over the remaining metals and the ring.

Donny was informed that the ring had a core of titanium, for the strength, since he had some, as well as it had been strengthened using a special titanium gas coating. He was also told that all the names had been engraved as large as possible with a laser, and would easily be seen with a magnifying glass, but to the naked eye it just looked like neat designs. Donny thanked the computer generated man, and left the room, turning it off and clearing the program from the memory. Captain Casey could still see it if he wanted to, but hopefully it would be a few days before he checked up on it.

Donny had been staring at the ring though when he left, hoping that it would stay intact, and it did, so a sigh of relief escaped. He rushed back up to his room to be there when the captain came to wake everyone up, and of course to hide the ring. After the morning exercises were over, everyone asked Donny how it looked, and he told them all in whispers that it looked really nice. Everyone said that they would come see it somehow either tonight or tomorrow, so he told them to all be careful, but that they would love it.

The next couple days flew by, and before they knew it, it was Christmas morning. Captain Casey had let the boys all sleep in, something he had never done before, and had left notes on their doors, telling them to meet him in the holographic room when they got up. Most of the boys were awake only a little after their normal wake up times, because it had become such a routine, and for those that did not wake up, the others woke them up excitedly, especially after they saw the notes attached on the insides of their doors. Together everyone met in the corridor and walked down to the holographic room, wearing the clothes they had recently got on Drandaria. When they got to the holographic room, they found the captain, Warren, and Will all waiting for them. It was currently a large cozy living room, with a huge decorated tree in the corner.

"Good morning guys." Everyone said as they entered.

"Merry Christmas or happy holidays don't you mean. Warren and I planned out this little surprise for you boys, but when we did it, I didn't think we could have a tree, and then I realized, what was I thinking, we could have nearly anything we wanted. Well, we don't have any gifts, but we can have a nice day together. Outside it's snowing, and we have a nice hill to sled and have fun on." Captain Casey said.

"Merry Christmas Sir, but you're wrong about one thing." Donny said and handed over the small box.

"What's this boys?" Captain Casey asked curiously.

"Open it and find out Sir." Franky said.

He opened it and saw the ring and just stared at it for a few minutes. Donny took out a magnifying glass and handed it over, and the captain took it, wondering why, but then used it to look closer. Tears came to his eyes when he realized what exactly he was looking at. He took the ring out of the box, and turned it over, looking at all the names on it.

"How! How did you guys ever do this?" Captain Casey asked.

"You remember the other day, when you kicked Will from the infirmary, to talk to Warren, well he came to the bridge and told us what he thought. We figured he was probably right. So, yeah, using a couple of the rocks of precious metals we've found, we programmed this very room with a forge and a jeweler, and had them make this for you. Personally I think it turned out very nice." Donny answered.

"I'm speechless. I don't know what to say." Captain Casey said with a few happy tears still leaking down his cheeks.

"Just say thank you." Kelly offered.

"Thank you isn't good enough, but I guess it'll have to do. Thank you all very much. You have no idea what this means to me."

"You're welcome Sir, try it on." Franky said.

Captain Casey nodded and slipped the ring on to the middle finger of his right hand.

"Very nice, it's a perfect fit, and it feels real nice as well."

"Will helped there, your exact body dimensions are stored in the computer, so we were able to get the exact size for the ring. The ring has a titanium core, for strength, and is twenty four carat gold. It was also strengthened with a special coating of titanium gas, so it should never scratch, and because of the core, it should never bend." Donny said.

"It's very nice, again, thank you boys very much. I wish I had have thought of something like this for you guys. Let's go have some breakfast. Warren already has it ready, and it's in the dining room on warmers, waiting for us." Captain Casey said.

They all got up and went to the dining room and found a lot of warmers, holding a lot of food. They all dished up and ate a nice big hearty breakfast. During the meal, Jonathon told the boys that they would be skipping lunch, that they were instead having an early big holiday dinner, so to eat as much as they wanted, and that afterward they would go out and play in the snow.

Once they were all full, they donned the snow suits that had been generated, and they all went outside to play in the computer generated snow. The boys however had a hard time telling the difference, and had a blast none the less, in the perfectly powdery snow. They spent hours sledding down the hills, throwing snowballs, building snowmen, and very near everything they could possibly do in the snow. Around 1400 hours, Warren and Will excused themselves to go start dinner, and left the others to continue in their fun. They did continue having fun, right up until Warren called them in for dinner.

They all exited the holographic room, and as soon as they exited, their snowsuits disappeared, and their clothes were dry and warm. They went up to the dining hall, and sat and enjoyed a nice large stuffed turkey and all the normal holiday fixings, including the captain's favorite dessert, pumpkin pie and whipped cream. The entire meal was delicious and everyone said so. After dinner, it was unanimously decided that games and movies was the way of the evening, so that was what they did. Captain Casey excused himself for a short while though, so that he could call home and wish everyone a merry Christmas.

"Merry Christmas mom and Dad. How has your day been, and how are all the others doing?" Jonathon asked as they came on the screen.

"Merry Christmas to you too Jon, everyone here's doing very well. Your brothers and sisters are all good, and they all wish you a merry Christmas as well. They all just left a few minutes ago, so you'll have to call them all at home to talk to them. How are the boys?" His mom asked.

"They're doing incredible. They've had a great day. We played out in the snow all afternoon, and had a nice big meal together. They also found a way to make me this wonderful ring, just wait until you actually see it." Jonathon said, showing the ring on his finger.

"How exactly did you play in the snow, and how did they manage that?" His dad asked.

"Do you think Earth is the only place with snow, or jewelers." Jonathon said cryptically, implying that they had maybe went down to a planet or something.

"Oh, that makes sense." His dad said, taking the bait, because Jonathon had still not told them a thing about the upgrades, he wanted to leave those as a giant surprise.

After taking a little more than an hour to make the calls he wanted, Jonathon went and joined the rest of his crew for the evening. After talking to his parents, he had of course called each of his siblings, as well as a few close friends, and also wished them all a Merry Christmas. Once he was finished making all the calls, Jonathon went and joined the boys for the rest of the evening in playing and relaxing. They all had a very nice Christmas together, and took a total of three days to relax.

For the next couple months nothing much happened, and the crew of the UE1 were enjoying themselves a great deal on their exploration mission. They met a few new people, but none near as friendly as the Drandarians. They saw many things, and had gone a considerable distance further than any Earth ship had ever gone before. The amount of information that they had gathered on the trip out was astonishing, and all the Earth scientists would be kept busy for many months. The boys had continued to learn quickly, to the point that Jonathon was certain that not one of his boys would pass at anything less than two to three years above their actual level. Not to mention their ship handling and their command knowledge was beginning to be nearly as good as his was, to the point he could easily hand any of the boys a ship to command, and they could do it. Not that he would though, because they were not ready for that yet, not quite, mostly because they were still not as comfortable around others, but they were getting even better there as well.

At the end of February, it was decided by all that they would turn around and head home, taking a different course of course. Again, on their trip back they saw and did many new things, and again met a few new races, one of them was not in the least bit friendly, but at least they did not outright attack them, just threatened them to get out of their space, or else.

The boys did not like this, and almost told them where to go, but restrained themselves, falling back on the diplomacy lessons their captain had been teaching them. The rest of the people were nice enough, and one even invited them to their planet. It was a tiny planet though, that was so packed with people that they were very nearly stacked on top of each other, it was not a pleasant place to visit, but they made the most of it. It was now two months later, and they were on the opposite side of Drandaria than they had started from, except there was another solar system between them, when they ran into a bit of a snag.

CHAPTER 26

ABDUCTION

Franky had had team three move the ship into a nearby asteroid field, so that they could sit for a day or two and relax, it was Saturday evening, and they had some maintenance to do to the hull. They had hit a small asteroid a few days before, and it had caused a small tear in the hull, so they were going to go out and repair it. So Sunday morning, it was decided that Team Two would go out and check the hull over, fix that area, and do any other repairs that they found as well. Team Two suited up, and went out onto the hull to take care of the problem.

The boys had been out there for an hour, when all of a sudden they were gone. A Qaralon ship, as it turns out, had also been hiding in the field, and due to the nature of the field, with all the metals in it, they went undetected with their shields up. They however saw the UE1 come in, and they knew exactly who they were as well, for their captain had been one of the captains of the ships that they had defeated at Drandaria. By the time that the bridge even knew it had happened, it was too late, the Qaralon ship had hit them with a missile, and disabled their engines. Only the extra strength added to that section and the extra shield there saved them at all with their main shields down. The ship went into a fury of activity.

"What the hell just happened." Captain Casey shouted out. "Play everything back, I want to know now."

The entire thing was played back on the recorders, and the Qaralon ship had only appeared for maybe a second as they teleported the boys out, and then they launched the missile and took off.

"What happened Sir, how did they sneak up on us? We had our scanners at maximum Sir, they shouldn't have been able to sneak up on us like that." Franky said, nearly hyperventilating and crying all at once.

The rest of the boys were just plain in shock.

"I don't know what happened guys. They had to have been here before us, and they must have seen us coming in and hiding. They had to have been waiting for such a thing. As for not being able to see them, why do you think we were here, to not be seen as easily right. Now, we need to get ourselves together, get our ship back up and running, and go get our men. Everyone to the engine room, we don't sleep until our guys are safe and back on this ship." Captain Casey said sadly.

Jonathon would never say it, but this was his absolute biggest fear on this mission, to lose one of his boys, and to have five be taken from right under his nose, but not be able to do a thing about it, was nearly crushing him. He had to stay strong though for the others however, they were depending on him.

They all rushed to the engine room and got to work getting the engines back on line. As soon as they got there, they saw the damage.

"Sir, my team needs to get out there and get the hull repaired before we can do anything. The only thing holding it together now are the engine room shields that are always on." Brady said.

"Yes, I agree. Take your guns with you, I hope the boys had theirs, but I fear that using them could get them killed. Be careful." Captain Casey said.

The boys very quickly suited up and got outside to start the much needed repairs. Kelvin broke off to check to see if the other repair was finished, and it had been just about done, so he finished it off right away. The others had checked the rest of the ship first, and came back to it last to fix, so that was good. As soon as Kelvin had that done, he headed back to get the main issue resolved. Brady had already had a few pieces of hull plating sent up, and they were already in the process of moving them into place and welding them on. Less than an hour later, they were done and were headed back inside. They had worked fast and efficient to get it done, and it was almost perfect. The only thing to have truly saved their butts were the new upgrades to this section.

Meanwhile, Captain Casey and the rest of the crew were busy repairing the damaged portion of the engine. Luckily, with the structural strength that was added, and with the engine shields that now ran at all times, there was not as much damage as there could have been, and inside of two hours from the time that they were hit, they were off and running.

Warren had brought the boys' DNA up, and had the scanners searching for them at maximum. They had a trail, it was faint, but they had a direction. It was heading toward the Qaralon home world. Captain Casey left to go call home. As soon as he got to his office, he did a conference call to his parents and WSEC.

"We've been attacked and five of my boys were taken!" Jonathon said without greeting.

"Oh my, what happened Jon." His mom asked immediately.

Jonathon related the whole tale as to what had happened, and what they had had to do. Everyone was surprised that a direct, unshielded hit, had not destroyed them, they however still had no clue as to the upgrades, but said nothing, because it was not important at the time.

"Where are you now, help is already on the way?" His dad asked.

"Sending the coordinates now. We're going after them at maximum speed, we'll either get them back alive, or die trying, but I guarantee that I'll take as many of those vile beasts with me as I can." Jonathon vowed harshly.

"Calm down Jon, you know that you aren't thinking clearly, you're mad, and more than a little sad and very angry at yourself. Don't forget, I'm your mother, I can read you very well. Going into a fight mad will get you killed for sure, and that'll do no one any good at all. Clear your mind, focus on the positive, and then go after them. I have no doubt that you'll find the boys, and you'll destroy many of those vile beasts, as you say, but do so while thinking clearly." His mom said calmly.

"Thanks mom, I needed that. You're right, as always. I'm going to call the Drandarians and the Tenarians, they're probably a lot closer than you guys are. We're going after them, and I won't rest until my boys are safe and back on this ship." Captain Casey said, this time much more clearly.

"Good idea Jonathon. Call for help, and it'll come. We'll send everything we can afford to send, because you're heading straight for the lions den, and you could be heading into a world of hurt." His dad said.

"Captain Casey, we'll send everything we can, like your father said, to aid the retrieval of your people. We're at least two weeks away though, so be careful out there." An admiral at WSEC that Jonathon had never met said.

"Thanks. I have to make a couple more calls. Talk to you later." Jonathon said and disconnected without waiting for an answer. As soon as he disconnected from them, he contacted Drandaria.

"Prime Minister Raindrop, I wish I was calling you for a better reason, but we need your help as quick as you can get here." Jonathon said as soon as the prime minister came on screen.

"Captain Casey, what is it, what's the matter, how can we help?" He asked, clearly seeing the distress in the captain.

Jonathon told him the entire story. The prime minister sat there in shock for a few moments before he spoke.

"Captain, we'll be there as quick as we can. We have fourteen of the new ship design ready and willing, as well as thirty two of the shuttles, to go with them. We'll get to you as quickly as we can possibly make it. I'm sure I'll have to beat off the captains to come to your aid." Prime Minister Rain Drop said.

"Don't send everything you have, you have to keep your planet protected as well. I'm also calling the Tenarians, and Earth are sending what they can, but they're the furthest away, so will take some time. I'll send you the coordinates for where I'm at currently, and where we're going, if that changes, I'll inform your people. Thanks." Jonathon said thankfully.

"I'll only send our new ships, the old ones will be sufficient to protect the planet, should the need arise." The prime minister stated.

"Thanks Sir. I have to go ask the Tenarians next, so I'll call if anything changes." Jonathon said, and then disconnected.

He had almost the same conversation with the the Tenarians, and they said they would send at the very least a few dozen ships to help out. Once finished, Captain Casey went back out to the bridge, to see how the boys were doing. Will and Alex were by far the worst, because their brother was one of the ones taken, and the others were trying to console them as best they could, as was Warren. As soon as the captain came on the bridge, both boys wrapped themselves around the captain, and cried into him. Jonathon knelt down with both boys, hugged them tight, and got them calmed down after a few minutes. As soon as they were able to let him go, Jonathon stood and motioned for the boys to listen.

"Okay guys, help is on the way. The Drandarians are the closest, so they'll be here the quickest. We aren't going to rest until we get our boys back. Now, I know you're all very angry right now. Put that anger aside though, it'll do none of us any good. Look how well making the enemy angry has helped us in the past, it's a useful tool, against the enemy. We can't have it though. We're on a rescue mission, plain and simple, same as if we didn't know who it was that we were rescuing. It just so happens they're family, and when we find them, we won't take pleas of pity, we'll only accept cries of pain, once our boys are safely on board." Captain Casey said gently.

"Yes Sir!" They all said softly.

"I know it's hard, and it'll be hard on all of us, but it's our best tool, to use our anger in a positive way." Captain Casey said calmly.

Meanwhile, on the Qaralon ship that abducted the boys, they were teleported to a small room, and that was where they had stayed, no contact by anyone as of yet.

"Okay guys, we've been taken, by the Qaralon no doubt. I've been in a place just like this before. Don't panic, and don't over react. The captain won't rest until he gets us back, so do nothing to cause us pain, they won't harm us, yet, at any rate. Let me do all the talking, assuming of course they come to see us. And don't eat anything they give us, no matter how hungry we get, drink only the water, however, even that'll be bad, but we have to drink to survive." Jamie said, keeping his cool amazingly well. It was five hours before a pair of Qaralon came to the small room the boys were being kept in. More than one of the boys felt like vomiting the first time they saw one of the ugly beasts again. Jamie stepped forward.

"What do you want, and why did you take us?" Jamie asked harshly.

"Because you make fine meal, and better hostage." The lead beast said with a sick grin.

"You'll find we're going to be your worst nightmare. If you knew what you just got yourselves into, you'd be crying like a baby. Our captain will hunt you down, and make you wish you were never born, but he won't kill you, oh no, the fate for you'll be far worse." Jamie said calmly.

"We destroyed you ship after we took you, there be no one coming for you, you little brats, you be fattened up and given as feast to our leaders, because you ship destroyed many ours." The vile being spat out.

"Oh, so you know us, yet you attacked us anyway. I knew you Qaralon were stupid, but I didn't think you had no brains at all. How many hits did you hit our ship with?" Jamie asked condescendingly.

"One, right to engine, ship not shielded. We not have stay an watch, we know it destroy." The beast stated in confidence.

"Are you dense. Our ship is the strongest of the fleet, it could easily take two blows to the engine rooms, without main shields, and still not be destroyed. Four hours tops is all it'd take to repair the damage. They'll be following you already, and your ships are forty percent slower than ours is. How far is it until we reach your home world, what, about two weeks right? Well, in one, our captain's going to catch up to you, and he'll remove your still beating heart from your chest, and then feed it to you just before you die. Now as for fattening us up, don't even think of it, we won't touch your food, we'd rather starve to death before ever eating anything you give to us. We'll be nothing but a shell, if and when you do make it to your planet. We'll be unfit to feed to your most hungry peasants." Jamie spat out.

"You know nothing, we make you eat, you not stop from feeding you, or we torture you." The beast snarled.

"By all means torture us, beat us, electrocute us, rape us, make us into your little pets, it'll do no good, we'll throw up anything you feed to us, and we'll fight you to within an inch of your lives if you come near us. Leave us alone, and your people will be left alive. Turn around and take us back to our ship, and we might even think of sparing your ship." Jamie said softly, dangerously.

"Oh, we do that for sure, except turn round, you will eat, and you eat it all. You make a satisfying meal to leaders, and you no say in it." The beast snarled out.

Jamie turned around whipped his pants down and growled out. "Go ahead, rape me now, find out what it gets you."

The beast took one step forward, probably to do just that, so Jamie whipped his pants back up, spun around, and in one swift move, hit the creature in the chest with his open palm. The beast stumbled backwards, his eyes rolled into his head, and he was unconscious.

"Take this pathetic excuse of a warrior back up to your captain, and tell it that the next creature that passes through that door will be killed without mercy. Unfortunately this one will wake in an hour or two." Jamie said, and then took the door and slammed it in the face of the beast that stood there, with an even more stupid look on its face than it normally had.

"That was fun." Jamie said as he brushed his hands together.

"I'm glad you considered that fun. I thought I was going to pee myself, but I just stood staring at the ugly beasts." Alex said.

"Worked out a lot of anger that way. Now let's just hope that my times were correct. Depending on how hard they were hit, I figure two to three hours to repair, and then they were on their way, and we all know they'll be coming at maximum speed. I sure wouldn't want to be this ship when Captain Casey gets here though. As soon as the fighting starts, we break out and take out as many as we can to get to a teleporter to get out of here. We all still have our weapons, the stupid beasts didn't even bother to check us, so we can cause a lot of damage when the time comes, but not 'til then, you all hear me?" Jamie asked seriously.

"Yes Sir!" They all said.

For the next few days the boys were left almost entirely to themselves. The guard that Jamie had hit was unwilling to go back, it seems that he was very fearful of the boys, and the captain was amazingly smart enough to listen to the warning, the guard having told him the warnings, and Jamie had meant what he had said. The only time the boys saw the beasts were when they dropped off food and water. The boys just threw the food out the door, as whoever had brought it was closing the door, more than once hitting the thing that had brought it to them. As it was feared, even the water tasted horrible, but they had no choice but to force it down. They were all getting very hungry, and more than a little ready to go, but they kept their spirits up the entire time. They managed to tell jokes and talk a lot, and even though they hated the situation they were in, they made the best of it.

The crew of the UE1 spent those few days searching, and it was, at times, a fight to make the boys eat and to participate in anything, other than searching for their friends and brother. It was only at the captain and Warren's prompting, that the boys actually talked or did anything, none of them even watched a movie or went to the holograph room, none of them felt it fair when the others were having a horrible time.

It was five days later that that UE1 had caught a glimpse of the ship on their scanners at their maximum range. A few hours later, when they were only about an hour away, Captain Casey had Kelly give them a call.

"Come out, come out wherever you are. You didn't hit us near as hard as you thought you did, and now we're back, and we want to play with you. You had better give us our people back, or we'll do a lot more than just play with you." Kelly said sweetly.

Teams one and four had gone to the cargo bay and got the shuttles all powered up, and started to launch. All of a sudden the Qaralon ship had three ships after them. Although they figured that the small ships would be no threat to them, but they could not have been more wrong, then again, they were too stupid to believe that smaller was more powerful, they thought that the bigger you were, the more powerful you were.

"You not destroy us, we gots you people on board." The beast snarled.

"Oh really, why don't you go ask them, I dare you, send one of your stupid people down there and verify that they'd gladly give up their lives to see the likes of you destroyed. It'll take only a minute." Kelly said sweetly.

They then heard the captain give the order to go and check, he was not taking any chances with these humans, they had already destroyed so many of their ships, and too easily, even for such a puny ship. They heard a communicator go off, and then the voice confirming they meant it. What the captain did not know, was that as soon as that was said, the messenger was laying on the floor, dead. The boys that had been their captives were now loose, and were now their worst enemy.

"I heard that, you have your confirmation, so it would be in your best interest to surrender now, before your captives make it to your bridge, and slaughter you in your stupid incompetence. They've almost certainly escaped, using the guns that they were wearing when they were abducted. I'm certain that you're too stupid to have checked them, they were just kids after all." Kelly said sweetly.

"You lie. They not escape, my people too smart for that, and we not surrender. It you will surrender, or I send someone down kill you crew." The beast snarled.

"You heard what your vile disgusting beast said, they confirmed what I told you. I know my friends far better than you do, and believe me, they're loose, and at the very least, one of your men is now dead. You will be soon too. If you surrender now, we might even let you live. Your ship will only just barely make it home, but it will. Do it now, or else." Kelly snapped out.

The beast went to reply, and only got out, "We not . . . ." and Kelly cut the communications off in mid sentence of the beast, this made it very angry.

Team two, however, was now loose on his ship, and by now ten beings were dead, but no one knew about it, because all that saw them died before they could even make a sound. Jamie had found a teleporter console, and found the UE1, but it was still too far away using the minimal teleporters the Qaralon had. He got the layout of the ship from it though, and they made a mad dash for the bridge, meeting and killing another five beasts on the way, and they too all died before they even had a chance to realize that the boys were there. They reached the bridge, and shot three of the things that were smart enough to draw a weapon, but were not fast enough to even fully pull them out.

"Who's in charge of this poor excuse for a ship?" Jamie asked happily, each of the five boys aiming at one of the beasts on the bridge.

"I captain, how you get out?" He asked, panicking, realizing that what the UE1 had told him, was in fact true.

"We escaped right after that pathetic excuse for a guard asked us if we would gladly die to see all of you dead. While it's true, we'd really rather stay alive, so we killed him, and here we are. How many of you were there on this flying death trap?" Jamie asked smiling.

"Twenty five." The captain said, realizing he was probably going to be dead real soon.

"Well then, including the three currently lying dead on your bridge, we have killed nineteen of your people, there are four of you left on the bridge, that means there are only two more of your people elsewhere. Stop the ship now, and bring up the communications?" Jamie demanded.

"What if I not do?" The captain asked bravely, or at least what he tried to make it sound like, because the puddle of urine that was collecting below him told the boys otherwise.

"Then I'll feel no pity about shooting you where you stand, and if any of the others even think of raising a weapon, we'll shoot them as well. Now do it, because I won't ask again, then I'll shoot you, and do it myself, you pathetic excuse for a leader. Just look at you, you can't even hold your pee under stress." Jamie hissed out, and he meant it, he had no problem at all with killing them all without mercy. They were all starving, so wanted to get home, and quick. Plus he was quickly losing his patience.

"Fine, not kill us." The beast said.

"Do as I say, and you'll be left alive, against my better judgment." Jamie said.

The captain nodded, and both orders were done by the couple remaining people on the bridge. As soon as the communications was up, Jamie stepped up, and called out to the UE1.

"Jamie, it's so good to see you guys, are all of you alright?" Captain Casey asked, thoroughly glad to see the boys looking well.

"Yes Sir, we're all very hungry, and we want to come home. The Qaralon have been kind enough to stop so that you can come get us. I've promised them that we won't kill them, so we probably shouldn't, but then again, we've already killed nineteen of the twenty five the captain claims to have had on board. I'm not so sure

I should trust him, but whatever. Come and get us please?" Jamie asked happily.

"Be right there, have them drop their shields and engines, and we'll get you right away." Captain Casey told the relieved boys.

"You heard him captain, shut em down or else, and remember, I won't ask a second time!" Jamie said threateningly.

"Fine." It said, and nodded to the others, so they did it.

Within a minute, all five boys were back on the bridge of their ship. Hugs were passed all around, and the boys were welcomed home, then they were sent promptly to the infirmary, and then the kitchen for some much needed food and a checkup. The boys almost all wanted to say kitchen first, but thought better of it. They trudged off, and the captain and team three were left with the mess in front of them.

"Kelly, if you would, put them up on screen please?" Captain Casey asked.

"Yes Sir!" He said.

"Qaralon ship, you took my people, and you tried to destroy us. We'll now pay upon you the same courtesy that you gave to us. You however probably won't be able to repair your engines as easily as we were able to. If you have any people in your engine room, I'd suggest you get them out of there, now." Captain Casey said sweetly.

"You wouldn't." It said in a last ditch hope.

"Don't try me. You have five minutes to comply, and then your engines will be destroyed. Try me, and it'll gladly be the whole ship. I really wouldn't try me, my two little ships you see buzzing around me, well they'd enjoy taking you apart, piece by piece." Captain Casey dangerously.

"No, you'll have to kill us, you not take another ship from me, they kill me at home this time." It said and disconnected.

They brought their shields and engines back on line, and fired a couple shots off. Before doing that though, they placed a call home for help, saying they were being attacked. They had called earlier and help was already on its way, but their help was closer than Captain Casey's help was, a lot closer.

Teams one and four did not take too kindly to the Qaralon firing, so went and attacked the ship, and together they destroyed the ship in under thirty seconds. All they did was circle around and around the large ship, both firing repeatedly, not that it actually took too many shots, and the Qaralon never even got off another shot before they were destroyed. They came back and docked in the cargo bay, and then went to find team two and welcome them home.

"Where are they Captain?" Alex asked as soon as they arrived on the bridge.

"I sent them down to the infirmary, and then the kitchen to get some food. They were starving. Were you the one that fired the last shot?" Captain Casey asked gently, but pretty sure he knew the answer.

"No Sir, I couldn't do it, not for revenge. They deserved nothing less, but not from me." Alex said proudly.

"Good, I'm glad for you. Go, go see your brother." Captain Casey said, and Alex just turned and ran out of the bridge to see his brother.

"You guys did good, quick and indecisive!" Captain Casey said to his boys proudly.

"Thanks Sir." Brady said.

"Let's go guys." Captain Casey said.

"Um Sir, I don't think we can. I have a hundred or so ships just coming into range." Matthew said.

"Well then, let's get out of here as fast as we can, because we can still out run them, and I don't want to be fighting a hundred or more ships, since we couldn't hope to win that." Captain Casey said simply.

"Yes Sir!" Everyone on the bridge said.

The emergency systems were activated, and Cullen got them moving as fast as they could, as quick as he could. The problem was that the Qaralon were forcing them into an asteroid field, so it would slow them a great deal. It was an immense field, and the ships had them pretty much surrounded, and they knew it. They headed to the field, seeing as how that was their only hope at survival. The field was only a day away, they would make it long before the Qaralon did, and they might even be able to make it through the field in time, but not likely. The only good thing was that the Qaralon would have to slow down to go through as well, and given that their ships were quite a bit larger, they would have to take greater care.

As soon as the boys had everything under control, Captain Casey went to his office to send out the distress call. As soon as he arrived, he did a conference call to his parents, WSEC, Tenaria, and Drandaria.

"Emergency, we have our people, and the ship that took them is destroyed. Everyone is alive and healthy, if not a bit hungry. We however have in excess of one hundred ships forcing us into an asteroid filed, at least a few light years across in every way. We're currently ahead of them, and can get through the field faster than they can, however, we still have a hundred ships after us. Anyone that can help, as soon as possible, would be greatly appreciated." Jonathon said calmly as soon as everyone was online.

"Our ships are two days from your location." Prime Minister Rain Drop said.

"Our ships are three to four days." The prime Minister of Tenaria said.

"We are still about a week out Jonathon, hold tight, we have over a hundred ships coming." His father said.

"Thanks, we'll evade them as best we can until help arrives then, thanks everyone." Jonathon said, and then disconnected. He very quickly headed back out to the bridge.

"Okay guys, here's the plan, not much, but it'll have to do. We're going to stay in the field and keep them at bay as best we can. The Drandarians are two days out, and the Tenarians three to four days, the Qaralon are still almost two days behind us, and we're faster." Captain Casey told the boys as soon as he made it back out to the bridge.

"Sir, why don't we just get through the field as fast as we can?" Franky asked.

"Because, I think that there's a reason that they're forcing us this way. I think that they know a fast way through, maybe a cleared path that their computers know, and can get them through really fast. If that were the case, we wouldn't stand a chance. It's the only reason they'd herd us right to here that I can think of. If anyone can think of anything else, I'd welcome your input right about now?" Captain Casey asked the boys for their opinion.

"If you're right, and I see no reason why you'd be wrong, because it makes perfect sense, and it'd be what I'd do, then we just have to get through first. I didn't think that they were smart enough for that though. Anyway, would there be a way for our computers to find a clear path through, and let it take over on autopilot to get us through even faster than they can?" Jesse asked hopefully.

"It's an extremely large asteroid field, and I bet our scanners can scarcely see half way into it, let alone all the way through it. It is however our best option, and we have about a day to do it, so I want everyone good at puzzles, staring at screens, and getting the computer to help to see if we can find this elusive path. I want the night crew to get their butts to bed, we don't stop for anything." Captain Casey commanded.

"Yes Sir!" Team four said and headed to bed, it was going to be a long night. Franky also followed, since he was going to be the night crew watch.

Almost everyone else on board, including Warren and Will, were staring at sections of the asteroid field, looking to see if they could find any patterns that looked suspiciously like a trail through it. As the captain had suspected though, the field was so dense with metals, and other scanner dampening materials, that they could not even see half way through it. So the problem became, even if they did find something like a path, how would they know it went all the way through, but they also all thought that if they could make it half way through at a high rate of speed, they would still easily exit out the other side long before the Qaralon did. It was during the night shift, nearly half way through it, that Bobby thought he found the path.

"Franky, I think I found it. As far in as I can see, there's a very clear path, and there are traces of debris left from many asteroids being destroyed all the way in as far as I can see. I say we take it, at the very least, even if we're wrong, it gets us deeper into it to hide, and a lot faster at that, or we can still make it through before they do. By the time that the Qaralon get here, we could be so deep inside that they might never find us." Bobby said very convincingly.

"Well, it sounds like a heck of a lot better plan than anything else we have so far, so I say we do it. Does everyone else agree, because it's all our necks on the line here?" Franky asked seriously.

"Yes Sir!" They said.

"Good work kid. If you found the actual path, you might have just saved us all, and even if you didn't, you're right about the other things as well. As soon as we reach it guys, we go in at full speed, so keep your eyes peeled, and the scanners looking only forward at their maximum. We already know what's behind us anyway, so no point in looking back there. Let's just make sure nothing in front of us can do us any harm. Weapons, make sure you watch like a hawk too, the second you see anything in front of us that can do us harm, blast it outta the way." Franky said.

Not one of the boys even answered, they knew it was their only hope, so just kept watching the screens, every last one of them. They had figured that by no later than 0600 hours they would reach the field, and Captain Casey had instructed them to go in as fast, and as careful as they possibly could anyway, so that was what they did.

At 0515, they entered the field at maximum speed, and the path stayed thankfully clean and clear all the way that their scanners could see, and by the time the captain and the rest of the crew came to the bridge, they were well inside. Franky briefed the others while he watched the screens, as were the others, to make sure nothing popped up in their way, in fact, so far not one of them even looked up, just continued watching.

"Well Bobby, it looks like your keen sight could have saved us. Thanks. You guys head on up to get some food, I know you probably didn't eat all night, and then go for a swim or something and relax, we'll take care of the rest of this." Captain Casey said.

"Thanks Sir, we will, because we're all quite hungry I'm sure, and I know my eyes are killing me. I don't think I've blinked in at least four hours." Bobby answered for them all.

"Of that I have little doubt. You boys go and get some rest." Captain Casey said warmly, and the boys did as they were told.

Captain Casey went and sent a message to the fleets telling them where to meet them. Due to the field dampening the signal so much, it would take probably half an hour, or more, for the fleet to receive the message, but it was good enough.

Twelve hours into the asteroid field, they were nearly half way through, and could just make out the other side, the problem was, that that was not the only thing that they could see.

CHAPTER 27

A TRAP IS SET

Ryan sat looking at the screen he was staring at, hoping and praying that what he had just seen come on screen was not what it was. So he looked again, and sure enough, it was as he feared.

"Um Sir, you better come take a look at this!" Ryan said worriedly.

"What is it Ryan?" Captain Casey asked, going over to see just what it was that Ryan was seeing.

"Well, the other side of the asteroid field just came into view, finally, but with it a whole lotta ships, and they aren't ours either. They have us trapped Sir." Ryan said looking ghostly white.

"No time to panic, we'll get through this. The Drandarians are coming up behind them and should be there soon, they won't get us without a fight. Full stop, then move us into the field as deep as you can get us, but don't stop, just keep us moving." Captain Casey said.

"Yes Sir!" All of team three said, the rest were all resting.

"Crew of the UE1, rest time is over, we're being pushed into an even larger trap, I need all hands on the bridge to help figure this one out." Captain Casey called out.

"Kelly, see if we can get the Drandarian fleet yet?" Captain Casey asked.

"Drandaria fleet, can you hear me, this is the UE1, and we're in serious trouble, please come in." Kelly called out, not letting any panic into his voice, even though he was certainly feeling it.

"This is Captain Cloudburst, we see them, we're coming up right behind them, what are your orders?" Captain Cloudburst asked.

"Do you think they've seen you yet?" Kelly asked.

"They've made no indication that they have as of yet." The captain answered.

"Hold back, hide until the Tenarians reach us, all together we have no hope in beating this number, even if we're superior in fighting skills." Kelly said calmly.

"You got it, I'll call the Tenarians and home, and get even more people on the way." Captain Cloudburst said.

"Good idea, but don't take everything you have from your planet though. We'll evade them as best as we can, you guys only come if we call. As soon as the Tenarians arrive, we'll start the attack." Kelly said and then disconnected.

"Good call Kelly, now let's all figure out what the heck we're going to do to get us out of this mess." Captain Casey said, now that the rest of the crew had made it up to the bridge.

It only took one look at the view screen for all the others that had just arrived, to see what the fuss was all about. They could clearly see the ships ahead of them, as well as all the ships that were still behind them, so they too knew they had gotten into a bit of a situation.

"Captain, what are we going to do?" Donny asked, taking in the gravity of the situation first.

"I wish I knew Donny, I wish I knew. There are about a hundred ships behind us, and at least three times that number waiting for us. We're moving into the asteroid field as deeply as we can right now, to get what little protection that it offers. From now on, we're at maximum alert, and the bridge is to be manned by a full team at all times, meals will be brought up to the team on duty whenever necessary. Now, we have to figure out how we're going to get out of this seemingly impossible situation, alive, because personally, I'd rather stay that way." Captain Casey said, and the boys all agreed wholeheartedly with that.

"Sir, it's plainly obvious that taking the path was a mistake. They were hoping we'd find it. All we can do now, is cut straight through the field as fast as we possibly can, and hide in the most dense part we can find." Bobby said simply.

"Bobby, if you're trying to blame yourself for this, don't, we took the best option that we had at the time, and it turned out to be wrong, it happens. How were we to know that the Qaralon had thought this out so well. Well, actually, I can guarantee that it wasn't them, the Framgar had to have helped, since there are as many ships of theirs out there as Qaralon, so we know who the brains of the attack is. Now, I think Bobby you're right, for now, that's our best hope. The Tenarians are still a day away, and our people at least three days away, but probably closer to four, if not five. I want the best eyes on the scanners looking for paths through the rocks, make the fit as tight as you can, so that the Qaralon have a very tough time trying to follow us, if they're stupid enough to even do so. And we all know they are."

"Yes Sir!" They all said.

"Warren and Will, I'm afraid that very soon your services may be required, because I doubt very seriously that we can make it out of this without a few injuries." Captain Casey warned.

"We're prepared Sir, the infirmary is stocked, and is set and ready to go, should we be needed. If required, teleport anyone directly to us, and we'll get them back on their feet and helping as soon as we can." Will said, Warren just nodded.

"Good." Captain Casey said, and then turned his eyes to the scanners as well, sending every bit of information he could to navigation, who was translating the information everyone was giving them into a course. A couple times the fit was just a touch too tight, and they felt when they bumped an asteroid, there would be many small injuries to the ship to be repaired soon, but right now that was of little concern. The shields were at maximum anyway, so mostly it was their shields hitting, so the damage to the ship itself should be minimal, at least they all hoped so.

As soon as they disconnected from talking to Kelly, the person on communications of Captain Cloudburst's ship, contacted everyone they could. As soon as they were connected, Captain Cloudburst sent out his instructions.

"Tenarian and Earth Fleets, this is Captain Cloudburst of the Drandarian Star Fleet, Captain Casey and his crew are in even greater peril than previously suspected. There's an armada of ships waiting for them, our systems peg them at close to three hundred and fifty ships strong, plus the approximately hundred that were following them. We've been instructed to hold back until reinforcements arrive, as together we don't stand a chance against those numbers. I've been requested to call out more people, send everything you can afford, this is full scale war by the looks of it."

"Acknowledged." Both fleet leaders said.

"We'll be at your location in less than twenty hours, and we have eighty three ships with us, so once we get there, the battle starts." A Tenarian captain said.

"Good. See you soon then."

"And our fleet is over a hundred strong, but we're still more than two days away ourselves, however we're going just as fast as we can. Hold them off as best you can, and we'll get there to reinforce as soon as possible." Earth fleet said, and they all disconnected.

He then made a call to his home world to inform Prime Minister Rain Drop of the severity of the situation, and that sending as many ships as could be spared, might be wise.

"Another three ships are just being tested, and four shuttles to go with each of them are already tested and ready to go. We'll send those, plus twenty of the old ships. We'll barely have crews to supply the ships, but we're on our way." The prime minister said.

"Remember what Captain Casey said though, don't leave our planet with no defenses, he'd be very upset. Send the new ones plus ten, and that should be good." Captain Cloudburst warned.

"You're right, he'd be upset, but we owe him. I'll send what you suggest, and then start training every person willing to operate the ships left for security." Prime Minister Rain Drop said.

"Sounds good Sir, see you soon." Captain Cloudburst said, and then disconnected.

Both the Earth and Tenarian fleets also called home and told them what they knew, and also requested that more ships be sent. What Jonathon had not known though, was that it was his own parents that were leading the Earth fleet, and were in the most brand new, top of the line ship, and were ready, willing, and more than able to fight off three times the numbers currently attacking.

Back on the EU1, Captain Casey figured that they had all best get very well prepared, so called out to a few of the boys.

"Team three and Franky, you're with me. I want to get our shuttles fully prepared for battle."

"Yes Sir!" The six boys said, and were already heading out.

"The rest of you, keep your eyes peeled and keep us safe."

"Yes Sir!" The rest of the crew said, not even looking up from their duties though, because that was far more important.

The seven of them went down to the cargo bay and started loading the shuttles with everything that they could possibly need. The missiles were all changed out to the highest yield Nutronium missiles and were fully stocked, the kitchen was fully stocked, just in case, and the first aid supplies were checked carefully. Then they went to the weapon storage area, and Captain Casey took down four crates. The boys had no idea what was in these crates, because they were told not to open them when they had come on board, but they were now opening them. It was in fact an in case of emergency pack, a very large one, being a few large crates.

"Okay boys, I was hoping that we'd never need what's in these boxes, it seems however that good planning was, as always, wise. What we have in these boxes are the most powerful Nutronium rifles, and hand grenades that there are. There are belts to hold it all, they'll also hold all your normal gear, as well as some other survival gear. I'll show you how to run a diagnostic on each item to make sure it's fully powered and working, and then we have to take them and hand them out to everyone on board." Captain Casey said, starting to remove some items from the first crate.

He spent five minutes showing the boys how to test everything, and then they spent almost fifteen minutes testing it all, because there was no sense in not testing them, and then have them fail when and if they were needed. Once all the tests were run, the captain showed the boys how to put on the belts. The new one snapped to the ones they already wore, and crisscrossed their chest and back. The rifle was attached over their shoulder, whichever one the wearer preferred, but you could take two if you wanted as well, and then the grenades were attached to the chest belts. There were pockets on the belt that held meal packs and first aid supplies, as well as a number of other survival gadgets that always came in handy, including a good knife, something that every survival kit should have. The belts had been designed to fit everyone, but given just how small some of the boys were, it would look very odd, as Kelly now did, as he suited up. The rifle was very nearly as large as he was, but he showed proficiency well beyond his years, in detaching and attaching the rifle at need. The crates were packed back up lightly, and then Captain Casey teleported them up to the bridge, where all the boys wondered for a second what they were for. They figured, correctly, that they would find out soon enough, and they did.

Captain Casey and the others arrived on the bridge only minutes after the supplies arrived, and then he went over everything with the rest of the boys, while Franky and team three watched and navigated. Soon everyone was suited up, and they all looked very formidable, and more than a bit scary. Even the youngest of them looked real scary, since they had all become quite muscular with the workouts they had done, and then strapped with all the gear they were currently wearing, well, it was a scary sight for sure. The captain figured these boys would have little to no problems dealing with any situation they should have to face, and he felt that the Qaralon had no idea what they were up against. He had a crew of very mean little boys that hated the Qaralon with a passion that a scarce few could imagine, especially after the kidnapping.

"Okay guys, two full teams are going to be on watch tonight, and they should be heading to bed now, because it's already getting late. Remember to be fully prepared, even in bed." Captain Casey warned.

Teams one and two, and Franky, left the bridge without prompting, went to the kitchen, grabbed some food, inhaled it, and went to bed, still in their uniforms. The only thing they did was to hang their weapon belts within very easy reach, so that if they needed them, all they had to do was grab them as they hopped out of bed.

The rest of the day, and well into the next morning, the crew of the UE1 worked their way deeper and deeper into the asteroid field. They could not see any ships following them, but that did not mean that they were not there, so they kept at full alert. Finally, at 0500 hours, they were informed that the Tenarians were there and waiting.

"Sir, I hate to wake you, but the Tenarians have arrived." Devon called to the captain.

"That's okay Devon, I wanted you to call me as soon as they arrived. We'll all be down in a few minutes."

The captain jumped out of bed, went and woke the boys, and told them to get ready in record time to meet him on the bridge. He then went back to his room to clean up a bit and change, and then headed to the bridge himself. If it had not been such a grave situation, he would have enjoyed the ride up to the bridge, since the lifts were going at maximum speed, and he always enjoyed that.

"Are they still up?" Captain Casey asked as soon as he entered the bridge, asking if there was anyone still in communication.

"Yes Sir, just waiting for your orders." Devon said.

"We'll turn and get out of here at the nearest point, and then we attack, you guys start moving in, and we'll meet you hopefully at the exact same time." Captain Casey ordered.

"Okay, exactly what Devon said, just wanted to verify." Captain Cloudburst said, and then the lines went blank.

"Let's get out of here as fast as we can boys, but watch for traps. Teams one and two and Franky, head to bed and catch a couple hours sleep while you can. We'll be in full attack mode in less than six hours." Captain Casey said.

"Yes Sir!" They all said.

"The rest of you, just do what you do best, and we'll survive this mess." Captain Casey said, pumping as much confidence into the boys as he could.

Though the mood was somber, and all were nervous and somewhat scared, they all knew that they were good enough to win, but could they do so without injury or possible death was what they all wondered.

CHAPTER 28

ATTACK!

Four and a half hours later, they were about thirty minutes from the edge of the asteroid field. They could clearly see that the Qaralon and Framgar ships were still waiting for them, but it appeared as if they had not spotted them yet. They had however spotted the Drandarian and Tenarian ships, but were not moving, they were just waiting, holding their lines. The rest of the ships that had been following them as well from Drandaria and Tenaria were almost there as well, having flown hard to meet up with their two fleets, and would commence battle as soon as all were ready. Captain Casey was happy for this. Teams two and four said that they were heading to the shuttles, that they would launch just as soon as they cleared the asteroid field, and then they would attack.

"You boys be careful. Franky and Donny, you go as well. Remember, that if anything happens, abandon the ship, and teleport back here immediately. If you get injured, teleport direct to the infirmary." Captain Casey said.

"Yes Sir!" They all said.

So half an hour later they emerged and teams two and four launched. The timing had been perfect, and they came out at the exact same time that the reinforcements arrived. The Drandarians launched their shuttles as well, and then all of a sudden the numbers had doubled. The Qaralon almost surrendered right there, because of the final reports from the last ship to see the little shuttles was not at all promising to the weaker Qaralon, but the Framgar forced them to stay put. None of them moved either though to attack, so Captain Casey moved into the front of the defenders.

"Okay, Kelly, you're up, do your stuff." Captain Casey said.

"Gladly Sir." Kelly said, and pulled up the communications. "Qaralon and Framgar attacking fleet, back off and move back into the asteroid field and go home, if you don't, well then, we'll be forced to act." He said quietly, almost dangerously.

"We outnumber you two to one, and all those tiny little ships are only but a nuisance to us, you can't stop us. It's you that'll surrender, or be destroyed." A Framgar said menacingly.

"Ah, now you see, that's where you're wrong. Those little tiny ships are going to be your worst nightmare. And remember, you may outnumber us, but we're smarter, and have better ships. We'll win if you wish to push us, now back off, this is your last warning." Kelly said gently.

They responded by launching a full out attack. The UE1 was hit with three missiles, and it was almost damaged seriously, but they held together, it did however make the boys really upset. The lead ship that had launched the missiles though, was destroyed in only four seconds, because the UE1 and both its shuttles fired everything they had at the ship. So far they had not even moved.

The attackers took a second to take in what had just happened, but in their incompetence, decided that even under such wanton brutality, that they would continue the attack, without their leaders. So, the battle commenced.

Both sides were now going at it full on, and both sides were taking losses, the Qaralon and Framgar however were taking the heaviest losses, but they could afford it. Sadly two of the defending ships were destroyed, one Drandarian and one Tenarian. The battle went on for roughly four hours, little skirmishes back and forth. The battle was hard and fierce, it was a no holds barred battle in fact, and the UE1 and both its shuttles were the leaders in that. They were wailing on the enemy with fists of fury at every opportunity. Every one of the defending ships were mounting massive wins though against the Framgar and especially the Qaralon. For every ten ships that they took out, eight of them were Qaralon, but five out of ten ships were not destroyed outright, they would still be able to eventually limp home. The Framgar though were not being so courteous, every chance they had, they shot to kill, so as such, those ships that were playing dirty, were dispatched without a second thought. More than half the time, it was Captain Casey or his boys that took the final shot. The entire battle spanned an area covering well in the range of a full light year next to the asteroid field.

The UE1 shuttles were whipping around everyone and blowing whatever they could out of the sky, and hit nearly every mark they targeted. They were not aiming to disable though, they were aiming to destroy, and their aims were straight and true. In fact, the two UE1 shuttles probably took out as many enemy ships as at least four or five of the other large ships had together. They would have tried disabling only, as they always tried to do, but the Framgar and the Qaralon were trying with everything they had to take out the UE1 and their shuttles, so the boys had no choice but to go at it full on. It was mostly the Framgar going after them, they had seen all the battle recordings and knew that if left to their own, that those three ships would take out most of their ships, so they were trying their best to take them out, to at least try and even the battle. Of course, this was impossible, or as close to it as you can get.

All the defending ships were taking on two and three attacking ships at almost any given time, they were ducking and weaving in and around the Qaralon and Framgar ships. They were firing everything that they had at them, hitting almost every time. Still they were taking heavy losses, yet the battle never seemed to end. All of a sudden two Framgar ships left an opening to a Qaralon ship, so one of the shuttles took what appeared to be an easy shot, but realized too late that they had been trapped, the Framgar had sacrificed a Qaralon ship in order to try and destroy the nasty little shuttle that had almost destroyed them already.

It was one of the UE1 shuttles that had taken the pair of direct hits, it was team two. The hits did not destroy them as the Framgar had obviously hoped it would, because the boys limped back to the ship, and docked. The two ships though that hurt their shuttle, were very quickly dispatched, and they would not be able to do any more harm.

Dillon went up to the infirmary, as soon as he was able to get out out of the damaged shuttle, to have what was suspected to have been a broken arm and rib mended. The rest of the crew got to work on patching up the shuttle, as soon as they were able to, so that they could get back out there.

Then, all of a sudden, the Qaralon and the Framgar ships retreated back into the asteroid field, just as suddenly as the battle had started, it had seemed to end.

"What was that all about?" Captain Casey asked to no one in general.

"I don't know Sir, but I'm not so sure it's a good thing. We should probably all get into the asteroid field though, and wait it out, so that we can get some rest while we can." Captain Cloudburst suggested.

"Good idea, this way we can get a few repairs done, as well as mourn the loss of the souls lost today. Thankfully our losses don't appear to be too high, however, the loss of even a single one of our ships is too much" Captain Casey said sadly, and the agreements rained in for a few moments after.

Team four docked in the cargo bay, and they too started to do the repairs on the shuttle that needed to be done. Once they had been cleared to re-enter, team two went back in and started working as well. Dillon joined them a short time later with a small cast on his arm, just to hold it properly for a couple days, so that it could mend how it was supposed to. As soon as he was able to, Captain Casey found where Dillon was and headed to see him.

"Dillon, I understand you didn't get out of the fight without a taste of pain, how are you doing?" He asked as he entered the cargo bay.

At the time that the accident happened, he was unable to really ask any questions, he just saw the shuttle take the hits, and it was he that fired the two killing blows, from his own personal chair, that removed the two ships to have done the damage.

"I'm fine Sir. I was standing when we were hit, and was thrown quite viciously against the ceiling. It looks worse than I do, to tell you the truth. In the end, all it'll do is teach me to hold on just a little better next time. We have to get these repairs done though, so that we can get back out there as soon as we can."

"I won't stop you, so please continue." Captain Casey said warmly to the brave boy, ruffling his hair affectionately, and then calling out to the others, "How are they looking guys?"

"Amazingly well, considering what we just went through Sir. It's a good thing they were built so tough, or we would've all been killed a few times." Donny answered truthfully, because when the Framgar had realized their error in judgment of the little ships, they and the Qaralon had started almost totally targeting them, since they were the largest threat, even if they were the smallest ones out there.

"Us too, that first hit should've killed us, but the new structural increases, and shield additions helped a great deal. We too have a few repairs that need to be done though, and team one's going to go do them as soon as we're safe."

"We should be done here soon Sir, so we can go out too and help to get it done quicker." Donny offered, and all of team four nodded their agreement.

"Okay then, as soon as you're back in though, we all go for a bit of a rest."

"Sounds good Sir." Donny agreed, because he knew that most of them were only going on pure adrenalin now.

An hour later the entire fleet was nestled in the asteroid field, and were all huddled in a large nest of ships, but every scanner was running at maximum. Every ship had people out on the hulls doing repairs, as well as people inside doing the same, mostly on their shuttles, but lots of work also being done elsewhere. Due to the size of the shuttles though, they took very little damage in comparison to what had been thrown at them, since they had proven to be very difficult to target. The Qaralon and Framgar were certainly starting to see that underestimating the small ships was not wise. This was the reason for the quick retreat, but not surrender. As it turns out, they had put another call out to send in the next wave, so unbeknownst to the defenders hiding and repairing, six hours later the next wave would be there.

The Earth ships called a short while later, saying that they were only twenty four hours out, and that they would be there as soon as they could make it. They were informed as to what had happened so far, and they too did not like the sounds of the retreat. They all knew that the Qaralon and Framgar had to have something else planned.

Once the repairs were done, all the ships went on rolling sleep periods, and everyone got almost two hours of rest, as well as everyone ate and replenished what energy they could, for they knew the worst of the battle was yet to come.

Four hours after they finished their needed repairs, they saw the attacking fleet emerge again from the asteroid field. So they went out to meet them. There were no more ships than there had been before, so no one suspected that there were more hiding in waiting.

The battle commenced without a word, and it got brutal almost right away. Three of the defending ships were soon disabled, and one more was destroyed, one of the Drandarian shuttles. The Qaralon ships were dropping like flies, and then finally, an hour into the renewed battle, they were sickened to see another three hundred ships emerge from the asteroid field.

"Retreat, we can't hope to win against that. Everyone, as fast as you can, go, head toward the Tenarian section." Captain Casey yelled out.

The fighting broke off suddenly, and the ships hit maximum LYS as fast as they could, and sped away. The Qaralon and Framgar ships however followed. The Earth fleet however knew full well that the Qaralon ships were not nearly as fast, while the Framgar were almost as fast, but still not quite.

The shuttles were following the big ships, since they were unable to dock, given the fast pace of the retreat. The Framgar tried to send missiles their way, and a few even hit the shuttles or ships, but nothing was damaged. The three ships that had been disabled, had quickly teleported their crew to the nearest ship soon after they found themselves unsafe, so they were safe and sound aboard other ships for now. The disabled ships would hopefully still be there when they got back, but they were not worried about that right then. They knew that if it were them, they would have destroyed the disabled ships, had they had a chance, and wondered if the Framgar would think about it, but they were also certain that the Qaralon would not.

So a little over a four hundred attacking ships were pursuing a little over a hundred defending ships, and they were gaining distance away from the combined Qaralon/Framgar fleet. They kept on the path for a full day, at maximum speed, until the fleet came to another asteroid field, where they entered the somewhat safe confines, and stopped. All the shuttles docked in their mother ships, and the crews got back together. They performed some very quick maintenance on the ships, to make sure they were prepared for almost anything, they all spent a little more than two hours doing this. A couple of the ships were showing more damage than could be fixed by a small crew on the hull, they needed a full team, so as people freed up from repairing damage elsewhere, they helped to patch up, to the best of their abilities, the ships that needed it the most.

The attacking ships could still be seen gaining on them, but they could also see the reinforcements coming. There were the hundred and twelve ships that were coming in from Earth, there were another sixty three coming from Tenaria, and then the few extra ships coming from Drandaria. Once everyone was close enough, Captain Casey, and all the other ships exited the asteroid field, and regrouped with the fresh members of the defense team.

"Well boys, here we go again. They just don't want to quit, so here we make hopefully our final stand. You all stay safe out there, you hear me, and that's an order I expect you to obey." Captain Casey said to his boys just before they headed back down to the shuttle bay to disembark again.

"And the same goes for you guys in here, and that too is an order." Donny said firmly, and they all headed off.

CHAPTER 29

REGROUP

Captain Casey led his group of ships to the rendezvous point that had already been agreed upon. Who it was leading the fresh group of ships that Earth were sending, he did not know. He had been sent messages personally by the captains of the lead ships from both Drandaria and Tenaria, and he thanked them personally, but as of yet, he had only received messages from the communications officer of the lead Earth ship. As they were coming closer to each other though, the lead Earth ship pinged them, asking to talk, so they were put up on screen.

"Hi Jonathon, help has arrived." Admiral Casey said as his ship pulled along side the UE1.

"Mom, Dad, what are you guys doing here?" Jonathon asked in surprise.

"What, and leave you to fight this all alone, not a chance. Besides, both your mother and I've been wanting to get back into space for a while now. We may be old, but we're not dead, yet, and we've been missing the action. I think I have no intention of growing old somewhere without a fight, and if I'm gonna go out, I'm goin out in style, takin' as many of the enemy with me as these old bones can." Admiral Casey said honestly, and Jonathon knew just what his dad meant, because he felt the same way.

"Well, I'm glad to see you here, I just wish it weren't for this reason. At least with all of us here now, the playing field has become a bit more fair, even if they still outnumber us almost two to one. I hope your crew and ship are ready for this." Jonathon said.

"Oh yes, we're very much ready. This is a brand new ship, and it has some very nice additions to it that should help, and the crew have been trained using the techniques your boys have perfected, they should prove to be very formidable." Admiral Casey said happily.

"Good, we've made some very major improvements to this old girl as well, that we'll go over, but at another time, I hope you understand why. I think that when you see it all, you'll agree that we can have them added to all the new ships, as well as retrofit older ones as time allows, once we deal with this little problem of course."

"Good, I can't wait, so let's do it. You're in command of this little shin dig, so give the word." Admiral Casey saluted.

"Yes Sir! Fleet, attack, disable only if possible, destroy if you have to." Jonathon said, and the fleet advanced to the field of battle.

The Qaralon and Framgar fleet should have retreated as soon as they saw the group of ships advancing on them. The Qaralon were normally not bright enough to do so by themselves, but the Framgar really should have known better. They were at least quite smart enough to know when they were fighting a losing battle. They too advanced forward and met the defending fleet.

The shuttles had all been launched half way there, and then suddenly there were even more defenders. The attacking fleet, however, did not ignore them this time. As soon as they were in range, the Qaralon and Framgar ships started throwing whatever they could at the small ships, now knowing that they had to be the first to go. Again, given their small size, the shuttles were only hit maybe once out of every ten times that they were targeted, and most of those were glancing blows that did not affect them, even if it did throw the crew around a bit. While the ships were engaged with the shuttles, the rest of the fleet took advantage of the fact that they were very nearly being ignored, and fired repeatedly on the attackers, because they were being almost totally ignored.

The shuttles were buzzing around, in and out of the larger ships, firing at whatever they could hit, and as always, their aim was straight and true. Between the UE1 shuttles, and all the Drandarian shuttles, the numbers of ships that they had disabled was more than twice that of all the larger ships put together, and they were triple the size in numbers. Admiral and Captains Casey, as well as the rest of the Earth and Tenarian fleets, were more than a little surprised to have seen the little shuttles to begin with, but were even more so when they saw how well they worked. There were times when people aboard the ships had to stop themselves from watching in awe, as the little ships buzzed in and around the larger ships, wailing upon the enemy with a fury they could hardly understand.

After almost three hours, the Qaralon and Framgar fleet had dropped in size to almost half the size that they had started out with, yet only around a hundred of them had been destroyed, the rest were floating dead in space. Given how poorly the battle was going, it was not a surprise when the Qaralon and Framgar ships just stopped fighting, turned tail, and ran. It was however a very welcome retreat.

"Good fight everyone. I'm happy to report that this round there were no ships lost, although many were damaged, some severely. Let's get back into the asteroid field, because I don't believe that that was the end of it. We need to get all the ships repaired as best we can, and then a little rest if we can afford it. Now Jonathon, where exactly did your little shuttles come from?" Admiral Casey asked curiously.

"All in good time Dad, all in good time, we have other things that need to be done first. Let's get going, so that we can get the repairs done, and get people some rest before we talk about things like that."

"You're right, come on everyone, into the field." Admiral Casey ordered.

All the shuttles docked quickly, and then the ships moved deep into the asteroid field. Captain Casey went down to the cargo bay, leaving team one in charge of the bridge for the time being.

"Hi boys, good to see you back. A couple of those hits looked pretty bad, are you all alright?" Captain Casey asked as soon as he entered the cargo bay, finding the boys already starting their repairs.

"Hello Sir, yeah, we're fine. Jamie and Teddy got a little banged up, but they're fine, and as soon as we finish getting the ship repaired, they're going to head up to the infirmary to get checked out. I tried to tell them to go right away, but they said that this was far more important than a few bruises." Donny said.

"Bobby and I got a little banged up as well, and my eye is already swelling shut, but we too will head up as soon as we're finished here

Sir, because this is really only a little issue, these shuttles need to be repaired first, they're more important right now." Franky said.

"Okay boys, I guess you're right, a few bruises are nothing compared to getting our ships back in order." He conceded. "No one feels the fight is anywhere close to finished yet, but we'll however take the time to clean up and rest a bit, after we get the ships repaired. How much time do you feel you need for your repairs guys?"

"Half an hour Sir." Donny said.

"Maybe an hour Sir." Franky said.

"As soon as we're finished, we'll help them as well, and then go help the others do any repairs to the ship that are needed." Donny said.

"No need, team three is out there already, and I was informed that the repairs will take ten to fifteen minutes to complete, and then they'll inspect the hull to make sure that everything else is still good, so they should be back in in less than an hour."

"That's good Sir. So you weren't even hit then!" Donny asked.

"We got hit once, but we were able to move mostly out of the way, so we were hardly affected. I'll leave you boys to your work, but remember, as soon as you're done, I want any of you with injuries straight to the infirmary to get fixed up. Oh and Dillon, how's your arm?" Captain Casey asked.

"It would've been fine, except the hit that got Bobby, also made me bang my arm, and it hurts again, but don't worry, I was going to go with the others to get it checked out." Dillon answered.

"Good. I'm proud of all of you guys. You guys will all be on the ship the next rotation, so the others can get out and use the shuttles as well. Donny and Franky, you'll of course stay and command the shuttles. I'll let you guys get back to work, but come see me once you're done."

"Yes Sir!" They all said.

As promised, just a little more than half an hour later, team three was finished inspecting the hull and fixing the three small sections that needed it. Teams two and four had finished only shorty thereafter, and joined everyone in the dining hall to have a quick lunch, and then get some rest and a good cleaning, as well as the injured getting fixed up. Dillon's arm had to be repaired again, because it had in fact been broken, again.

After everyone had had two, two hour naps each, the ship and shuttles were fully restocked, and all diagnostics were done, they then offered their help to repair other ships that still needed it. All ships that had no damage had also done the same thing, so the ships that still needed it, were now being patched up. Everyone had been enjoying the temporary peace, but they all knew that it would not last.

But it did. Three days went by, and there was no sign of the Qaralon or the Framgar. No one minded this, but knew that it probably spelled more than a little trouble. Captain Casey was the first to break the rest, so called out to the fleet.

"Well I don't know about you guys, but sitting here doing nothing, is doing nothing for my nerves. We're going to go out and destroy all the Qaralon and Framgar ships, except a few to put the survivors in."

"We'll come with you, just in case, because we feel the same way." Admiral Casey said.

All told, half the ships went out and followed the UE1 to where the stranded Qaralon and Framgar ships were.

"All Qaralon and Framgar ships, you're going to be destroyed, but first we're going to teleport all of you onto a few of the ships that still have engines that might be capable once you repair them." Kelly said.

"You'd better not do that. Our people will be back with even more ships, and you'll all be destroyed." One of the beasts stated strongly.

"Funny, I don't feel scared. Look around you. See just how many ships we have, we still have the same number as when we started. You tried, and failed to beat us down, and even if you sent out even more ships, do you honestly think you can win against us." Kelly said as condescendingly as he could.

"You should be crying and peeing yourself, you're nothing but a small child, we're the Framgar, and we're feared." The beast said again.

"Yeah, thing is though, I'm not afraid of you, and I may be a small child, but I have a very big ship, and this ship has spanked you a number of times, so will continue to do so. Now, what I said earlier wasn't a request, I was simply being polite and telling you what we're going to do, you may have noticed already that some of your people have disappeared. As soon as you're all safe on a few ships, we're going to destroy the remainder of your ships, and you'll see it happen as well." Kelly said happily.

"I'll find you and rip your heart out, and eat it while your dying body watches." The beast tried.

"I welcome you to try. You won't get within twenty feet of me before I kill you, and I can, with my very big gun. This conversation is over now, enjoy your new ship." Kelly said sweetly, and then cut the communications.

"You know, if I had to guess, I'd say that that particular Framgar doesn't like you very much Kelly." Jamie said in a deadpan voice.

"I know, ain't it great. I really like pushing their buttons like that, do you think it shows too much?" Kelly asked with a grin.

"Oh no, not at all. No one would be able to tell that you enjoy doing that to them." Jamie said sarcastically, and then started laughing.

Once all the Framgar and Qaralon people were teleported to the four ships needed to hold them all, they started destroying the remaining ships. Each ship was hit with just one low yield missile, and each one just disintegrated upon impact. The beings that were now trapped upon four ships watched helplessly as their ships were totally destroyed, yet they were left alive. None of them could figure out why the humans would leave an enemy alive. The Qaralon were not used to being packed into such tight spaces, and were not liking the fact that the ships were now packed with ten times the amount of people than they were designed to hold. Fights started breaking out, and an all out mutiny was brewing upon the ships. Everyone in the Earth and ally fleet was more than aware of the fact that this could happen, but they cared not, it was not their problem. Once that was taken care of, Admiral Casey sent out a message to the entire fleet.

"Attention everyone please!"

All people on all of the ships went to the nearest communications port to see what the admiral had wanted. Once everyone was gathered, the admiral started.

"Within the next few days, an entire army of ships will be coming from Earth, and another from Tenaria. The Drandarians have already sent all that they could spare, and we thank them a great deal. The reason I say this, is because this has been considered war, and as soon as we're all regrouped, we're to take the fight to them. We'll go through the asteroid field and finally disarm the Qaralon, and then if the Framgar don't surrender and offer peace, we'll go to their home world and do the same to them." Admiral Casey informed everyone. He had received the orders from Earth, he was told that this was the final stand, and it would not, could not continue.

"Um Sir, I don't think it'll be necessary to take the fight to them, because here they come." Marty said.

Everyone saw the admiral turn and look at his screens, and then turn back, and he actually smiled a nice predatory smile.

"Marty, it appears as if you have keen eyes. We do in fact have several hundred ships coming out of the asteroid field now. Everyone get battle ready, the fight is back upon us." Admiral Casey said happily, because he had not felt so alive for a while, and was enjoying this.

Instead of waiting for the attacking fleet of ships to come to them this time, they went to them, and then stopped. Kelly, who was once again on communications, took the honor of calling out.

"You may have noticed that where all of your ships were, there are now only four, and a debris field. That was because we destroyed all your ships. You'll however find all your people aboard the four ships. You're instructed to take those people now and go back home, and never bother us again, ever. If however you fail to listen to this warning, we'll attack, and we'll destroy you." Kelly snapped out.

"They were helpless, and you destroyed them, we'll destroy you." A voice said.

"Apparently you're too dense to understand what I told you, the ships were destroyed, your people were moved to the four ships that you see where you left them, all your people are alive. Again, you're instructed to get your people and go home, and never bother us again, or we'll destroy your fleet, and then go to your home world and destroy every ship you have there, as well as all your ship building factories. This isn't a threat, it's a promise." Kelly said slowly, so that they could understand.

"It not us that dense, it you for still being here, you should left, now you be destroyed." The voice said.

"Again, you're wrong. It'll be us winning this battle, and it'll be all your ships destroyed. You were warned, so now we feel no remorse." Kelly said and cut the signal.

With the end of the communications, it was the defenders that made the first move this time. Working quickly to disable every ship that they could. They attacked in such a manner that they had left the attacking ships still bunched together at the exit of the asteroid field, so this meant that they had little room to maneuver, and the defenders had no problem taking full advantage of this. In fact, that was the plan, though no one ever actually laid out any real plans, it just worked out that way, and it worked to everyone's favor, and they liked it.

Again the small shuttles showed their strength in this matter, and because they were so fast and agile, they were able to get right in there and disable ship after ship after ship, yet every time they were fired upon, a poor unsuspecting asteroid took the brunt of the explosion, or in several cases, one of their own ships managed to take the hit instead. Either way, this was more than okay by the pilots of the war shuttles. Of the defending ships, only one had received any actual damage to it, whereas the Qaralon and the Framgar ships were dropping left, right and center, faster than they could count. Only half an hour into this more than brutal assault, the Qaralon and Framgar fleet retreated back through the asteroid field path, leaving behind almost three hundred disabled ships, and untold amounts of soldiers.

Of all the Framgar and Qaralon ships that had been hit by the combined forces, only two of them had been outright destroyed. The Earth, Tenarian and Drandarian ships, however, received no damage that resulted in a ship having to back off, and of the damage that had been caused, none of it was major enough to even effect them any, mostly it just bruised them a bit. Once again, everyone was more than happy with that. It had been a quick and almost brutal assault, yet the defenders never were brutal, though they hit without remorse, just they also did not hit to destroy.

Once they were sure that the Qaralon and Framgar were not coming back out right away, Admiral Casey ordered everyone back, so that they could regroup. All the shuttles docked in their mother ships and the crews headed up to their bridges to be briefed. Captain Casey's boys had just made it to their bridge themselves.

"Well guys, as usual, you've proven that you're exceptional at battle. I think, therefore, that tonight we're going to cuddle in the middle of the other ships and try and rest a bit for the night. None of you has had any proper rest for a couple weeks now, and you're all getting tired." Captain Casey said.

"Captain, we're fine, we don't need the rest." Donny tried, but he and everyone knew he was lying.

No sooner had he said this though, when one boy yawned, causing a chain reaction through almost all the boys. Captain Casey chuckled.

"I know you guys could keep going, but for how long. You're all young still, and need a lot more rest than adults do, and eventually, without the sleep you need, you could just pass out, and we certainly don't want that." Captain Casey said gently.

"Okay Sir, I guess you're right. A little rest would probably feel real nice right about now." Donny said, and Captain Casey nodded, so put a call through to his parents ship.

"Hey Dad, my boys need a good rest, so we're all going to go to bed after having a good meal. We'll curl up in the middle of all you guys, and you can give us a call if we're needed for any reason."

"They deserve the rest, you guys go, and I promise that unless necessary, no one will contact you for at least twelve hours. Have a good night guys."

"Thanks Dad. I hope that they won't be stupid enough to come back, but I know they are. Our attack forces are still a few days out, otherwise we stay here I guess, so we'll find out just how stupid they are."

"You're welcome, and sadly, I'm certain you're right. I've dealt with their stupidity for many years, and even at eighty, I'm willing to bet I'll see it for many more years to come." Admiral Casey said, and then disconnected.

As soon as he was off line with his dad Captain Casey turned to the boys.

327

"Okay boys, get us in the midst of all the ships while I call Warren and Will, and get them started on some good food for all of us, then we can eat and go to bed."

"Yes Sir!" They all said, happy with the arrangements.

A few minutes later they were parked in the middle of a large nest of ships, and everyone went down to the dining hall. Captain Casey, Donny, Franky, Jamie and Kelly all went to the kitchen to help, while the rest said that they would get the tables all set and ready.

"What's cooking in here guys?" Captain Casey asked as they entered.

"Just a quick simple pasta dish, good and filling. Just what everyone needs, lots of protein and carbs." Warren answered.

"Good, what can we help with?"

"If you guys want to get some bread and salad ready, that should help a lot thanks." Will answered.

"Consider it done." Captain Casey said, and he and the boys got started helping out with what was requested, while Warren and Will were getting the pasta and the chicken that was to go along with it finished up.

A short time later the food was served, and everyone sat down and ate and ate and ate, because they were all very hungry. It was a very good thing indeed that easily three times too much food had been made for them to eat, because they ate it all. That was the problem with the battles and repairs they had been doing, they were getting the food and rest that they needed, but only just barely enough to survive. Once the meal was finished, and everyone finished cleaning up, they all went up to their rooms, and they all enjoyed extremely long hot showers before climbing into bed without even bothering to get dressed. Not one of the crew was awake for more than a minute after laying in their beds, and it was only just a few minutes past 2000 hours.

It was almost exactly twelve hours later when the first of the crew stirred, and it was not even the captain, it was Brad, and that was only to go to the washroom. He did look at the clock though, and figured that they should all get up, so he called out to the others to get up. They all sat up and stretched and yawned.

"What time is it?" Pete asked when he finished his yawning and stretching.

"0830 hours and I only woke up about ten minutes ago. I saw the time and figured we should probably get up and get our butts in gear." Brad said.

"Yeah, we probably should. I wonder why the captain hasn't come in to wake us up yet. It sure was nice sleeping as long as that though, I feel a lot better, as if I could go out and kick some serious enemy butt all day long." Zach said, and the others agreed.

"For sure. Captain Casey either decided to let us sleep, or he's still asleep as well, which is kind of what I figure. Either way, I don't mind either." Pete said.

"Me neither!" The others all said.

"I'm hungry, let's go down to the kitchen and see if Warren's up yet, and if he's not, we can get breakfast started for everyone." Pete said.

"Okay." Everyone said.

They all went and got themselves quickly ready for the day, then headed down to the kitchen, and found that there was no one there, so they started making up a huge breakfast for everyone. They were halfway through, when Warren stumbled in.

"Oh, good morning boys. How long have you been up for?" He asked sleepily, a large yawn escaping him as he was still stretching.

"About half an hour Sir." Pete answered.

"Okay, is anyone else up yet?"

"Not that we know of, we aren't even sure if Captain Casey's awake yet."

"Oh, okay then. I'll go get the others up then, if you guys have everything under control here."

"That'd be fine Sir. Breakfast should be ready in fifteen minutes or less, tell them to come right down." Lance said, Warren just nodded and headed right out.

His first stop was the captains suite. He knocked, but there was no answer, so he opened the door

"Good morning Captain, are you awake." Warren asked.

"Huh, what. Oh what time is it Warren?" Captain Casey asked groggily.

"Almost 0900 hours Sir. Pete and his team were already in the kitchen getting breakfast ready when I came in, so I said I'd come get the rest of you up. They said that it'll be ready in a few minutes, so go straight there. You go ahead and get ready, and I'll get the others all up going."

"Thanks Warren, you go ahead and do just that, and I'll meet you all down there."

"Will do Sir."

Warren took a few minutes to go and wake all the boys, and told them to get ready and go for breakfast right away. Not even ten minutes later, everyone was seated, and team four was bringing the food out. They all sat and ate in near silence, and had a good meal together. As soon as they were all done, Captain Casey stood and got everyone's attention.

"Well guys, I hope you all enjoyed your good rest, I know I sure did, and thanks team four for getting breakfast for everyone. I'm sure that it was appreciated by all."

"We did Sir." Everyone said.

"No problem Sir." Team four said.

"On the agenda today are repairs, restocking and diagnostics. All of the major repairs are already done, but there are a few things that are mostly minor that need to be done. Team one on the hull, team two on shuttle one, team three on shuttle two, and team four you guys are on all three ships diagnostics. Let's make the ships perfect. Donny and Franky, you're with me to restock. Now if any team finishes up, split up and join another team. If we all get done early enough, we'll offer our services to the other ships as needed, to get everyone up to their best."

"Yes Sir!" They all said.

"Good, let's go." Captain Casey said, and they all started to take off, but stopped when Warren started to talk.

"Captain, as soon as Will and I are done cleaning up in here, we can come help you guys as well." He offered.

"Okay, make sure the infirmary and the kitchen are fully stocked first, and then go ahead and join whomever you wish to join."

"Not a problem Sir, but the infirmary and kitchen we keep fully stocked at all times, so as soon as we're finished cleaning the kitchen up, we can join you guys." Warren said.

"Great, then let's get going boys." Captain Casey said, and then everyone went about their business.

Team one went and got suited up, went out onto the hull, and spent the better part of two hours scouring the entire hull, looking for anything that was not perfect, and fixing it. They found only maybe twenty minor issues that they were able to fix right away.

Team two did the same for shuttle one, but took only an hour to do their chore, while team three took a few minutes longer on shuttle two. As soon as they were all done, Jamie called team one to see if they needed help.

"No thanks guys, go ahead and help elsewhere. We're about half way done out here, but everything's been real easy little fixes. If no one needs any help first, then come on out." Brady said.

Team four was working on the ship diagnostics, and had found a few errors, so were working on them when Jamie called them to ask the same question.

"Actually, if you guys would do the diagnostics on the shuttles, that'd be great. We keep getting errors and fixing things all over the ship, mostly with the scanners, seems they took a bit of a beating, it's a wonder they still worked at all, but they had backups in triplicate, so I guess that's why." Pete said.

"Okay, will do. Good luck." He said to Pete, and then turned to the rest of his team when he disconnected. "Okay, let's do the diagnostics on the shuttles guys."

They went about doing the shuttle diagnostics, and a little under an hour later they were done. Only shuttle one did not pass, and it was only a minor fix on an internal computer system.

Warren and Will had joined the Captain, Donny and Franky as soon as they were finished, and together they went about getting everything restocked in the ship, and cleaned it up a bit as well, since it had not taken long to restock the power cells and the weapons.

Once everyone was finished, they went to the bridge as was normal, and waited for the others, they all came in within minutes of each other.

"So how did everything go?" Captain Casey asked once everyone was gathered.

"Well, with all the errors we found in the scanners on the ship here, I'm surprised they even worked at all. It took us two hours just to run the diagnostics and fix the problems. We didn't even get a chance to do the shuttle diagnostics." Pete said.

"But we did them, and everything on the shuttles are now at peak performance Sir." Jamie said quickly before Captain Casey could ask.

"And we found about twenty or so little things on the hull, and quickly repaired them. Most of that was just cleaning up previous quick repairs and patches." Brady said.

"Okay, good. We restocked the power cells, and made sure the weapons were all in good order, and fully stocked. We're getting critically low on them though. I'm pretty sure the new fleet coming in will be carrying a huge supply to restock us all, so we should be fine. How are the missiles in the shuttles?" Captain Casey asked.

"We restocked them, probably before you got to the weapons room, since that was the first thing we did." Jamie answered.

"Good. Well then, I'm going to put a call out to the fleet then and see who else needs some assistance. Is there anything else that anyone can think of that we should do here first?" Captain Casey asked.

"No Sir!" Everyone answered.

"Good. Kelly, seeing as how you're standing next to the communications center, as you usually are, would you please bring up the fleet?" Captain Casey asked with a smile.

"Yes Sir!" Kelly answered and then did just that.

"Hi everyone. We're all fresh and ready to help whoever needs it. Our ship has been gone over with a fine tooth comb this morning, so it's in as perfect a condition as we can possibly make it. Just send us requests, and we'll send a team to whomever needs it the most." Captain Casey, said and then Kelly closed the communications off.

Not even five minutes later, they had requests enough to keep them busy for the next three days. Captain Casey went through the requests quickly on his screen, and then assigned three of the teams three different ships to help out. They would rotate every few hours or so, so that everyone got the extra help they needed. He and team three stayed aboard, as did Warren and Will. They mostly just spent the time cleaning the rest of the ship, and then went and made lunch when it was that time. Captain Casey called the boys back for lunch, and once they were finished, team four stayed behind, while the others went to three new ships.

During the next twenty four hours, they did much the same, and while everyone was happy of the break, and the time to get their repairs done, they were more than a little surprised that the Qaralon and Framgar had not come back to try and finish the fight, as they normally did.

CHAPTER 30

A TACTICAL RETREAT

That peace was short lived however, because everyone was awakened at 0300 hours when one of the ships on watch saw the attacking fleet emerge from the asteroid field. It became plainly obvious why it took so long though, because when all the ships came out, in total, there had to have been a thousand ships or more. As soon as the entire attacking fleet was gathered, Admiral Casey came on the screens.

"We're going to have to retreat a bit here, until the rest of the Earth ships come to join us. We're good, very good, but against these numbers we'd fail rather quickly. We'll try and lead them right to a rendezvous point where the rest of our fleet can meet us, hopefully they can hide somewhere and then we can surround and surprise them. Everyone stay close and we'll keep just out of range of them." Admiral Casey said.

His ship started to pull away and everyone else started to follow.

As soon as they were on their way, Captain Casey got the boys' attention.

"So who wants to pull the night shift?"

"We will Sir." Jamie answered.

"I will Sir." Franky said.

"Okay, we'll go and get some more sleep, you guys have a good night, and make sure and call me the second you need me okay. I dislike being shaken out of bed, so try and warn me first if we're about to be hit, but I doubt we will though."

"We'll try Sir, but you know as well as I do how unlikely I'd have the time to do that, but we'll keep near the front, so it's unlikely that we'd get hit anyway. You guys just go get a good sleep." Franky said.

"I know. Have a good night boys, and you guys, let's get back to bed." Captain Casey first said to the night shift, and then turned to the rest and finished.

"Good night." They all said.

"Well I don't know about you guys, but I could use a midnight snack. Anyone else want anything while I'm gone?" Dillon asked.

"Yeah, why don't you just do up a tray of sandwiches then, and bring some drinks? That should last us all through the night. Thanks." Jamie answered.

Dillon headed down to the kitchen and made up the sandwiches, grabbed some drinks, and went back up to the bridge. The boys sat around eating and chatting the rest of the night, while they kept up with the ships around them. Amazingly enough, the Qaralon and Framgar ships actually followed them. They had no idea they were being led right into a trap. Admiral Casey had called within an hour of them all leaving, telling them that the rest of their fleet was going to hide in a few hours, because they were coming up to another large asteroid field, and then they would sit and wait.

For the most part though, the night was uneventful, which everyone was thankful for of course. The boys just stayed mostly where they were all night long, laughing and talking They almost did not realize the time until Captain Casey and the rest of the crew walked in later that morning.

"Good morning boys. Were there any problems during the night?"

"No Sir! We've kept just ahead of the attacking ships, and stupidly enough, they've followed us. About an hour after you guys went up to bed though, your dad called and said the ambush would be set, and we have the coordinates as to where to go. I think because we have a shortage of missiles though, that we should break off and head to the meeting place as fast as we can go, to get some more weapons. We're a little over three hours away now." Franky answered.

"Well, we all knew they weren't very smart, and I think your idea is a good one. A few of the other ships could probably go for a refill as well, so we'll try and get there first then. I'll call my dad and talk it over with him. In the meantime, if you guys are still okay, we'll all go for our morning exercises and then breakfast, and someone will bring yours up to you."

"Sounds fine Sir. We had a midnight snack, so we're all good for now." Jamie said.

"Good, see you in a bit then. I'm gonna call my dad though before I head down. You guys go ahead and head down and get started, and I'll meet you there." Captain Casey told the rest of the crew.

"Yes Sir!" Everyone said.

The boys headed to the holographic room and set a nice tropical beach to exercise on, and Donny led them to start. After the boys left, Captain Casey went to his office and called his dad.

"Good morning Dad, how was your night?" Jonathon asked.

"Pretty good, and yours?"

"Pretty good. As you know, we're getting a bit short on weapons, and Franky had a good idea. We'd like to break off and head to the rendezvous point early, so that we can restock. I know a few of the other ships were getting low as well, so a few of us could stand to go."

"Okay, there was only five of you short, so that shouldn't be a problem. I'll call the fleet and tell them what you're coming for then, and you call the other ships and tell them to go with you."

"Okay Dad, we'll meet you there then. Have fun." Jonathon said and signed off.

Captain Casey then took a couple minutes to call the other four ships and told them the plan, so then he called up to Franky and told him it was a go, and that four ships would be following. Once all that was taken care of, he went down to join the others for their morning exercises.

Almost three hours later, they were at the rendezvous point with the other four ships. They greeted each other, and relayed a few of the goings on, then they were fully stocked with missiles. They then waited with the ships for the others to come by. It was only an hour long wait, and as soon as the procession passed, they exited the field and pursued the pursuers.

CHAPTER 31

BATTLE WORTHY OF TELLING
FOR YEARS TO COME

As the two separate fleets of ships passed, the newest fleet and their additions watched and waited. It did not appear at all as if the enemy ships had even noticed them, which was pretty sad, considering none of them were really all that well hidden, Captain Casey had thought to himself. Oh well, everyone was okay with that. As soon as the Qaralon and Framgar fleet was well passed them, Captain Casey turned to the boys.

"Okay boys, let's deploy our little toys and go kick some scum butt. I want you guys to be very careful out there. I know you always are, but still, be careful."

"Yes Sir!" Donny said.

"Team two, you're with me." Donny said.

"Team four, you're with me." Franky said.

Teams two and four followed Franky and Donny, while teams one and three stayed on the bridge. Team two had refused to go take a nap, because they all said they were wide awake and would be fine until a while later. Kelly was told to bring up the fleet, so he did, and as soon as Kelly had the fleet up, Captain Casey started.

"Okay, it doesn't appear as if they've even noticed we're behind them yet, so let's go give them a bit of a wake up call. Disable everything without question, there'll be no talking this time. We've given them enough warnings."

He got confirmation from everyone, and then they started. Because they had not even known that the Earth ships were behind them, since they never watch their tails, it was easy for them to sneak up on them, and then they all started opening fire as soon as they were in range. Due to the sheer surprise of the attack, and the very brutal nature of it, well over a hundred ships were disabled before they even knew what was happening. In this first attack, only two of the attacking ships were destroyed, but the entire fleet turned to attack the attackers, which probably sealed their fate.

As soon as they turned around, the Qaralon and Framgar forgot about the ships that they had been following, and then those ships also turned and started attacking from behind again, and the numbers of enemy ships dropping, started rising. Qaralon and Framgar ships were being disabled or destroyed by the dozen. The small shuttles however, as in every battle they had been in so far, were doing far more of the damage than anyone else.

Donny and team two were doing exceptionally well, within five minutes of starting the fight, they had disabled ten ships, and were now whipping in and around all the other ships, throwing everything they had at the attackers and hitting with ninety nine percent accuracy.

"Okay guys, let's really show these things what we're made of." Donny said, he had brought in Franky for that.

They teamed up together and started doing even more damage, together they were taking out an average of eight ships for every ten minutes. Within an hour, together they had taken out a little more than fifty ships, while the rest were also mounting high amounts of good hits.

All of a sudden the tables turned on Donny and team two. They got separated a little from Franky and team four, and then four ships started pelting them. They were getting hit rapidly, and even though they were able to keep from being destroyed, by moving rapidly, they were still being hit, and their shields were going down quickly.

"Someone get us out of this trap, our shields aren't going to hold out much longer." Donny called out.

"We're trying to get there, but they're starting to get desperate, I think they're trying to just keep us away from you, so that they can destroy you." Franky said.

"Gee, that's comforting." Donny deadpanned.

"We're coming for you, and we'll persuade them to let you go" Kelly said.

A few seconds later all four ships were blown out of the sky as the UE1 barged right through, and threw no less then five maximum yield missiles at each ship. The shuttle, however, took a couple very direct hits right at the end, tossing the little shuttle around like a small child's toy. Donny had been knocked unconscious when he was quite violently thrown with the last hit, and Teddy was also lying on the floor, bleeding and moaning, when the console he was at exploded with the last hit.

"Captain, we have seriously injured, and the shuttle can't hold up to anything more, we need to come in!" Jamie called out.

"Leave the shuttle and teleport in, I'll lower the shields for a second to get you guys back. We can't lower them long enough to get the shuttle in though." Captain Casey said.

"Okay, send us directly to the infirmary then." Jamie said.

"Already on it. Shut it down, and as soon as you do, you're out of there." Kelvin said.

"Done, get us out of here." Jamie said a few seconds later, and then they were in the infirmary.

Warren and Will got to work right away, each picking up an injured boy, and taking them to a bed. They both got to work on Teddy first to stop the bleeding, and scan him to make sure there was no internal damage. There was, and Warren got to work on that right away, while Will went and started the scans on Donny. The rest of the team had left almost right away, so that they would not be in the way, and so that they could help somewhere else. They were bruised and bashed, and they each had a couple little scrapes and cuts, but not one of them felt anywhere near bad enough to stay in the infirmary, what they wanted was to go beat up more Qaralon.

"Warren, Donny has some bleeding on the brain, as well as a cracked shoulder, and a couple broken ribs." Will said as soon as the scan completed.

"Okay, I'll be right there. I'm almost finished with Teddy."

"I can get started on the bones, you've shown me how to do that already, but the bleeding I'll let you fix."

"Okay, go ahead and ask if you need any help."

He got to work on Donny doing what he could. Because he was still unconscious, they did not need to worry about him being uncomfortable or anything, Teddy however required a good dose of pain killers and sedatives. A few moments later the captain came in.

"How are they Warren?" Captain Casey asked.

"They'll live Sir. Donny will be down for at least two to three days, and Teddy probably only two days. How's it going out there?" Warren asked.

"Okay, doctors orders will be followed. We're doing pretty good. One of our ships was lost unfortunately, and another six, including our shuttle, were disabled. The Qaralon and Framgar however are taking heavy losses, and I feel that they'll probably try and run any time now, we are, however, not going to let them run anymore. We've already committed to destroying their whole fleet, and we'll do so. They'll regret ever trying to fight us again." Captain Casey said with conviction. He was not at all happy that two of his boys were injured, and that one of his shuttles lay damaged and currently floating in space.

"Well I'm sure you're needed on the bridge far more than here, so go!" Warren ordered.

Captain Casey gave a salute and a yes Sir, and turned and headed out.

"Hows the fight going up here guys?" Captain Casey asked as he entered the bridge again.

"Pretty good Sir, over a quarter of the ships have been disabled or destroyed. Another of our ships was disabled, but otherwise everything is going as good as can be hoped for. How are Donny and Teddy?" Jamie asked.

"They're in rough condition, and will be out of commission for a few days, but they'll be fine. Let's go get these beasts."

And with that the UE1 and their shuttle went back into the fight with a vengeance. They started mounting even higher numbers of disabled ships. Finally, after three hours of the brutal punishment they were being dealt, the Framgar and Qaralon decided that they would not win, so took off. They were more than a little frightened though, when the ships they had attacked did something they rarely did, they turned and went after them. Captain Casey took the lead, and he and his crew thoroughly enjoyed picking off the slower moving ships, one by one.

"Uh Uh Uh, there's nowhere to run, we're gonna get you." Kelly called out sweetly to the Framgar and Qaralon, just to try and tick them off even more.

An hour later, realizing that the Earth ships and their allies were not going to give up, they stopped and continued the fight, realizing that Kelly had really meant it.

Warren and Will had gotten both Donny and Teddy all fixed and stabilized, and they were awake and chatting quietly about how they wanted to get back out there, and kick some more butt. Warren though had other ideas about that.

"You'll be doing no such thing young men. You're staying here and getting better for at least two days. Will and I have to go get some food for everyone, you're to stay here, but don't move too much. The only time that you're allowed out of those beds is to go to the washroom, is that understood."

"Yes Sir!" They both said drearily.

"Good. We'll be back with some food for you in a bit." Warren said, and then the two of them left.

As soon as both of them had left the infirmary, Donny turned to Teddy.

"Well that sucks. I feel well enough to get back out there, but I bet the captain wouldn't let us either!"

"Yeah me too, but we have to listen to Warren, and he's probably right anyway."

"I know. Still sucks though, we should be out there helping, instead of sitting around in here being lazy. I feel bad even though I know I shouldn't."

"No, you shouldn't feel bad, and right now I doubt we could even be of much help. I can move, but it doesn't feel very nice, so I'm sure I wouldn't be moving very fast."

"Yeah, me too. We should at least ask for some cards or a couple games to keep busy, because this is boring."

"We can ask Warren when he comes back." Teddy said.

A short while later Will brought in some light supper for the boys, and was about to leave, when he was stopped.

"Will, could you maybe get us some cards, and or a couple games, we're kinda bored here?" Teddy asked.

"Sure, let me help take the food up to the others first, and then we can arrange something. You could've always turned on the T.V., or the view screens and watched the battle you know." Will said.

"Never even thought of that. Guess I'd be no use on the bridge right now if I can't even think of that, huh!" Donny said.

"No, you probably wouldn't, but what'd you expect, you had a major concussion, as well as a bleed on the brain. It's bound to scramble you at least a little." Will said softly.

"I guess so." Donny admitted humbly.

A few minutes later Warren and Will were taking the food up to the bridge for the others. They stood well out of the way and watched the others work. They had uncovered all the food, and as one of the guys got a spare second, they rushed over, grabbed something, stuffed it into their mouths, and ate it quickly. This method of eating and fighting went on for at least half an hour, and Warren and Will just stood and watched. They were still amazed at how well everyone worked together, and with very little talking, they were able to move fluidly, and fire at and hit just about anything in sight. Captain Casey was mainly sitting in his chair, just watching, and would occasionally do something on his computer screen, like send a missed ship to weapons, or send a command to another ship to do a certain thing, but otherwise he sat and did almost nothing except watch. Once everyone had their fill, and the food was gone, Warren and Will excused themselves to go clean up, and tend to their patients.

As they were walking, heading back to the kitchen, Will told Warren that he was going to get some games for their patients, because they had asked for something so that they would not be bored. Warren was good with this and said he would meet him later then. Warren decided to check on the patients first, so headed right there.

"So how are you guys feeling?" He asked when he walked into the infirmary.

"A little sore and tender, but otherwise fine I guess." Teddy answered.

"Same here." Donny also answered.

"That's to be expected. I see you're watching the battle. Let me guess, if you can't be there yourselves, you may as well watch it right?" Warren asked.

"Something like that, ya. Better than laying around doing nothing. Hey, where's Will?" Donny asked.

"He said something about going to get some games for you, and that he'd be right down. He should be here in a couple minutes."

"Oh, okay. He said he would for us. Thanks a lot." Donny said.

That battle was going well, or at least as well as a battle can go. The Earth fleet was handing out a beating the likes of which had never been heard of before. The Framgar and Qaralon were starting to lose hope, they were dropping far faster than they could comprehend, and as they got more tired and desperate, they were getting worse, and considering how poor the Qaralon performed at the best of times, that was bad. With that weariness on their part, they were getting more and more sloppy, hitting less and less ships, and the Earth fleet was holding up surprisingly well. They had a couple more ships disabled, but none were destroyed. A few injuries of course were to be expected, but thankfully, in the past several hours that they knew of, no one had been killed. All were happy with that.

The UE1 shuttle was handing out the single largest beating though, they were whipping around so fast and so tight to the enemy ships now that the Framgar and Qaralon hardly knew they were there before they lost a propulsion pod or their engine room, or whatever the boys could hit at the time. All this was making the boys hungry though.

"Zach and Lance, you're on food duty, I'm getting very hungry here, and it looks like it's going to be a long night." Franky said.

"Okay." Both boys said, and went to the little galley and started preparing a quick dinner.

"I wonder how Donny and Teddy are doing?" Zach asked.

"I don't know, why don't you call and ask real quick." Franky said.

"Okay."

He called the UE1 and talked to Kelly for a couple minutes and got the basic rundown. They talked for a few seconds more, but he found out all that they wanted and needed to know.

"Kelly said they're fine, but they'll be off duty for a couple or a few days, while they heal. He said that Donny had a real bad concussion and bleeding in his head, and Teddy had some broken bones and some internal bleeding. Other than that though, everything's going good." He turned and told the others.

"Well that's good to hear. I bet Donny's not too happy about having to do nothing for at least a couple days to heal. Somehow I don't think he's the type of person to just lay back and relax." Franky chuckled.

"No kidding, Teddy won't be much better though. Most of us wouldn't be I think." Bobby admitted as he shot down yet another Qaralon ship.

Soon dinner was ready and Franky, Zach and Lance quickly ate while the others kept up the fight. As soon as they were finished, they took over, while the other three ate their dinner. Once they finished, they gave the galley a very quick cleaning, and then joined the others to continue the attack.

"I hope this doesn't last too much longer, we're slaughtering them, but I'm getting a bit tired." Lance said.

"Yeah me too. I'm pretty sure that the admiral will have thought of something for that though." Franky said as he was firing information back and forth between the different consoles.

"I hope so!" Lance said.

"He's too good to overwork his people, and Captain Casey's the same. We really should call in and say we're getting tired over here though, the others will be able to switch off more often, so will be fresher, whereas we don't have that luxury." Franky said.

"On it!" Zach said.

He again called the UE1 and talked to the captain this time, and explained to him that they were all getting a bit tired, and could use some rest real soon. He was told that something would be worked out shortly, and to keep up the good work.

As soon as he was disconnected from the communications with Zach, Captain Casey told the boys on the bridge that they had the ship, and to keep it in one piece. The boys nodded or called out, 'Yes Sir', and he was gone. He headed to his office and called up his parents ship and asked to speak to his dad in private for a moment.

"Hey Dad, glad you could finally join me, what took you so long?" Jonathon teased his dad for taking a whole two minutes to get to his office.

"You always were a brat, I have no idea where you get it from. What are you harassing me for this time?"

"Yeah right, you know exactly where I get it from, because mom says we're exactly alike." Jonathon said with a smile.

"Oh yeah, you're right. Anyway what's up?"

"Nothing much, except my guys are getting a bit tired. Let's say we back off and let them think we decided that we've done them enough damage, let them get home, then we can turn back, and clean up the mess a bit tomorrow. Many of us could also stand for some repairs, and I'm willing to bet that many are in need of a good sleep." Jonathon suggested.

"It's scary just how much like me you really are! I was just telling your mom, not ten minutes ago, that that's what we were going to do real soon. Why don't we call it now then, and find ourselves a nice hole to sleep in for the night, do some much needed repairs and cleaning tomorrow, and then go for the rest of the fleet the day after. Give them enough of a head start that they figure we aren't going to follow."

"Excellent, my guys will appreciate it. You send out the order then, and we can hit that asteroid field that's about an hour from here, it should be nice and safe." Jonathon said, and then disconnected after their goodbyes.

Seconds later, the admiral sent the orders. "All ships, this is Admiral Casey, we're going to do a fake retreat, and head to the asteroid field an hour behind us, so that we can rest and do some repairs, and then clean up a bit. Let's go."

And just like that, they broke off the fight and pulled back. The Framgar and Qaralon ships never even thought twice about it, they just tucked tail and ran, as fast as their pitiful ships could carry them, leaving all their people that were stranded behind, not caring about them at all. They had figured, incorrectly, that the Earth ships thought they had done enough, as Captain and Admiral Casey had hoped they would. Less than an hour later, all the ships were tucked inside the asteroid field, and getting some much needed rest and relaxation, it had been a long day. All told they lost three ships completely, and another ten were currently floating in space, their crews automatically teleporting to other ships for protection, and to be of use elsewhere.

"Alright everyone, we're tucked in the middle of the nest, since we have the smallest crew, so can't have an actual night shift. I want everyone to go get cleaned up and meet me in the theatre in twenty minutes, we need to wind down a bit." Captain Casey told everyone, except the two boys and their minders in the infirmary.

As soon as everyone was gone, he relayed the same message to Warren, and Warren said he would bring Donny and Teddy no problem.

Everyone met in the theatre less than twenty minutes later, including Donny and Teddy, who were in wheelchairs.

"Teddy, since you got the worst injury, you get to pick the movie tonight." Captain Casey offered.

He went to the console and looked through it for a few minutes, before deciding on something, and then started it. For the rest of the evening they watched the movie, ate lots of snack foods, and drank lots. Not even one of the boys whispered a complaint when the captain called bedtime. So shortly after that, they were all in bed and sound asleep for the night. Every last one of the boys was well beyond exhausted, they had been running and fighting very nearly non stop all day, and it showed. The captain had actually been amazed that not one of the boys had fallen asleep during the movie, but they were all awake, though not one of them looked to be fully awake either. None the less, every one of them walked to their rooms of their own accord, with of course the exception of their two injured, but they too were still wide awake.

They all slept peacefully through the night, none of them bothered by anything at all. Once again, probably not so surprisingly, they all slept in quite late for them, and by the time they all woke up, it was nearing 0900 hours. They all got cleaned and dressed, made sure their rooms were good, and then headed for some good filling breakfast once they were informed that it was ready. Warren and Will had out done themselves this morning, because there was a lot there, and it was all very good as well. Every last one of them appreciated it though, but appreciated more that there was at least twice as much as normal, because they all needed it, a great deal in fact. As soon as they were done filling themselves past decent, Captain Casey stood and got everyone's attention.

"First order of business this morning will be repairs. Teams two and three, you have the shuttle, make it perfect. The rest of you are on the hull, and Franky, Warren, Will, and I'll be inside getting things in order here. Once this is done, regardless of how the others are doing, we start out looking for enemy ships to destroy."

"Yes Sir!" Everyone said.

"Sir, can Teddy and I at least help by running the ship diagnostics. We won't even need to get out of these chairs to do them, and any repairs we can't do ourselves easily, we'll ask for help, we promise." Donny nearly pleaded.

"What do you say Warren?" Jonathon asked.

"As long as they do nothing strenuous, and take it easy, I see no reason why not."

"Thanks Sir. Teddy, you take the shuttle, and I'll get the bridge." Donny said.

"Sure." Teddy said, happy to just have something constructive to do.

"Remember boys, take it real easy, and Teddy, no stretching your arms at all, you probably won't like that too much." Warren warned.

"Okay Sir." Teddy answered and turned and wheeled off.

They all went about their chores, and considering just what all they had went through, they actually had less to do than they had thought they might need. They were all of course good with this, but there was still plenty to do. Teddy had gone right to the shuttle and had started the diagnostics on it, when he ran into a bit of a snag.

"Dillon, can you come in here and give me a hand for a few minutes please?" He asked once he finished running the shuttle diagnostics a little while later.

"Sure Teddy," He called out, and then, "what do you need?" Once he made it inside the shuttle.

"The weapons guidance system is out of alignment, and the power cells are only at seventy eight percent, but both are in areas I can't get at to work on, so I need your help with those please, while I get the inertia compensator's back to a hundred percent."

347

"Okay, consider it done." Dillon said with a salute.

"Ah knock it off and get to work." Teddy said and then stuck his tongue out at the older boy.

Together they got all the internal systems back up to peak performance in short order, and were finished only minutes before the rest of the guys finished up on the hull. They all met up with each other inside the shuttle, because the boys working outside came in.

"How was it out there guys?" Teddy asked.

"It was starting to look pretty beat up. If it hadn't been for the extra strength and shields, they would have been toasted out there I'm thinking." Tristan said.

"All fixed now though?" Teddy asked.

"Yep, all good. Everything inside all fixed now?" Tristan asked.

"Yeah, we're all set, let's go see how the others are doing." Teddy said.

Donny had started the scans as soon as he made it to the bridge, and within just a few minutes, three minor issues popped up, and he was able to fix them from the bridge. Once the scan was completed though, he found a further eight problems that needed working on. One in the power systems, four in the engines, and the rest in weapons. With that information, he went to get to work. He soon realized he was going to need some help though.

"Captain, I could use a little help in the engine and power rooms please, if you have a spare hand to send, I could use it?" Donny asked.

"Okay, I can send Franky." Captain Casey said.

"Thanks." Donny said.

A few minutes later, Franky arrived.

"Hey Donny, what did you need help with?"

"I was able to get everything else done, but the problems in the engine and power rooms are all things I'm not allowed to do right now. Here's the list of the problems, so if you could get them done, it'd be great."

"Okay, thanks. Hmm, this should only take a few minutes each." Franky said after looking at the list for a minute.

"None of them are major problems, so no, it shouldn't take long. Normally I would've just done it myself, but I'm not allowed to get out of the chair and crawl through access panels and stuff." Donny said, and then Franky went to work, crawling through things, to get to the places he needed to go, to get to them.

Less then fifteen minutes later he was done.

"Well, Captain Casey and the rest of us were almost finished when you called, so they should be done now. I wonder how the guys on the hull are doing? We got hit a few times, but nothing major. I hope it's not too bad." Franky said when he exited the last access tunnel.

"Let's head up to the bridge and wait for everyone, since that's where we'll all be meeting anyway I'm sure."

"Lead the way wheels." Franky teased. Donny just shook his head, but did lead the way to the bridge

"Oh, I didn't expect you guys to be finished already." Franky said as they came onto the bridge to find everyone already there and waiting for them.

"We just finished the repairs, and walked on the bridge not even a minute before you came in." Brady said.

"Well, how was it out there?" Franky asked.

"We were just about to tell the others when you so rudely interrupted." Pete teased.

"Well then, please don't let us ruin your story." Donny said with a mock bow in his chair.

"Hmph." Pete snorted. "It wasn't too bad actually. We only had one major repair, and about fifteen smaller ones. How was the shuttle and the internal systems?" He asked.

"Internal systems weren't too bad, only some minor adjustments, only two actual issues." Donny answered.

"The shuttle systems took a beating, but Dillon and me fixed them all up." Teddy said.

"The hull of the shuttle was looking a little worse for wear as well, but it's as good as we can make it, so we're good to go there as well. Now all we need is our other shuttle." Jamie answered.

"And everything else in the ship's in good shape. Our shuttle is the first place we're heading. As soon as we retrieve it, teams three and four will be sent down to get it fixed, while we clean up some of the mess out there. We'll of course do any cleaning along the way that we can." Captain Casey told everyone.

"By cleaning, I assume you mean pack the enemies onto as few a number of ships as we can get away with, and destroy the rest?" Alex asked with an evil grin.

"What else would I mean!" Captain Casey said, matching the evil grin.

"Good, let's go then!" Alex said.

"Kelly, go tell the others our plan then, and let's get out of here." Captain Casey said.

"You got it Sir." Kelly answered, and then went and did as he was asked.

It took them nearly three hours to make the one hour trip to where their shuttle was stranded, because they stopped twenty two times to clean up the mess left behind. The Qaralon were not at all pleased, and the Framgar were absolutely furious with what the UE1 was doing to all their ships, packing them into their worst off ships, like the animals they thought they were not. Not once did they even bother telling the enemies what they were doing though, they just did it, they were for the most part sick of talking to them, only to hear them whine and lie and threaten, so they just did not bother. They were pinged by many of them though, but Kelly ignored them completely. They finally made it to where their shuttle was.

"Given the amount of damage that little shuttle dealt out, I'm more than a bit surprised that the Framgar didn't destroy it once it was helpless. They really should have, now it'll come back to haunt them. Who wants the first haunting?" Captain Casey asked with a glint in his eyes.

"Me." Everyone answered, this of course came as no surprise to the captain.

"Well, let's get it inside then, and teams three and four go do your magic, and bring the little beast back to life."

"Yes Sir!" They all said.

As soon as Captain Casey had word that the shuttle was safely inside, they continued on their cleanup mission. Alone they spent the entire rest of the day teleporting beings to single ships, and destroying the vast majority of the rest. In total they destroyed over a hundred ships, but they lost count after eighty somewhere. The rest of the fleet was out there doing the exact same thing, and the stranded ships were the first places everyone headed, so that they could get them repaired. Many ships helped those ships as they needed it. Between all the ships that were able to help, in an area where there had been over six hundred disabled ships, there were now maybe fifty. As soon as they were finished cleaning up, and their own disabled ships were fixed up, Admiral Casey called the whole fleet.

"Good work guys. This should really start to hurt them. There are still two of our ships that are in pretty rough shape, but are at least able to move under their own power now. Let's get them in the middle, and we can get as many people out there helping as we can. UE1, you're of course exempt, you don't have the man power to spare, or should I say boy power. Even though boy power seems to be ten times more potent." Admiral Casey said with a chuckle.

"Ha ha, very funny Dad. Boy, am I ever glad I didn't inherit your sense of humor."

"Yeah, right, who says!" His mom snorted. He could hear all the other captains laughing at them as well.

"Yeah, well, what can I say. The boys I'm sure appreciate the compliment none the less. In the morning, assuming everything's ready, I'm guessing we head out and show them who's boss in their own territory?" Jonathon asked.

"Oh we'll be ready all right, and then we show them why we won the war to begin with. They really shouldn't have done what they did. They had already lost far too many ships in the war, now we're going to take the very last ones we can manage." Admiral Casey smiled.

"Can't wait." Captain Casey said, and more than a few approvals were heard from the others also.

"Okay, well whomever can spare a repair crew, send them out to help, and then get as much rest as you can. Tomorrow morning we head out." Admiral Casey said and disconnected.

"Okay boys, I think a nice swim is called for. Go get suited up and meet me in the pool." Captain Casey ordered.

"Does that mean us too Sir?" Teddy asked.

"Yes, swimming is very good for rehabilitation, so it certainly includes you two."

"Good. Meet you there." Teddy said.

"Get someone to help you get undressed and dressed Teddy, because your arm will still really hurt if you move it too much the wrong way." Warren said.

"Okay." Teddy said, not caring, just glad he could go swimming.

"I'll help you out Teddy." Jamie said.

"Thanks. I hate being injured, I feel like a baby half the time, 'cause I can't do anything right now." Teddy said, but with no real bite to it.

"Yeah, well next time it could be me, and you'll be helping me. In this line of work it comes with the territory little buddy, we just have to deal with it. Just be thankful, it could've been far worse." Jamie said as they headed to their room.

"Yeah, I know, that's why I'm not complaining. At least I'll be all better real soon. Warren said I should be able to go back to light duty tomorrow, and full duty in two or three more days. He says my ribs are fine now and my shoulder's almost all better. At least I don't have to use the chair anymore." Teddy said.

"True." Jamie said.

A few minutes later, when they arrived, Jamie helped Teddy to pull off his shirt and then he got himself changed, because Teddy said he should be able to manage the pants and shorts by himself. He did manage, but it pulled and hurt a bit when he fully extended his arm, but it was not too bad, almost back to normal.

Everyone met in the pool and they swam and played for a good hour and a half before the captain called showers and bed.

The rest of the fleet had teams working through the night to get the last of the ships all ready for the up and coming final battle, and by morning, every ship was as close to a hundred percent as they possibly could be.

CHAPTER 32

THE FINAL STAND

The following morning, everyone got their morning chores and breakfast out of the way and got ready for the day ahead. They all knew that it was going to be a very long day, but they all knew it needed to be done. At 0900 hours, Admiral Casey called up the fleet.

"Okay, here's the plan everyone. We're going to break into three groups, we're going to each head in a different direction, and then hide as close as you can without being detected. I'll send out the order once everyone's in place, and then we hit from three different sides. We want to try and sneak in as close as possible though, to make this as much a sneak attack as we can possibly get away with."

Everyone agreed with the plan, so the groups were formed, and then they headed off to the three different locations that were chosen to be the best. Because one of the groups was to go to the far side, and another group was also pretty far away, the attack would end up happening the following day, since it would take almost eighteen hours for the ships that had to go the furthest, to get there. Captain Casey and his crew, as well as his parents ship and crew, and the rest of their group had drawn the long straw, and got to stay the closest, so they were hidden deep inside the asteroid field that the Qaralon thought was their main protection. And then they waited.

The following morning after everyone got a good nights sleep, Admiral Casey gave the command and all of a sudden the Qaralon home world was being attacked. They did not sink as low as the Qaralon themselves had done though, by sending missiles at the poor innocent people on the planet. They did not however show any sympathy toward the ships. As before, they tried not to destroy the ships unless necessary, and they were pounding what ships they had left into the ground, as they say. The Qaralon and Framgar simply did not have enough ships left to take the abuse they were given, and they had every last ship available out and fighting, even old broken down war horses were being sent in to fight. They lasted even less time than the newer ones. All told, there were about a thousand ships left defending the planet when they arrived. Within five hours that number was less than half that.

Another three hours later, and there was only about three hundred left, when they shut down their engines, and cut their shields, signaling defeat.

"Kelly, you're up." Admiral Casey said happily.

"You bet Sir." Kelly said with a mile wide grin.

"Qaralon home world come in." Kelly said clearly.

The leader came on screen with a look that crossed somewhere between disgust and total fear.

"You were warned the last time we saw you, that the next time you attacked our people, that we'd remove your ability to fight us again. You didn't heed that warning, what do you have to say for yourselves?" Kelly asked calmly.

"We strong and proud race, you not tell us what do." The leader attempted pitifully.

"Really. We did tell you what to do after the war though, we made it very clear in fact. Leave us alone, leave our friends alone, and you'd be left alone. I'm sorry, I thought you were smart enough to at least comprehend basic instructions. Now tell me, what did we tell you would happen if you ever attacked us again?" Kelly asked slowly, clearly.

"You say you destroy all ships, but you not do that." The leader snarled.

"Really. You really shouldn't test us. How many times have we handed you your heads on a platter now anyway? Now, you have some very simple instructions, I'll spell them out very simply, so your little mind can understand. Nod if you understand." Kelly said in a voice reserved for talking down to the lowliest of beings, of which in his mind he was.

"Don't talk me like that, I ruler this planet, I not stand it."

"I asked a simple yes or no question, in a way I hoped you would understand, but from where I'm sitting right now, it doesn't look as if you have the power to stop me from talking to you in any way I see fit. Now, do you understand?" Kelly snarled, and then asked again, this time even slower.

He nodded this time, which was a really good thing.

"Good. Now step one is to get all of your people off your ships and ship factories, and get them all on the planet. Step two, all, and I do mean all people that do not belong on your planet, that you have captured, you are to teleport up to one of your ships. Two simple things, this is all we ask. If however you fail to do so, or even think of harming one prisoner, we have ten missiles locked on your compound as we speak, and we will use them without mercy. Were those instructions clear enough, or should I break them down further?" Kelly asked slowly, menacingly.

"Yes, we understand. What you plan do after that?" He spat out.

"Oh, that's a surprise, I'm sure you'll like it. You have ten minutes to get those two things done, and remember, we're watching, and ten missiles are pointed right at you. So no trying me, because I won't stand for it, and I'll personally push the button if I suspect anything." Kelly snapped out, and then closed communications with the planet.

"Oh you are an evil little so and so aren't you. Now I know why I like you so much." Admiral Casey laughed.

"Thanks Sir, but I was telling the truth, in case you wondered. I can and will push that button too, and I know that someone already has them loaded for me." Kelly answered smoothly.

"Oh I don't even doubt it. Have fun when you call them back." Admiral Casey said.

"Thanks, I will." Kelly said.

"You really do enjoy that too much, you know that right!" Captain Casey said as he ruffled the boys hair lovingly.

"Na, you can't love something that fun too much. Who started the timer and how much time we got left?"

"I did, and we have eight minutes left." Bobby answered.

"Good, I'll be right back." Kelly said and then headed out.

"I wonder where he went in such a hurry?" Tony asked.

"To the nearest washroom to throw up. He was ash white the entire time the beast was on the screen. That was the first time he'd ever had one of them on screen, and it made him a bit sick seeing that thing." Captain Casey said calmly, not worrying about it.

"Can't say as I blame him. I almost wanted to throw up at the first sight too." Tony said.

"No, and I'd never hold it against any of you, or anyone for that matter."

A few minutes later Kelly came back and took up the communications console again, looking more normal again.

"How much time we got left?" Kelly asked once he was settled in again, as if he had not even left to go empty the entire contents of his stomach.

"Just under a minute left Kelly, I'll give you the thumbs up when it's time." Bobby said.

"Thanks."

The almost minute almost seemed to drag by as they all waited for the thumbs up sign, it finally came.

"Qaralon leader, have you complied with both orders?" Kelly asked.

"Yes, all is done you asked. Now what going you do?" He asked again, this time sounding more down.

"You'll have to wait for the surprise, I promise you that you'll love it." Kelly said with a grin, all happy.

"Admiral Casey, if you would please get our people off that filth of a ship, and somewhere nice and cozy?" Kelly asked.

"Sure thing kiddo, we'd be happy to do that, just give us a minute or two please." Admiral Casey said happily.

Within three minutes, all the prisoners were teleported to four of the Earth ships, and one of the Tenarian ships, as well as two that belonged to the Drandarians. As soon as everyone was clear, the nod was given, and all the ships opened fire on the now empty ships and factories, and blew them all into space dust. Kelly, instead of watching the ships, was watching the face of the Qaralon leader, as were more than a few of the others. The look on his face went from shock, to fear, to anger, and then to something in the middle of it all.

"Did you like your little surprise?" Kelly asked in a nice cheery voice.

"You destroy all our ships!" It said in astonishment.

"Yes, it really shouldn't have come as much of a surprise to you, you were told at the end of the war what would happen. You were also told a couple times today already what we told you then. So why are you now surprised? You should know by now that we don't give idle threats. Now for the next part, and listen very closely, because we won't tolerate further attacks on any people. If we ever see any of your ships outside of your own solar system, they'll be escorted back home, and then after getting your people safely on the planet, we'll destroy said ship. If we even hear a rumor that you're building another fleet of ships to attack anyone ever again, we'll come in and wipe out the entire planet. I can't say this strongly enough, don't mess with us. You've done it twice, and there won't be a third chance. Am I making myself perfectly clear?" Kelly said calmly.

"Yes. We understand, but we not have 'nough resources our solar system, we starve if you not let us leave." The leader said.

"I'm sorry, that's not of any of our concern. Your people got into this mess yourselves, and you can get yourselves out of it. There's an empty system right next to you, it has lots of resources you can use. To show that we aren't the beasts that you are, we'll allow you to use that system as well, you may not claim it however, you may simply use it. The same warning however, leave that system, or your own, and you know the results." Kelly said quietly.

"What we to do about population though, we not all fit our planet no more, and you stranded Framgar here too?" The panic of the situation was setting in now.

"You'll have to deal with your population issues on your own. You have a few planets that, with some work, could suitably house many of your people, use them. The same warning will be delivered to the Framgar home world, and all their ships neutralized. You'll soon have some ships limping home, we didn't destroy all of them. The Framgar are welcome to head home, as long as they call for an escort first. They may also use the solar system next to them, and it alone. As I said, we aren't beasts. Any other questions?" Kelly asked.

"No." He said and then signed off.

"Very well done Kelly. You showed compassion when none was warranted, and a firm hand when it was needed. You'll make an excellent captain one of these days." Captain Casey said lovingly, rubbing the still sick boy on the back.

"I second that motion, and all that you told them has been entered, and it's now a contract that has been sent to the planet, as well as to Framgar. They'll know why we're there when we arrive." Admiral Casey said.

"Good and thanks. Now can we get out of here? I hate this place!" Kelly asked.

"You got it, lead the troops out of here Kelly." Admiral Casey offered.

"Yes Sir! You heard him guys, let's get going. We have one more stop, and then home, well Earth, because this is home." Kelly told the entire fleet.

"Yes Sir!" Everyone shouted.

CHAPTER 33

SHOWING OFF

They led the fleet from the Qaralon system, and headed toward one of the asteroid fields they had used once before to rest. A few hours later, when they arrived, they all parked with the UE1 in the center. Admiral and Captain Casey came on board the UE1 to congratulate everyone.

"Hello everyone, I hope everyone is well?" Admiral Casey asked as he appeared on the bridge with his wife.

"Hi Mom and Dad, I'm glad we made it through this in one piece, so we're all well. My two injured are almost healed and all my ships are intact, so we're good. We lost a few ships, and those people will be missed, but they died doing what they loved, and could any crew hope for anything more. Well I have a few upgrades in the ship I'd love to show you guys. Let's say it's a much more comfortable ship than it was when I borrowed it." Jonathon told his parents.

"Yes, they fought the good fight, and will be honored for it. Well show me my baby, and let's see how much you've messed it up?" Admiral Casey grinned.

Jonathon and all his boys led the captain and admiral on a tour of the ship. First was the new shuttle bay. They both thought it impressive. Next was the engine and power rooms, and they loved those modifications as well. Then the shields and inertia compensator's, and they were told how much better they performed now. Next was the pool, and both were speechless at this, but they asked how they could contain all the water, it was Jamie who explained it to them. Then for the biggest one, the holographic room. They entered, and both had a puzzled look on their faces, because at the moment it was just an empty room.

"You said this room was the most impressive thing, but I don't see anything special about it!" Captain Casey said to her son.

"Ah, but you haven't let us turn it on yet, would somebody do the honors please. Let's say a nice sandy beach somewhere nice and warm." Captain Casey said, and then a few seconds later they were standing on a gorgeous sandy beach, with the most beautiful blue ocean water lapping at their feet.

"W-w-w-what is this, is this a dream?" Admiral Casey stuttered out.

"No, not a dream, a holographic representation that both looks and feels completely real. Go ahead, feel the water." Jonathon told his parents.

They did so, even felt the sand, then kicked off their shoes, and sampled it that way too.

"This was a little gift, as was the pool, from the Drandarians, we think it's pretty neat, and we sure have enjoyed it ever since we installed it. The technology is actually quite simple and easy to make, so all our ships could have this put in with ease." Jonathon told his parents.

"Well this is possibly the most amazing thing I've ever seen. What else can these rooms do?" Admiral Casey asked.

"Let's see, we've gone sledding in the winter, remember my telling you about that, as well we've been swimming in many tropical locations, traveled fabled cities, and hiked huge mountains. The most interesting thing though is this." Captain Casey said while handing his parents his ring.

"It's a ring, the ring the boys got for you for Christmas, but what of it?" His mom asked.

"This ring was made in here. The boys used some precious metals we found, and made programs to have this created. Anything that's made in here stays in here, if it was only created in here. But things using materials from outside of here, can be brought in and made, and they stay. Up 'til they did this, we had no idea it could be done, but it can. Oh and the craftsmanship on it's superb as well." Jonathon told his parents.

"I'll say, this is a very neat room, and I can't wait to explore it further." Admiral Casey said in pure awe.

"You're of course welcome to come use it at any time." Jonathon offered his parents.

"Of course we are, it's our ship. Well it was. Your father and I've decided to give it to you guys, the boys need it more than we do." His mom said.

"Thanks guys, but you don't have to do that though. I'm sure that if I asked, they'd build us a new ship." Jonathon said.

"True, but we've already been given the ship that we have now, and we were told it was a replacement for your ship. It seems everyone at the top wants these boys out here. They were almost begging us to give it to you and everything. Well, seeing as how we have such a nice beach, why don't we all go swimming? Can you program a nice cabana with swimsuits for everyone, and maybe even a little food stand or something?" Admiral Casey asked curiously.

"Fine, we'll take it, the boys already consider this home anyway, so they'll agree I'm sure, and I notice an awful lot of nodding heads that say yes. As for the cabana, that can be done, but don't leave here with those shorts on, or you'll find yourself naked as soon as you exit. A couple of the boys accidentally found that out once, it was really quite comical. As for food and drinks, you can't do that. It'll come up, but anything you eat or drink in here does nothing for you, so it's no point. We can go for some food first or after." Jonathon said.

"Or Will and I can go get everyone something, it's one of our jobs after all." Warren offered.

"If you don't mind, that'd be great." Jonathon said.

They nodded and then turned and left. Donny was already at the console working on adding a large cabana with everything they would need, and in a minute it appeared.

"It's all ready Sir, a large mens change room, and a small woman's one, all the suits are there, and are to size."

"Amazing." Admiral Casey whispered.

A few minutes later everyone exited the cabana and ran to the nice warm inviting water, and splashed and played until the food arrived. Warren and Will had already gotten changed, so were ready to swim as well, as soon as the meal was finished of course. Donny went back to the console and programmed a huge table and chairs to seat everyone, and he placed it right in the water, so that everyone's feet were still in the water, it was really quite nice. They enjoyed a very nice meal together, and talked and ate, and ate and talked. Once satisfied, they all laid down on the soft warm sand and rested for a while, before going back in the water to play for a while longer. They ended up staying there for the most part of the day, just resting and relaxing, all of them feeling that it was a very well deserved rest.

CHAPTER 34

FINALLY, IT'S OVER!

The next three days went by with not so much as a whisper of a problem. They were now heading to the Framgar planet to destroy all their ships, and while they figured they might have a little bit of a fight, it would not be large. The Drandarians had excused themselves to go home as soon as they left the Qaralon system, since they felt that the rest could handle the situation quite nicely, and they just wanted to go home. They were thanked repeatedly for the great help that they provided, offered condolences for the brave men and woman that would never fight again, and were told that should they ever need a hand, to call at any time. They were thankful as well, but were soon gone.

Finally they reached the Framgar home world, and found all the ships ready and waiting for them, but not in the way they expected. They were all empty. As soon as they were stopped in front of the empty fleet of ships, the planet contacted them.

"Earth ships, we've received your demands, and have decided that you've taken enough of our lives already while we were helping the Qaralon. We'll allow you to destroy our ships, and we'll no longer pose a threat to you. We'd ask though, that you leave us at least a few ships if you could?" The Framgar leader asked humbly, knowing when he was soundly beat.

"We accept your total surrender, and because you did so without a fight, we'll leave all your ships intact, however, remember the warning, the next time we won't be so kind." Admiral Casey said.

"We understand, and we thank you. We'll heed your warnings, and won't bother you at all, we'll also sever all ties with the Qaralon." The leader added.

"Good, then our work here is done." Admiral Casey said, and then closed contact with the planet.

"Well that went surprisingly well. I'm not really surprised though, but I'm very happy for it. Tenarian ships, again we thank you more than you can know, for your help, and we wish you a safe trip home." Admiral Casey said.

"And we thank you too Sir, and you too have a safe trip home as well." The lead Tenarian smiled.

They then started back on their way out, the Earth and Tenarian ships heading in different directions.

"Well everyone, I think it's about time we headed home. We've been gone long enough, and we have much to celebrate, and many to mourn." Admiral Casey said.

Admiral Casey in the lead, pointed everyone toward home, and they took a nice leisurely pace. They were only at half speed. Many of the captains from the fleet were coming and going from the UE1 over the next few days to do a couple things, first and foremost was to congratulate the boys on their exceptional skills, and second was to see the new toys that the ship now had.

Every single captain said they would love to have the holographic suite on their ship, and the pool would be nice, but why bother with the pool when you have the holograph suite they all asked. They were all told the same thing, it was real, and this way it allowed one group to be using the pool, while another could use the holograph room. This seemed like a reasonable explanation to all and thought it made sense, so that was good.

"Jonathon, your father and I'd like for you and your crew to join us and a few of the captains for a dinner this evening." His mom asked.

"Okay, is it a formal dinner?"

"Yes, full dress uniforms will be required, your dad wasn't happy, but he'll survive." She said with a chuckle.

"Yeah, he still can't stand the formal stuff, but he's so good at it." Jonathon added with a smile.

"Dinner will be at 1800 hours sharp."

"Okay Mom, we'll be there."

"Good, see you later, oh, and be here an hour early will you." His mom said and then disconnected.

"Yes Ma'am." He chuckled after she was gone.

"Everyone meet me on the bridge please." Captain Casey called out on his communicator.

"Hey Captain, what's happening?" Donny asked once they were all on the bridge.

"Not much, other than the fact that we've been invited to a formal dinner on my parents ship this evening. We're to be there by 1700 hours and dinner will commence at 1800 hours. We're to be in full dress uniforms, so an hour before we're to leave, we'll all take the time to get completely cleaned and polished up, to be ready to go." Captain Casey said.

"Yes Sir!" Everyone said.

"Good. We have three hours 'til then, so for the rest of the time, I'll take the bridge alone, and you guys can go and relax a bit and have some fun." Captain Casey said.

"Okay Sir." They all said.

The boys all headed down to the holographic room and did a little mountain hike they all liked, while the captain watched the bridge. A few minutes before they were to start getting ready, he called his parents up.

"Hi Dad, I know you guys don't need to stop to get ready, but we do, so should we all just park for the night here?" Jonathon asked.

"We could do that, or I could have someone go to your ship and get us a couple hours closer. No, let's just go ahead and stop for the night. I'll call the halt then, and we'll see you guys in a little while." Admiral Casey said.

"Okay then, see you in a while." Jonathon said and then disconnected.

A few moments later the command came through, so everyone halted, and then parked. Captain Casey called the boys, and told them all it was time to get ready for dinner, and to go to their rooms to do so. He then went to his own room and first got his uniform out, to inspect it to make sure it was perfectly clean. He knew he would not have to worry about it being wrinkled. He then checked his shoes, and noticed that they needed a good polish, so put them into his cleaner to clean and polish them while he went for a nice long hot shower.

The boys arrived in their rooms and did much the same, checking their uniforms first, and then polishing their shoes, and then into the showers to get ready.

Once everyone was clean, they all spent a while getting their hair dried and done, then they all got dressed, and then everyone met in the hallway almost at the same time.

"Line up for inspection boys." Captain Casey said.

They quickly lined up right in the corridor, and their captain proudly gave them a very thorough inspection, only having to adjust a couple very minor things.

"Looking good boys, let's go for dinner. Now, it's an hour before dinner, so that means that you're to get into the crowd and mingle. I don't want to see anyone sitting back in a corner or anything. Remember to be polite, and answer any questions as best you can. And most important, have some fun tonight, these are all nice people, and they all like a good joke, so just be yourselves." Captain Casey said to his boys proudly.

"Yes Sir!" They all said, a lot less nervous than they would have been a year ago.

Captain Casey smiled to himself thinking that the boys would be perfectly fine; they were all becoming very self assured young men, and very little would, or could make them lose their cool.

"Okay, come on then, my parents don't go for fashionably late, so we better get moving."

He turned and started toward the nearest teleporter console, and got them all over to his parents ship. He then asked the computer for the location of his parents, and he was told his father was on the bridge, so that was where they headed. Because it was a different design than their own ship, they had to use directions given to them by the computer. Though the ship was of a different design, most everything they saw though was very nearly identical to all the other ships. The walls were the same, the doors were the same, even the colours for the most part were the same. They felt that they could feel just as at home in this ship as they could their own, only the physical layout and sizes were actually different. They arrived a few minutes later on the bridge. As soon as they entered, everyone rose and saluted them. They saluted back, but were not sure why.

"Hi Admiral, what's going on here?" Captain Casey asked warily.

"Nothing much, don't worry about it." Admiral Casey smiled.

"I think that worries me more than being saluted by everyone when I enter the bridge of an admirals ship, and then to be told by the admiral to not worry about it." Captain Casey said with a wary smile.

"You worry too much kid. Let's go to the dining hall, your mother's already there and waiting for us." Admiral Casey said, clapping his son on the back.

He did not wait for an answer, and turned and left the bridge, so the crew of the UE1 just followed. He took them down a couple dozen levels, near to the bottom of the ship, and then to a corridor that looked as if it had been recently changed, since there was still minor finishing work being done. He then went to the only door on the left side; it opened and he entered, they followed.

"Very nice. I knew all of your engineers and scientists had gotten the technical specifications for the holographic room from me, but I didn't think you guys would've had all the parts to build one this quickly." Jonathon said.

What they had walked into was a large forest clearing with a large waterfall and pool to the left of them. It had been decorated very nicely to enhance the natural surroundings, and there were tables placed in strategic places, but all facing a very large table near to the large natural pool. On the opposite side of the clearing, there was a large outdoor cooking area set up, and a dozen cooks were very busy cooking a very large amount of food. Over all the feel of the area was very nice and relaxing.

"Yeah, they've all been working non stop manufacturing everything they needed, you have no idea how excited everyone was about this. They finished this morning, hence the dinner being tonight, and not a few nights ago like I wanted."

"I bet I can guess. The people I gave the pads to were almost vibrating when I handed them over, they were so excited. So who designed the scene for tonight?"

They all turned as they got their answer.

"Your father and I did this, we had a little fun. We were the first to get to test it out, and this was what we did. Everyone should be showing up very soon, so we should go ahead and get out of the doorway and look around a little." His mom said as she strolled up to all the guys.

"You did a very nice job, but yes, we should, so let's go." Jonathon said.

"Thanks. We put in a few really nice trails, so that people can take nice walks on, and there's lots of wildlife around as well, so we could have visitors for dinner." She said as they walked.

The boys moved away from the adults, and spent a few minutes looking around as well. When they heard everyone else arriving, they went back to the clearing, where they found Admiral and Captains Casey greeting everyone that were just entering.

"Come on over boys and meet our other guests!" Admiral Casey called out.

For the next several minutes the boys were all introduced to almost a hundred of the captains from the Earth fleet. They were all doing well with the introductions and the praises. Most of them had already met over the past few weeks, or months, the boys were no longer sure, but not all, and the boys were fairly comfortable in the situation.

"Please, everyone wander around and enjoy the trails and the nature, and we'll all be called when dinner's ready." Admiral Casey called out.

Everyone dispersed into the crowd just talking and laughing, and the boys were the main guests of honor. Jonathon and his parents went and sat on a nice bench near to the waterfall and started a conversation.

"The boys seem so much more social now than when we first met. You've done a wonderful job with them. I can also tell you that I wouldn't want to get any of them mad, especially if the tongue of the youngest one says anything about the rest of them." Admiral Casey said.

"Thanks, they deserve most of the credit though, I haven't had to do much with them. They're all naturally very bright, and they grabbed on to what I taught them, then took it upon themselves to take it further. The past eleven months they've seen and done much, a lot more than even you've been told, the full report will be finished soon, and I'm at over a thousand pages already. You know all of the major things already of course, but there's lots more. Just working with the Drandarians, who treated them like heroes and or gods, helped them so much more than I could've ever done alone. As for getting them mad, I wouldn't suggest it either. Kelly, however, has the nastiest little tongue of the bunch, as you've quite clearly heard yourself. The others would probably just beat you up instead." Captain Casey laughed.

"I can't wait to read the report, that is if your mother let's me first, she doesn't usually let me pull rank on her." Admiral Casey said with a mock pout.

"You know full well that at home I outrank you old man. And I'm sure Jonathon will send us two copies to read, won't you Jonathon!" His mom said, his dad just shook his head.

"Yes mommy." Jonathon said in his best pouty voice he could manage, both parents laughed.

The boys had of course dispersed amongst the other captains and were just walking around, chatting to whomever they came across.

"Your name's Kelly right, I'm Captain Greene, and I'd love to talk with you for a few minutes if I could!" He said, offering his hand to shake.

"Yes I'm Kelly, Captain, how can I help you?" He asked, shaking the offered hand.

"Oh, I don't need any help. I just wanted to talk to the young man who could out talk an enemy leader the way you did. I also hear that that wasn't the first time you did that, and that you enjoy doing it too. From what I understand, Jonathon found all of you on the streets, living for yourselves, is that where you learned to talk like that?"

"Yeah, I liked telling them off like that, it's great stress relief the captain says. Yes we were all street rats, but I hardly ever talked back then, and don't really like to think back to how it was."

"Great stress relief, yeah, I can see that. As for your being a street rat, and not wanting to dwell on the past, I can understand that as well, and with as good as you boys now are, you'll never have to go anywhere you don't want. So if you hardly ever talked back then, how did such a young man as yourself develop such a sharp tongue then?"

"Well the first time I had to deal with a tough situation, I happened to be at communications, so it was my job to deal with it. I just pushed aside my fear and started talking, as I went on it became easier and more forceful, now I just find it fun." Kelly giggled, remembering back to that first time and how scared he was.

"Well I must say that I'm surprised at that, but given what all of you've been through, and to come as far as you have, then I guess that I shouldn't be, but I am. Well I've taken up more than enough of your precious time young man, it was a pleasure talking to you." Captain Greene said and then stood, from the bench they sat at, to leave.

"Wait, you haven't told me anything about yourself. Like what ship was yours, and were any of your people hurt? Also do you have a wife or any children?" Kelly asked.

"Well if you want to talk to a boring old guy like me, then I'll stay." He smiled. "I'm the captain of the UE256, we got a bit beat up, and we had a couple minor injuries, but from what I understand, a couple of your people got worse, so it wasn't too bad. I do have a wife back on Earth, and we wanted children, but sadly weren't blessed with the ability, so we've had a number of children through our home over the years, trying to help where we could. Many of them right off the street in fact."

"I'm sorry to hear that you couldn't have children of your own, but at least you and your wife helped other needy children out, that has to feel nice. I know that Captain Casey feels good about what he's done for us."

"There I'm afraid you might be wrong. Good isn't quite strong enough to begin with, and by the way he talks about you guys, it's you who've given him far more than he could've ever given to you guys."

"Yeah, we all know he feels that way, but he's wrong. We were alive when he found us, if you wish to call it that. Now we're living. There's a big difference, and nothing we can do can possibly be more than that."

"You sure do speak well for an eight-year-old. I understand you were seven when you started, so must be eight now."

"I think I'm eight now anyway, not too sure when my birthday is. I'm not that smart, those are Donny's words, but they're true anyway."

"I think you're smarter than you think you are, but that's fine. The statement's true though, especially for you boys. I've known Jonathon for many years, and he's far happier now than he's ever been before, because you guys have lifted him higher than anything else possibly could, so don't sell yourselves short." Captain Green said, and then stood and walked off.

Kelly just sat there and thought about what he was told for a few minutes, then stood and started to walk down the trail when he heard the call for dinner.

"It didn't feel that long." He said to himself.

The others had all stood around, or walked with one or more of the captains, and talked until the call for dinner came. All the boys had a good time, and talked a lot about themselves, as well as learned a lot from the captains they were speaking to.

"Would the crew of the UE1 join my wife and myself at the head table please?" Admiral Casey said as everyone came into sight.

A few moments later, once everyone was seated, the admiral stood up again.

"We're holding this little get together this evening to have a small celebration for the victory, and of course we'll have a toast to those who were lost, for they should never be forgotten. So the first toast of the night will be to our fallen people. We thank you for being the great people you were, and you will be sorely missed, we hope that the loss of your lives was not in vain. We won the war, but at what cost, the cost of even one life is too great, but to save the lives of millions, it is but a small price to pay. To the fallen, we raise our glasses to you. A moment of silence please."

At the end of the silence everyone drained their glasses, to celebrate the lives.

"And now we celebrate our guests of honor, the crew of the UE1. Would everyone please rise to give praise to the crew that took out possibly more ships than everyone in this room combined. To Captain Jonathon Casey and your crew, we thank you for your hard work, and the skills you used to win this battle. To the Captain, you have a very fine crew, and should be very proud. To the crew of the UE1, you have the best captain there is, I know, I trained him." Admiral Casey said, and then raised his glass.

Everyone raised their glasses as well, and gave their agreement to the toast, and then drained their glasses again. Captain Casey then stood up once everyone sat back down.

"We thank you for your kind words Sir, and I wish I could take even half the credit. The simple fact of the matter is, these boys don't even need me anymore, they could do very well on their own. I taught them everything I knew, and they drank it up, now I find them teaching me. They've given to me far more than they could ever know, more than I could ever give to them." Captain Casey said, and then sat down.

"You're wrong Sir, it's you that's given us more than you could know. Yes, we might be able to go out on our own, but without you, we're nothing. You taught us everything you knew, yet everyday you teach us more. Don't be thinking that you can get rid of us that easily Sir, we're not going anywhere. And the credit is all yours, only under your command could we have done what we did, and we're forever in your debt." Donny stood and said.

"Well it seems that you're all thankful for each other, and don't be fooled boys, you couldn't get rid of him that easily either. The UE1 is officially yours, to use for many years to come. Once you're all ready, I fully expect to see each and every one of you as a captain, and I expect nothing less. Now, unless I'm much mistaken, our dinner is ready and waiting for us, so I say, let's eat." Admiral Casey said with a grand gesture.

With that, twenty people came out carrying large trays filled with many different foods, and stopped at the head table first. Once everyone had their food, they started eating, and while everyone chatted, they enjoyed the very good food. It was a very slow meal and everyone took their time, and finally, almost an hour after they started, the dessert was being served, in the same manner. Once everyone was finished being stuffed far more full than is normally healthy, Admiral Casey stood up.

"Well I don't know about the rest of you, but that was a most excellent meal, and I'm full beyond belief, so could use a nice walk along a nice sandy beach somewhere." Admiral Casey said.

"Sounds good Sir." A few people said.

As soon as all the food was cleared out, Admiral Casey changed the scene to a nice sandy beach with a beautiful sunset low over the water. The admiral kicked off his shoes and socks, rolled up his pant legs, and started walking, the rest followed suit a few seconds later.

"So Donny, are you ready for all the media attention that you guys are going to get when we get home?" Admiral Casey asked when Donny came up beside him a few minutes later.

"I hope so, it'll still be rough, but we'll manage. Tonight was bad enough, but I have a feeling that when we get back, it'll be far worse. I hope that they just don't crowd us and make us tell of our past, and things like that. I don't think some of us would be able to handle that very well, especially the younger ones. Kelly of course will have no problem telling them where to go and how to get there." Donny said with a smile.

"I'd actually enjoy seeing that. However, I'm sure that that won't be a problem. WSEC has been hounded for information ever since the media found out about this little experiment, that turned out to be a massive success. They were all told, however, that any badgering of you guys, or asking questions about your past would land them in jail with fines, and removal of their licenses, permanently. Somehow I don't believe that they'll be any problem. Not to mention, your captain, his mom, and myself will be with you at all times, and believe me when I say, I have a lot of weight to throw around, so no one will bother you guys. We'll have to have a press conference though, and you'll all be asked questions, but if we think that a question is inappropriate, we'll step in and strike the question."

"We all thank you for that, and I also can't say that I'd mind seeing Kelly go at one of those guys, they wouldn't even know what hit them. You know just as well as I do though, that some of the more slimy reporters, that don't have a license, or a brain, will have no fear about grilling us, if given half a chance, so I'll instruct all the guys to stay close together at all times." Donny said seriously.

"That's true, they wouldn't hesitate if they had the chance to do so, anything to get a good juicy story some of them say. It's a very good idea to stick together as much as possible though, because like they say, there's strength in numbers. You're right though, they'd have no idea what hit them if they had a go at Kelly, he'd tear them to shreds, maybe make them cry, now that'd be too funny. So what do you think you guys are going to do once you get back into space?"

"Not too sure. I have no idea what, if any plan Captain Casey has. He always said that we'd go home after a year, but what home. We have none, and I know for a fact he wouldn't leave us now, and his apartment's barely large enough for him. Not to mention that we'd all miss being in space too much to stay on the planet for too long. We really have nothing to be going back for, this is mostly for the captain. If I had any say, I'd want to collect more kids, go back out, train a new batch of kids, and see where life takes us." Donny answered after a few moments of thought.

"I bet that if you mentioned all this to Jonathon, that he'd go with it, you have a lot more say than you probably know, he respects you a great deal. Why don't you tell him this, and you might be surprised, he might've already been thinking about it for all you know."

"Maybe, I'll talk to him, but we all respect him a lot too."

"I know." Admiral Casey said, patting Donny on the shoulder.

For the next half an hour they walked in silence, enjoying the cool evening air, the warm ocean water, and the starlight in the sky.

Soon though they returned and exited the holographic room, and everyone started going back to their ships. Captain Casey and his crew were the last to leave, with thanks all around. As soon as they all made it back to their ship, Captain Casey and the boys all headed to their rooms to get changed and put their uniforms in the laundry to get them all taken care of. Within just a few seconds of each other, they all met in the hall outside their rooms, all of them figuring that they would go do something together for the night.

Donny was the last one out of his room, and as soon as he saw the captain, he asked, "Captain, could I talk to you a few minutes?"

"Sure Donny, let's go to my office, we can speak there."

"We'll be in the theatre watching a movie when you guys are done then, just meet us there, okay." Franky told them.

"Okay, sounds good." Both Donny and the captain said.

They all split up from there, Donny and the Captain to the captains office, while Warren and the rest of the boys all headed to the theatre to pick out and watch a movie. As soon as they made it there, they both sat down and got comfortable.

"So what is it that you wanted to talk about?" Captain Casey asked.

"Well Sir, I was wondering if you had any plans after our visit to Earth?"

"I've been thinking about what we should do, and I haven't come up with anything really. Because you're asking me, I'm willing to bet you have an idea that you'd like to share. What is it?" Captain Casey asked.

"You know me so well Sir. Well, as you're more than aware, none of us have a home, this is our home really. Well, even if we did get homes on the planet, I know I'd miss being in space too much, and I'd want to be back. So that isn't an option I'd really like. Not to mention, I'd like to stay with you, and I know all the others feel the same way about all of this. I was kind of hoping that once we visit, and get all the icky stuff over with, we could come back out and head out the other way and just keep exploring. We've been in space for many years, but due to the war, we've seen and done very little. I was also thinking that why don't we find some more crew members, and train the next generation. I know we could help out a great deal there, we still have lots to learn, but we also have lots to teach." He said quite convincingly.

"That was a few of the many ideas I'd thought of, and since you've brought that very idea to me, we can all talk it over, over the next few days, and then make a decision. I know that this is your home now, and I also know none of you could really live on Earth again, not for some time yet, if at all. You all still have a lot of growing up to do, and the emotional hurt that you have is still too close to the surface to allow Earth to be home for a while. Maybe when you're older you could again, maybe it never will really be home for any of you, maybe space will always be home. Soon enough, if you choose to stay in space, you'll all be in command of ships yourself, and I'm willing to bet that you're the youngest space captain there ever is. I'm certain that you could easily take over command now, but deep down, you don't feel that you're ready, and maybe you're not." Captain Casey said.

"I know I could physically do it Sir, but I'm not really mentally ready to do it yet I think. Maybe in a few years like you said. I don't know about the others, but I really have no desire to ever go back to the planet for more than just visits. I have a feeling though, that none of us could ever leave space for long. We can talk it out, but I can tell you what the answers will be, they'll all be yes, and I'm willing to bet on it." Donny said with a smile.

"I wouldn't bet against you, but we have to make it fair. Not to mention we should get everyone elses ideas and opinions as well. Together we can come up with a good plan of action."

"You're right, as always Sir, and we could probably get lots of good ideas that way. Well why don't we go join the others then, and we can talk after breakfast in the morning!"

"You know it's supposed to be me dismissing people right, but let's go." Captain Casey said with a nice warm smile, Donny just grinned back.

They left and headed to the theatre and joined the others in a movie and popcorn. After the movie finished, they all headed to bed early, and slept straight through the night.

CHAPTER 35

HOME AT LAST, WELL, MAYBE NOT

The next morning, everyone got cleaned and dressed, did their morning exercises and had breakfast as usual. It was about as routine as any morning can be on a space ship that seemed to find more than it's fair share of trouble. They had just finished breakfast when Captain Casey stood, getting everyone's attention just by doing so.

"Before we start the day guys, Donny has a couple questions to ask you."

"What, hey, Captain, that was cruel! Well fine then. Okay guys, as you know, we're heading back to the planet, but has anybody given it any thought as to what would happen once we got there?" He asked the whole crew.

"Yes." Everyone said.

"Well so did I. Admiral Casey got it out of me, and I gave him my idea, so he told me to talk to Captain Casey, and that was what we talked about last night. My idea was to go back out after a short visit, and continue our exploration mission. Maybe go somewhere no one's ever been before, the universe is a large place, and we've seen almost nothing of it. I also asked if we could gather other boys just like us, and we can help to train them. We agreed that this had to be a decision among all of us, and that we should get everyone elses ideas and opinions about this. So first, all in favor of going back out, let's say for another year?"

Every hand in the room, including Will and Warren's, shot up as one lightning fast movement.

"Well I guess that was unanimous. Next, all in favor of getting more crew members?" Donny asked.

Again all hands in the room shot up, as if attached to each other.

"Now an open floor discussion. Please keep it to one at a time on the questions or ideas, and we can all work out an answer." Donny said and then sat down.

"I'd like to go first." Kelly said after standing up. "This is my home now, and no other place will ever be home to me. I like both of the ideas, so I say we go for it. When we choose the others to come with us, I say you let us kids go out and get them. I don't know about the others, but I was very scared when you came up to us. Adults were very scary at that time, and even though you got us to trust you enough to talk at the time, I think we might have an easier time of it."

"I think that's a good idea, this way we can get our crew even faster, and like you said, probably easier, and hopefully with less hassle and pain on our parts." Jamie said while rubbing his side from the memory of the hit.

"Yeah, I can see how you might feel that way." Captain Casey said with a laugh.

"Okay, so how many more people should we add to our crew then?" Brady asked.

"Good question. We haven't thought about that yet. What does everyone think is a good number to add?" Donny asked.

"How about another ten." Dillon asked.

"Or maybe twenty." Ryan said.

"I think twenty would be good as well." Cullen said.

"I say ten." Marty said.

"Why not right in the middle at fifteen then!" Brad said.

"Here's what we're going to do. We'll cast a silent vote, and we can decide that way. I'll program this pad real quick, then we can pass it around so that you can enter your vote, then I'll compile the list, and we'll have the number." Donny said.

He spent the next few minutes programming the pad he had. He entered his number, and then passed it around. Even Warren and the captain were handed the pad for this, and when everyone was finished, it was handed back to Donny to compile the list.

"Okay, five members has two votes, ten has five votes, fifteen has ten votes, twenty has seven votes and we have one vote for twenty five. We have a clear winner. We'll choose fifteen new crew members then." Donny said.

"What about adding another person to help in the kitchen?" Lance asked.

"Why, is my cooking not good enough for you?" Will asked with the best pout he could, even sniffling a bit for effect.

"No, that's not it, and you know it. The reason is simple. If you guys are needed in the infirmary, that's just a bit more important, and this way you have a helper that can still do meals, so the rest of us can do our duties without having to stop and make something to eat." Lance said with a shake of his head.

"I was just teasing you, but I think it's a good idea. Hopefully of course our services there'll no longer be needed, but a helper would be kind of nice. What do you think Warren?" Will asked.

"Probably not such a bad idea. You could probably go out and find our helper. Maybe an older street kid who's interested in cooking, maybe even an ex street kid like me." Warren said.

"Sounds good to me, how about you Captain." Donny asked.

"We could do that." Captain Casey said.

"Okay, any other bright ideas?" Donny asked.

Everyone looked around for a moment, checking to see if anyone else could think of anything. Finally, after almost a minute, they all shook their heads no.

"Then let's go ahead and get this day started. If anyone has any other ideas, let me know, and we can put them out. We have until we get back to the planet to get this all figured out. How much longer at the pace we've kept have we got?" Donny asked.

"A little over two weeks." Tony answered.

"Okay then, lots of time to figure things out." Donny said.

They all went about their days, and the next two weeks flew by, so before they knew it, they were above the planet. No one was able to come up with any other ideas, other than a couple little things that were decided against, since they did not really make sense to do.

"Well guys, we're back. We've been gone almost a year, in two weeks I believe is the day I started looking for you. So how does it feel?" Captain Casey asked.

"You'd think I'd feel like I was coming home, but it doesn't, I'm home already and Earth is just a nice place to visit." Franky said.

"Me too." Everyone said, including Warren.

"I know how you feel, I was born and raised on this very ship, and even though I lived on the planet for a few years, it never felt like home, and it was getting almost unbearable, hence the reason for this mission, as you all already knew." Captain Casey agreed.

"Well I guess we should get this over with huh!" Donny said.

"Yep, let's all go get changed, and then we can go. By now I'm sure the press conference is already ready for us, and waiting, and probably not so patiently." Captain Casey said.

"Yes Sir!" Everyone said.

A short while later everyone was scrubbed and dressed and ready to go, so they all teleported right into the lobby of WSEC, where the press conference was being held.

Almost immediately they were being barraged with questions from every direction, and it was not an adult, but Kelly, who got them to back off.

"We just got here, back off now and let us breath for a minute. This is a press conference, and you'll all have your chance to ask questions. There'll be rules that need to be followed before we start, failure to comply by any, and we leave without warning, now back up." Kelly snapped.

They all went silent almost immediately, and most even backed off a few steps, and everyone in the room was surprised at how well Kelly had controlled the situation. They all went to the podium area that had been set up, and shook hands with Admiral Casey and a few other admirals that were there.

"Very well handled Kelly, we already told them not to do that, but they didn't listen to us." Admiral Casey laughed as Kelly came up to him.

"It was fun Sir. Well, let's get this party started shall we." Kelly said with a grin and stepped up to the microphone.

"Alright everyone, listen up. None of us really wants to be here doing this, so we're imposing a few rules. As I mentioned before, if you do anything that's on the list, we'll leave, and you'll never get to talk to us again. Rule one is, our past is our past, and you don't need to know about it, plain and simple, don't ask. Second, when we give you an answer, it's good enough, if we don't elaborate, it's for a reason, again you don't need to know. Third, when we say we've had enough, there are to be no more questions. Fourth, you're to ask one question at a time, from one person, however you wish to work that out's your problem, not ours. Fifth, after this press conference, we won't speak to any reporters at all, so don't approach us and ask us questions, you won't like the results, I can promise you that. You may start." Kelly said.

One reporter put up his hand, so Kelly pointed to him, and he pushed forward a bit.

"We're reporters and it's our duty to get all the information. How is it you feel that you can place so many restrictions?"

"Simple, it's our lives, not yours, and we'll put any restrictions on questions that we see fit." Kelly answered simply. Another reporter put up her hand, Kelly pointed to her.

"I understand that you were all street children before Captain Casey took you all in for this mission. I don't want to know your past, I simply want to know how it was he found all of you, if you don't mind my asking?"

"I'll take that question." Captain Casey said, coming forward. "I decided on what to do, and then I went searching the streets where I knew that children had a tendency to live. I talked to them, we made the deal, and then they became my crew." Captain Casey answered. She nodded her head and backed off, and another put up her hand.

"Did any of you have any training of any sort to work a star ship before going up?"

"I'll take that one." Devon said, moving forward. "No, none of us had even been on a ship before then. Most of us had little to no actual schooling, and we're still working on that, but we're doing very well on that too I might add. All of the things that we've learned, Captain Casey taught to us all on the ship. We stayed in our system while we were learning, and once he felt we were ready, the captain set us on our journey."

"I'd like to know how it was that you boys were the only other ones to have beaten a training simulation that was designed to put the most experienced crew through their paces, and probably fail, as almost every crew has done?" Another reporter asked after getting the nod.

"Not only did we have a good teacher, but we all trust and like each other. We all learned together, and knew what each and every person was supposed to be doing. By being able to trust that that was going to be done, we were able to work together as one, to defeat an almost impossible enemy. We actually didn't find it very difficult at all when we did it for the first time. We've also taught this same method to some friends, and they too have increased their performance a considerable amount." Matthew said.

"Who were these friends, and why did you teach them this information?" Another asked after getting approval.

"I'm sorry, I won't allow that question. I said that if we didn't elaborate, it was for a reason." Kelly answered.

"Okay, fine, then I would like to ask a different question if I could?" He asked.

"That's fine, but please don't reword the question a different way, we won't answer it, and we'll leave."

"That's okay, it's a different question. We've all been shown a few of your battle recordings over the past few months, and we've all noticed the same things. How is it that you can all work together and hardly even say a word to each other? Even your captain was not yelling out commands."

"It comes down to the same answer as was given a few moments ago. Trust. We trust each other to do what they're supposed to do. We all have the same learning, and we can all run every system on the ship, so we know what can and needs to be done, and we know that everyone can do it. It just feels normal to us. We're aware that this probably wouldn't work on most ships, because the people weren't all trained the same way, and the same trust may or may not be there. They can learn to work with each other, but still need some form of command and or communication to know where to go." Tony said.

The rest of the conference went on for another hour before Kelly called the end, and even though everyone groaned, no one tried to ask any more questions. As soon as they were finished, they left the large conference area and into a private area, where they could talk more easily. Captain Casey started out almost as soon as they were free.

"You guys did very well today, I'm proud of you, and you should be proud of yourselves as well. As a treat, my parents have informed me that we get to have a very nice dinner tonight, on them, at the same restaurant they took us to before. The reservations are for in an hour, so we have an hour to kill. I say we go walk around for a bit." He told the boys proudly.

"Okay Sir." They all said.

They took a walk around the area, just looking in and around the shops on the street front, until it was time for dinner. They arrived a few minutes early, but were shown in anyway and seated at a very large head table. A few people were already there, including the prime minister and his wife, and about a dozen or so admirals, as well as their husbands or wives. Oddly enough though, Jonathon's parents had yet to arrive. They ended up arriving a few minutes late, but carrying a large box between them, they went right up to the head table and set it down on the end of the table, and then went to their table.

Once everyone that was supposed to be there, was there, and seated, Prime Minister Stevens stood to get everyone's attention.

"I thank you all for coming this evening. By now, nearly everyone on the planet knows Captain Casey and his crew, and how it was that they contributed to the battles that we've recently won. To the crew of the UE1, planet Earth thanks you. Without your help, and the knowledge that you've been so kind to share with everyone, we were able to defeat the enemy, and hopefully it'll be permanent this time. Given the very strong warnings that Kelly gave to them, they'd be foolish to ignore it. And just so everyone's aware, those warnings will be upheld as well, we won't go through another war just to feed them. Now, I know that none of you guys liked having to go through that press conference today, but I have to say that you all did exceptionally well, and for possibly the first time I've ever seen, you guys controlled them, instead of the other way around. I think no one really wants to hear me talk all evening long, so I'll stop now, before everyone falls asleep, that way we can eat."

With that statement, the kitchen doors opened, and a couple dozen waiters and waitresses at least came out, bearing large trays of food and drink. They stopped at the head table first, and the crew of the UE1 took what they wanted, and then the trays were carried off to the various tables in the room. Once everyone had been served their food, the whole room started to eat. Everyone enjoyed the meal thoroughly, but then the dessert trays were brought out, and when those were tasted, everyone forgot how good dinner was, because the desserts were even better yet. Once again, once everyone was satisfied, the prime minister stood and got everyone's attention.

"Now that everyone has enjoyed the delicious meal, I have a little ceremony to perform."

The prime minister and Admiral Casey stood and went to the large box on the table. The prime minister opened the box and started taking out boxes, each box was ornately engraved with a crew members name.

"When I call out your name, would you come forward please?" Prime Minister Stevens said.

He called out Kelly first, since he was the youngest, and Kelly came up and took the box and shook the prime ministers hand, and then Admiral Casey's hand as well. The prime minister called out each of the crew members names one by one, and each one came up and shook the Prime Minister's and the Admiral's hands, and then took their box and went back to their seat. Everyone in the crew was called up, including Warren and Captain Casey himself. Once everyone had been given the box with their name on it, and they were all seated, the prime minister went and stood back by his seat.

"Now, only one of you has ever received a box like this before, and he probably already knows one of the things that he'll find in it. I'd very much like for you to all open your boxes now, and find your brand new rank, and our highest achievement award for meritorious services in there. All of you young men, except three of you, are now Junior Lieutenants, and the three boys in already higher positions, are now your lieutenants. Your Doctor has been bumped all the way to Lieutenant Commander, and your Captain has been promoted to Rear Admiral, but will still stay as Captain of the UE1. To the entire crew of the UE1, you've done your planet proud, and it was with great honor that I bestowed upon you these small tokens of our appreciation. Now remember that these are very real positions that you now hold, and with those positions comes respect and responsibility. Don't abuse the privilege, and you boys will go far in this world." Prime Minister Stevens said.

"Yes Sir!" They all said, a few of the boys with tears.

"I understand that you guys are going to collect some more recruits, and then go back out again, so I'll give you all the help I can give. WSEC has been instructed to give you any supplies you need, and you're to call at any time should you be in need of any assistance, and we'll come as soon as we can. It's getting late now, and understandably you'll want to get started on your recruiting very soon, so I think that unless anyone else has anything to say, we should call this a night." Prime Minister Stevens said.

"I do have a few words Sir. If I may of course?" Rear Admiral Casey asked.

"Of course Rear Admiral. It's your party after all." Prime Minister Stevens smiled.

"Thank you Sir. On behalf of my entire crew and myself, we thank you for everything this evening. I'd also like to point out something. There are many kids still on the street, many more than I myself can help. There are also many orphans in the orphanages. Now obviously not all will either be suited for it, or will want to do it, but why not set up a school for those that are interested. You'll need to make sure that the instructors are well trained in dealing with troubled youth, and to give the kids the time that they need to adjust. I chose all boys for my mission for some pretty obvious reasons, but there's no reason that girls couldn't also be included. Right now we have no actual schools set up to train ships crews, they're mostly just trained on the fly as it were, but I think we should. The war necessitated the fast paced training that we've had to do, however, a good school that'll start kids young, to learn all that they need to know to become part of the space fleet, would not be a bad idea" Rear Admiral Casey said.

"We'll most certainly look into that, because you're right, there are a lot of orphans out there, and even others that would be very interested. Sadly though, the war actually totally sidetracked the starting of training for our crews, it was going to be done once we knew if we could actually go anywhere and do anything, but alas, it never got started, we just didn't have the time. I'd like for you to write up a proposal for me however, send it to me as soon as you're done, we can go over it together, and then we'll go from there. Now I'm pretty sure I know your reasoning, but tell me, why is it you didn't choose girls?" Prime Minister Stevens asked curiously.

"Simple hormones Sir, and lack of manpower to supervise. Let's just say that opposites attract, and on a ship with only two adults, there were just not enough barriers to dissuade those attractions." Jonathon grinned. "My entire team will go over the proposal for you Sir, and we'll try and have it to you in just a few days."

"I like how you put that so politely. I was right in my suspicions, and I can understand why it was you made that decision." Prime Minister Stevens laughed.

"Thank you Sir. Well as you said before, we'll want to get started soon, so I'm going to say excuse us for the evening, and we'll contact you just as soon as we have a proposal for you."

"Then I can't wait to hear from you guys, you all have a good night."

With all the pleasantries done for the time, the crew of the UE1 teleported up to the ship and all went to one of the lounges and sat down.

"Well, today was an interesting day. How do you all feel about being actual ranked officers in the space fleet?" Rear Admiral Casey asked his fine crew.

"I'm not sure Sir. Both nervous and excited I guess. Given the rank I was given, and what little I know of officer ranking, I'd say that we all jumped forward a few steps." Donny said.

"Yes you did, and I'd expect nothing less. It's a bit frightening, especially at first. I wasn't really expecting a promotion myself, and while I suspected that they might do something like that for you guys, I never expected it to be quite that high. However, even though I'm now a Rear Admiral, I'm still Captain Casey to you guys, and to most. Mostly only higher ranking officials will use my true rank, as I'm still officially a captain. Now for the reason we're here. Let's go ahead and see how much of this new training proposal we can get done tonight. I want your ideas please?"

"Why not just do it like you did it Sir. Keep most everything the same as how you did it. Depending upon the crew size, and the

ship size, you could go from just a few students, to a lot of students."
Franky said.

"That'll be one of the proposals we send through of course, seeing as how we know it worked so well with you guys, all hands on training. Problem is of course, most captains and crews won't be able to cope with some of the difficulties that kids with your unique backgrounds can pose. It'd take some very specialized training. I have that training, but most don't, therefore I was able to make it very easy on you guys. Should someone else try it, it might not work as well, or at all."

"I think I understand what you mean, but tell me what do you mean by street kids possibly being difficult?" Jamie asked.

"I know you understand, all of you do. First is your lack of trust, I was able to work quickly with you to get the trust base started, but you had to learn to trust me, and that took a while. Because of who I am, and the training I've had, I knew exactly how to work with you guys to build the trust again. Second is the little attitudes that street kids quite often have. You all had them, some worse than others. Now, a strong attitude can both help and hinder you in life, you needed to learn how to focus it. I was able to teach you that, again others would find this difficult. Third is your education, or lack thereof. You need to be very smart and to be able to think on your feet. Well that part street kids generally have lots of, they just don't have the actual learning. That takes a long time, as you're all finding out."

"We can teach you everything you need to know to fly a ship, no problem there, that's really pretty easy, but how and why it flies, now that's a bit more tricky. So as you can see, there are a lot of reasons to not do it on a ship, but then again, there's one really good reason to do it on a ship. You were all used to a huge amount of freedom. You could come and go as you pleased, do pretty much anything you wanted whenever you wanted and no one would or could truly stop you. Well in an actual school, students like yourselves might be tempted to just walk out and come back as they pleased, this just wouldn't do. But where can you really go on a ship?" Captain Casey grinned.

"Okay, thank you Sir. You're right about all of that." Jamie said.

"Okay Sir. Then if on the ground isn't a great idea, and if on a ship isn't a great idea, what if they did it on a space station. They could maybe use the Jupiter Space Station, or build another one just for schools. For training purposes, they could use limited range shuttles just like ours." Bobby said.

"Well that sounds like a good idea, we'll put that down as well." Captain Casey said.

"Thanks Sir. They'd of course have to have a lot of really good teachers trained a lot like you were though. I also think they should have at least a couple full sized ships for training missions, once the better students are ready for it." Bobby said.

"Okay, I'll add that as well." Captain Casey said.

"I like the idea of a space station school, I think it'd work the best. Having ships to use is good as well, but I'd recommend making them not only limited range, but remote controlled as well, so that you don't get the possibility of someone stealing one of them. I know that there are a lot of street kids who have no problems stealing what they want and need. I'd also maybe add quite a few holographic rooms, so that you can simulate the bridge, engine and power rooms, as well as other key areas, and things like that, so that much of the training is still hands on, but isn't at all dangerous if someone manages to screw up somehow." Ryan added.

"Okay, consider that added. These are some good ideas guys, the Prime Minister will be very pleased."

"If at all possible Sir, keep the class sizes as small as possible, only ten to twenty students per instructor, so that everyone can get the attention they need. For certain things you could combine a number of classes together, but not for most." Brad said.

"Good idea, but might be a little difficult, depending upon the amount of students, and the size of the school. Also finding suitable teachers might be tough, until they get people trained in special teaching methods. To start, I suppose they could only take smaller numbers of students though."

"Sir, I know that for now this is supposed to be to get kids off the streets, but what about those kids that aren't on the streets that'd like to join as well, 'cause you know they'll want to once they hear about it!" Devon asked.

"That's a good question Devon, and for now, we won't worry about it, because for now it'd still be an experiment. For those kids though, they could probably just go to a school on the planet near their homes, so that they can still live at home with their parents, since that'd be more preferable to them, otherwise they can have much the same things. Maybe I'll just add that into the proposal as well, so that they can look into that as well." Captain Casey said and then added it.

"Well I don't know about the others Sir, but I think that's a good proposal. Unless anyone has any other ideas of course." Donny said.

"No Sir!" Everyone said.

"Then we have our proposal. Well there's still a little over an hour before you guys have to be up to your rooms, so why don't you guys all go down and go swimming for the rest of the night, while I write up the full proposal." Captain Casey said.

"Yes Sir!" Everyone said, and then they left the room, only Warren stayed behind.

"Hey Warren, why don't you go join the others and relax a bit as well, and if I get done early enough, I'll join you there as well." Captain Casey said.

"I will, but I just had another idea for the proposal. Your schools should also be training people in cooking and medical studies, as well as other various fields, so I'd also add those training options into it as well."

"Okay Warren, that's a good idea. So you haven't said much since you got a nice promotion, how are you holding up?" Captain Casey asked.

"Fine, I guess. Still kind of in shock really. I mean, it's not like I really helped all that much in all that you guys did. I would've been perfectly happy being a lowly ensign, but not this." Warren said quietly, rubbing his new rank insignia.

"You helped a lot more than you know. You may have only been helping on the sidelines, but remember, without sideline support, a team can, and will fail. You kept us all fed and in good shape, if it hadn't been for Will and yourself, then it would've fallen upon the rest of us to do what you guys did. Don't worry, you deserved the promotion and the recognition, as well as the pay raise that came with it."

"What do you mean pay raise, I thought it was you paying me?"

"Well it had been. The government has taken this project on, and they're paying everything now, even the boys, although they don't know it yet, are on the payroll. Problem with them of course, is some don't even know their last names, and the others have buried them too deeply to find anymore, and we need to get their last names so that they can get paid, but for now, until they're nineteen, all their money is going into accounts under my name. My dad asked me about this just before we left, it's why he pulled me off to the side for a few minutes, it was to tell me he was going to do that until we figured something else out. So yeah, I'm no longer paying you, and even I'm on a full rear admirals pay scale now, kinda nice."

"Um wow, okay, so how much am I getting paid?" Warren asked.

"I should just let you find out when your first payment is made, but it's almost twice what I was paying you, because you're pulling double duties." Captain Casey grinned.

"Wow, the government sure pays their doctors well don't they."

"Yes they do, now go, I'm going to my office to write this all up and send it out." Captain Casey said.

"Yes Sir!" Warren said and turned and left.

Jonathon went to his office and wrote out the proposal quickly, and put all the information in, so once he was finished, which only took twenty minutes, he sent it to the prime minister. He then went to his room and got changed really quickly, to join the boys for the remaining forty minutes of the evening. He found the boys in the pool, and they were all swimming laps, getting their exercise for the night. He joined them in the pool and started swimming as well. Finally, what felt like a short time later, he called bedtime, and everyone got out of the pool, dried off quickly, and went to their rooms to get showered and ready for bed.

CHAPTER 36

PICKING THE NEW GENERATION

The following morning everyone got their morning routines over with, then the captain told everyone to help clean up, and even he himself helped clean. When it was done he told everyone to meet back in the dining room.

"Okay guys, here's the plan for the day. Teams one, two and three will each go out and look for five young men just like you were. Team four, you're with me. We need to restock on supplies, and you're going to help me get them. Franky and Donny, you'll be running backup for the search teams, when they find candidates, and they pass the tests, then you'll come and collect them and get them up to the ship and prepared. Warren and Will, you'll be out finding yourselves a suitable chef trainee. You're all to be in full dress uniforms with your decorations on them. Now very important, you need to stick together in your teams. You'll scare most people off, but you could attract unwanted attention as well. If you get into any situation you don't believe you can easily get out of, call me, and then feel free to use your sidearm to stun the situation, or if that's deemed too extreme, use other methods as you see fit."

"Yes Sir!" Everyone said.

"Because I'm sure none of you remembers the entrance test that I gave to you, I have it on pads for all of you to use, you can just do it verbally, and then score it that way. I require a minimum ninety percent to pass. That's all, go get changed, and go do your assigned chores."

"Yes Sir!" They all said again.

Everyone left right away to go to their rooms to get changed. He got into his full dress uniform, then added his new rank insignia, as well as his new decoration, and then he was ready to go. He waited in the hall for team four to be ready, and when they exited their rooms, he looked them over to make sure their ranks were shown in the proper location, and their decorations were placed correctly. Once he was satisfied they were all ready to go, he turned wordlessly, and they followed. Jonathon teleported he and his team to WSEC. They went in and went straight to the warehouses to get the required stock.

Each of the teams was ready in their own time, and as soon as they were, they went down to the planet as well, and started their search. Team three went toward where Tristan used to crash, and they found a group of three boys from about eleven years old, to thirteen years old.

"Guys, look who it is. Those are the guys from the UE1, Tristan, Ryan, Matthew, Cullen and Kelly, I can't believe they're coming down here." They all heard the smallest boy say excitedly.

"This used to be my home too, and I used to sit right where you're sitting now. I know exactly what you guys do to live out here, how would you like to have a chance to join us?" Tristan asked gently.

"Who do I have to kill?" The oldest boy asked.

"No one, in fact, I'd rather you never have to do that. All you have to do is pass a test, and then you could become crew members, and train to run a star ship just like us."

"I'd like to take the test." The youngest boy said quickly. The others all nodded their agreement. The three boys were quickly given the test, and they all passed easily.

Team one had went to where Brady used to hang out, but they found no one around, yet the entire team felt as if they were being watched, not even ten minutes after they came down. Brady whispered to the guys to be prepared, because he felt that something was not quite right. They looked all around, and suddenly Brady found what it was.

"Who are you, and why are you following us like a sneaking thief? Hey, I recognize you. You're that reporter that was all mad that we had the nerve to restrict what you guys could ask. So you're a sleaze ball journalist aren't you?" Brady spat out.

"No, I'm just a journalist who wants to get the full story, and I'll get it."

"No, I'm afraid you got all that you can or will get from us, now get lost before I get angry!" He snarled.

"Oh come on, I'm a nice guy. I just want an interview with you guys, get the full story." He said slickly. "But really, what can you do to me?"

"Nice guy my butt, you're following us around like a rat on a trail of breadcrumbs, and as for the interview, you won't get it, no one will. We gave all the information we care to give at the press conference. Now, as for what can we do to you, you have no idea. It'd be in your best interest to leave at once though." Brady said calmly.

"Boy, you're messing with the wrong person. I get all the best exclusives, because I'm not afraid to get my hands dirty, and all five of you together offer no threat to me. Now give me the interview, or I'll keep following you until I get all the information I need, in any way I can." He threatened, which very seriously ticked the boys off.

"I think you have it wrong there, it's you that doesn't know what you're messing with. If you don't leave now, or insist on following us, not only will I be calling the Prime Minister and Admiral Casey, I'll stun you." Brady said and raised his gun, the others followed suit immediately after.

"Go ahead and call them, I'm not scared of those jumped up little pencil pushers, and those aren't even real guns, no one would give children real guns to use." He said, sounding very sure of himself.

"Again you're very much mistaken, they are real. I'm not sure if you noticed our ranks, but they're very real, and with the ranks come the weapons, and to prove that they are real, why don't you just try and follow us." Brady said sweetly, and then he turned to walk away and the others followed.

Brady and the rest of his team started walking away, and the man started to follow them. Brady heard him, he turned and saw what he needed to see, took aim, and fired, stunning the man instantly. He slumped to the ground as if boneless.

"Captain Casey, we have an issue here." Kelvin said into his communicator.

"Yes Kelvin, what is it?" He asked.

Kelvin took a few moments to relay the information.

"Okay, stay put and watch over him, and I'll call the prime minister and have him deal with it."

"Thanks Sir."

They waited for about twenty minutes before Prime Minister Stevens and Admiral Casey, as well as a few police officers entered the alley they were in.

"Good morning gentlemen. I hear this man didn't take no for an answer, and you were forced to stun him when he went to follow you?" The prime minister asked.

"That's correct Sir." Brady answered.

"Good enough for me, gentlemen, please take this thing away and charge him with everything you can, including harassment and assault." Prime Minister Stevens asked.

"Yes Sir!" They said and picked the man up and carried him away.

"Sorry about that boys, these guys were warned what would happen, so now he's going to find out. His license, which was only hanging on by a thread to begin with, will be revoked, and every news media will be forced to never accept a story from him, no matter how good it is. And they'll listen too, or I'll pull their operating licenses, and they don't want that. Well I know you have better things to be doing this morning, so we'll leave you to your work. Have a pleasant day." Prime Minister Stevens said.

"Thank you Sir, and you too." Brady said.

Within four hours the boys had their five team members each, to make the total of fifteen people they wanted to recruit. Donny and Franky were kept very busy teleporting between locations to give the new boys their communicators, and get their information, and got the new crew members and their enlisting team teleported up to the ship. All three teams had no problems getting the street boys to talk to them, some of them knew them from the past, but all of them knew of the stories of Captain Casey and his crew, and all lined up excitedly to take the test. It had in fact been a huge amount faster and easier than when Captain Casey had done the same thing, because all the street kids knew the stories of the crew of the UE1, most importantly though, where they had come from and went on to do.

Warren and Will had spent almost three hours scouring the city looking for a suitable candidate and they finally found someone. He was still living on the street, but worked in a soup kitchen as often as he could, to help cook for the others. He too jumped at the chance to come and help, and they all teleported up to the ship.

Captain Casey and team four spent a little over three hours getting all the new supplies they needed and getting them teleported up to the ship. Their new uniforms would not be ready until the following day though, but Captain Casey did not mind, because they still had enough to last for a while, and as long as the new boys were about the same sizes as the others were, then they would all have uniforms. Almost all their supplies were now aboard the ship, so the captain and his team went up as well to get the fun started, once again.

It had been an incredible year, full of fun and fear, everyone learned far more than they ever thought was possible, and they had done far more than even that. Such a simple experiment, such a simple idea, but with an outcome far outweighing the energy put into it.

Author Bio

Native Canadian Michael Lee-Allen Dawn loves to read and write and hopes that his wife and two children love what he wrote for them. He was born and raised in the mainland of British Columbia, Canada, and never plans to leave.